THE WI

# THE WRECK OF THE MARY DEARE

## Hammond Innes

Thorndike Press
Thorndike, Maine USA

This Large Print edition is published by Thorndike Press, USA.

Published in 1999 in the U.S. by arrangement with Curtis Brown UK.

U.S. Softcover ISBN 0–7862–1713–8 (General Series Edition)

The text of this Large Print edition is unabridged.
Other aspects of the book may vary from the original edition.

Set in 16 pt. New Times Roman.

Printed in Great Britain on acid-free paper.

**Library of Congress Cataloging-in-Publication Data**

Innes, Hammond, 1913–
    The wreck of the Mary Deare / Hammond Innes.
      p.   cm.
    ISBN 0–7862–1713–8 (lg. print : sc : alk. paper)
    1. Large type books.    I. Title.
    [PR6017.N79W74    1999]
    823'.912—dc21                   98–44590

*To the Mate and Crew of*
*TRIUNE OF TROY*
*and the memory of a gale off the Minkies*

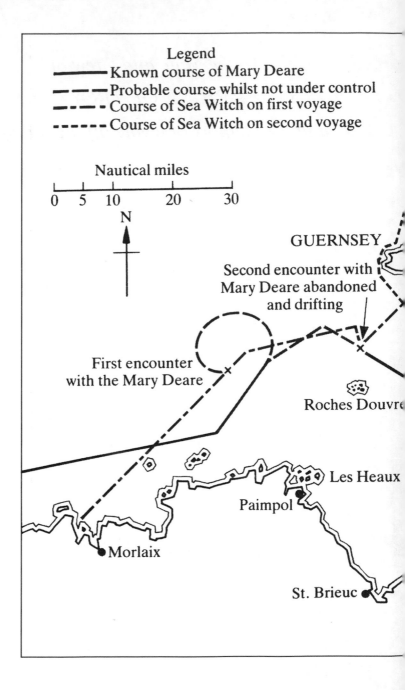

Legend
———— Known course of Mary Deare
— — — Probable course whilst not under control
—·— · Course of Sea Witch on first voyage
· · · · · · Course of Sea Witch on second voyage

Nautical miles

| | | | |
|0|5|10|20|30|

N

GUERNSEY

Second encounter with
Mary Deare abandoned
and drifting

First encounter
with the Mary Deare

Roches Douvre

Les Heaux

Paimpol

Morlaix

St. Brieuc

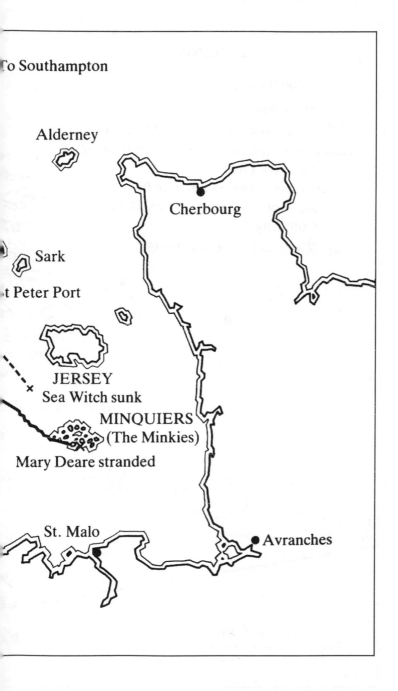

To Southampton

Alderney

Cherbourg

Sark

t Peter Port

JERSEY

Sea Witch sunk

MINQUIERS
(The Minkies)

Mary Deare stranded

St. Malo

Avranches

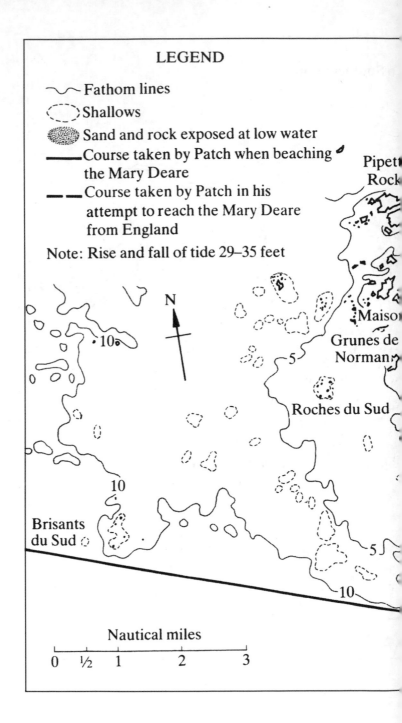

LEGEND

〜〜 Fathom lines

⊂ ⊃ Shallows

▨ Sand and rock exposed at low water

—— Course taken by Patch when beaching
the Mary Deare

— — Course taken by Patch in his
attempt to reach the Mary Deare
from England

Note: Rise and fall of tide 29–35 feet

N

Pipett
Rock

Maiso

10

5

Grunes de
Norman

Roches du Sud

10

Brisants
du Sud

5

10

Nautical miles

0   ½   1        2        3

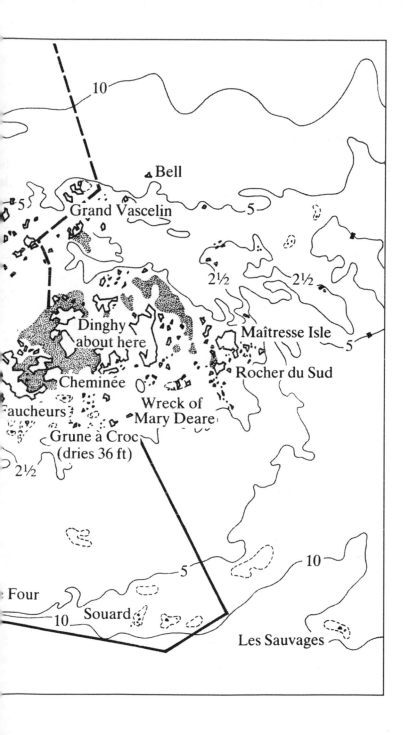

10

Bell

5
Grand Vascelin
5

2½
2½

Dinghy
about here
Maîtresse Isle
5

Cheminée
Rocher du Sud

Faucheurs
Wreck of
Mary Deare

Grune à Croc
(dries 36 ft)

2½

5
10

Four
10
Souard
Les Sauvages

# CONTENTS

# Part One

# THE WRECK

# CHAPTER ONE

I was tired and very cold; a little scared, too. The red and green navigation lights cast a weird glow over the sails. Beyond was nothing, a void of utter darkness in which the sea made little rushing noises. I eased my cramped legs, sucking on a piece of barley sugar. Above me the sails swung in a ghostly arc, slatting back and forth as *Sea Witch* rolled and plunged. There was scarcely wind enough to move the boat through the water, yet the swell kicked up by the March gales ran as strong as ever and my numbed brain was conscious all the time that this was only a lull. The weather forecast at six o'clock had been ominous. Winds of gale force were reported imminent in sea areas Rockall, Shannon, Sole and Finisterre. Beyond the binnacle light the shadowy outline of the boat stretched ahead of me, merging into the clammy blackness of the night. I had dreamed of this moment so often. But it was March and now, after fifteen hours at sea in the Channel, the excitement of owning our own boat was gone, eaten up by the cold. The glimmer of a breaking wave appeared out of the darkness and slapped against the counter, flinging spray in my face and sidling off into the blackness astern with a hiss of white water. God! It was cold! Cold and clammy—and not a star anywhere.

The door of the charthouse slammed back to give me a glimpse of the lit saloon and against it loomed Mike Duncan's oilskin-padded bulk, holding a steaming mug in either hand. The door slammed to again, shutting out the lit world below, and the darkness and the sea crowded in again. 'Soup?' Mike's cheerful, freckled face appeared abruptly out of the night, hanging disembodied in the light from the binnacle. He smiled at me from the folds of his balaclava as he handed me a mug. 'Nice and fresh up here after the galley,' he said. And then the smile was wiped from his face. 'What the hell's that?' He was staring past my left shoulder, staring at something astern of us on the port quarter. 'Can't be the moon, can it?'

I swung round. A cold, green translucence showed at the edge of visibility, a sort of spectral light that made me catch my breath in sudden panic with all the old seamen's tales of weird and frightful things seen at sea rushing through my mind.

The light grew steadily brighter, phosphorescent and unearthly—a ghastly brilliance like a bloated glow-worm. And then suddenly it condensed and hardened into a green pin-point, and I yelled at Mike: 'The Aldis—quick!' It was the starboard navigation light of a big steamer, and it was bearing straight down on us. Her deck lights were

4

appearing now, misted and yellow; and gently, like the muffled beat of a tom-tom, the sound of her engines reached out to us in a low, pulsating throb.

The beam of the Aldis lamp stabbed the night, blinding us with the reflected glare from a thick blanket of mist that engulfed us. It was a sea mist that had crept up on me in the dark without my knowing it. The white of a bow wave showed dimly in the brilliance, and then the shadowy outline of the bows themselves took shape. In an instant I could see the whole for'ard half of the ship. It was like a ghost ship emerging out of the mist, and the blunt bows were already towering over us as I swung the wheel.

It seemed an age that I watched *Sea Witch* turn, waiting for the jib to fill on the other tack and bring her head round, and all the time I could hear the surge of that bow wave coming nearer. 'She's going to hit us! Christ! She's going to hit us!' I can still hear Mike's cry, high and strident in the night. He was blinking the Aldis, directing the beam straight at her bridge. The whole superstructure was lit up, the light reflecting back in flashes from the glass windows. And the towering mass of the steamer kept on coming, thundering down on us at a good eight knots without a check, without any alteration of course.

The main and mizzen booms swung over with a crash. The jib was aback now. I left it like that for a moment, watching her head pay off. Every detail of *Sea Witch*, from the tip of her long bowsprit to the top of her mainmast, was lit by the green glow of the steamer's starboard light now above us. I let go the port jib sheet, hauling in on the starboard sheet, saw the sail fill, and then Mike screamed, 'Look out! Hold on!' There was a great roaring sound and a wall of white water hit us. It swept over the cockpit, lifting me out of my seat, tugging at my grip on the wheel. The sails swung in a crazy arc; they swung so far that the boom and part of the mainsail were buried for a moment in the back of a wave whilst tons of water spilled across our decks; and close alongside the steamer slid by like a cliff.

Slowly *Sea Witch* righted herself as the water poured off her in a white foam. I still had hold of the wheel and Mike was clutching the backstay runner, shouting obscenities at the top of his voice. His words came to me as a frail sound against the solid thumping of the ship's engines. And then another sound emerged out of the night—the steady thrashing of a propeller partly clear of the water.

I shouted to Mike, but he had already realized the danger and had switched the Aldis on again. Its brilliant light showed us plates pitted deep with rust and a weed-grown Plimsoll mark high above the water. Then the plates curved up to the stern and we could see

6

the propeller blades slashing at the waves, thumping the water into a swirling froth. *Sea Witch* trembled, sails slack. Then she slid off the back of a wave into that mill race and the blades were whirling close along our port side, churning white water over the cabin top, flinging it up into the mainsail.

It was like that for a moment and then they flailed off into the darkness beyond the bowsprit and we were left pitching in the broken water of the ship's wake. The Aldis beam picked out her name—*MARY DEARE—Southampton*. We stared dazedly at her rust-streaked lettering while the stern became shadowy and then vanished abruptly. Only the beat of her engines remained then, throbbing gently and gradually dying away into the night. A faint smell of burning lingered on for a while in the damp air. 'Bastards!' Mike shouted, suddenly finding his voice. 'Bastards!' He kept on repeating the word.

The door of the charthouse slid back, and a figure emerged. It was Hal. 'Are you boys all right?' His voice—a little too calm, a little too cheerful—shook slightly.

'Didn't you see what happened?' Mike cried.

'Yes, I saw,' he replied.

'They must have seen us. I was shining the Aldis straight at the bridge. If they'd been keeping a lookout—'

'I don't think they were keeping a lookout.

7

In fact, I don't think there was anybody on the bridge.' It was said so quietly that for a moment I didn't realize the implication.

'How do you mean—nobody on the bridge?' I asked.

He came out on to the deck then. 'It was just before the bow wave hit us. I knew something was wrong and I'd got as far as the charthouse. I found myself looking out through the window along the beam of the Aldis lamp. It was shining right on to the bridge. I don't think there was anybody there. I couldn't see anybody.'

'But good God!' I said. 'Do you realize what you're saying?'

'Yes, of course, I do.' His tone was peremptory, a little military. 'It's odd, isn't it?'

He wasn't the sort of man to make up a thing like that. H. A. Lowden—Hal to his friends—was an ex-Gunner, a Colonel retired, who spent most of the summer months ocean racing. He had a lot of experience of the sea.

'Do you mean to say you think there was nobody in control of that ship?' Mike's tone was incredulous.

'I don't know,' Hal answered. 'It seems incredible. But all I can say is that I had a clear view of the interior of the bridge for an instant and, as far as I could see, there was nobody there.'

We didn't say anything for a moment. I think we were all too astonished. The idea of a

8

big ship ploughing her way through the rock-infested seas so close to the French coast without anybody at the helm . . . It was absurd.

Mike's voice, suddenly practical, broke the silence. 'What happened to those mugs of soup?' The beam of the Aldis lamp clicked on, revealing the mugs lying in a foot of water at the bottom of the cockpit. 'I'd better go and make another brew.' And then to Hal who was standing, half-dressed, his body braced against the charthouse: 'What about you, Colonel? You'd like some soup, wouldn't you?'

Hal nodded: 'I never refuse an offer of soup.' He watched Mike until he had gone below and then he turned to me. 'I don't mind admitting it now that we're alone,' he said, 'but that was a very unpleasant moment. How did we come to be right across her bows like that?'

I explained that the ship had been down-wind from us and we hadn't heard the beat of her engines. 'The first we saw of her was the green of her starboard navigation light coming at us out of the mist.'

'No fog signal?'

'We didn't hear it, anyway.'

'Odd!' He stood for a moment, his long body outlined against the port light, and then he came aft and seated himself beside me on the cockpit coaming. 'Had a look at the barometer during your watch?' he asked.

'No,' I said. 'What's it doing?'

'Going down.' He had his long arms

wrapped round his body, hugging his seaman's jersey. 'Dropped quite a bit since I went below.' He hesitated and then said, 'You know, this gale could come up on us pretty quickly.' I didn't say anything and he pulled his pipe out and began to suck on it. 'I tell you frankly, John, I don't like it.' The quietness of his voice added strength to his opinion. 'If the forecast turns out right and the wind backs north-westerly, then we'll be on a lee shore. I don't like gales and I don't like lee shores, particularly when the lee shore is the Channel Islands.'

I thought he wanted me to put back to the French coast and I didn't say anything; just sat there staring at the compass card, feeling obstinate and a little scared.

'It's a pity about the kicker,' he murmured. 'If the kicker hadn't packed up—'

'Why bring that up?' It was the only thing that had gone wrong with the boat. 'You've always said you despise engines.'

His blue eyes, caught in the light of the binnacle, stared at me fixedly. 'I was only going to say,' he put in mildly, 'that if the kicker hadn't packed up we'd be halfway across the Channel by now and the situation would be entirely different.'

'Well, I'm not putting back.'

He took his pipe out of his mouth as though to say something and then put it back and sat there, staring at me with those unwinking blue

10

eyes of his.

'The real trouble is that you're not used to sailing in a boat that hasn't been kept up to ocean racing pitch.' I hadn't meant to say that, but I was angry and my nerves were still tense from the steamer incident.

An awkward silence fell between us. At length he stopped sucking on his pipe. 'It's only that I like to arrive,' he said quietly. 'The rigging is rusty, the ropes rotten and the sails—'

'We went over all that in Morlaix,' I said tersely. 'Plenty of yachts cross the Channel in worse shape than *Sea Witch*.'

'Not in March with a gale warning. And not without an engine.' He got up and went for'ard as far as the mast, bending down and hauling at something. There was the sound of splintering wood and then he came back and tossed a section of the bulwarks into the cockpit at my feet. 'The bow wave did that.' He sat down beside me again. 'It isn't good enough, John. The boat hasn't been surveyed and for all you know the hull may be as rotten as the gear after lying for two years on a French mud bank.'

'The hull's all right,' I told him. I was calmer now. 'There are a couple of planks to be replaced and she needs restopping. But that's all. I went over every inch of her with a knife before I bought her. The wood is absolutely sound.'

11

'And what about the fastenings?' His right eyebrow lifted slightly. 'Only a surveyor could tell you whether the fastenings—'

'I told you, I'm having her surveyed as soon as we reach Lymington.'

'Yes, but that doesn't help us now. If this gale comes up on us suddenly ... I'm a prudent mariner,' he added. 'I like the sea, but it's not a creature I want to take liberties with.'

'Well, I can't afford to be prudent,' I said. 'Not right now.'

Mike and I had just formed a small salvage company and every day we delayed getting the boat to England for conversion was a day lost out of our diving season. He knew that.

'I'm only suggesting you steer a point off your direct course,' he said. 'Close-hauled we can just about lay for Hanois on Guernsey Island. We'll then be in a position to take advantage of the wind when it backs and run for shelter to Peter Port.'

Of course ... I rubbed my hand over my eyes. I should have known what he was driving at. But I was tired and the steamer incident had left me badly shaken. It was queer the way the vessel had sailed right through us like that.

'It won't help your salvage venture if you smash the boat up.' Hal's voice cut across my thoughts. He had taken my silence for refusal. 'Apart from the gear, we're not very strongly crewed.'

That was true enough. There were only the

12

three of us. The fourth member of the crew, Ian Baird, had been sea-sick from the time we had left Morlaix. And she was a biggish boat for three to handle—a forty-tonner. 'Very well,' I said. 'We'll head for Guernsey.'

He nodded as though he'd known it all along. 'You'll need to steer North 65° East then.'

I turned the wheel, giving her starboard helm, and watched the compass card swing to the new course. He must have been working out the course in the charthouse just before the steamer came up on us. 'I take it you worked out the distance, too?'

'Fifty-four miles. And at this rate,' he added, 'it'll be daylight long before we get there.'

An uneasy silence settled between us. I could hear him sucking at his empty pipe, but I kept my eyes on the compass and didn't look at him. Damn it, I should have thought of Peter Port for myself! But there'd been so much to do at Morlaix getting the boat ready . . . I'd just about worked myself to a standstill before ever we put to sea.

'That ship.' His voice came out of the darkness at my side, a little hesitant, bridging the gap of my silence. 'Damned queer,' he murmured. 'You know, if there really was nobody on board . . .' He checked and then added, half-jokingly, 'That would have been a piece of salvage that would have set you up for life.' I thought I sensed a serious note

13

underlying his words, but when I glanced at him he shrugged his shoulders and laughed. 'Well, I think I'll turn in again now.' He got up and his 'good night' floated back to me from the dark gap of the charthouse.

Shortly afterwards Mike brought me a mug of hot soup. He stayed and talked to me whilst I drank it, speculating wildly about the *Mary Deare*. Then he, too, turned in and the blackness of the night closed round me. Could there really have been nobody on the bridge? It was too fantastic—an empty ship driving pell mell up the Channel. And yet, cold and alone, with the pale glimmer of the sails swooping above me and the dismal dripping of mist condensed on the canvas, anything seemed possible.

At three Hal relieved me and for two hours I slept, dreaming of blunt, rusted bows hanging over us, toppling slowly, everlastingly. I woke in a panic, cold with sweat, and lay for a moment thinking about what Hal had said. It would be queer if we salvaged a ship, just like that, before we'd even . . . But I was asleep again before the idea had more than flickered through my mind. And in an instant I was being shaken and was stumbling out to the helm in the brain-numbing hour before the dawn, all recollection of the *Mary Deare* blurred and hazed by the bitter cold.

Daylight came slowly, a reluctant dawn that showed a drab, sullen sea heaving gently, the

14

steepness flattened out of the swell. The wind was northerly now, but still light; and some time during the night we had gone over on to the other tack.

At ten to seven Hal and I were in the charthouse for the weather report. It started with gale warnings for the western approaches of the Channel; the forecast for our own area of Portland was: *Wind light, northerly at first, backing north-westerly later and increasing strong to gale.* Hal glanced at me, but said nothing. There was no need. I checked our position and then gave Mike the course to steer for Peter Port.

It was a queer morning. There was a lot of scud about and by the time we had finished breakfast it was moving across the sky quite fast. Yet at sea level there was scarcely any wind so that, with full main and mizzen set and the big yankee jib, we were creeping through the water at a bare three knots, rolling sluggishly. There was still a mist of sorts and visibility wasn't much more than two miles.

We didn't talk much. I think we were all three of us too conscious of the sea's menace. Peter Port was still thirty miles away. The silence and the lack of wind was oppressive. 'I'll go and check our position again,' I said. Hal nodded as though the thought had been in his mind, too.

But poring over the chart didn't help. As far as I could tell we were six miles north-north-

15

west of the Roches Douvres, that huddle of rocks and submerged reefs that is the western outpost of the Channel Islands. But I couldn't be certain; my dead reckoning depended too much on tide and leeway.

And then Mike knocked the bottom out of my calculations. 'There's a rock about two points on the starboard bow,' he called to me. 'A big one sticking up out of the water.'

I grabbed the glasses and flung out of the charthouse. 'Where?' My mouth was suddenly harsh and dry. If it were the Roches Douvres, then we must have been set down a good deal farther than I thought. And it couldn't be anything else; it was all open sea between Roches Douvres and Guernsey. 'Where?' I repeated.

'Over there!' Mike was pointing.

I screwed up my eyes. But I couldn't see anything. The clouds had thinned momentarily and a queer sun-glow was reflected on the oily surface of the sea, merging it with the moisture-laden atmosphere. There was no horizon; at the edge of visibility sea and air became one. I searched through the glasses. 'I can't see it,' I said. 'How far away?'

'I don't know. I've lost it now. But it wasn't more than a mile.'

'You're sure it was a rock?'

'Yes, I think so. What else could it be?' He was staring into the distance, his eyes narrowed against the luminous glare of the

16

haze. 'It was a big rock with some sort of tower or pinnacle in the middle of it.'

The Roches Douvres light! I glanced at Hal seated behind the wheel. 'We'd better alter course,' I said. 'The tide is setting us down at about two knots.' My voice sounded tense. If it was the Roches Douvres and the wind fell any lighter, we could be swept right down on to the reef.

He nodded and swung the wheel. 'That would put you out by five miles in your dead reckoning.'

'Yes.'

He frowned. He had taken his sou'wester off and his grey hair, standing on end, gave his face a surprised, puckish look. 'I think you're under-rating yourself as a navigator, but you're the boss. How much do you want me to bear up?'

'Two points at least.'

'There's an old saying,' he murmured: 'The prudent mariner, when in doubt, should assume his dead reckoning to be correct.' He looked at me with a quizzical lift to his bushy eyebrows. 'We don't want to miss Guernsey, you know.'

A mood of indecision took hold of me. Maybe it was just the strain of the long night, but I wasn't sure what to do for the best. 'Did you see it?' I asked him.

'No.'

I turned to Mike and asked him again

17

whether he was sure it was rock he'd seen.

'You can't be sure of anything in this light.'

'But you definitely saw something?'

'Yes. I'm certain of that. And I think it had some sort of a tower on it.'

A gleam of watery sunlight filtered through the damp atmosphere, giving a furtive brightness to the cockpit. 'Then it must be the Roches Douvres,' I murmured.

'Look!' Mike cried. 'There it is—over there.'

I followed the line of his outstretched arm. On the edge of visibility, lit by the sun's pale gleam, was the outline of a flattish rock with a light tower in the middle. I had the glasses on it immediately, but it was no more than a vague, misty shape—a reddish tint glimmering through the golden haze. I dived into the charthouse and snatched up the chart, staring at the shape of the Roches Douvres reef. It marked drying rock outcrops for a full mile north-west of the 92 ft. light tower. We must be right on the fringe of those outcrops. 'Steer north,' I shouted to Hal, 'and sail her clear just as fast as you can.'

'Aye, aye, skipper.' He swung the wheel, calling to Mike to trim the sheets. He was looking over his shoulder at the Roches Douvres light as I came out of the charthouse. 'You know,' he said, 'there's something odd here. I've never actually seen the Roches Douvres, but I know the Channel Islands pretty well and I've never seen any rock that

18

showed up red like that.'

I steadied myself against the charthouse and focused the glasses on it again. The gleam of sunlight had become more positive. Visibility was improving all the time. I saw it clearly then and I was almost laughing with relief. 'It's not a rock,' I said. 'It's a ship.' There was no doubt about it now. The rusty hull was no longer blurred, but stood out clear and sharp, and what I had taken to be a light tower was its single funnel.

We were all of us laughing with the sense of relief as we turned back on to the course. 'Hove-to by the look of it,' Mike said as he stopped hauling in on the main-sheet and began to coil it down.

It certainly looked like it, for now that we were back on course her position didn't seem to have altered at all. She was lying broadside on to us as though held there by the wind and, as we closed with her and her outline became clearer, I could see that she was stationary, wallowing in the swell. Our course would leave her about half a mile to starboard. I reached for the glasses. There was something about the ship . . . something about her shape and her rusty hull and the way she seemed a little down at the bows.

'Probably pumping out her bilges,' Hal said, his voice hesitant as though he, too, were puzzled.

I focused the glasses and the outline of the

19

vessel leaped towards me. She was an old boat with straight bows and a clean sweep to her sheer. She had an old-fashioned counter stern, an untidy clutter of derricks round her masts, and too much superstructure. Her single smoke stack, like her masts, was almost vertical. At one time she had been painted black, but now she had a rusty, uncared-for look. There was a sort of lifelessness about her that held me with the glasses to my eyes. And then I saw the lifeboat. 'Steer straight for her, will you, Hal,' I said.

'Anything wrong?' he asked, reacting immediately to the note of urgency in my voice.

'Yes. One of the lifeboats is hanging vertically from its davits.' It was more than that. The other davits were empty. I passed him the glasses. 'Take a look at the for'ard davits,' I told him and my voice trembled slightly, the birth of a strange feeling of excitement.

Soon we could see the empty davits with the naked eye and the single lifeboat hanging from the falls. 'Looks deserted,' Mike said. 'And she's quite a bit down by the bows. Do you think—' He left the sentence unfinished. The same thought was in all our minds.

We came down on her amidships. The name at her bows was so broken up with rust streaks that we couldn't read it. Close-to she looked in wretched shape. Her rusty bow plates were out of true, her superstructure was damaged and she was definitely down by the bows, her stern standing high so that we could see the top of her screw. A festoon of wires hung from her mast derricks. She was a cargo ship and she looked as though she'd taken a hell of a hammering.

We went about within a cable's length of her and I hailed her through our megaphone. My voice lost itself in the silence of the sea. There was no answer. The only sound was the sloshing of the swell against her sides. We ran down on her quickly then, Hal steering to pass close under her stern. I think we were all of us watching for her name. And then suddenly there it was in rust-streaked lettering high above our heads just as it had been during the night: *MARY DEARE—Southampton*.

She was quite a big boat, at least 6,000 tons. Abandoned like that she should have had a salvage tug in attendance, ships standing by. But there wasn't another vessel in sight. She was alone and lifeless within twenty miles of the French coast. I glanced up along her starboard side as we came out from under her stern. Both davits were empty, the lifeboats gone.

'You were right then,' Mike said, turning to Hal, his voice tense. 'There wasn't anybody on the bridge last night.'

We stared up at her in silence as we slipped away from her, awed by the sense of mystery.

21

The rope falls hung forlornly from the empty davits. A thin trailer of smoke emerged incongruously from her funnel. That was the only sign of life. 'They must have abandoned ship just before they nearly ran us down,' I said.

'But she was steaming at full ahead,' Hal said, speaking more to himself than to us. 'You don't abandon ship with the engines going full ahead. And why didn't she radio for help?'

I was thinking of what Hal had said half-jokingly last night. If there was really nobody on board . . . I stood there, my hands braced on the guardrail, my body tense as I stared at her, searching for some sign of life. But there was nothing; nothing but that thin wisp of smoke trailing from the funnel. Salvage! A ship of 6,000 tons, drifting and abandoned. It was unbelievable. And if we could bring her into port under her own steam . . . I turned to Hal. 'Do you think you could lay *Sea Witch* alongside her, close enough for me to get hold of one of those falls?'

'Don't be a fool,' he said. 'There's still quite a swell running. You may damage the boat, and if this gale—'

But I was in no mood for caution now. 'Ready about!' I called. And then, 'Lee ho!' We came about on to the other tack and I sent Mike below to get Ian out of his bunk. 'We'll jog up to her close-hauled,' I told Hal. 'I'll jump for the ropes as you go about.'

'It's crazy,' he said. 'You've a hell of a height to climb to the deck. And supposing the wind pipes up. I may not be able to get you—'

'Oh, to hell with the wind!' I cried. 'Do you think I'm going to pass up a chance like this? Whatever happened to the poor devils who abandoned her, this is the chance of a lifetime for Mike and myself.'

He stared at me for a moment, and then he nodded. 'Okay. It's your boat.' We were headed back for the ship now. 'When we get under her lee,' Hal said, 'we'll be pretty well blanketed. I may have some difficulty—' He stopped there and glanced up at the burgee.

I had done the same, for there was a different feel about the boat now. She was surging along with a noise of water from her bows and spray wetting the foredeck. The burgee was streamed out to starboard. I checked with the compass. 'You'll have no difficulty standing off from her,' I said. 'The wind's north-westerly now.'

He nodded, his eyes lifting to the sails. 'You're still determined to go on board?'

'Yes.'

'Well, you'd better not stay long. There's some weight in the wind now.'

'I'll be as quick as I can,' I said. 'If you want to recall me in a hurry signal on the fog-horn.' We were doing all of four knots now and the ship was coming up fast. I went to the charthouse door and yelled to Mike. He came

23

almost immediately. Ian was behind him, white-faced and still sweaty-looking from his bunk. I gave him the boat-hook and told him to stand by in the bows ready to shove off. 'We'll go about just before we get to her. That'll take the way off her and you'll be all set to stand-off again.' I was stripping off my oilskins. Already the rusty sides of the *Mary Deare* were towering above us. It looked a hell of a height to climb. 'Ready about?' I asked.

'Ready about,' Hal said. And then he swung the wheel. *Sea Witch* began to pay off, slowly, very slowly. For a moment it looked as though she was going to poke her long bowsprit through the steamer's rusty plates. Then she was round and I made up the starboard rudder as the boom swung over. There was little wind now that we were close under the *Mary Deare*. The sails flapped lazily. The cross-trees were almost scraping the steamer's sides as we rolled in the swell. I grabbed a torch and ran to the mast, climbed the starboard rail and stood there, poised, my feet on the bulwarks, my hands gripping the shrouds. Her way carried me past the for'ard davit falls. There was still a gap of several yards between me and the ship's side. Hal closed it slowly. Leaning out I watched the after davit falls slide towards me. There was a jar as the tip of our cross-trees rammed the plates above my head. The first of the falls came abreast of me. I leaned right out, but they were a good foot beyond my reach.

'This time!' Hal shouted. The cross-trees jarred again. I felt the jolt of it through the shroud I was clinging to. And then my hand closed on the ropes and I let go, falling heavily against the ship's side, the lift of a swell wetting me to my knees. 'Okay!' I yelled.

Hal was shouting to Ian to shove off. I could see him thrusting wildly with the boat-hook. Then the end of the boom hit me between the shoulder-blades, the jar of it almost making me lose my hold. I hauled myself upwards with desperate urgency, afraid that the stern might swing and crush my legs against the ship's side. There was the slam of wood just below my feet and then I saw *Sea Witch* was clear and standing out away from the ship. 'Don't be long,' Hal shouted.

*Sea Witch* was already heeling to the wind, the water creaming back from her bows and a white wake showing at her stern as she gathered speed. 'I'll be as quick as I can,' I called back to him, and then I began to climb.

That climb seemed endless. The *Mary Deare* was rolling all the time, so that one minute I'd be swung out over the sea and the next slammed against the iron plates of her side. There were moments when I thought I'd never make it. And when, finally, I reached the upper-deck, *Sea Witch* was already half a mile away, though Hal had her pointed up into the wind and was pinching her so that her sails were all a-shiver.

25

The sea was no longer oil-smooth. Little waves were forming on the tops of the swell, making patterns of white as they broke. I knew I hadn't much time. I cupped my hands round my mouth and shouted: '*Mary Deare!* Ahoy! Is there anybody on board?' A gull shifted his stance uneasily on one of the ventilators, watching me with a beady eye. There was no answer, no sound except the door to the after deck-house slatting back and forth, regular as a metronome, and the bump of the lifeboat against the port side. It was obvious that she was deserted. All the evidence of abandonment was there on the deck—the empty falls, the stray pieces of clothing, a loaf lying in the scuppers, a hunk of cheese trampled into the deck, a half-open suitcase spilling nylons and cigarettes, a pair of sea boots; they had left her in a hurry and at night.

But why?

A sense of unease held me for a moment—a deserted ship with all its secrets, all its death-in-life stillness—I felt like an intruder and glanced quickly back towards *Sea Witch*. She was no bigger than a toy now in the leaden immensity of sea and sky, and the wind was beginning to moan through the empty ship—hurry! hurry!

A quick search and then the decision would have to be made. I ran for'ard and swung myself up the ladder to the bridge. The wheelhouse was empty. It's odd, but it came as a shock to me. Everything was so very normal there; a couple of dirty cups on a ledge, a pipe carefully laid down in an ash-tray, the binoculars set down on the seat of the Captain's chair—and the engine-room telegraph set to *Full Ahead*. It was as though at any moment the helmsman might return to take his place at the wheel.

But outside there was evidence in plenty of heavy weather. All the port wing of the bridge had been stove in, the ladder buckled and twisted, and down on the well-deck the seas had practically stripped the covering from the for'ard holds and a wire hawser was lying uncoiled in loops like dannert wire. And yet that in itself didn't account for her being abandoned; another tarpaulin hatch cover had been partly rigged and fresh timbering lay around as though the watch on deck had just knocked off for a cup of tea.

The chartroom at the back of the wheelhouse shed no light on the mystery; in fact, the reverse, for there was the log book open at the last entry: *20.46 hours—Les Heaux Light bearing 114°, approximately 12 miles. Wind south-east—Force 2. Sea moderate. Visibility good. Altered course for the Needles—north 33° east.* The date was March 18, and the time showed that this entry had been made just an hour and three-quarters before the *Mary Deare* had almost run us down. Entries in the log were made every hour so that whatever

27

it was that had made them abandon ship had occurred between nine and ten the previous night, probably just as the mist was closing in.

Checking back through the log I found nothing to suggest that the ship would have to be abandoned. There had been constant gales and they had taken a bad beating. But that was all. *Hove-to on account of dangerous seas, waves sometimes breaking against bridge. Making water in No. I hold. Pumps not holding their own.* That entry for March 16 was the worst. Wind strength was given as Force 11 for twelve solid hours. And before then, ever since they had left the Mediterranean through the Straits, the wind had never fallen below Force 7, which is moderate gale, and was several times recorded as Force 10, whole gale. The pumps had been kept going all the time.

If they had abandoned ship in the gale of March 16 it would have been understandable. But the log showed that they had rounded Ushant on the morning of March 18 in clear weather with seas moderate and the wind Force 3. There was even a note—*Pumps making good headway. Clearing wreckage and repairing Number One hatch cover.*

It didn't make sense.

A companionway led to the upper or boat-deck level. The door to the Captain's cabin was open. The room was neat and tidy, everything in its place; no sign of hurried departure. From the desk a girl's face in a big silver frame smiled at me, her fair hair catching the light, and across the bottom of the picture she had scrawled: *For Daddy—Bons voyages, and come back soon. Love—Janet.* There was coal dust on the frame and more of it on the desk and smudged over a file of papers that proved to be the cargo manifest, showing that the *Mary Deare* had loaded cotton at Rangoon on January 13 and was bound for Antwerp. On top of a filing tray filled with papers were several air mail letter-cards slit open with a knife. They were English letter-cards post-marked London and they were addressed to Captain James Taggart, *S.S. Mary Deare* at Aden, addressed in the same uneven, rather rounded hand that had scrawled across the bottom of the photograph. And below the letters, amongst the mass of papers, I found report sheets written in a small, neat hand and signed James Taggart. But they only covered the voyage from Rangoon to Aden. On the desk beside the tray was a sealed letter addressed to Miss Janet Taggart, University College, Gower Street, London, W.C.1. It was in a different hand and the envelope was unstamped.

All those little things, those little homely details . . . I don't know how to express it— they added up to something, something I didn't like. There was that cabin, so quiet, with all the decisions that had driven the ship throughout her life still there in the

29

atmosphere of it—and the ship herself silent as the grave. And then I saw the raincoats hanging on the door, two blue Merchant Navy officers' raincoats hanging side by side, the one much bigger than the other.

I went out and slammed the door behind me, as though by closing it I could shut away my sudden, unreasoned fear. 'Ahoy! Is there anyone on board?' My voice, high and hoarse, echoed through the vaults of the ship. The wind moaned at me from the deck. Hurry! I must hurry. All I had to do was check the engines now, decide whether we could get her under way.

I stumbled down the dark well of a companionway, following the beam of my torch, flashing it through the open doorway of the saloon where I had a glimpse of places still laid and chairs pushed hastily back. A faint smell of burning lingered on the musty air. But it didn't come from the pantry—the fire was out, the stove cold. My torch focused on a half-empty tin of bully lying on the table. There was butter, cheese, and a loaf of bread with the crust all covered in coal dust; coal dust on the handle of the knife that had been used to cut it, coal dust on the floor.

'Is there anybody about?' I yelled. 'Ahoy! Anyone there?' No answer. I went back to the 'tween-decks alley-way that ran the length of the port-hand midships section. It was as silent and as black as the adit of a mine. I started down it, and then I stopped. There it was again—a sound I had been conscious of, but had not thought about; a sound like the shifting of gravel. It echoed within the ship's hull as though somewhere the steel plates were shifting on the bottom of the sea. It was a strange, uncanny sound, and it stopped abruptly as I walked on down the alley-way so that, in the vacuum of abrupt silence, I heard the wind's howl again.

The door at the end of the alley-way swung open to the roll of the ship, letting in a glimmer of daylight. I started towards it, conscious that the acrid smell of burning had increased until it quite overlaid the fusty mixture of hot oil, stale cooking and sea water dampness that permeates the 'tween-decks of all cargo ships. A fire-hose, fixed to a hydrant near the engine-room door, snaked aft through pools of water and disappeared through the open door, out on to the well-deck beyond. I followed it. Out in the daylight I saw that Number Three hatch was burned and blackened, eaten half away by fire, and Number Four had been partly opened up. Fire hoses curled round the deck, disappearing into the open inspection hatch of Number Three hold. I went a few rungs down the vertical ladder, flashing my torch. But there was no smoke, no lurid glow, and the acrid fumes of fire had a stale, washed-out smell, mixed with the pungent odour of chemicals. An empty foam extinguisher toppled on its side, clattering against the steel of the bulkhead plating. My torch showed the black pit of the hold piled high with charred and sodden bales of cotton and there was the sound of water slopping about.

The fire was out—dead—not even a wisp of smoke. And yet the ship had been abandoned. It didn't make sense. I was thinking of last night, how the smell of burning had lingered in the mist after the ship had gone past us. And there was the coal dust on the captain's desk and in the galley. Somebody must have put that fire out. I ran back to the engine-room door, remembering the grating sound of gravel shifting. Could it have been coal? Was there somebody down in the stoke-hold? Somewhere in the ship a hatch slammed, or maybe it was a door. I went in, on to the catwalk that hung over the black abyss of the engine-room, criss-crossed with the steel of gratings and vertical ladders. 'Ahoy!' I yelled. 'Ahoy there!'

No answer. My torch showed a glint of polished brass and the duller gleam of burnished steel amidst the shadowy shapes of the engines. No movement either . . . only the sound of water that made little rushing noises as it slopped about to the roll of the ship.

I hesitated, wondering whether to go down to the stoke-hold, held there by a sort of fear. And it was then that I heard the footsteps.

They went slowly along the starboard alley-way—boots clanging hollow against the steel flooring; a heavy, dragging tread that passed the engine-room door, going for'ard towards the bridge. The sound of the footsteps gradually faded away and was lost in the slapping of the water in the bilges far below me.

It couldn't have been more than twenty seconds that I remained there, paralysed, and then I flung myself at the door, dragged it open and dived out into the alley-way, tripping over the step in my haste, dropping my torch and fetching up against the farther wall with a force that almost stunned me. The torch had fallen into a pool of rusty water and lay there, shining like a glow-worm in the darkness. I stooped and picked it up and shone it down the passage.

There was nobody there. The beam reached the whole shadowy length as far as the ladder to the deck, and the corridor was empty. I shouted, but nobody answered. The ship rolled with a creak of wood and the slosh of water, and above me, muffled, I heard the rhythmic slamming of the door to the after deckhouse. And then a faint, far-distant sound reached me, a sound that had a note of urgency in it. It was *Sea Witch's* fog-horn signalling me to return.

I stumbled for'ard and as I neared the ladder to the deck, the fog-horn's moan was mingled with the noise of the wind soughing through the superstructure. Hurry! Hurry! There was a greater urgency in it now; urgency in the noise of the wind, in the fog-horn's blare.

I reached the ladder, was starting up—when I saw him. He was outlined for an instant in the swinging beam of my torch, a shadowy figure standing motionless in the recess of a doorway, black with a gleam of white to his eyes.

I checked, shocked into immobility—all the silence, all the ghostly silence of that dead ship clutching at my throat. And then I turned the beam of the torch full on him. He was a big man, dressed in reefer and sea boots, and black with coal dust. Sweat had seamed his face, making grime-streaked runnels as though he had wept big tears and the bone of his forehead glistened. All the right side of his jaw was bruised and clotted with blood.

He moved suddenly with great rapidity, came down on me with a rush. The torch was knocked from my hand and I smelt the stale smell of sweat and coal dust as his powerful fingers gripped my shoulders, turning me like a child, twisting my head to the cold daylight that came down the ladder. 'What do you want?' he demanded in a harsh, rasping voice. 'What are you doing here? Who are you?' He shook me violently as though by shaking me he'd get at the truth.

'I'm Sands,' I gasped out. 'John Sands. I came to see—'

'How did you get on board?' There was a note of authority, as well as violence, in the

34

rasp of his voice.

'By the falls,' I said. 'We sighted the *Mary Deare* drifting and when we saw the lifeboats gone, we came alongside to investigate.'

'Investigate!' He glared at me. 'There's nothing to investigate.' And then quickly, still gripping hold of me: 'Is Higgins with you? Did you pick him up? Is that why you're here?'

'Higgins?' I stared at him.

'Yes, Higgins.' There was a sort of desperate violence in the way he said the man's name. 'But for him I'd have got her safe to Southampton by now. If you've got Higgins with you . . .' He stopped suddenly, his head on one side, listening. The sound of the fog-horn was nearer now and Mike's voice was hailing me. 'They're calling you.' His grip tightened convulsively on my shoulders. 'What's your boat?' he demanded. 'What sort of boat is it?'

'A yacht.' And I added inconsequentially: 'You nearly ran us down last night.'

'A yacht!' He let go of me then with a little gasp like a sigh of relief. 'Well, you'd better get back to it. Wind's getting up.'

'Yes,' I said. 'We'll have to hurry—both of us.'

'Both of us?' He frowned.

'Of course,' I said. 'We'll take you off and when we reach Peter Port . . .'

'No!' The word exploded from his lips. 'No. I'm staying with my ship.'

'You're the Captain, are you?'

'Yes.' He stooped and picked up my torch and handed it to me. Mike's voice came to us faintly, a strangely disembodied shout from the outside world. The wind was a low-pitched, whining note. 'Better hurry,' he said.

'Come on then,' I said. I couldn't believe he'd be fool enough to stay. There was nothing he could do.

'No. I'm not leaving.' And then a little wildly, as though I were a foreigner who had to be shouted at: 'I'm not leaving, I tell you.'

'Don't be a fool,' I said. 'You can't do any good here—not alone. We're bound for Peter Port. We can get you there in a few hours and then you'll be able to—'

He shook his head, like an animal at bay, and then waved an arm at me as though signalling me to go.

'There's a gale coming up.'

'I know that,' he said.

'Then for God's sake, man . . . it's your one chance to get clear.' And because he was the Captain and obviously thinking about his ship, I added, 'It's the one hope for the ship, too. If you don't get a tug out to her soon she'll be blown right on to the Channel Islands. You can do far more good—'

'Get off my ship!' He was suddenly trembling. 'Get off her, do you hear? I know what I have to do.'

His voice was wild, his manner suddenly menacing. I stood my ground for a moment

36

longer. 'You've got help coming then?' I asked. And when he didn't seem to understand, I said, 'You've radioed for help?'

There was a moment's hesitation and then he said, 'Yes, yes, I've radioed for help. Now go.'

I hesitated. But there was nothing else I could say, and if he wouldn't come . . . I paused halfway up the ladder. 'Surely to God you'll change your mind?' I said. His face showed in the darkness below me—a strong, hard face, still young but with deep-bitten lines in it, made deeper by exhaustion. He looked desperate, and at the same time oddly pathetic. 'Come on, man—whilst you've got the chance.'

But he didn't answer; just turned away and left me there. And I went on up the ladder to meet the weight of the wind howling along the deck and find the sea a mass of whitecaps with *Sea Witch* pitching violently two cables off.


## CHAPTER TWO

I had stayed too long. I knew as soon as *Sea Witch* turned to pick me up. She came roaring down-wind, the big yankee jib burying her bows deep into the wind-whipped waters, her long bowsprit thrusting into the backs of the waves, spearing them and coming out in a

37

welter of spray. Hal had been right. I should never have boarded the ship. I ran to the falls, damning the crazy madman who'd refused to be taken off. If he had come with me, there would have been some point.

*Sea Witch* heeled over in a gust as Hal fought the wheel, bringing her round through the wind, all her sails flogging madly. The big yankee filled with a crack like a pistol shot, heeling the boat over till all the weed-grown boot-topping showed in the trough of a wave; and then the big sail split across and in an instant was blown to tatters. The wind was strong to gale in the gusts and she should have been reefed by now, but they hadn't a hope of reefing, just the three of them. It was madness for them to attempt to come alongside. I had never seen a sea whipped up so quickly. But Mike was waving to me, signalling downwards with his hand, and Hal was braced at the wheel, edging her up towards the ship's side, mainsail shivering, barely filled, the remnants of the yankee fluttering in streamers from the forestay. I caught hold of one of the falls then and swung myself out over the side, slithering down hand over hand until the surge of a wave soaked me to the waist and I looked up and saw that the rusty plates stood above me, high as a cliff.

I could hear *Sea Witch* now, hear the slap of her bows as she hit a wave and the solid, surging noise of her passage through the water.

There were shouts and over my shoulder I saw her coming up into the wind, very close now, her head unwilling to pay off, the bowsprit almost touching the steamer's side. A gust of wind buffeted me, the main boom slammed over, sails filling suddenly, and she went surging past me a good twenty yards out from where I clung, swinging sickeningly in mid-air. Hal was shouting at me. 'The wind . . . strong . . . the ship turning round.' That was all I caught and yet he was so close I could see the water dripping off his oilskins, could see his blue eyes wide and startled-looking under his sou'wester.

Mike eased the sheets and the boat roared off down-wind. Hanging there, soaked with sea water thrown up from the wave tops breaking against the ship's side, I felt the weight of the wind pressing me in towards the rusty hull. At each roll I had to brace myself to meet the shock of my body being flung against her. Gradually I realized what had happened. The wind was swinging the *Mary Deare* broadside on; and I was on the windward side, exposed to the full force of the rising gale.

*Sea Witch* went about again and I wanted to shout to Hal not to be a fool, that it was no good. Now that the *Mary Deare* had swung, it was dangerous to come alongside with the wind pressing the yacht down on to the ship. But all I did was pray that he'd make it, for I knew I couldn't hang there much longer. The ropes were getting slippery with water and it was bitterly cold.

I don't know how Hal managed it, but despite the lack of headsails to bring her bow round, he got her about with almost no way on her a short stone's throw from where I was clinging. Then he let her drift down-wind. It was a superb piece of seamanship. There was a moment when her stern was almost within my reach. I think I might have made it, but at that moment the roll of the *Mary Deare* swung me against her side and I was held fast against the wet chill of her hull, whilst the familiar counter of my boat slid away as Hal got her moving again to prevent her from being battered to pieces against the ship. 'No good . . . daren't . . . too dangerous . . . Peter Port.' The ragged snatches of Hal's shouts reached me through the wind as I was freed from the ship's side and swung out over the water, right over the spot where *Sea Witch's* stern had been only a few seconds before. I wanted to shout to him to try again, just once more. But I knew it was risking the boat and their lives as well. 'Okay,' I yelled. 'Make Peter Port. Good luck!'

He shouted something back, but I couldn't hear what it was. *Sea Witch* was already disappearing beyond the steamer's bows, going fast with all her sheets eased and the wind driving at the great spread of her mainsail. I glanced up quickly at the towering wall of iron above my head and then I began to climb whilst I still had some strength left.

But each time the ship rolled I was flung against the side. It gave me extra purchase, flattened hard against the rusty plates, but it battered me, knocking the wind out of me. And each time I was swung clear the loss of purchase almost flung me off, for my fingers were numbed with cold and my arms and knees trembled with the strain of clinging there too long. The waves broke, engulfing me in ice-cold spray, and sometimes green water sloshed up the side of the ship and gripped me about the waist, plucking at me as it subsided.

I made only a few feet, and then I was finally halted. I could climb no further. Flattened against the ship's side, I gripped the rope with my shaking legs and, letting go with one hand, hauled up the free end, pulling it up between my legs and wrapping it over my shoulder. It took the strain off my arms. But it didn't get me back on to the ship's deck. I began to shout then, but the sound of my voice was whipped away by the wind. I knew the man couldn't possibly hear me, but I still went on shouting, praying that he'd come. He was my only hope. And then I stopped shouting, for I had no breath left—jarred and bruised, swung one moment out over the tumbled waters, the next slammed against the ship's side, it came to me slowly that this was the end.

It is difficult to be scared of something that is inevitable. You accept it, and that is that. But I remember thinking how ironical it was; the sea was to me a liquid, quiet, unruffled world through which to glide down green corridors to the darker depths, down tall reef walls with the fish, all brilliant colours in the surface dazzle, down to the shadowy shapes of barnacle-crusted wrecks. Now it was a raging fury of a giant, rearing up towards me, clutching at me, foaming and angry.

And then hope came suddenly in the graze of my hand against the rusty plates. Blood oozed in droplets from my knuckles, to be washed away by a blinding sheet of spray, and I stared, fascinated, as a flake of rust was peeled off by the upward scrape of my body. I didn't look up. I didn't move for fear I had imagined that I was being hauled up. But when the sea no longer reached me as it burst against the ship's side, I knew it was true. I looked up then and saw that the davits had been hauled inboard, saw the ropes move, taut, across the rail-capping.

Slowly, a foot at a time, I was hauled up, until at last my head came level with the deck and I looked into the haggard face and the wild, dark eyes of the *Mary Deare's* captain. He dragged me over the side and I collapsed on to the deck. I never knew till then how comfortable iron deck plates could be. 'Better get some dry clothes,' he said.

He pulled me to my feet and I stood there, trying to thank him. But I was too exhausted, too numbed with cold. My teeth chattered. He got my arm round his neck and half dragged me along the deck and down to one of the officers' cabins. 'Help yourself to what you want,' he said as he lowered me on to the bunk. 'Rice was about your height.' He stood over me for a moment, frowning at me as though I were some sort of a problem that had to be worked out. Then he left me.

I lay back, exhaustion weighting my eyelids, drowning consciousness. But my body had no warmth left in it and the cold cling of sodden clothes dragged me up off the bunk, to strip and towel myself down. I found dry clothes in a drawer and put them on; woollen underwear, a shirt, a pair of trousers and a sweater. A glow spread through me and my teeth stopped chattering. I took a cigarette from a packet on the desk and lit it, lying back again on the bunk, my eyes closed, drawing on it luxuriously. I felt better then—not worried about myself, only about *Sea Witch*. I hoped to God she'd get safe to Peter Port.

I was drowsy with the sudden warmth; the cabin was airless and smelt of stale sweat. The cigarette kept slipping from my fingers. And then a voice from a great distance off was saying: 'Sit up and drink this.' I opened my eyes and he was standing over me again with a steaming mug in his hand. It was tea laced with rum. I started to thank him, but he cut me short with a quick, angry movement of his hand. He didn't say anything; just stood there, watching me drink it, his face in shadow. There was a strange hostility in his silence.

The ship was rolling heavily now and through the open door came the sound of the wind howling along the deck. The *Mary Deare* would be a difficult tow if it blew a gale. They might not even be able to get a tow-line across to us. I was remembering what Hal had said about the Channel Islands as a lee shore. The warmth of the drink was putting new life into me; enough for me to consider what faced me, now that I was marooned on board the *Mary Deare*.

I looked up at the man standing over me, wondering why he had refused to leave the ship. 'How long before you expect help to reach us?' I asked him.

'There won't be any help. No call went out.' He leaned suddenly down towards me, his hands clenched and his jaw, thrust into the grey light coming in through the porthole, showing hard and knotted. 'Why the hell didn't you stay on your yacht?' And then he turned abruptly and made for the door.

He was halfway through it when I called after him. 'Taggart!' I swung my legs off the bunk.

He spun round on his heels as though I'd punched him in the back. 'I'm not Taggart.' He came back through the doorway. 'What made you think I was Taggart?'

'You said you were the captain.'

44

'So I am. But my name's Patch.' He was standing over me again, a dark shadow against the light. 'How did you know about Taggart? Are you something to do with the owners? Is that why you were out there . . .' The wildness went out of his voice and he wiped his hand across the coal dust grime of his face. 'No. It couldn't be that.' He stared at me for a moment and then he shrugged his shoulders. 'We'll talk about it later. We've plenty of time. All the time in the world. Better get some sleep now.' He turned then and went quickly out.

Sleep! Five minutes ago that was what I'd wanted most in the world. But now I was wide awake. I won't say I was scared; not then. Just uneasy. That the man should behave oddly was not surprising. He had been twelve hours alone on the ship. He'd put out a fire single-handed and he'd stoked furnaces till he was on the brink of exhaustion. Twelve hours of hell; enough to unbalance any man. But if he was the captain, why wasn't he Taggart? And why hadn't the ship radioed for assistance?

I got up stiffly off the bunk, pulled on a pair of sea boots that were lying under the desk and staggered out into the corridor. There was a lot of movement on the ship now. Lying broadside to the seas, she was rolling heavily. A rush of cold air brought with it the battering noise of the wind. I went straight up to the bridge. It was raining and visibility was down to less than a mile; the whole sea was a dirty white of breaking water with the spray smoking from the crests and streaming away before the wind. It was already blowing gale force in the gusts.

The compass showed the ship lying with her bows to the north. The wind had backed into the west then; almost a dead run to Peter Port. I stood there working it out, listening to the thundering of the gale, staring out at that bleak waste of tumbled water. If Hal made it—if he got under the lee of Guernsey and made Peter Port . . . But it would take him several hours and he wouldn't realize at first that no distress signal had been sent out. Even when he did, the lifeboat would have to fight the gale to reach us; it would take them six hours at least, and by then it would be dark. They'd never find us in the dark in this sort of weather.

I turned abruptly and went through into the chartroom. A new position had been marked on the chart; a small cross two miles north-east of the Roches Douvres with 11.06 pencilled against it. It was now eleven-fifteen. I laid off the line of our drift with the parallel rule. If the wind held westerly we should drive straight on to the Plateau des Minquiers. He had discovered that, too, for a faint pencil line had been drawn in and there was a smudge of dirt across the area of the reefs where his fingers had rested.

Well, at least he was sane enough to appreciate the danger! I stood, staring at the chart, thinking about what it meant. It wasn't a pleasant thought. To be driven ashore on the rocky cliffs of Jersey would have been bad enough, but the Plateau des Minquiers . . .

I reached out to the bookshelf above the chart table, searching for Part II of the Channel Pilot. But it wasn't there. Not that it mattered. I knew them by reputation: a fearful area of rocks and reefs that we call the Minkies.

I was thinking about the Minkies and how it would feel to be on board a ship being pounded to pieces in such a maelstrom of submerged rocks when I noticed the door at the back of the chartroom with W/T stencilled on it. There was a steep ladder with no door at the top and as soon as I entered the radio shack I knew why no distress call had been sent out. The place had been gutted by fire.

The shock of it halted me in the doorway. The fire in the hold, and now this! But this was an old fire. There was no smell of burning, and planks of new wood had been nailed over the charred gaps that the fire had burned in roof and walls. No attempt had been made to clear the debris. The emergency accumulators had come through the burned-out roof and lay on the floor where they had fallen; one had smashed down on to the fire-blackened table and had crushed the half-melted remains of the transmitter. Bunk and chair were scarcely recognizable, skeletons of blackened wood, and the radio equipment fixed to the walls was distorted beyond recognition and festooned with metal stalactites where solder had dripped and congealed; more equipment lay on the floor, black, twisted pieces of metal in the debris of charred wood. Whatever had caused the fire, it had burned with extraordinary ferocity. Water had seeped in through the gaps in the walls, streaking the blackened wood. The wind stirred the sodden ashes, shaking the rotten structure as it howled round the bridge.

I went slowly back down the ladder to the chartroom. Maybe the log book would tell me something. But it was no longer open on the table. I went through to the wheelhouse and was halted momentarily by the sight of a shaggy comber rearing up out of the murk to the port bow, spindrift streaming from its crest. It crashed down on to the iron bulwarks, and then the whole fore part of the ship, all except the mast and derricks, disappeared beneath a welter of white water. It seemed an age before the shape of the bows appeared again, a faint outline of bulwarks rising sluggishly, reluctantly out of the sea.

I hurried down the companionway and made straight for the captain's cabin. But he wasn't there. I tried the saloon and the galley, and then I knew he must be down in the stoke-hold again. There was no doubt in my mind what had to be done. The pumps had to be got

48

going. But there was no light in the engine-room, no sound of coal being shovelled into the furnaces. I shouted from the catwalk, but there was no answer; only the echo of my voice, a small sound lost in the pounding of the waves against the outside of the hull and the swirl of water in the bilges.

I felt a sudden sense of loss, a quite childish sense of loneliness. I didn't want to be alone in that empty ship. I hurried back to his cabin, the need to find him becoming more and more urgent. It was empty, as it had been before. A clang of metal aft sent me pushing through the door to the boat deck, and then I saw him. He was coming towards me, staggering with exhaustion, his eyes staring and his face dead white where he had wiped it clean of sweat and coal dust. All his clothes were black with coal and behind him a shovel slid across the deck. 'Where have you been?' I cried. 'I couldn't find you. What have you been doing all this time?'

'That's my business,' he muttered, his voice slurred with fatigue, and he pushed past me and went into his cabin.

I followed him in. 'What's the position?' I asked. 'How much water are we making? The seas are breaking right across the bows.'

He nodded. 'It'll go on like that—all the time now—until the hatch cover goes. And then there'll only be the shored-up bulkhead between us and the sea-bed.' It was said flatly, without intonation. He didn't seem to care, or else he was resigned.

'But if we get the pumps going . . .' His lack of interest checked me. 'Damn it, man,' I said. 'That was what you were doing when I came aboard, wasn't it?'

'How do you know what I'd been doing?' He suddenly seemed to blaze up, his eyes angry and wild. He seized hold of my arm. 'How do you know?' he repeated.

'There was a wisp of smoke coming from the funnel,' I said quickly. 'And then all that coal dust; you were covered with it.' I didn't know what had roused him. 'You must have been down in the stoke-hold.'

'The stoke-hold?' He nodded slowly. 'Yes, of course.' He let go of my arm, his body gradually losing its tautness, relaxing.

'If the pumps could keep her afloat coming up through the Bay . . .' I said.

'We had a crew then, a full head of steam.' His shoulders drooped. 'Besides, there wasn't so much water in the for'ard hold then.'

'Is she holed?' I asked. 'Is that the trouble?'

'Holed?' He stared at me. 'What made you . . .' He pushed his hand up through his hair and then down across his face. His skin was sallow under the grime; sallow and sweaty and tired-looking. The ship lurched and quivered to the onslaught of another wave. I saw his muscles tense as though it were his own body that was being battered. 'It can't last long.'

I felt suddenly sick and empty inside. The

man had given up hope. I could see it in the sag of his shoulders, hear it in the flatness of his voice. He was tired beyond caring. 'You mean the hatch cover?' He nodded. 'And what happens then?' I asked. 'Will she float with that hold full of water?'

'Probably. Until the boiler-room bulkhead goes.' His tone was cold-blooded and without emotion. That hold had been flooded a long time. The ship had been down by the bows when we had sighted her through the mist. And last night ... I was remembering the draught marks high out of the water at her stern and the blades of the propeller thrashing at the wave tops. He had had time to get used to the idea.

But I was damned if I was going to sit down and wait for the end. 'How long would it take to get steam up—enough to drive the pumps?' I asked. But he didn't seem to hear me. He was leaning against the deck, his eyes half-closed. I caught hold of his arm and shook him as though I were waking him out of a trance. 'The pumps!' I shouted at him. 'If you show me what to do, I'll stoke.'

His eyes flicked open and he stared at me. He didn't say anything.

'You're just about all in,' I told him. 'You ought to get some sleep. But first you must show me how to operate the furnace.'

He seemed to hesitate, and then he shrugged his shoulders. 'All right,' he said, and

51

he pulled himself together and went out and down the companion ladder to the main deck. The weight of the wind was heeling the ship, giving her a permanent list to starboard. Like that she rolled sluggishly with an odd, uneven motion that was occasionally violent. His feet dragged along the dark, echoing alley-way; at times he seemed uncertain of his balance, almost dazed.

We turned in through the engine-room door, crossed the cat-walk and descended an iron ladder into the dark pit of the engine-room, the beams of our torches giving momentary glimpses of vast shadowy machinery, all still and lifeless. Our footsteps rang hollow and metallic on the iron gratings as we made our way for'ard through a litter of smaller machinery. There was a sound of water moving in little rushes and heavy thuds echoed up the tunnel of the propeller shaft.

We passed the main controls with the bridge telegraph repeaters and then we reached the doors leading in to the boiler-room. Both doors were open, and beyond, the shapes of the boilers loomed bulky and majestic, without heat.

He hesitated a moment, and then moved forward again. 'It's this one,' he said, pointing to the port-hand of the three boilers. A dull red glow rimmed the furnace door. 'And there's the coal.' He swung the beam of his torch over the black heap that had spilled out of the coal-box opening. He had half-turned back towards the furnace, when he checked and stood staring at the coal as though fascinated, slowly lifting the beam of his torch so that the white circle of it shone on plate after plate, all black with dust, as though he were tracing the line of the coal coming down from the bunkering hatch at deck level. 'We'll work two-hour shifts,' he said quickly, glancing at his watch. 'It's nearly twelve now. I'll relieve you at two.' He seemed suddenly in a hurry to go.

'Just a minute,' I said. 'How do you operate the furnace?'

He glanced impatiently back at the boiler with its temperature gauge and the levers below that operated the furnace doors and the dampers. 'It's quite simple. You'll get the hang of it easily enough.' He was already turning away again. 'I'm going to get some sleep,' he muttered. And with that he left me.

I opened my mouth to call him back. But there seemed no point. I should probably find out easily enough and he needed sleep badly. For a moment, as he passed through the stokehold doors, his body was sharply etched against the light of his torch. I stood there listening to the sound of his feet on the steel ladders of the engine-room, seeing the faint reflection of his torch limning the open doorway. Then it was gone and I was alone, conscious suddenly of the odd noises about me—the murmur of water, the queer booming of waves breaking against the ship's hull and the sudden little rushes of coal tipping in the chutes as she rolled; conscious, too, of a sense of claustrophobia, of being shut in down there below the waterline. Beyond the boilers were the baulks of timber shoring the bulkhead, and beyond the rusty plates was water. I could see it trickling down the seams.

I stripped off my borrowed jersey, rolled up my sleeves and went over to the furnace. It was barely warm. I could put my hands on the casing of it. I found the lever and flung open the furnace door. A pile of ash glowed red. There was no rush of flame, no sign of it having been stoked in hours. I picked up one of the crowbar-like slices that lay about and prodded the glowing mass. It was all ash.

I had a look at the other two furnaces then, but their draft vents were all wide open, the fires burned out, the boilers cold. There was just that one furnace still alive, and it was alive because the dampers were shut right down. I remembered then how his footsteps had dragged past the engine-room door that first time I had stood on the catwalk calling into the abyss below. He hadn't been down here—then or at any time. Yet he was covered in coal dust. I stood there, leaning on my shovel, thinking about it until the noise of the waves booming against the hollow hull reminded me that there were other, more urgent matters, and I began shovelling in coal.

I piled it in until it was heaped black inside the furnace. Then I shut the door and opened all the dampers. In a few minutes the furnace was roaring, the bright light of flames showing round the edges of the door and lighting the stoke-hold with a warm glow, so that the shapes of the boilers emerged, dim and shadowy, from the darkness that surrounded me. I opened the door again and began shovelling hard, the shovel and the black coal lit by the lurid glow. Soon I was stripped to the waist and the sweat was rolling off me so that my arms and body glistened through their coating of coal dust.

I don't know how long I was down there. It seemed like hours that I shovelled and sweated in the cavernous inferno of the stoke-hold. The furnace roared and blazed with heat, yet it was a long while before I noticed any change in the pressure gauge. Then slowly the needle began to rise. I was standing, leaning on my shovel, watching the needle, when faint above the furnace roar I heard the slam of metal against metal and turned.

He was standing in the rectangle of the stoke-hold doors. He didn't move for a moment and then he advanced towards me, reeling drunkenly to the movement of the ship. But it wasn't the rolling that made him stagger. It was exhaustion. I watched him as he came towards me with a sort of fascination. The furnace door was open and in the glow I saw his face sweating and haggard, the eyes sunk into shadowed sockets.

He stopped as he saw me staring at him. 'What's the matter?' he asked. There was a nervous pitch to his voice, and his eyes, turned now to catch the furnace glow, had a wild look in them. 'What are you staring at?'

'You,' I said. 'Where have you been?'

He didn't answer.

'You haven't been to sleep at all.' I caught hold of his arm. 'Where have you been?' I shouted at him.

He shook me off. 'Mind your own damn' business!' He was staring at me wildly. Then he reached for the shovel. 'Give me that.' He snatched it out of my hand and began to feed coal in through the open furnace door. But he was so exhausted he could hardly balance himself to the roll of the ship. His movements became slower and slower. 'Don't stand there watching me,' he shouted. 'Go and get some sleep.'

'It's you who need sleep,' I told him.

'I said we'd take it in two-hour shifts.' His voice was flat, his tone final. Coal spilled suddenly out of the chute, piling over his feet to a heavy roll. He stared at it with a sort of crazy fascination. 'Get out of here,' he said. And then, shouting: 'Get out! Do you hear?' He was leaning on the shovel, still staring down at the coal spilling out of the chute. His

56

body seemed to sag and he brushed his arm across his sweaty face. 'Go and get some sleep, for God's sake. Leave me here.' The last almost a whisper. And then he added, as though it were a connected thought: 'It's blowing full gale now.'

I hesitated, but he looked half-crazed in that weird light and I picked up my jersey and started for the door. I checked once, in the doorway. He was still watching me, the furnace-glow shining full on his haggard face and casting the enormous shadow of his body on the coal chute behind him.

Clambering up through the gloom of the engine-room I heard the scrape of the shovel and had one last glimpse of him through the open door; he was working at the coal, shovelling it into the furnace as though it were some sort of enemy to be attacked and destroyed with the last reserves of his energy.

The sounds of the gale changed as I climbed up through the ship; instead of the pounding of the waves against the hull, solid and resonant, there was the high-pitched note of the wind and the hissing, tearing sound of the sea. Cold, rushing air hit me in a blast as I stepped out into the corridor and made my way for'ard to my borrowed cabin. I had a wash and then lay back on the bunk, exhausted.

But though I was tired and closed my eyes, I couldn't sleep. There was something queer about the man—about the ship, too; those two fires and the half-flooded hold and the way they had abandoned her.

I must have dozed off, for, when I opened my eyes again, I was suddenly tense, staring at the dim-lit unfamiliarity of the cabin, wondering where I was. And then I was thinking of the atmosphere in that other cabin and, in the odd way one's mind clings to a detail, I remembered the two raincoats hanging on the door, the two raincoats that must belong to two different men. I sat up, feeling stale and sweaty and dirty. It was then just after two. I swung my feet off the bunk and sat there staring dazedly at the desk.

Rice! That was the name of the man. Less than twenty-four hours ago he had been on board, here in his cabin, perhaps seated at that desk. And here was I, dressed in his clothes, occupying his cabin—and the ship still afloat.

I pulled myself up and went over to the desk, drawn by a sort of fellow-feeling for the poor devil, wondering whether he was still tossing about on the sea in one of the lifeboats. Or had he got ashore? Maybe he was drowned. Idly I opened the desk top. There were books on navigation; he'd been an orderly man with a sense of property for he had written his name on the fly-leaf of each—John Rice, in the same small, crabbed hand that had made most of the entries in the bridge log book. There were paperbacks, too, mostly detective fiction, exercise books full of trigonometrical

58

calculations, a slide rule, some loose sheets of graph paper.

It was under these that I found the brand-new leather writing case, the gift note still inside—*To John. Write me often, darling. Love—Maggie.* Wife or sweetheart? I didn't know, but staring up at me was the last letter he had written her. *My darling Maggie* it began, and my eyes were caught and held by the opening of the second paragraph: *Now that the worst is over, I don't mind telling you, darling, this has been a trip and no mistake. Nothing has gone right.*

The skipper had died and they had buried him in the Med. And out in the Atlantic they had run into heavy weather. On March 16 they were hove-to—*a real buster*—the pumps unable to hold their own, Numbers One and Two holds flooded, and a fire in the radio shack whilst they were trying to shore up the boiler-room bulkhead, with the crew near panic *because that bastard Higgins, had told them that explosives formed part of the cargo, whatever the manifest said.* A Mr Dellimare, whom he referred to as *the owner*, had been lost overboard that same night.

Patch he described as having joined the ship at Aden as first officer in place of *old Adams who was sick.* And he added this: *Thank God he did or I don't think I'd be writing this to you. A good seaman, whatever they say about his having run the* BELLE ISLE *on the rocks a few years back.* And then this final paragraph: *Now Higgins is first officer and honestly, Maggie, I don't know. I've told you how he's been riding me ever since we left Yokohama. But it isn't only that. He's too thick with some of the crew—the worst of them. And then there's the ship. Sometimes I think the old girl knows she's bound for the knacker's yard. There's some ships when it comes to breaking up . . .*

The letter ended abruptly like that. What had happened?

Was it the shout of Fire? There were questions racing through my mind, questions that only Patch could answer. I thrust the letter into my pocket and hurried down to the stokehold.

I had got as far as the engine-room before I stopped to think about the man I was going to question. He'd been alone on the ship. They'd all abandoned her, except him. And Taggart was dead—the owner, too. A cold shiver ran through me, and on the lower catwalk I stopped and listened, straining my ears—hearing all the sounds of the ship struggling with the seas, all magnified by the resonance of that gloomy cavern, but unable to hear the sound I was listening for, the sound of a shovel scraping coal from the iron floors.

I went down slowly then, a step at a time, listening—listening for the scrape of that shovel. But I couldn't hear it and when I finally reached the door to the stoke-hold, there was the shovel lying on the coal.

I shouted to him, but all I got was the echo of my own voice, sounding thin against the pounding of the seas. And when I flung open the furnace door, I wondered whether he existed at all outside of my imagination. The fire was a heap of white-hot ash. It looked as though it hadn't been stoked since I had left it.

In a frenzy, I seized the shovel and piled on coal, trying to smother my fears in physical exertion, in satisfaction at the sound of the coal spilling out of the chute, at the roar of the furnace.

But you can't just blot out fear like that. It was there inside me. I suddenly dropped the shovel, slammed the furnace door shut and went rushing up through the ship. I had to find him. I had to convince myself that he existed.

You must remember I was very tired.

He wasn't on the bridge. But there were pencil marks on the chart, a new position. And the sight of the seas steadied me. They were real enough anyway. God! they were real! I clung to the ledge below the glass panels of the wheelhouse and stared, fascinated, as a wave built up to port, broke and burst against the ship's side, flinging up a great column of smoking water that crashed down on the foredeck, blotting everything out. The sea rolled green over the bows. And when the outline of the bulwarks showed again and she struggled up with thousands of tons of water spilling off her, I saw that the for'ard hatch was a gaping rectangle in the deck.

There was no litter of matchwood. The deck was swept clear of all trace of the hatch covers. They had been gone some time. I watched the water spilling out of the hold as the ship rolled. But as fast as it spilled, the angry seas filled it up again. The bows were practically under water. The ship felt heavy and sluggish under my feet. She didn't feel as though she could last much longer.

I glanced round the bridge, rooted to the spot by the strange emptiness of it and the sudden certainty that the ship was going to go down. The spokes of the wheel were flung out in a forlorn circle. The brass of the binnacle gleamed. The telegraph pointers still stood at Full Ahead. The emptiness of it all . . . I turned and went down to the captain's cabin. He was there, lying back in the arm-chair, his body relaxed, his eyes closed. A half-empty bottle of rum stood on the desk at his elbow. The glass was on the floor, spilling a brown wet stain across the carpet. Sleep had smoothed out the lines of his face. Like that he seemed younger, less tough; but he still looked haggard and his right hand twitched nervously where it lay against the dark leather arm of the chair. The two blue raincoats still hung incongruously side-by-side on the back of the door. The girl still smiled at me sunnily from her silver frame.

A big sea broke against the ship's side, darkening the portholes with upflung water. His eyelids flicked back. 'What is it?' He seemed instantly wide awake, though his face was still puffed with sleep, flushed with the liquor he'd drunk.

'The for'ard hatch covers have gone,' I said. I felt a strange sense of relief. He was real and it was his responsibility, not mine. I wasn't alone after all.

'I know that.' He sat up, pushing his hand across his face and up through his black hair. 'What do you expect me to do about it—go out and rig new ones?' His voice was a little slurred. 'We did that once.' He pulled himself up out of the chair and went over to the porthole and stood there, looking at the sea. His back was towards me, his shoulders slightly hunched, hands thrust into his pockets. 'It was like this all the way up through the Bay—heavy seas and the ship making water all the time.' The daylight filtering through the porthole shone cold and hard on his exhausted features. 'And then that storm! God! What a night!' He stared out through the porthole.

'You'd better get some more sleep,' I said.

'Sleep?' His hand went to his eyes, rubbing them, and then pushing up through his hair again. 'Maybe you're right.' His forehead wrinkled in a frown and he smiled so that his face had a surprised look. 'You know, I can't remember when I last slept.' And then he added: 'There was something . . .' He was frowning. 'God! I can't remember. Something I was going to look up.' He stared down at the chart and books that lay on the floor beside the arm-chair. The chart was Number 2100, the large-scale chart of the Minkies. And then he was looking at me again and in an odd voice he said, 'Who exactly are you?' He was a little drunk.

'I told you that earlier,' I replied. 'My name is—'

'To hell with your name,' he shouted impatiently. 'What were you doing out there in that yacht? What made you board the ship?' And then before I had time to say anything, he added, 'Are you something to do with the Company?'

'What company?'

'The Dellimare Trading and Shipping Company—the people who own the *Mary Deare*.' He hesitated. 'Were you out there, waiting to see if—' But then he shook his head. 'No, it couldn't have been that. We weren't steaming to schedule.'

'I'd never heard of the *Mary Deare* until last night,' I told him. And I explained how we'd almost been run down. 'What happened?' I asked him. 'How was it that the crew abandoned her with the engines still running and you on board? Was it the fire?'

He stared at me, swaying a little on his feet. And then he said, 'She was never meant to

64

make the Channel.' He said it with a sort of smile, and when I asked him what he meant, he shrugged his shoulders and turned back to the porthole, staring out at the sea. 'I thought we were in the clear when I'd got her round Ushant,' he murmured. 'God damn it! I thought I'd taken all the knocks a man could in the course of a single voyage. And then that fire.' He turned and faced me again then. He seemed suddenly to want to talk. 'It was the fire that beat me. It happened about nine-thirty last night. Rice rushed in here to say that Number Three hold was ablaze and the crew were panicking. I got the hoses run out and part of Number Four hatch cleared so that we could play water on the bulkhead. And then I went down the inspection ladder into Number Four to check. That's how they got me.' He pointed to the bloodied gash on his jaw.

'You mean somebody hit you—one of the crew?' I asked in astonishment.

He nodded, smiling. It wasn't a pleasant smile. 'They battened the inspection hatch down on top of me when I was unconscious and then they drove the crew in panic to the boats.'

'And left you there?'

'Yes. The only thing that saved me was that they forgot we'd cleared part of the hatch cover. By piling bales of cotton up—'

'But that's mutiny—murder. Are you suggesting Higgins . . .'

He lurched towards me then, sudden violence in his face. 'Higgins! How did you know it was Higgins?'

I started to explain about the letter Rice had written, but he interrupted me. 'What else did he say?' he demanded. 'Anything about Dellimare?'

'The owner? No. Only that he'd been lost overboard.' And I added, 'The Captain died, too, I gather.'

'Yes, damn his eyes!' He turned away from me and his foot struck the overturned glass. He picked it up and poured himself a drink, his hands shaking slightly. 'You having one?' he didn't wait for me to reply, but pulled open a drawer of the desk and produced a glass, filling it almost to the brim. 'I buried him at sea on the first Tuesday in March,' he said, handing the drink to me. 'And glad I was to see the last of him.' He shook his head slowly. 'I was glad at the time, anyway.'

'What did he die of?' I asked.

'Die of?' He looked up at me quickly from under his dark brows, suddenly suspicious again. 'Who the hell cares what he died of?' he said with sudden truculence. 'He died and left me to face the whole . . .' He made a vague gesture with the hand that held his glass. And then he seemed suddenly to notice me again, for he said abruptly: 'What the hell were you doing out there in that yacht of yours last night?'

66

I started to tell him how we'd bought *Sea Witch* in Morlaix and were sailing her back to England for conversion into a diving tender, but he didn't seem to be listening. His mind was away on some thought of his own and all at once he said: 'And I thought it was decent of the old bastard to get out and make room for a younger man.' He was laughing again as though at some joke. 'Well, it's all the same now. That bulkhead will go soon.' And he looked at me and added, 'Do you know how old this ship is? Over forty years old! She's been torpedoed three times, wrecked twice. She's been rotting in Far Eastern ports for twenty years. Christ! She might have been waiting for me.' And he grinned, not pleasantly, but with his lips drawn back from his teeth.

A sea crashed against the ship's side and the shudder of the impact seemed to bring him back to the present. 'Do you know the Minkies?' He lunged forward and came up with a book which he tossed across to me. 'Page three hundred and eight, if you're interested in reading the details of your own graveyard.' It was the Channel Pilot, Part II.

I found the page and read: *PLATEAU DES MINQUIERS.—Buoyage.—Caution.—Plateau des Minquiers consists of an extensive group of above-water and sunken rocks and reefs, together with numerous banks of shingle, gravel and sand . . . The highest rock, Maîtresse Île, 31 feet high,* on which stand several houses, is situated near the middle of the plateau... There were details that showed the whole extent of the reefs to be about 17 1/2 miles long by 8 miles deep, and paragraph after paragraph dealt with major rock outcrops and buoyage.

'I should warn you that the so-called houses on Maîtresse Ile are nothing but deserted stone shacks.' He had spread the chart out on the desk and was bending over it, his head in his hands.

'What about tide?' I asked.

'Tide?' He suddenly seemed excited. 'Yes, that was it. Something to do with the tide. I was going to look it up.' He turned and searched the floor again, swaying slightly, balanced automatically to the roll of the ship. 'Well, it doesn't matter much.' He downed the rest of his drink and poured himself another. 'Help yourself.' He pushed the bottle towards me.

I shook my head. The liquor had done nothing to the chill emptiness inside me—a momentary trickle of warmth, that was all. I was cold with weariness and the knowledge of how it would end. And yet there had to be something we could do. If the man were fresh; if he'd had food and sleep ... 'When did you feed last?' I asked him.

'Oh, I had some bully. Sometime this morning it must have been.' And then with sudden concern that took me by surprise, he said, 'Why, are you hungry?'

It seemed absurd to admit to hunger when the ship might go down at any moment, but the mere thought of food was enough. 'Yes,' I said. 'I am.' Anyway, it might get him away from the bottle, put something inside him besides liquor.

'All right. Let's go and feed.' He took me down to the pantry, holding his glass delicately and balancing himself to the sluggish roll. We found a tin of ham—bread, butter, pickles. 'Coffee?' He lit a primus stove he'd found and put a kettle on. We ate ravenously by the light of a single, guttering candle; not talking, just stuffing food into our empty bellies. The noise of the storm was remote down there in the pantry, overlaid by the roar of the primus.

It's surprising how quickly food is converted into energy and gives a man back that desperate urge to live. 'What are our chances?' I asked.

He shrugged his shoulders. 'Depends on the wind and the sea and that bulkhead. If the bulkhead holds, then we'll be driven on to the Minkies sometime during the night.' The kettle had boiled and he was busy making the coffee. Now that the primus was out, the pantry seemed full of the noise of the gale and the straining of the ship.

'Suppose we got the pumps working, couldn't we clear that for'ard hold of water? There was a good deal of pressure in the boiler when I was down there and I stoked before I left.'

'You know damn' well we can't clear that hold with the hatch cover gone.'

'Not if we ran her off before the wind. If we got the engines going . . .'

'Look,' he said. 'This old ship will be weeping water at every plate joint throughout her whole length now. If we ran the pumps flat out, they'd do no more than hold the water that's seeping into her, let alone clear Number One hold. Anyway, how much steam do you think you need to run the engines and the pumps as well?'

'I don't know,' I said. 'Do you?'

'No. But I'm damn' sure it would need more than one boiler; two at least. And if you think we could keep two boilers fired . . .' He poured the coffee into tin mugs and stirred sugar in. 'With one boiler we could have the engines going intermittently.' He seemed to consider it, and then shook his head. 'There wouldn't be any point in it.' He passed me one of the mugs. It was scalding hot.

'Why not?' I asked.

'For one thing the wind's westerly. Keeping her stern to the wind would mean every turn of the screw would be driving her straight towards the Minkies. Besides . . .' His voice checked, ceased abruptly. He seemed to lose himself in some dark thought of his own, his black brows furrowed, his mouth a hard, bitter line. 'Oh, to

70

hell with it,' he muttered and poured the rest of his rum into his coffee. 'I know where there's some more liquor on board. We can get tight, and then who the hell cares?'

I stared at him, my bowels suddenly hot with anger. 'Is that what happened last time? Did you just give up? Is that what it was?'

'Last time?' He was frozen to sudden immobility, the mug of coffee halfway to his lips. 'What do you mean—last time?'

'The *Belle Isle*,' I said. 'Did she go down because . . .' I stopped there, checked by the sudden, blazing fury in his eyes.

'So you know about the *Belle Isle*. What else do you know about me?' His voice was shrill, uncontrolled and violent. 'Do you know I was on the beach for damn' near a year? A year in Aden! And this . . . This first ship in a year, and it has to be the *Mary Deare*, a floating bloody scrap-heap with a drunken skipper who goes and dies on me and an owner . . .' He pushed his hand up through his hair, staring through me, back into the past. 'Fate can play dirty tricks, once she's got her claws into you.' And then, after a pause: 'If I could keep this old tramp afloat . . .' He shook his head. 'You wouldn't think it would happen to a man twice, would you,' he murmured. 'Twice! I was too young and green to know what they were up to when I got command of the *Belle Isle*. But I knew the smell of it this time. Well, they got the wrong man.' He gave a bitter laugh. 'A lot

71

of good it did me, being honest. I got her up through the Bay. God knows how I did it, but I did. And round Ushant I headed for Southampton.' His eyes focused on me again and he said, 'Well, now I don't care any more. You can't go on fighting a thing. This gale has finished me. I know when I'm licked.'

I didn't say anything, for there wasn't anything I could say. It had to come from him. I couldn't drive him. I knew that. I just sat there and waited and the silence tightened between us. He finished his coffee and put the mug down and wiped his mouth with the back of his hand. The silence became unbearable, full of the death-struggle sounds of the ship. 'Better come and have a drink,' he said, his voice tense.

I didn't move. I didn't say anything either.

'It's tough on you, but you didn't have to come on board, did you? He stared at me angrily. 'What the hell do you think I can do?'

'I don't know,' I said. 'You're the captain. It's for you to give the orders.'

'Captain!' He laughed without mirth. 'Master of the *Mary Deare*!' He rolled it round his tongue, sneeringly. 'Well, at least I'll have gone down with the ship this time. They said she was jinxed, some of them.' He seemed to be speaking to himself. 'They were convinced she'd never make it. But we're all jinxed when times get hard; and she's been kicked around the world for a good many years. She must

72

have been a crack cargo liner in her day, but now she's just a rusty old hulk making her last voyage. We'd a cargo for Antwerp, and then we were taking her across the North Sea to Newcastle to be broken up.' He was silent after that, his head on one side, listening. He was listening to the sounds of the ship being pounded by the waves. 'What a thing it would be—to steam into Southampton with no crew and the ship half-full of water.' He laughed. It was the drink in him talking, and he knew it. 'Let's see,' he said, still speaking to himself. 'The tide will be turning against us in a few hours. Wind over tide. Still, if we could hold her stern-on to the wind, maybe we could keep her afloat a little longer. Anything could happen. The wind might shift; the gale might blow itself out.' But there was no conviction in the way he said it. He glanced at his watch. 'Barely twelve hours from now and the tide will be carrying us down on to the rocks and it'll still be dark. If visibility is all right, we should be able to see the buoys; at least we'll know—' His voice checked abruptly. 'The buoys! That's what I was thinking about before I went to sleep. I was looking at the chart . . .' His voice had become animated, his eyes suddenly bright with excitement. And then his fist crashed against the palm of his hand and he jumped to his feet. 'That's it! If we were to hit the tide just right . . .' He pushed by me and I heard his feet take the steps of the ladder leading to the

73

bridge two at a time.

I followed him up and found him in the chartroom, poring over a big book of Admiralty tide-tables. He looked up and for the first time I saw him as a leader, all the fatigue wiped out, the drink evaporated. 'There's just a chance,' he said. 'If we can keep her afloat, we might do it. It means working down in that stoke-hold—working like you've never worked in your life before; turn-and-turn about—the stoke-hold and the wheel-house.' He seized hold of my arm. 'Come on! Let's see if we've got sufficient head of steam to move the engines.' A wave hit the side of the ship. Sheets of water fell with a crash, sluicing into the wheel-house through the broken doorway leading to the port wing of the bridge. Out of the tail of my eye I saw water thundering green across the half-submerged bows. And then I was following him down the ladder again into the body of the ship and he was shouting: 'By God, man, I might cheat them yet.' And his face, caught in the light of my torch as it was turned momentarily up to me, was filled with a sort of crazy vitality.

## CHAPTER THREE

The darkness of the engine-room was warm with the smell of hot oil and there was the hissing sound of steam escaping, so that the place seemed no longer dead. In my haste I let go at the bottom of the last ladder and was pitched a dozen feet across the engine-room deck, fetching up against a steel rail. There was a prolonged hiss of steam as I stood there, gasping for breath, and the pistons moved, thrusting their arms against the gleaming metal of the crankshaft, turning it—slowly at first, and then faster and faster so that all the metal parts gleamed in the light of my torch and the engines took on that steady, reassuring thump-thump of vitality and power. The hum of a dynamo started and the lights began to glow. The humming became louder, the lights brighter, and then abruptly they snapped full on. Brass and steel work gleamed. The whole lit cavern of the engine-room was alive with sound.

Patch was standing on the engineer officer's control platform. I staggered down the catwalk between the two big reciprocators. 'The engines!' I shouted at him. 'The engines are going!' I was beside myself with excitement. For that one moment I thought we could steam straight into a port.

But he was already shutting off the steam, and the beat of the engines slowed and then stopped with a final hiss. 'Don't stand there,' he said to me. 'Start stoking. We want all the steam we can get.' For the first time he looked like a man in control of the situation.

But stoking was more difficult now; dangerous, too. The movements of the ship were unpredictable. One moment I would be flinging a shovelful of coal high up against the thrust of gravity, the next I would be pitched towards the flaming mouth of the furnace and the coal would seem to have no weight at all as it left the shovel.

I don't know how long I was working there alone before he joined me. It seemed a long time. I didn't see him enter. All my mind was concentrated on the coal and that gaping furnace door, concentrated on gauging the pitch of the ship, avoiding being flung against the red-hot fire. I felt a hand on my arm and I looked up to find him standing over me. I straightened up and faced him, panting, with the sweat pouring off my body. 'I've got the pumps going,' he said.

I nodded, too short of breath to waste it in speech.

'I've just been up to the bridge,' he went on. 'Half the time the bows are right under. Any moment that bulkhead may go. Do you think you could hear the engine-room telegraph from in here?'

'I don't know,' I said. 'I expect so.'

He took me through into the engine-room then and showed me the engine controls and the voice pipe that connected with the bridge. 'I'll go up to the bridge now,' he said. 'You go back to the boiler-room and start stoking. I'll give you a ring on the engine-room telegraph. If you don't hear it after two minutes come to the voice pipe. Okay?'

I nodded and he went clambering up the ladder, whilst I returned to the stoke-hold. Even in that short time my arms and back had stiffened. I had to force myself to start shovelling again. I was beginning to get very tired and I wondered how long we could keep this up. Faint above the roar of the furnace and the sounds of the engine-room came the jangling of the bridge telegraph. I flung the furnace door to and went through to the engineers' control platform. The pointer stood at Full Ahead. I spun the control wheel, opening up the steam valves, and for the first time I understood the thrill and pride an engineer officer must feel; the hiss of steam, the pistons moving and the engines taking up a steady, pulsating beat, vibrant with power. The heart of the ship had come alive, and it was I who had made it alive. It was satisfying.

Back in the stoke-hold the shovel felt strangely light. I barely noticed the aching of my arms. Confidence and the will to fight back had returned. I was suddenly full of energy.

It worked out that about every ten minutes or so the engines had to be run; it took about three minutes to get her stern-on again. Those three minutes produced a big drop in the pressure gauge. Only by keeping the furnace full and roaring could that pressure be built up again in time to meet the next demand from the bridge. At 15.30 he called me up to take over the wheel. 'Watch the spindrift,' he said. 'That will tell you the wind direction. Lay her exactly along the direction of the wind. If you're a fraction out the stern will swing almost immediately. And have full rudder on from the moment you order me to start the engines—and don't forget she'll carry way for a good five minutes after the engines have stopped.' He left me then and I was alone at the wheel.

It was a welcome relief to be able to stand there with nothing heavier than the wheel to shift. But whereas in the stoke-hold with the roar of the furnace and the periodic sound of the engines, there had been a sense of security and normality, here I was face to face with the reality of the situation. A grim half light showed the bows so badly down in the water that they barely lifted above the marching wave tops even when running dead before the wind, and, as soon as the ship swung and I had to use the engines, the whole deck for'ard of the bridge became a seething welter of water. The sweat cooled on my body, an ice-cold, clammy coating to my skin, and I began to shiver. I found a duffle coat in the chartroom and put it on. A new position had been marked in on the chart. We were lying just about halfway between the Roches Douvres and the Minkies. The congested area of submerged reefs was looming rapidly nearer.

At 16.30 he relieved me. He stood for a moment looking out across the bows into the faded daylight of that wretched, gale-swept scene. His face and neck glistened with sweat and his eyes were deep-sunk in their sockets, all the bone formation of his face standing out hard and sharp. 'Come through into the chartroom a minute,' he said, taking hold of my arm—whether out of a need for the companionship of physical contact or to steady himself against the roll of the ship, I don't know. 'The wind is westerly now,' he said, pointing to our position on the chart. 'It will probably back farther into the south-west. If we're not careful we're going to be driven slap into the middle of the Minkies. What we've got to do now is to inch our way to the south'ard. Every time we run the engines we've got to make full use of them.'

I nodded. 'Where are you heading for—St Malo?'

He looked at me. 'I'm not heading anywhere,' he said. 'I'm just trying to keep afloat.' He hesitated and then added, 'In four hours the tide will start running against us. It'll be wind over tide then and throughout most of the night. It'll kick up a hell of a sea.'

I glanced out of the chartroom window and my heart sank, for it didn't seem possible that the sea could be worse than it was now. I watched him work out the dead reckoning and mark in another cross about five miles west and a little south of the other. 'We can't have moved that much in an hour,' I protested.

He flung down the pencil. 'Work it out for yourself if you don't believe me,' he said. 'The tide's running south-easterly three knots. Allow two miles for wind and engines, and there you are.'

I stared at the chart. The Minkies were getting very close. 'And in the next two hours?' I asked.

'In the next two hours the tide slacks off considerably. But my reckoning is that we'll be within a mile or so of the southwest Minkies buoy. And there we'll stay for the first half of the night. And when the tide turns . . .' He shrugged his shoulders and went back again into the wheelhouse. 'Depends whether we've managed to edge south at all.'

With this cheerful prospect I went below again, back to the familiar, aching grind and blazing heat of the stoke-hold. One hour in the stoke-hold; one on the bridge. Turn and turn about; it became a routine. Dazed with tiredness we did it automatically, unconsciously adjusting ourselves to the greater movement of the bridge and then readjusting ourselves to the quicker, less predictable and much more dangerous motion of the stoke-hold.

I remember being at the wheel when darkness fell. It seemed to steal up on us almost imperceptibly. And then suddenly I couldn't see the bows, couldn't tell where the wind was because I couldn't see the spume flying off the wave tops. All I could see was darkness shot with the white-tumbling wave tops. The deck sloped forward under my feet and, with broken water all round the ship, it was as though we were running the rapids of a giant river, slipping downhill at tremendous speed. I steered by the compass and the feel of the ship then, all the time pushing her towards the south with every burst of the engines

At the helm just after midnight a glimmer of light showed for an instant in the rushing, wind-torn darkness beyond the bows. I hoped to God I had imagined it. I was very tired by then and it had just been a momentary gleam, indistinct and ephemeral. But a little later I saw it again, a flash of light about two points off the starboard bow. It showed intermittently, often obscured by the backs of the waves.

By the end of my watch it was possible to identify it as group-flashing two. The chart showed the south-west Minkies buoy as Gp.fl.(2). 'About what we expected,' Patch said when he relieved me. His voice showed no lift of interest; it was flat and slurred with weariness, his face gaunt in the light of the binnacle.

And after that the light was always with us, getting a little nearer, a little clearer until it began to fade with the first grey glimmer of dawn as I took over the wheel at five-thirty in the morning. I was almost dead with exhaustion then, hardly able to stand, my knees trembling. The night in the stoke-hold had been hell, the last hour almost unendurable, shovelling coal with rivulets of water spilling across the floor and spitting steam as they whirled round the hot base of the furnace.

The tide had turned now and the double flash of the Minkies buoy began to come down on us fast, and on the wrong side of us. Soon, as the daylight strengthened, I could see the buoy itself, one of those huge pillar buoys that the French use, and, even above the wind, I thought now and then I could catch the mournful, funeral note of a whistle. We were going to pass at least half a mile inside it. I had a look at the chart and then got Patch on the voice pipe and told him to come up.

It seemed a long time before he appeared on the bridge, and when he came he moved slowly, his feet dragging as though he were just out of a sick bed. Changing watches during the night, he had been just a shadowy shape in the pale, reflected glow of the binnacle light. Now, seeing him suddenly in the cold light of day, I was shocked. He looked ghastly. 'You're just about out on your feet,' I said.

He stared at me as though he hadn't understood. I suppose I looked pretty bad myself. 'What is it?' he asked.

I pointed to the Minkies buoy, now almost four points on the starboard bow. 'We're passing too far inside it,' I said. 'At any moment we may hit the Brisants du Sud rocks.'

He went into the chartroom and I waited, expecting him to send me running below to get the engines going. He was gone a long time. Once I shouted to him, afraid that he must have gone to sleep. But he answered immediately that he was watching the buoy through the window and working something out. The tide had got a firm hold of us now. I watched the bearing of the buoy altering rapidly. It was almost abeam of us before he emerged from the chartroom. 'It's all right,' he said. 'There's water enough at this stage of the tide.' His voice was quite calm.

The wind had caught our stern now and we were swinging. Not two cables' length away an eddy marked a submerged rock and the heavy overfalls broke against each other in violent collision, sending up great gouts of water. And beyond was a cataract of broken water where the waves spilled in tumbled confusion, raging acres of surf. A big sea hit us, thudding against the ship's side and rolling in a white tide across the foredeck. Tons of water crashed down on the bridge. The whole ship shuddered. 'Aren't you going to get the engines started?' I demanded.

He was standing with his back to me, staring

83

out to starboard. He hadn't heard me. 'For God's sake!' I cried. 'We're being carried right on to the Minkies.'

'We're all right for the moment.' He said it quietly, as though to soothe me.

But I didn't believe him. How could we be all right? All ahead of us was nothing but reefs with the seas pouring white across miles of submerged rock. Once we struck . . . 'We've got to do something,' I said desperately.

He didn't answer. He was staring through the glasses out beyond the starboard bow, his legs straddled against the sickening lunges of the ship.

I didn't know what to do. He seemed calm and in control of the situation, and yet I knew that he had gone physically beyond the limits of endurance—mentally, too, perhaps. 'We've got to get clear of the Minkies,' I told him. 'Once we're clear of the Minkies we're all right.' I let go of the wheel and started for the companion ladder. 'I'm going to start the engines.'

But he grabbed hold of my arm as I passed him. 'Don't you understand?' he said. 'We're sinking.' His face was as stony as the gaze of his dark eyes. 'I didn't tell you before, but water is flooding through that bulkhead. I had a look at it just before I relieved you.' He let go of my arm then and stared through the glasses again, searching for something in the grey, scudfilled dawn.

'How long—' I hesitated, unwilling to put it into words. 'How long before she goes down?'

'I don't know. A few minutes, an hour, maybe two.' He lowered the glasses with a little grunt of satisfaction. 'Well, it's a slender chance, but . . .' He turned and stared at me as though assessing my worth. 'I want pressure in that boiler for ten to fifteen minutes' steaming. Are you prepared to go below and continue stoking?' He paused and then added, 'I should warn you that you'll stand no chance at all if that bulkhead goes whilst you're down there.'

I hesitated. 'For how long?'

'An hour and a half I should say.' He glanced quickly away to starboard, half nodded his head and then caught hold of my arm. 'Come on,' he said. 'I'll give you a hand for the first hour.'

'What about the ship?' I asked. 'If she strikes on one of these reefs . . .'

'She won't strike,' he answered. 'We're drifting down just about a mile inside the buoys.'

Down in the stoke-hold there was a strange sense of remoteness from danger. The warmth and the furnace glow and the blaze of the lights were comfortingly normal. Now that I could no longer see the seas thundering over the reefs I was enveloped in a false sense of security. Only the boom of the waves crashing against the hollow sides of the ship and the bright rivulets of water streaming from the

85

started rivet holes reminded us of the danger we were in; that and the forward slant of the decks and the water sluicing up out of the bilges, black with coal dust, filthy with oil.

We stoked like madmen, shoulder-to-shoulder, flinging coal into the furnace with utter disregard of exhaustion. It seemed an eternity, but that bulkhead held and finally Patch looked at his watch and flung his shovel down. 'I'm going up to the bridge,' he said. 'You'll be on your own now. Keep on stoking until I ring for full speed. Then, when you've got the engines going, come straight up to the bridge. All right?'

I nodded, not trusting myself to speak. He was pulling his clothes on and I watched him as he staggered through to the engine-room and disappeared. The sound of the waves thundering against the hull seemed louder now. I looked down at my wrist watch. It was twenty past seven. I started to shovel coal again, conscious all the time of the hull plates towering above me and of the slope of the decks; conscious that at any moment this lit world might plunge below the seas. Water was sloshing about in the bilges, spilling over on to the plates and swirling round my feet.

Half-past seven! Quarter to eight! Would he never ring for the engines? Once I paused, leaning on my shovel, certain that the deck below my feet was at a steeper angle, watching that streaming bulkhead and wondering what the hell he was doing up there on the bridge. What was this slender chance he had talked of? Exhausted, my nerves strung taut with fear and the long wait, I suddenly wasn't sure of him any more. What did I know about him? My first impressions—of a man unbalanced by circumstances—returned, stronger now because more dangerous.

And then suddenly, faint above the booming of the waves, came the jangle of the telegraph. It was almost eight o'clock. I flung my shovel down, slammed the furnace door shut and, with my clothes in my hand, staggered quickly through into the engine-room. The telegraph indicator was at Full Ahead. I turned the steam full on and as I raced up the ladders, the whole steel-traceried vault of the engine-room became alive with the pounding of the engines.

He was standing at the wheel, steering the ship, as I panted up the ladder on to the bridge. 'Are we clear of the Minkies yet?' I gasped.

He didn't answer. His hands were gripped tight on the wheel, his whole body tense as he stared out ahead. The ship heeled in a long agonizing roll and I staggered down the slope of the bridge-deck to the starboard windows. A buoy, painted red and white, was sliding past us. The bows were completely submerged.

'Almost there now.' His voice was taut, barely audible. His eyes looked out of their sunken sockets, staring fixedly. And then he shifted the balance of his feet and the wheel spun under his hands. I couldn't believe it for a moment. He was turning the wheel to port. He was turning the ship to port, turning her in towards the rock outcrops of the Minkies. 'Are you crazy?' I shouted at him. 'Turn to starboard! To starboard, for God's sake!' And I flung myself at the wheel, gripping the spokes, trying to turn it against the pressure of his hands.

He shouted something at me, but it was lost in the noise of a big sea crashing against the bridge. I wouldn't have heard him anyway. St Malo was only twenty miles away and the beat of the engines throbbed through the deck plates, beating a message of hope against the soles of my feet. We had to turn to starboard— away from the Minkies, towards St Malo. 'For Christ's sake!' I screamed at him.

Fingers gripped my hair, forcing my head back. He was shouting at me to let go of the wheel, and my eyes, half-closed with pain, caught a glimpse of his face, set and hard and shining with sweat, the lips drawn back from his teeth and the muscles of his jaw knotted. 'It's our only chance.' His voice was barely audible above the roar of the seas. And then the muscles of my neck cracked as he flung me back and I was caught on a downward plunge and fetched up against the window ledge with such force that all the breath was knocked out of me. A patch of broken water slid past on the port side and almost ahead of us the sea flung a curling wave-top round a little huddle of rocks that were just showing their teeth. I felt suddenly sick.

'Will you take the wheel now?' His voice was distant, quite cool. I stared at him, dazed and not understanding. 'Quick, man,' he said. 'Take the wheel.' He was on his own bridge, giving an order, expecting it to be obeyed. The acceptance of obedience was implicit in his tone. I dragged myself to my feet and he handed over to me. 'Steer north ten degrees east.' He fetched the hand-bearing compass from the chartroom and went out with it on to the starboard wing of the bridge. For a long time he stood there, quite motionless, occasionally raising the compass to his eye and taking a bearing on some object behind us.

And all the time I stood there at the wheel, holding the ship to ten degrees east of north and wondering what in God's name we were doing sailing straight in towards the reefs like this. I was dizzy, still a little sick, too scared now to do anything but hold on to the course I had been told, for I knew we must be in among the rocks and to try to turn the ship would mean certain disaster. And through the windows, out in that maelstrom of white water that filled all my horizon, there gradually emerged the shapes of more rocks, whole masses of rocks, getting nearer and nearer every minute.

89

'Steer due north now.' His voice was still calm. Yet all ahead of us was nothing but waves tumbling and falling and cascading on the half-exposed reefs. There was one lone island of rock nearer than the rest and, as the ship drove towards it, he was back at my side. 'I'll take her now.' There was a gentleness in the way he spoke and I let him have the wheel, not saying anything, not asking any questions, for his face had a strange, set look as though he were withdrawn inside himself, out of reach of any human.

And then we struck—not suddenly with an impact, but slowly, gently, a long grinding to a halt that sent me staggering forward until I was brought up against the window ledge. The ship checked, her keel making a noise that was felt in vibration rather than heard above the roar of the storm. For a moment she seemed to tear herself loose and go reeling on through the water; then she struck again and ground to a sudden, sickening halt. The engines continued without pause as though the heart of her had refused to recognize death.

It was a queer moment. Patch was still standing there at the wheel, still staring out ahead with set face and the knuckles of his hands white with the violence of his grip on the wheel spokes. The wheelhouse looked exactly the same, and for'ard, through the glass windows, the bows remained submerged with the waves rolling across them. The deck under my feet still pulsed with life. Nothing had changed; only that we were now motionless and at rest.

Trembling, I wiped the cold sweat from my forehead with my hand. We were aground on the Minkies now. I felt a sense of finality. I turned and looked at him. He seemed dazed. His face, where it had been wiped clear of coal dust, was chalk-white, his dark eyes staring. He was gazing out across the tumbled waste of the sea. 'I did what I could,' he breathed. And then again, louder: 'God in heaven, I did what I could.' There was no blasphemy in the way he said it; only the sense of a man in torment. And finally his hands dropped slackly from the spokes of the wheel as though relinquishing at last his command of the ship and he turned away and walked, slowly and deliberately in the manner of a sleep-walker, through into the chartroom.

I pulled myself together then and followed him.

He was bent over the chart and he didn't look up. A wave crashed against the ship's side, throwing a solid mass of water against the chartroom window, momentarily blocking out the daylight. As it fell away he pulled the log book towards him and, picking up the pencil, began to write. When he had finished, he closed the book and straightened up, as though he had written *Finis* to that section of his life. His eyes came slowly round and met mine. 'I'm

91

sorry,' he said. 'I should have explained what I was going to do.' He was like a man woken from a dream and suddenly rational. 'It was a question of hitting the tide just right.'

'But we should have headed towards St Malo.' I was still dazed, a little stupid—I didn't understand.

'In just over two hours, if we'd lasted that long, the tide would have turned and driven us north across the reefs.' He slid the chart along the table towards me. 'See for yourself,' he said. 'The only chance was to beach her here.' And he put his pencil on the spot where the ship was lying.

It was about a mile south of the main body of the reefs in an area showing 2 1/4 fathoms depth at low water. 'That rock away on the port bow is Grune à Croc,' he said. It was marked as drying 36 ft. 'And you'll probably find Maîtresse Ile just visible away to starboard.' His pencil point rested for a moment on the high point to the east of the main reefs. 'At low water it should be reasonably sheltered in here.' He threw the pencil down and straightened up, stretching himself and rubbing his eyes. 'Well, that's that.' There was finality and the acceptance of disaster in the way he said it. 'I'm going to get some sleep.' He went past me then without another word, through into the wheelhouse. I heard his feet on the companion ladder descending to the deck below. I hadn't said anything or tried to stop him. I was too tired to question him now. My head throbbed painfully and the mention of sleep had produced in me an intense desire to close my eyes and slide into oblivion.

I paused on my way through the wheelhouse and stood looking out on the grey, desolate sea-scape of rock and broken water. It was queer to stand there by the wheel with the feel of the engines under my feet, knowing all the time that we were hard aground on the worst reef in the English Channel. Everything in the wheelhouse seemed so normal. It was only when I looked out through the windows and saw the rocks emerging from the tide and the ship's bows no more than a vague outline below the creaming break of the waves that I was able to comprehend what had happened.

But for six hours or more we should be safe; until the rising tide exposed us again to the full force of the seas. I turned and made my way below, moving as though in a dream, like a sleep-walker. Everything seemed vague and a little remote and I staggered slightly, still balancing automatically to the roll of a ship which was now as steady as a rock. As I reached my cabin I felt the beat of the engines slow and stop. Either we had exhausted the steam or else he had gone below and stopped the engines himself. It didn't seem to matter either way. We shouldn't be wanting the engines again, or the pumps. Nothing seemed to matter to me then but sleep.

That sleep should have been possible in those circumstances may seem incredible, but having thought him mad and then found him, not only sane, but capable of an extraordinary feat of seamanship, I had confidence in his statement that we should be sheltered as the tide fell. In any case, there was nothing I could do; we had no boats, no hope of rescue in the midst of those reefs, and the gale was at its height.

I woke to complete darkness with water running like a dark river down the corridor outside my cabin. It came from a broken porthole in the saloon—probably from other places, too. The seas were battering against the ship's side and every now and then there was a grumbling, tearing sound as she shifted her bottom on the shingle bed. I moved up to Patch's cabin then. He was lying on his bunk, fully clothed, and even when I shone my torch on him he didn't stir, though he had been asleep for over twelve hours. I made two trips below to the galley for food and water and the primus stove, and it was on the second of these that I noticed the little white rectangle of a card pinned to the mahogany of the door just aft of the captain's cabin. It was a business card: *J. C. B. Dellimare*, and underneath—*The Dellimare Trading and Shipping Company Ltd*. The address was St Mary Axe in the City of London. I tried the door, but it was locked.

It was daylight when I woke again. The wind had died down and the seas no longer crashed against the ship's side. A gleam of watery sunlight filtered in through the salt-encrusted glass of the porthole. Patch was still asleep, but he had taken off his boots and some of his clothes and a blanket was pulled round his body. The companion ladder leading to the saloon and the deck below was a black well of still water in which things floated. Up on the bridge, the sight that met my eyes was one of utter desolation. The tide was low and the rocks stood up all round us like the stumps of rotten teeth, grey and jagged with bases blackened with weed growth. The wind was no more than Force 5 to 6 and, though I could see the seas breaking in white cascades over the farther rocks that formed my horizon, the water around was relatively quiet, the broken patches smoothed out as though exhausted by their passage across the reefs.

I stood there for a long time watching the aftermath of the storm whirl ragged wisps of thin grey cloud across the sun, staring in the chaos of rocks that surrounded us, at the seas breaking in the distance. I felt a deep, satisfying joy at the mere fact that I was still alive, still able to look at sunlight glittering on water, see the sky and feel the wind on my face. But the davits were empty arms of iron uplifted over the ship's side and the boat that had been hanging by one of its falls was a broken piece of splintered wood trailing in the sea at the end of a frayed rope.

Patch came up and joined me. He didn't look at the sea or the sky or the surrounding rocks. He stood for a moment gazing down at the bows which now stood clear of the sea, the gaping hole of the hatch black and full of water. And then he went out to the battered port wing and stood looking back along the length of the ship. He had washed his face and it was white and drawn in the brittle sunlight, the line of his jaw hard where the muscles had tightened, and his hands were clenched on the mahogany rail capping.

I felt I ought to say something—tell him it was bad luck, that at least he could be proud of an incredible piece of seamanship in beaching her here. But the starkness of his features checked me. And in the end I went below, leaving him alone on the bridge.

He was there for a long time and when he did come down he only said, 'Better get some food inside you. We'll be able to leave in an hour or two.' I didn't ask him how he expected to leave with all the boats smashed. It was obvious that he didn't want to talk. He went and sat on his bunk, his shoulders hunched, going through his personal belongings in a sort of daze, his mind lost in its own thoughts.

I got the primus going and put the kettle on whilst he wandered over to the desk, opening and shutting drawers, stuffing papers into a yellow oilskin bag. He hesitated, looking at the photograph, and then he took that, too. The tea was made by the time he had finished and I opened a tin of bully. We breakfasted in silence, and all the time I was wondering what we were going to do, how we were going to construct a boat. 'It's no good waiting to be taken off,' I said at length. 'They'll never find the *Mary Deare* here.'

He stared at me as though surprised that anybody should speak to him in the dead stillness of the ship. 'No, it'll be some time before they find her.' He nodded his head slowly, still lost in his own thoughts.

'We'll have to build some sort of a boat.'

'A boat?' He seemed surprised. 'Oh, we've got a boat.'

'Where?'

'In the next cabin. An inflatable rubber dinghy.'

'A rubber dinghy—in Dellimare's cabin?'

He nodded. 'That's right. Odd, isn't it? He had it there—just in case.' He was laughing quietly to himself. 'And now we're going to use it.'

The man was dead and I saw nothing funny about his not being here to use his dinghy. 'You find that amusing?' I asked angrily.

He didn't answer, but went to the desk and got some keys, and then he went out and I heard him unlock the door of the next cabin. There was a scrape of heavy baggage being

97

moved and I went to give him a hand. The door was opened and, inside, the cabin looked as though a madman had looted it—drawers pulled out, suitcases forced open, their hasps ripped off, their contents strewn over the floor; clothes and papers strewn everywhere. Only the bed remained aloof from the chaos, still neatly made-up, unslept-in, the pillow stained with the man's hair oil.

He had the keys. He must have searched the cabin himself. 'What were you looking for?' I asked.

He stared at me for a moment without saying anything. Then he shifted the big cabin trunk out of the way, toppling it on to its side with a crash. It lay there, a slab of coloured hotel labels—Tokyo, Yokohama, Singapore, Rangoon. 'Catch hold of this!' He had hold of a big brown canvas bundle and we hauled it out into the corridor and through the door to the open deck. He went back then and I heard him lock the door of Dellimare's cabin. When he returned he brought a knife with him. We cut the canvas straps, got the yellow dinghy out of its wrappings and inflated it.

The thing was about twelve feet long and five feet broad; it had paddles and a rudder and a tubular telescopic mast with nylon rigging and a small nylon sail. It even had fishing tackle. 'Was he a nervous sort of man?' I asked. For a shipowner to pack a collapsible dinghy on board one of his own ships seemed odd behaviour—almost as though he suffered from the premonition that the sea would get him.

But all Patch said was, 'It's time we got moving.'

I stared at him, startled at the thought of leaving the comparative security of the ship for the frailty of the rubber dinghy. 'The seas will be pretty big once we get clear of the reefs. Hadn't we better wait for the wind to drop a bit more?'

'We need the wind.' He sniffed it, feeling for its direction with his face. 'It's veered a point or two already. With luck it will go round into the north-west.' He glanced at his watch. 'Come on,' he said. 'There's four hours of tide with us.'

I tried to tell him it would be better to wait for the next tide and get the whole six hours of it, but he wouldn't listen. 'It would be almost dark then. And suppose the wind changed? You can't beat to windward in this sort of craft. And,' he added, 'there may be another depression following on behind this one. You don't want to be caught out here in another gale. I don't know what would happen at high water. The whole bridge deck might get carried away.'

He was right, of course, and we hurriedly collected the things we needed—food, charts, a hand-bearing compass, all the clothes we could clamber into. We had sou'westers and sea boots, but no oilskins. We took the two raincoats from the cabin door.

It was nine forty-five when we launched the dinghy from the for'ard well-deck. We paddled her clear of the ship and then hoisted sail. The sun had disappeared by then and everything was grey in a mist of driving rain, the rocks appearing farther away, vague battlement shapes on the edge of visibility; many of them were already covered. We headed for Les Sauvages and in a little while the flashing buoy that marked the rocks emerged out of the murk. By then the *Mary Deare* was no more than a vague blur, low down in the water. We lost her completely as we passed Les Sauvages.

There was still a big sea running and, once we cleared the shelter of the Minkies, we encountered the towering swell left by the gale. It marched up behind us in wall upon wall of steep-fronted, toppling water, and in the wet, swooping chill of that grey day I lost all sense of time.

For just over four hours we were tumbled about in the aftermath of the storm, soaked to the skin, crammed into the narrow space between the fat, yellow rolls of the dinghy's sides, with only an occasional glimpse of Cap Frehel to guide us. And then, shortly after midday, we were picked up by the cross-Channel packet coming in from Peter Port. They were on the look-out for survivors, otherwise they would never have sighted us, for they were passing a good half mile to the west of us. And then the packet suddenly altered course, coming down on us fast, the bows almost hidden by spray flung up by the waves. She hove-to a little up-wind of us, rolling heavily, and as she drifted down on to us rope ladders were thrown over the side and men came down to help us up, quiet, English voices offering words of encouragement, hands reaching down to pull us up.

People crowded us on the deck—passengers and crew, asking questions, pressing cigarettes and chocolate on us. Then, an officer took us to his quarters and the packet got into her stride again, engines throbbing gently, effortlessly. As we went below I caught a glimpse of the dinghy, a patch of yellow in the white of the ship's wake as it rode up the steep face of a wave.

## CHAPTER FOUR

A hot shower, dry clothes and then we were taken into the officers' saloon and a steward was bustling about, pouring tea, bringing us plates of bacon and eggs. The normality of it— the incredible normality of it! It was like waking from a nightmare. The *Mary Deare* and the gale and the tooth-edged rocks of the Minkies seemed part of another life, utterly

101

divorced from the present. And then the Captain came in. 'So you're the survivors from the *Mary Deare*.' He stood, looking from one to the other of us. 'Is either of you the owner of the yacht *Sea Witch*?'

'Yes,' I said. 'I'm John Sands.'

'Good. I'm Captain Fraser. I'll have a radio message sent to Peter Port right away. A Colonel Lowden brought her in. He was very worried about you. He and Duncan were on board yesterday, listening to the radio reports of the search. They had planes out looking for you.' He turned to Patch. 'I take it you're one of the *Mary Deare*'s officers?' His voice was harder, the Scots accent more pronounced.

Patch had risen. 'Yes. I'm the master of the *Mary Deare*. Captain Patch.' He held out his hand. 'I'm most grateful to you for picking us up.'

'Better thank my first officer. It was he who spotted you.' He was staring at Patch, small blue eyes looking out of a craggy face. 'You say your name is Patch?'

'Yes.'

'And you're the master of the *Mary Deare*?'

'Yes.'

The iron-grey brows lifted slightly and then settled in a frown. 'I understood that a Captain Taggart was master of the *Mary Deare*.'

'Yes, he was. But he died.'

'When was that?' There was a sharpness in the way the question was put.

102

'Just after we cleared Port Said—early this month.'

'I see.' Fraser stared at him stonily. And then, consciously relaxing: 'Well, don't let me interrupt your meal. You must be hungry. Sit down. Sit down, both of you.' He glanced at his watch and then called to the steward to bring another cup. 'I've just time before we go into St Malo.' He sat down, leaning his elbows on the table, his blue eyes staring at us, full of curiosity. 'Well now, what happened, Captain Patch? The air has been thick with messages about the *Mary Deare* for the last twenty-four hours.' He hesitated, waiting. 'You'll be glad to know that a boatload of survivors was washed up on Ile de Brehat yesterday afternoon.' Patch still said nothing. 'Oh, come; you can't expect me not to be curious.' His tone was friendly. 'The survivors report that there was a fire and you ordered the crew to abandon ship. That was Thursday night and yet Lowden told me—'

'I ordered them to abandon ship?' Patch was staring at him. 'Is that what they say?'

'According to a French report, yes. They abandoned ship shortly after 22.30 hours. Yet at 09.30 the following morning Lowden saw the *Mary Deare* . . .' He hesitated, silenced by Patch's hard, uncompromising stare. 'Damn it, man!' he said in sudden exasperation. 'What happened? Is the *Mary Deare* afloat or sunk or what?'

Patch didn't say anything for a moment. He seemed to be thinking it out. Finally he said, 'A full statement will be made to the proper authorities. Until then—' He was still staring at Fraser. 'Until then you'll excuse me if I don't talk about it.'

Fraser hesitated, unwilling to let it go at that. Then he glanced at his watch again, drank up his tea and rose to his feet. 'Very proper of you, Captain,' he said, his voice formal, a little huffed. 'Now I must go. We're just coming into St Malo. Meantime, please accept the hospitality of my ship. Anything you want, ask the steward.' As he went out, he paused in the doorway. 'I think I should tell you, Captain, that we have a young lady on board—a Miss Taggart. She's Captain Taggart's daughter. She flew out to Peter Port yesterday, and when she heard survivors had come ashore on the coast of France, she came on with us.' He paused, and then came back a few steps into the saloon. 'She doesn't know her father is dead. She's hoping he's amongst the survivors.' Again a slight hesitation. 'I presume you notified the owners?'

'Of course.'

'I see. Well, it's a pity they didn't see fit to inform his next-of-kin.' He said it angrily. 'I'll have my steward bring her to you.' And then in a softer tone: 'Break it to her gently, man. She's a nice wee thing and she obviously adored her father.' He left then and a silence descended on the room. Patch was eating with the concentration of a man shovelling energy back into his body. There was nothing relaxed about him.

'Well, what did he die of?' I asked him.

'Who?' He looked at me with a quick frown.

'Taggart.'

'Oh, Taggart. He died of drink.' He resumed his eating, as though dismissing the matter from his mind.

'Good God!' I said. 'You can't tell her that.'

'No, of course not,' he said impatiently. 'I'll just tell her he died of heart failure. That was probably the medical cause anyway.'

'She'll want to know details.'

'Well, she can't have them.' I thought he was being callous and got up and went over to the porthole. The engines had been slowed. We were coming into the *Rade* and I could see the tourist hotels of Dinard climbing the hill from the quay, deserted and forlorn in the rain. 'He was running around the ship, screaming like a soul in torment.' He pushed his plate away from him. 'I had to lock him in his cabin, and in the morning he was dead.' He pulled out the packet of cigarettes he had been given and opened it with trembling fingers, tearing at it viciously. His face was deathly pale in the flare of the match.

'D.T.s?' I said.

'No, not D.T.s. I only discovered afterwards . . .' He dragged on his cigarette, pushing his

105

hand up through his hair. 'Well, it doesn't matter now.' He pulled himself to his feet. 'We're nearly in, aren't we?'

The ship was moving very slowly now. Lock gates glided past. Boots rang on the deck overhead and there was the clatter of a donkey engine. 'I think we're going into the basin now,' I told him.

'You're lucky,' he said. 'You're through with the *Mary Deare* now.' He had started pacing restlessly up and down. 'God! I almost wish I'd gone down with the ship.'

I stared at him. 'It's true then ... You did order the crew to take to the boats. That story about your being knocked out—'

He turned on me, his face livid. 'Of course, I didn't order them to take to the boats. But if they stick to that story ...' He flung away towards the other porthole, staring out at the grey daylight.

'But why should they?' I demanded. 'If it isn't true—'

'What's truth got to do with it?' He stared at me angrily. 'The bastards panicked and now they're saying I ordered them to abandon ship because they've got to cover themselves somehow. A bunch of damned cowards— they'll cling together. You'll see. When it comes to the Formal Enquiry ...' He gave a little shrug of his shoulders. 'I've been through all this before.' He said it slowly, half to himself, his head turned away, staring out

106

through the porthole again at the waste ground with the rusty railway wagons. He muttered something about it being a strange coincidence, and then a door slammed and there was the sound of voices, a medley of French and English. He swung round, staring at the door and said, 'You will, of course, confine yourself to a statement of the reasons for your presence on board the *Mary Deare*.' He spoke quickly, nervously. 'You are in the position of a passenger and any comments—' The door opened and he half turned, facing it.

It was Captain Fraser, and with him were two French officials. Smiles, bows, a torrent of French, and then the shorter of the two said in English: 'I regret, Monsieur le Capitaine, I have bad news for you. Since half an hour I have heard on the radio that some bodies have been washed ashore on Les Haux. Also some wreckage.'

'From the *Mary Deare*?' Patch asked.

'Mais oui.' He gave a little shrug. 'The lighthouse men on Les Heaux have not identified them, but there is no other ship in distress.'

'Les Heaux is an island just north of the Ile de Brehat—about forty miles west of here,' Fraser said.

'I know that.' Patch moved a step towards the official. 'The survivors,' he said. 'Was there a man called Higgins amongst them?'

The officer shrugged. 'I do not know. No

official list of survivors is yet completed.' He hesitated. 'Monsieur le Capitaine, if you will come to the Bureau with me it will assist me greatly. Also it will be more simple. The formalities, you understand . . .' He said it apologetically, but it was clear he had made up his mind.

'Of course,' Patch said, but I could see he didn't like it. His eyes glanced quickly from one to the other of them, and then he went across the room and passed through the lane they opened out for him to the door.

The official turned to follow him, but then stopped and looked back at me. 'Monsieur Sands?' he enquired.

I nodded.

'I understand your boat is waiting for you in Saint Peter Port. If you will give my friend here the necessary particulars and your address in England, I do not think we need detain you at all.' He gave me a quick, friendly smile. 'Bon voyage, mon ami.'

'Au revoir, monsieur,' I said. 'Et merci, mille fois.'

His assistant took the particulars, asked a few questions and then he, too, departed. I was alone, and I sat there in a sort of coma, conscious of the bustle and hubbub of passengers descending to the quay, yet not sure that it was real. I must have dozed off for the next thing I knew the steward was shaking me. 'Sorry to wake you, sir, but I've brought

Miss Taggart. Captain's orders, sir.'

She was standing just inside the door; a small, neat girl, her hair catching the light from the porthole just the way it had done in that photograph. 'You're Mr Sands, aren't you?'

I nodded and got to my feet. 'You want Captain Patch.' I started to explain that he had gone ashore, but she interrupted. 'What happened to my father, please?'

I didn't know what to say. She should have been asking Patch, not me. 'Captain Patch will be back soon,' I said.

'Was my father on the *Mary Deare* when you boarded her?' She stood there, very straight and boyish, and quite determined.

'No,' I said.

She took that in slowly, her eyes fixed steadfastly on mine. They were grey eyes, flecked with green; wide and startled-looking. 'And this Captain Patch was in command?' I nodded. She stared at me for a long time, her lip trembling slightly. 'My father would never have abandoned his ship.' She said it softly and I knew she had guessed the truth, was bracing herself for it. And then: 'He's dead—is that it?'

'Yes,' I said.

She took it, dry-eyed, standing there, stiff and small in front of me. 'And the cause of death?' She tried to keep it formal, impersonal, but as I hesitated, she made a sudden, small feminine movement, coming towards me: 'Please, I must know what happened. How did he die? Was he ill?'

'I think it was a heart attack,' I said. And then I added, 'You must understand, Miss Taggart, I wasn't there. I am only passing on what Captain Patch told me.'

'When did it happen?'

'Early this month.'

'And this Captain Patch?'

'He was the first mate.'

She frowned. 'My father didn't mention him. He wrote me from Singapore and Rangoon and the only officers he mentioned were Rice and Adams and a man named Higgins.'

'Patch joined at Aden.'

'Aden?' She shook her head, huddling her coat close to her as though she were cold. 'My father always wrote me from every port he stopped at—every port in the world.' And then she added, 'But I got no letter from Aden.' Tears started to her eyes and she turned away, fumbling for a chair. I didn't move and after a moment she said, 'I'm sorry. It's just the shock.' She looked up at me, not bothering to wipe away the tears. 'Daddy was away so much. It shouldn't hurt like this. I haven't seen him for five years.' And then in a rush: 'But he was such a wonderful person. I know that now. You see, my mother died . . .' She hesitated and then said, 'He was always coming back to England to see me. But he never did. And this time he'd promised. That's what makes it so

110

hard. He was coming back. And now—' She caught her breath and I saw her bite her lip to stop it trembling.

'Would you like some tea?' I asked.

She nodded. She had her handkerchief out and her face was turned away from me. I hesitated, feeling there ought to be something I could do. But there was nothing and I went in search of the steward. To give her time to recover I waited whilst he made the tea and brought it back to her myself. She was composed now and though her face still looked white and pinched, she had got back some of the vitality that there had been in that photograph. She began asking me questions and to keep her mind off her father's death I started to tell her what had happened after I boarded the *Mary Deare*.

And then Patch came in. He didn't see her at first. 'I've got to leave,' he said. 'A question of identification. They've picked up twelve bodies.' His voice was hard and urgent, his face strained. 'Rice is dead. The only one I could rely on—'

'This is Miss Taggart,' I said.

He stared at her. For a second he didn't know her, didn't connect her name; his mind was concentrated entirely on his own affairs. And then the hardness slowly left his face and he came forward, hesitantly, almost nervously. 'Of course. Your face . . .' He paused as though at a loss for words. 'It—it was there on his desk. I never removed it.' And then, still looking at her, as though fascinated, he added almost to himself: 'You were with me through many bad moments.'

'I understand my father is dead?'

The forthright way in which she put it seemed to shock him, for his eyes widened slightly as though at a blow. 'Yes.'

'Mr Sands said you thought it was a heart attack?'

'Yes. Yes, that's right—a heart attack.' He said it automatically, not thinking about the words, all his mind concentrated in his eyes, drinking her in as though she were some apparition that had suddenly come to life.

There was an awkward pause. 'What happened? Please tell me what happened?' She was standing facing him now and there was a tightness in her voice that betrayed her nervousness. I suddenly felt that she was afraid of him. A sort of tension stretched between them. 'I want to know what happened,' she repeated and her voice sounded almost brittle in the silence.

'Nothing happened,' he answered slowly. 'He died. That's all.' His voice was flat, without feeling.

'But how? When? Surely you can give me some details?'

He pushed his hand up through his hair. 'Yes. Yes, of course. I'm sorry. It was March 2nd. We were in the Med. then.' He hesitated as though searching in his mind for the words he wanted. 'He didn't come up to the bridge that morning. And then the steward called me. He was lying in his bunk.' Again a pause and then he added, 'We buried him that afternoon, at sea.'

'He died in his sleep then?'

'Yes. That's right. He died in his sleep.'

There was a long silence. She wanted to believe him, wanted to desperately. But she didn't. Her eyes were very big and her hands were pressed tightly together. 'Did you know him well?' she asked. 'Had you sailed with him before?'

'No.'

'Had he been ill at all—during the voyage, or before you joined the ship at Aden?'

Again the slight hesitation. 'No. He hadn't been ill.' He seemed to pull himself together then. 'I gather the owners didn't inform you of his death. I'm sorry about that. I notified them by radio immediately, but I received no reply. They should have notified you.' He said it without any hope that they would have done so.

'What did he look like—before his death? Tell me about him please. You see, I hadn't seen him—' The pleading sound of her voice trailed away. And then suddenly in a firmer voice she said, 'Can you describe him to me?'

He frowned slightly. 'Yes, if you want me to.' His tone was reluctant. 'I—don't quite know

113

what you want me to tell you.'

'Just what he looked like. That's all.'

'I see. Well, I'll try. He was small, very small—there was almost nothing of him at all. His face was red—sun-burned. He was bald, you know, but when he had his cap on and was up on the bridge he looked much younger than—'

'Bald?' Her voice sounded shocked.

'Oh, he still had some white hair.' Patch sounded awkward. 'You must understand, Miss Taggart, he wasn't a young man and he'd been a long time in the tropics.'

'He had fair hair,' she said almost desperately. 'A lot of fair hair.' She was clinging to a five-year-old picture of him. 'You're making him out to be an old man.'

'You asked me to describe him,' Patch said defensively.

'I can't believe it.' There was a break in her voice. And then she was looking at him again, her chin up, her face white. 'There's something more, isn't there—something you haven't told me?'

'No, I assure you,' Patch murmured unhappily.

'Yes, there is. I know there is.' Her voice had suddenly risen on a note of hysteria. 'Why didn't he write to me from Aden? He always wrote me . . . every port . . . and then dying like that and the ship going down . . . He'd never lost a ship in his life.'

114

Patch was staring at her, his face suddenly hard and angry. Then abruptly he turned to me. 'I've got to go now.' He didn't look at the girl again as he turned on his heels and walked quickly out.

She looked round at the sound of the door closing, staring at the blankness of it with wide, tear-filled eyes. And then suddenly she slumped down into her chair and buried her head in her arms, her whole body racked by a paroxysm of sobs. I waited, wondering what I could do to help her. Gradually her shoulders ceased to shake. 'Five years is a long time,' I said gently. 'He could only tell you what he knew.'

'It wasn't that,' she said wildly. 'All the time he was here I felt—' She stopped there. She had her handkerchief out and she began dabbing at her face. 'I'm sorry,' she whispered. 'It was silly of me. I—I was just a schoolgirl when I last saw my father. My impression of him is probably a bit romantic.'

I put my hand on her shoulder. 'Just remember him as you last saw him,' I said.

She nodded dumbly.

'Shall I pour you some more tea?'

'No. No thanks.' She stood up. 'I must go now.'

'Is there anything I can do?' I asked. She seemed so lost.

'No. Nothing.' She gave me a smile that was a mere conventional movement of her lips. She was more than dazed; she was raw and hurt inside. 'I must go—somewhere, by myself.' It was said fugitively and in a rush, her hand held out to me automatically. 'Good-bye. Thank you.' Our hands touched, and she was gone. For a moment her footsteps sounded on the bare wood of the deck outside, and then I was alone with the sounds of the ship and the dock. Through the porthole I saw the bare, grey walls of St Malo glistening wet in a fleeting gleam of sunlight—the old walls of the city and above them the new stone and roofing of buildings faithfully copied to replace the shattered wreckage that the Germans had left. She was walking quickly, not seeing the passengers or the French or the sombre, fortress-like beauty of the ancient city; a small, neat figure whose mind clung to a girl's memories of a dead father.

I turned away and lit a cigarette, slumping wearily into a chair. The crane, the gangway, the passengers in their raincoats and the French dock men in their blue smocks and trousers; it all seemed so ordinary—the Minkies and the *Mary Deare* were a vague dream.

And then Captain Fraser came in. 'Well,' he said, 'what *did* happen? Do you know?' The curiosity in his blue eyes was unveiled now. 'The crew say that he ordered them to abandon ship.' He waited and when I didn't say anything, he added, 'Not just one of them;

116

it's what they all say.'

I remembered then what Patch had said: *They'll cling together . . . because they've got to cover themselves somehow.* Who was right—Patch or the crew? My mind went back to that moment when we had grounded, when he had relinquished the wheel from the grip of his hands in the midst of that waste of sea and rock.

'You must have some idea what really happened.'

I was conscious of Fraser again and was suddenly and for the first time fully aware of the ordeal that Patch now faced. I pulled myself stiffly up out of the chair. 'I've no idea,' I said. And then, because I sensed in the man a sort of hostility towards Patch, I added quickly, 'But I'm quite certain he never ordered the crew to take to the boats.' It was an instinctive rather than a reasoned statement. I told him I was going ashore then to find a hotel, but he wouldn't hear of it and insisted on my accepting the hospitality of his ship, ringing for the steward and putting a cabin at my disposal.

I saw Patch once more before I took the plane for Guernsey. It was at Paimpol, twenty or thirty miles to the west of St Malo, in a little office down by the *bassin.* There were fishing vessels there, packed two and three-deep along the walls—tubby wooden bottoms, all bitumen-black, nudging each other like charladies, with mast-tops nodding, gay with

117

paint—and the water of the *bassin* was poppled with little hissing waves, for it was blowing half a gale again. As the police car that had brought me from St Malo drew up I saw Patch framed in the fly-brown office window; just his face, disembodied and white as a ghost, looking out like a prisoner on to the world of the sea.

'This way plees, monsieur.'

There was an outer office that served as a waiting-room with benches round the wall and a dozen men were seated there, dumb, apathetic and listless—flotsam washed in by the sea. I knew instinctively that they were all that remained of the *Mary Deare*'s crew. Their borrowed clothes breathed shipwreck and they huddled close together, like a bunch of frightened, bewildered sheep; some that were clearly English, others that might by any race under the sun. One man, and one man alone, stood out from the motley bunch. He was a great hunk of a brute with a bull's neck and a bull's head, all hard bone and folds of flesh. He stood with his legs spread wide, solid as a piece of sculpture on the pedestal of his feet, his huge meaty hands thrust inside his trousers, which were fastened with a broad leather belt that was stained white with a crust of salt and had a big square brass buckle that had turned almost green. He held his hands there as though trying to prevent the great roll of fat, like a rubber tyre, that was his belly escaping

118

entirely from the belt. His clothes were borrowed—a blue shirt that was too small for him and blue trousers that were too short. His thighs and legs tapered away like a bull terrier's hind quarters so that they looked on the verge of buckling under the weight of that great barrel of a body.

He started forward as though to bar my way. Tiny eyes, hard as flint, stared at me unwinking over heavy pouches of flesh. I half checked, thinking he was going to speak to me, but he didn't; then the gendarme opened the door to the inner office and I went in.

Patch turned from the window as I entered. I couldn't see his expression. His head and shoulders were outlined against the window's square of daylight and all I could see was the people in the road outside and the fishing boats moving restlessly in the *bassin* beyond. There were filing cabinets ranged against the walls under faded charts of the harbour, a big, old-fashioned safe in one corner, and, seated at an untidy desk facing the light, was a ferrety little man with twinkling eyes and thinning hair. 'Monsieur Sands?' He held out a thin, pale hand. He didn't rise to greet me and I was conscious of the crutch propped against the wooden arm of his chair. 'You will excuse me please for the journey you make, but it is necessary.' He waved me to a seat. 'Alors, monsieur.' He was staring at the sheet of foolscap in front of him that was covered with

119

neat, copper-plate writing. 'You go on board the *Mary Deare* from your yacht. C'est ça?'

'Oui, monsieur.' I nodded.

'And the name of your yacht, monsieur?'

'*Sea Witch.*'

He began to write slowly and with meticulous care, frowning slightly and biting softly at his underlip as the steel nib scratched across the surface of the paper. 'And your name—your full name?'

'John Henry Sands.' I spelt it for him.

'And your address?'

I gave him the name and address of my bank.

'Eh bien. Now, you boarded the *Mary Deare* how long after the crew had abandoned the ship?'

'Ten or eleven hours after.'

'And Monsieur le Capitaine?' He glanced at Patch. 'He was still on the ship, eh?'

I nodded.

The official leaned forward. 'Alors, monsieur. It is this that I have to ask you. In your opinion, did Monsieur le Capitaine order the crew to abandon ship or did he not?'

I looked across at Patch, but he was still just a silhouette framed in the window. 'I can't say, monsieur,' I replied. 'I wasn't there.'

'Of course. I understand that. But in your opinion. I want your opinion, monsieur. You must know what had happened. He must have talked about it with you. You were on that ship through many desperate hours. It must have occurred to you both that you might die. Did he not say anything that would enable you to form some opinion as to what really happened?'

'No,' I said. 'We didn't talk very much. There wasn't time.' And then, because it must seem extraordinary to him that we hadn't had time to talk in all the hours we had been on board together, I explained exactly what we had had to do.

He kept on nodding his small head whilst I was talking, a little impatiently as though he weren't listening. And as soon as I had finished, he said, 'And now, monsieur, your opinion. That is what I want.'

By then I had had time to make up my mind. 'Very well,' I said. 'I am quite convinced that Captain Patch never ordered his crew to abandon ship.' And I went on to explain that it was impossible to believe that he had done so since he himself had remained on board and, single-handed, had put out the fire in the after hold. All the time I was talking the steel pen scratched across the surface of the paper, and when I had finished the official read it through carefully and then turned the sheet towards me. 'You read French, monsieur?' I nodded. 'Then please to read what is written there and sign the deposition.' He handed me the pen.

'You understand,' I said, when I had read it through and signed it, 'that I wasn't there. I do

121

not *know* what happened.'

'Of course.' He was looking across at Patch. 'You wish to add anything to the statement you have made?' he asked him. And when Patch merely shook his head, he leaned forward, 'You understand, Monsieur le Capitaine, that it is a very serious charge that you make against your crew—your officers also. Monsieur 'Iggins has sworn that you gave the order to him, and the man at the wheel—Yules—has confirmed that he heard you give the order.' Patch made no comment. 'I think perhaps it will be best if we have Monsieur 'Iggins and the other man in here so that I can—'

'No!' Patch's voice trembled with sudden violence.

'But, monsieur.' The official's voice was mild. 'I must understand what—'

'By Christ! I tell you, no!' Patch had come forward to the desk in two strides, was leaning down over it. 'I won't have my statement queried in front of those two.'

'But there must be some reason—'

'No, I tell you!' Patch's fist crashed down on the desk. 'You have my statement and that's that. In due course there will be an Enquiry. Until then neither you nor anybody else is going to cross-examine me in front of the crew.'

'But, Monsieur le Capitaine, do you understand what it is you accuse them of?'

122

'Of course, I do.'

'Then I must ask you—'

'No. Do you hear me? No!' His fist slammed the desk again. And then he turned abruptly to me. 'For God's sake, let's go and have a drink. I've been in this wretched little office ...' He caught hold of my arm. 'Come on. I need a drink.'

I glanced at the official. He merely shrugged his shoulders, spreading his hands out palm upwards in a little gesture of despair. Patch pulled open the door and strode through the outer office, not glancing to left or right, walking straight through the men gathered there as though they didn't exist. But when I started to follow him, the big man blocked my path. 'Well, wot did you tell 'em?' he demanded in a throaty voice that was like steam wheezing up from the great pot of his belly. 'I suppose you told 'em that he never ordered us to abandon ship. Is that wot you said?'

I tried to push past him, but one of his great paws shot out and gripped me by the arm. 'Come on. Let's have it. Is that wot you told 'em?'

'Yes,' I said.

He let go of me then. 'God Almighty!' he growled. 'Wot the hell do you know about it, eh? You were there I s'pose when we took to the boats?' He was grinning, truculent, and the stubble mat of his face, thrust close to mine, was still grey with salt and dirt. For a man who had been shipwrecked he looked oddly pleased with himself. He oozed self-confidence like a barrel oozes lard and his small, blood-shot eyes glittered moistly, like a pair of oysters, as he said again, 'You were there, eh?' And he guffawed at his own heavy humour.

'No,' I told him. 'Of course I wasn't there. But I don't—'

'Well, we was there.' His voice was raised and his small eyes darted to the half-open door behind me. 'We was there an' we know dam' well wot orders were given.' He was saying it for the benefit of the French official in the inner office. 'It was the right order, too, with the ship half full of explosives and a fire on board. That's wot we felt at the time—me and Rice and the old Chief . . . everybody.'

'If it was the right order,' I said, 'how was it possible for Captain Patch to put the fire out on his own?'

'Ah. You'd better ask him that.' And he turned and looked at Patch.

Patch came slowly back from the street door. 'What exactly do you mean by that, Higgins?' he demanded. His voice was quiet, but it trembled slightly and his hands were clenched.

'Wot a man's done once, he'll do again,' Higgins said, and there was a gleam of triumph in his eyes.

I thought Patch was going to hit him. So did

124

Higgins, for he stepped back, measuring the distance between them. But Patch didn't hit him. Instead, he said, 'You deserve to be strung up for murder. You killed Rice and those others as surely as if you'd taken a gun to them and shot them down in cold blood.' He said it through clenched teeth and then turned abruptly to walk out.

And Higgins, stung, shouted hoarsely after him: 'You won't get away with it at the Enquiry—not with your record.'

Patch swung round, his face white, and he was trembling as he looked at the pitiful little gathering, his eyes passing from face to face. 'Mr Burrows.' He had picked on a tall, thin man with a sour, dissipated face. 'You know damn' well I never gave any orders to abandon ship.'

The man shifted his feet nervously, not looking at Patch. 'I only know what was passed down to me on the blower,' he muttered. They were all nervous, doubtful, their eyes on the floor.

'Yules.' Patch's gaze had switched to an under-sized little runt of a man with a peaked, sweaty face and shifty eyes. 'You were at the wheel. You heard what orders I gave up there on the bridge. What were they?'

The man hesitated, glancing at Higgins. 'You ordered the boats swung out and the men to stand by to abandon ship,' he whispered.

'You damned little liar!' Patch started to

move towards him, but Higgins stepped forward. And Yules said, 'I don't know what you mean.' His voice was high-pitched on a note of sudden spite.

Patch stared at him a moment, breathing heavily. And then he turned and went out quickly. I followed him and found him waiting for me on the pavement outside. His whole body was shaking and he looked utterly drained. 'You need some sleep,' I said.

'I need a drink.'

We walked in silence up to the square and sat at a little *bistro* that advertised *crêpes* as a speciality. 'Have you any money?' he asked. And when I told him Fraser had lent me some, he nodded and said, 'I'm a distressed seaman and a charge on the Consul. It doesn't run to drinks.' There was a note of bitterness in his voice. And then, when he had ordered cognac, he suddenly said, 'The last body wasn't brought in until two o'clock this morning.' His face looked haggard as it had done on the *Mary Deare*, the bruise along his jaw even more livid against the clean-shaven pallor of his face.

I gave him a cigarette and he lit it with trembling hands. 'They got caught in the tide-rip off the entrance to Lezardrieux.' The drinks came and he knocked his back and ordered two more. 'Why the hell did it have to be Rice's boat?' The palm of his hand slapped viciously against the table. 'If it had been Higgins . . .' He sighed and relapsed into silence.

I didn't break it. I felt he needed that silence. He lingered over his second drink and every now and then he looked at me as though trying to make up his mind about something. The little square bustled with life, full of the noise of cars hooting and the quick, excited chatter of French people as they hurried along the pavement outside. It was wonderful just to sit there and drink cognac and know that I was alive. But my mind couldn't shake itself free of the *Mary Deare*, and watching Patch as he sat, staring down at his drink, I wondered what had really happened on that ship before I boarded her. And that little huddle of survivors in the office overlooking the *bassin* . . . 'What did Higgins mean—about your record?' I asked. 'Was he referring to the *Belle Isle*?'

He nodded, not looking up.

'What happened to her?'

'Oh, she ran aground and broke her back . . . and people talked. That's all. There was a lot of money involved. It's not important.'

But I knew it was. He'd kept on talking about it, saying you wouldn't think it could happen to the same man twice. 'What's the connection between the *Belle Isle* and the *Mary Deare*?' I asked.

He looked up at me quickly. 'How do you mean?'

'Well . . .' It wasn't easy to put it into words with him staring at me like that. 'It's a pretty

127

strange story, you know—the crew saying you ordered them to abandon ship and you saying you didn't. And there's Taggart's death,' I added. 'Dellimare, too.'

'Dellimare?' The sudden violence of his voice shook me. 'What's Dellimare got to do with it?'

'Nothing,' I said. 'But . . .'

'Well, go on. What else are you thinking?'

It was a question that had been in my mind for a long time. 'That fire . . .' I said.

'Are you suggesting I started it?'

The question took me by surprise. 'Good God, no.'

'What are you suggesting then?' His eyes were angry and suspicious.

I hesitated, wondering whether he wasn't too exhausted to answer rationally. 'It's just that I can't understand why you put the fire out and yet didn't bother to get the pumps going. I thought you'd been stoking that boiler. But it hadn't been touched.' I paused there, a little uncertain because of the strange look on his face. 'What had you been doing?'

'God damn you!' His eyes suddenly blazed. 'What's it got to do with you?'

'Nothing,' I said. 'Only . . .'

'Only what? What are you getting at?'

'It was just the coal dust. You were covered with it and I wondered . . .' I saw his hand clench and I added quickly, 'You can't expect me not to be curious.'

His body relaxed slowly. 'No. No, I suppose not.' He stared down at his empty glass. 'I'm sorry. I'm a little tired, that's all.'

'Would you like another drink?'

He nodded, sunk in silence again.

He didn't speak until the drinks came, and then he said, 'I'm going to be quite honest with you, Sands. I'm in a hell of a spot.' He wasn't looking at me. He was looking down at his glass, watching the liquor cling to the sides of it as he swirled it gently round and round.

'Because of Higgins?'

He nodded. 'Partly. Higgins is a liar and a blackguard. But I can't prove it. He was in this thing right from the start, but I can't prove that either.' He looked at me suddenly. 'I've got to get out to her again.'

'To the *Mary Deare*?' It seemed odd that he should think that it was his responsibility. 'Why?' I asked. 'Surely the owners will arrange—'

'The owners!' He gave a contemptuous little laugh. 'If the owners knew she was on the Minkies . . .' And then abruptly he changed the subject and began questioning me about my own plans. 'You said something about being interested in salvage and converting that yacht of yours into a diving tender.' That had been up in his cabin when he'd been half-doped with liquor and exhaustion. I was surprised he remembered it. 'You've got all the equipment, have you—air pumps and diving suits?'

129

'We're aqualung divers,' I said. His sudden interest had switched my mind to the problems that lay ahead—the conversion, the fitting out, all the business of starting on our first professional salvage operation.

'I've been thinking...' He was drumming nervously on the marble-topped table. 'That boat of yours—how long will it take to convert her?'

'Oh, about a month,' I said. And then it dawned on me. 'You aren't suggesting that we take you out to the *Mary Deare*, are you?'

He turned to me then. 'I've got to get back to her,' he said.

'But, good God—why?' I asked. 'The owners will arrange for the salvage—'

'Damn the owners!' he snarled. 'They don't know she's there yet.' He leaned urgently towards me. 'I tell you, I've got to get out to her.'

'But why?'

His eyes gradually dropped from my face. 'I can't tell you that,' he muttered. And then he said, 'Listen, Sands. I'm not a salvage man. But I'm a seaman, and I know that ship can be refloated.'

'Nonsense,' I said. 'Another gale and she'll be flooded—she'll probably break up.'

'I don't think so. She'll have water in her, but she won't be flooded. It isn't as though she's sunk,' he added. 'At low water you could get pumps operating from her deck and, with all the apertures sealed up . . .' He hesitated. 'I'm trying to put it to you as a business proposition. That ship is lying out there and you and I are the only people who know she's there.'

'Oh, for God's sake!' I said. The effrontery of the proposition staggered me. He didn't seem to understand that there were laws of salvage, that even if it were possible to refloat the *Mary Deare*, it involved agreement between the owners, the insurance people, the shippers—everybody.

'Think it over,' he said urgently. 'It may be weeks before some fisherman finds her there.' He gripped hold of my arm. 'I need your help, Sands. I've got to get into that for'ard hold. I've got to see for myself.'

'See what?'

'That hold didn't flood because the ship was unseaworthy. At least,' he added, 'that's what I believe. But I've got to have proof.'

I didn't say anything, and he leaned towards me across the table, his eyes on mine, hard and urgent. 'If you won't do it . . .' His voice was hoarse. 'I've nobody else who'll help me. Damn it, man! I saved your life. You were dangling at the end of that rope. Remember? I helped you then. Now I'm asking you to help me.'

I looked away towards the square, feeling a little embarrassed, not understanding what it was that he was so worried about. And then

131

the police car that had brought me to Paimpol drew up at the curb and I watched with relief as the gendarme got out and came into the *bistro*.

'Monsieur—if you wish to catch your aeroplane . . .' He nodded towards the car.

'Yes, of course.' I got to my feet. 'I'm sorry. I've got to go now.'

Patch was staring up at me. 'What's your address in England?' he asked.

I gave him the name of the boatyard at Lymington. He nodded, frowning, and looked down at his empty glass. I wished him luck then and turned to go.

'Just a minute,' he said. 'You've got a bank, I suppose?' And when I nodded, he reached into his pocket and pulled out a package and tossed it on to the table. 'Would you have them lock that up for me?'

'What is it?' I asked as I picked it up.

He moved his hand in a vague, impatient gesture. 'Just some personal papers. Afraid they may get lost.' And then, without looking up at me, he added, 'I'll collect them when I see you.'

I hesitated, wanting to tell him it was no good his coming to see me. But he was sitting there, slumped in his chair, lost apparently in his own thoughts. He looked drawn and haggard and ghastly tired. 'You better get some sleep,' I said, and my words took me back again to the *Mary Deare*. He didn't

132

answer, didn't look up. I slipped the package into my pocket and went out to the car. He was still sitting there slumped over the table as I was driven away.

Two hours later I was in the air, high up over the sea. It was like a corrugated sheet of lead and out beyond the starboard wingtip was an area all flecked with white.

The Frenchman in the next seat leaned across me to peer out. 'Regardez, regardez, monsieur,' he whispered eagerly. 'C'est le Plateau des Minquiers.' And then, realizing I was English, he smiled apologetically and said, 'You will not understand, of course. But there are rocks down there—many, many rocks. Très formidable! I think it better we travel by air. Look, monsieur!' He produced a French paper. 'You 'ave not seen, no?' He thrust it into my hands. 'It is terrible! Terrible!'

It was opened at a page of pictures— pictures of Patch, of Higgins and the rest of the survivors, of a dead body lying in the sea, and of officials searching a pile of wreckage washed up on some rocks. Bold black type across the top announced: MYSTERE DU VAISSEAU BRITANNIQUE ABANDONNE.

'Interesting, is it not, monsieur? I think it is also a very strange story. And all those men . . .' He clicked his tongue sympathetically. 'You do not understand how terrible is this region of the sea. Terrible, monsieur!'

I smiled, overwhelmed by a desire to

133

laugh—to tell him what it had been like down there in the Minkies. But by now I was reading the statement made to the authorities by *le Capitaine Gideon Patch*, and suddenly it was borne in on me that he had not stated the *Mary Deare*'s position. He hadn't even mentioned that the ship was stranded and not sunk. '. . . *and you and I are the only people who know she's there.*' His words came back to me and I sat staring down at the paper, knowing suddenly that this wasn't going to be the end of the *Mary Deare*.

'A strange affair, is it not, monsieur?'

I nodded, not smiling now. 'Yes,' I said. 'Very strange.'

# Part Two

# THE ENQUIRY

# CHAPTER ONE

The formal enquiry into the loss of the *Mary Deare* was finally fixed for Monday, May 3rd, at Southampton. For a Ministry of Transport Enquiry, this must be considered unusually expeditious, but I learned later that the date had been brought forward at the urgent request of the insurance companies. The sum involved was a very large one and right from the start it was the question of insurance that was the vital factor.

In fact, we had only been in Lymington a few days when I had a visit from a Mr F. T. Snetterton representing the H. B. & K. M. Insurance Corporation of San Francisco. It was that section of the cargo consigned by the Hsu Trading Corporation of Singapore that interested him. Could I testify as to the nature of it? Had I been down into any of the holds? Had Patch talked to me about it?

There was a devil of a racket going on. *Sea Witch* had just been slipped and the yard men were drawing keel bolts for inspection and Mike and I were stripping the old engine out of her. I took him down to the waterfront, where we could talk in peace.

'You understand, Mr Sands,' he explained earnestly, 'I have to be sure that the cargo was exactly what the Hsu Trading Corporation claim. I have to establish the manifest, as it were. Now surely you must have seen something that would enable you to give an opinion as to the nature of the cargo? Think, sir. Think.' He was leaning forward, blinking in the bright sunshine, quite over-wrought by the urgency of his problem.

I told him I had been down the inspection hatch of Number Three hold. I described the charred bales to him. 'Please, Mr Sands.' He shook his head impatiently. 'It's the aero engines I am interested in. Only the aero engines.'

That was the first time anyone had mentioned aero engines to me. 'I heard she had a cargo of explosives.'

'No, no—aero engines.' He sat down on the railing of one of the pontoons where the boats were laid up, a neat, dapper man dressed in black with a brief-case. He looked entirely out of place. 'The ship herself,' he said in his precise way, 'is not important—twice the break-up value, that's all. And the cotton was insured by a Calcutta firm. No, it's the aero engines we're worried about. There were a hundred and forty-eight of them—surplus American stores from the Korean war—and they were insured for £296,000. I must be certain that they were on board at the time the ship went down.'

'What makes you think they weren't?' I asked him.

He looked at me quickly, hesitating and fidgeting with his brief-case. 'It's a little difficult,' he murmured. 'But perhaps—since you're not an interested party . . . perhaps if I explain, it may help you to remember something—some little thing . . . an unguarded word, perhaps.' He looked at me again, and then said, 'Shortly after the claim was filed, we heard from our agent in Aden that a man named Adams had been talking about the *Mary Deare* and her cargo in a Steamer Point bar. He was reported to have given it as his opinion that she contained nothing but bales of cotton at the time she went down.' And he added hastily, 'You understand, sir, this is in the strictest confidence.' And then he asked me again whether I couldn't remember some little detail that would help him. 'Surely if you were on that ship for forty-eight hours you must have learned something about the cargo?'

'There was a gale blowing,' I said. 'The ship was sinking.'

'Yes, yes, of course. But you must have talked with Mr Patch. You were with him through a critical period. A man will often say things in those circumstances that he would be reluctant . . .' He let the sentence go, staring at me all the time through his glasses. 'You're sure he said nothing about the cargo?'

'Quite sure.'

'A pity!' he murmured. 'I had thought . . .'

139

He shrugged his shoulders and stood up. I asked him then how he thought it was possible for a cargo consigned to a ship not to be on board her at a later date? He looked at me. 'All things are possible, Mr Sands, where a great deal of money is involved.' I remembered Patch saying the same thing about the loss of the *Belle Isle*. And then he suddenly asked me whether Patch had mentioned the name of another boat whilst we were together on the *Mary Deare*?

'I don't think so,' I said quickly. If Snetterton wanted to find out about the *Belle Isle*, he could find it out from somebody else.

But he wasn't to be put off so easily. 'You don't think so?' He was peering at me. 'I want you to be quite certain about this, Mr Sands. It may be vitally important.'

'I am quite certain,' I said irritably.

'Mr Patch never mentioned the name of another ship to you?'

Damn it, the man had no right to come here questioning me about what Patch had said. No, I told him. And I added that if he wanted to find out what ships Patch had been connected with why the devil didn't he go and ask him.

He stared at me. 'This isn't a ship that Mr Patch ever sailed in.'

'Well, what ship is it then?'

'The *Torre Annunziata*. Now please think back very carefully. Did Mr Patch ever mention the name *Torre Annunziata* to you?'

'No,' I said. 'Definitely not.' I felt relieved and angry. 'What's the *Torre Annunziata* got to do with it?'

He hesitated. 'It's a little delicate, you understand ... so much supposition ...' Then he suddenly made up his mind and said, 'The Dellimare Company owned only two ships— the *Mary Deare* and the *Torre Annunziata*. The *Torre Annunziata* was in the Rangoon River at the same time that the *Mary Deare* put in to load her cotton cargo.' He glanced at his watch and then rose to his feet. 'Well, sir, I won't trouble you any further for the moment.'

He turned then and began to walk back towards the slip, and as we negotiated the wooden duck-boards of the pontoons, he said, 'I'll be quite honest with you. This is a matter that might in certain circumstances ...' He hesitated there and seemed to change his mind. 'I am waiting for a report now from our agent in Rangoon. But ...' He shook his head. 'It's all very disturbing, Mr Sands. The *Torre Annunziata* has been sold to the Chinese. She has vanished behind what I believe is called the Bamboo Curtain—not only the ship, but her crew as well. And Adams has disappeared, too. We are almost certain that he shipped out in a dhow bound for Zanzibar. It may be weeks before we can contact him. And then there are these two fires on the *Mary Deare* and the loss of Mr Dellimare. A fire in the radio room is most unusual, and Mr Dellimare had been in the Navy. The possibility of suicide ... small firm, you know ... might be in difficulties ...' He tucked his brief-case more firmly under his arm. 'You see what I mean, Mr Sands. Little things in themselves, but together ...' He glanced at me significantly. And then he added, 'The trouble is the time factor. The H. B. & K. M. are making great efforts to increase their business in the Pacific. And Mr Hsu is a big man in Singapore—considerable influence in Eastern ports. They feel it calls for prompt settlement of the claim unless ...' He shrugged.

We had reached the slip and he paused for a moment to admire *Sea Witch*'s lines, asking questions about our diving plans, the aqualungs we were using and the depths at which we could work. He seemed genuinely interested and I explained how we had financed ourselves by salvaging bits and pieces from the wreck of a tanker in the Mediterranean and that we were now going to work on the wreck of an L.C.T. in Worbarrow Bay off the Dorset coast. He wished us luck and gave me his card. 'Think about what I've said, Mr Sands. If you remember anything— well, you have my card, sir.'

It was only after Snetterton had gone— when I had had time to think over what he had told me—that I began to understand what the loss of the *Mary Deare* was going to lead to. There would be other people besides

Snetterton coming to ask me questions. He was just the breeze before the storm. The newspaper reports I had read had all taken it for granted that the ship was sunk—so had Snetterton and the two reporters who had come to see me when I had arrived with *Sea Witch*. Everybody thought she was sunk. But sooner or later they would start probing, and before then I had to see Patch and find out his reasons for concealing her position.

I thought it must be connected in some way with his past record and when I was in London two days later to sign our salvage contract with the underwriters, I made a few enquiries about the *Belle Isle*. She had been wrecked on the Anambas Islands north-east of Singapore nearly ten years ago, and she was entered in the records as a 'total loss'. Her master was given as Gideon S. Patch. An Enquiry had been held in Singapore and the Court had found the stranding to be due to default of the Master and had suspended his Certificate for a period of five years. That was all. There were no details. But, discussing it with one of my friends in the marine section of Lloyd's, who specialized in the Far East, I learned that some ugly rumours had got about afterwards to the effect that the stranding had been a put-up job. The ship had been very heavily insured.

I was very close to St Mary Axe and I decided to have a look at the Dellimare Company office. It was partly that I was curious to see the sort of company it was, and also I wanted to find out where I could contact Patch. Their offices were at the Houndsditch end, on the fourth floor of a dingy building full of small trading businesses. I found myself in a poky little room with a desk and a gas fire and some filing cabinets. The single typewriter had its cover on and dirt-grimed windows looked out across a litter of chimney pots to the white-tiled rear of a big office block. There was a bell on the counter and amongst a litter of papers was some Dellimare Company notepaper. It gave the directors as J. C. B. Dellimare, Hans Gundersen and A. Petrie. When I rang the bell, the door of an inner office was opened and a full-bosomed, fleshy-looking woman appeared, dressed in black with a lot of cheap jewellery and blonde hair that was startling because it was clearly natural.

When I gave her my name, she said, 'Oh, are you the Mr Sands who was on board the *Mary Deare*? Then perhaps you can help me.' She took me through into the other office. It was a much brighter room with cream walls and a red carpet and a big green and chromium steel desk that was littered with Press clippings, mostly from French newspapers. 'I'm trying to find out what really happened to him,' she said. 'To Mr Dellimare, that is.' And she glanced involuntarily at a big photograph in an ornate silver frame that stood beside her on the desk. It was a head and shoulders portrait, showing a rather hard, deeply-lined face with a small straight mouth under the thin pencil-line of a moustache.

'You knew him well?' I asked.

'Oh, yes. We formed the Company. Of course, after Mr Gundersen joined, it was all different. Our main office became Singapore. Mr Dellimare and I just looked after the London end.' There was something entirely personal about the way she said 'Mr Dellimare and I', and after that she began asking me questions. Had Captain Patch said anything to me about how Mr Dellimare had been lost? Did I go into his cabin? Had I talked to any of the survivors? 'He had been in the Navy. He couldn't just have gone overboard like that?' Her voice trembled slightly.

But when she realized I could tell her nothing that she didn't already know, she lost interest in me. I asked her then for Patch's address, but she hadn't got it. 'He came in about three days ago to deliver his report,' she said. 'He's coming back on Friday, when he'll be able to see Mr Gundersen.' I gave her the address of the boatyard and asked her to tell Patch to contact me, and then I left. She came with me to the door. 'I'll tell Mr Gundersen you've been,' she said with a quick, brittle smile. 'I'm sure he'll be interested.'

Mr Gundersen! Perhaps it was the inflection of her voice, but I got the impression that she was a little nervous of him, as though he were

145

entirely remote from the Dellimare Company office that she knew with its silver-framed photograph and its view over the chimneys.

It never occurred to me that I should meet Gundersen, but on Friday afternoon the boy from the yard's office came down to the slip to say that a Mrs Petrie was calling me from London. I recognized the slightly husky voice at once. Mr Gundersen had just arrived by plane from Singapore and would like to have a talk with me. He was coming down to Southampton tomorrow, would it be convenient for him to call on me at the yard at eleven o'clock?

I couldn't refuse. The man had come all the way from Singapore and he was entitled to find out all he could about the loss of the Company's ship. But, remembering the things Snetterton had hinted at, I had a feeling of uneasiness. Also, my time and all my energies were concentrated on the conversion of *Sea Witch* and I resented anything which took my mind off the work that Mike and I had planned and struggled for over years of wreck-hunting. I was worried, too, about what I was going to tell him. How was I to explain to him that nobody had been notified of the position of the wreck?

And then early next morning Patch came on the phone from London. No, they hadn't given him any message from me. I thought then that he was ringing me about the package I had brought over for him and which I realized was still on board, locked away in my brief-case. But it wasn't that. It was about Gundersen. Had Gundersen been to see me? And when I told him that I was expecting him at eleven o'clock, he said, 'Thank God! I tried to get you last night—to warn you.' And then he added, 'You haven't told anybody where the *Mary Deare* is lying, have you?'

'No,' I said. 'Not yet.' I hadn't told anybody, not even Mike.

'Has a man called Snetterton been to see you—a marine insurance agent?'

'Yes.'

'You didn't tell him?'

'No,' I said. 'He didn't ask me. He presumed the ship was sunk.' And then I said, 'Haven't you notified the authorities yet? If you haven't, I think it's time—'

'Listen,' he said. 'I can't come down now. I've got to see somebody. And on Monday I've got to go to the Ministry of Transport. But I'll be able to come down and see you on Tuesday. Will you promise to say nothing until then?'

'But why?' I said. 'What's the point in concealing her position?'

'I'll explain when I see you.'

'And what about Gundersen? What am I to say to him?'

'Say anything you like. But for God's sake don't tell him where she is. Don't tell anybody. I ask you as a favour, Sands.'

'All right,' I said doubtfully.

He thanked me then and rang off.

An hour later Gundersen arrived. The boy came down to say that he was waiting for me in the yard manager's office. A big chauffeur-driven limousine stood outside and I went in to find Gundersen seated on the edge of the desk smoking a cigarette and the manager standing in front of him in uneasy silence. 'You're Mr Sands, are you?' Gundersen asked. He didn't offer me his hand or get up or make any move. The manager gave us the use of his office and slipped out. As soon as the door was shut Gundersen said, 'You know why I'm here, I imagine?' He waited until I had nodded and then said, 'I saw Mr Patch yesterday. I understand you were with him during the last forty-eight hours on the *Mary Deare*. Naturally I wanted to hear your version of what happened on our ship.' He asked me then to go through the whole sequence of events. 'I want every detail, please, Mr Sands.'

I went through the whole story for him, leaving out only the details about Patch's behaviour and what had happened at the end. He listened in complete silence, not interrupting once. His long, immobile face, tanned by the sun, showed no flicker of expression, and his eyes, behind their horn-rimmed glasses, watched me all the time I was talking.

Afterwards he asked me a series of

questions—straightforward, practical questions concerning course and wind strength and the length of time we had run the engines. The ordeal we had gone through seemed to mean nothing to him and I got the impression of a cold personality.

Finally, he said, 'I don't think you have yet understood, Mr Sands, what it is I wish to know.' His slight accent was more noticeable now. 'I want to discover the exact position in which the ship went down.'

'You don't seem to realize the conditions prevailing at the time,' I said. 'All I can tell you is that she was close to the Roches Douvres at the time I boarded her.'

He got up then. He was very tall and he wore a light-coloured suit of smooth material draped in the American fashion. 'You are not being very helpful, Mr Sands.' A signet ring on his finger flashed in the pale April sunlight. 'It seems odd that neither you nor Patch can say where the ship was at the time you abandoned her.' He waited, and then he said, 'I have also talked to Higgins. He may not have a Master's Certificate, but he's an experienced seaman. You may be interested to know that his calculations, based on wind strength, probable drift and tide, put the *Mary Deare's* final position a good deal to the east of where you and Patch seem to think you were. Have you any comment to make?' He stood facing me, his back to the window.

'None,' I said, nettled and a little angry at his manner. And then, because he was still staring at me, waiting, I said, 'I'd remind you, Mr Gundersen, that I am not concerned in this. I was on board your ship by accident.'

He didn't answer for a moment. Finally he said, 'That remains, perhaps, to be seen.' And he added, 'Well, at least I have got something out of you. Now that we have some idea of the length of time the engines were running and the course steered whilst they were in use, it should be possible to arrive at an approximation of the position.' He paused again. 'Is there anything further you would care to add to what you have already told me, Mr Sands?'

'No,' I said. 'Nothing.'

'Very well.' He picked up his hat. And then he paused. 'The manager here tells me that you're interested in salvage. You've formed a company—Sands, Duncan & Company, Ltd.' He stared at me. 'I think I should warn you that this man Patch has a bad record. Unfortunately our Mr Dellimare was inexperienced in matters connected with shipping. He employed this man when nobody else would, and the result has proved disastrous.'

'He did his best to save the ship,' I said angrily.

For the first time his face moved. An eyebrow lifted. 'After he had caused the crew to panic and take to the boats. I have yet to discover his precise motives, but if you're mixed up in this, Mr Sands . . .' He put his hat on. 'You can contact me at the Savoy Hotel if you should find you have some further information to give me.' He went out of the office then and I watched him drive away with an uneasy feeling that I was getting myself dangerously involved.

This feeling persisted, and it came between me and my work so that I was not in a particularly sympathetic mood when Patch finally arrived. We were living on board *Sea Witch* by then, which was fortunate because he didn't arrive until the evening. I had expected him to look rested, the lines in his face smoothed out. It came as a shock to me to find him looking just as haggard. We had only one light on board, an inspection lamp clamped to a half-erected bulkhead, and in its harsh glare he looked ghastly, his face quite white and a nervous tic at the corner of his mouth.

We cleared the saloon table of tools and wood-shavings, and I sat him down and gave him a drink and a cigarette and introduced him to Mike. It was neat rum I gave him and he knocked it straight back, and he drew on his cigarette as though it were the first he'd had in days. His suit was old and frayed and I remember wondering whether the Dellimare Company had paid him. Oddly enough, he accepted Mike at once and, without attempting to get me alone, asked straight out what Gundersen had wanted, what he had said.

I told him, and when I had finished, I said, 'Gundersen suspects something. He hinted as much.' I paused waiting for the explanation he had promised me. But all he said was, 'I'd forgotten that Higgins might work it out.' He was speaking to himself.

'What about that explanation?' I asked him.

'Explanation?' He stared at me blankly.

'You surely don't imagine,' I said, 'that I can be a party to a piece of deception that involves the owners, the insurance people, everybody with a financial interest in the ship, unless I know that there is some good reason?' I told him I considered that my duty was clear. 'Either you explain why you've withheld this vital information or I go to the authorities.' An obstinate, shut look had come over his face. 'Why pretend the ship went down, when at any moment she may be sighted lying there in the middle of the Minkies?'

'She could have been carried there by the tides,' he murmured.

'She could have been, but she wasn't.' I lit a cigarette and sat down opposite him. He looked so desperately tired of it all. 'Listen,' I said more gently. 'I've been trained in marine insurance. I know the procedure after the loss of a ship. Any moment now the Receiver of Wreck will start taking depositions under oath from everybody connected with the loss. And

152

under oath I've no alternative but to give the full—'

'You won't be called on to make a deposition,' he said quickly. 'You weren't connected with the ship.'

'No, but I was on board.'

'By accident.' He pushed his hand up through his hair in a gesture that brought it all back to me. 'It's not for you to make any comment.'

'No, but if I have to make a statement under oath . . .' I leaned across the table towards him. 'Try and see it from my point of view,' I said. 'You made me a certain proposition that day in Paimpol. A proposition which, in the light of your failure to notify the owners of the present whereabouts of the ship, was entirely crooked. And Gundersen is beginning to think—'

'Crooked?' He began laughing and there was a note of hysteria in his voice. 'Do you know what cargo the *Mary Deare* carried?'

'Yes,' I said. 'Aero engines. Snetterton told me.'

'And did he tell you that the other Dellimare ship was moored next to the *Mary Deare* for four days in the Rangoon River? Those aero engines are in China now—sold to the Chinks for a mint of money.'

The positiveness of his accusation took me by surprise. 'How can you be certain?' I asked him.

He looked at me, hesitating for a moment.

'All right. I'll tell you. Because Dellimare offered me five thousand quid to wreck the *Mary Deare*. Cash—in fivers.'

In the sudden silence I could hear the lapping of the water at the bottom of the slip. 'Dellimare? Are you serious?' I asked.

'Yes, Dellimare.' His voice was angry and bitter. 'It was after old Taggart died. Dellimare was desperate then. He had to improvise. And, by the luck of the devil, I was on board. He knew my record. He thought he could buy me.' He leaned back and lit another cigarette, his hands shaking. 'Sometimes I wish to God I'd accepted his offer.'

I poured him another drink. And then I said, 'But I still don't understand why you should conceal the *Mary Deare*'s position. Why haven't you told all this to the authorities?'

He turned and looked at me. 'Because if Gundersen knows where she is, he'll go out there and destroy her.'

That was nonsense, of course. You can't destroy a 6,000 ton ship just like that. I told him so. He'd only got to go to the authorities, demand an examination of the vessel and the whole thing would be decided. But he shook his head. 'I have to go back myself—with somebody like you that I can trust.'

'You mean you're not sure about what you just told me—about the cargo?'

He didn't say anything for a moment, but just sat there, hunched over his drink, smoking.

154

You could feel his nerves in the stillness of the cabin. 'I want you to take me out there,' he said finally. 'You and Duncan.' He turned, leaning towards us. 'You've been in marine insurance, haven't you, Sands? You know how to fix up a salvage contract. Now listen. When will your boat be ready?'

'Not till the end of the month,' Mike said, and the way he said it was a warning to me that he didn't want to have anything to do with it.

'All right. The end of the month. I'll come back then. Have you got an underwater camera?' And when I nodded he leaned forward earnestly. 'You could take a picture then of the damage to the for'ard holds. The insurance people would give you a lot of money for that—and for pictures of the cargo.' And then he added, 'And if I'm wrong, then there's quarter of a million pounds worth of aero engines—enough salvage to set you up in a big way. Well?' His eyes moved quickly, nervously, from one to the other of us.

'You know very well I can't agree to a proposition like that,' I said. And Mike added, 'I think you should put the whole matter in the hands of the authorities.'

'No. No, I can't do that.'

'Why not?' I asked.

'Because I can't.' The tension was building up in him again. 'Because I'm up against a company. I've a record behind me and they'll twist things ... I've been through all this

155

before.' Sweat was shining in beads on his forehead. 'And there's Higgins and the crew. Everything is against me.'

'But if the Receiver of Wreck made an examination—'

'I tell you, no. I'm not having the Receiver of Wreck out there—or anybody.' He was staring at me wildly. 'Can't you understand— I've got to go back there myself.'

'No, I can't,' I said. 'If you refused Dellimare's offer, you've nothing to worry about. Why conceal the fact that you beached her on the Minkies?' And when he didn't answer, I said, 'Why do you have to go back? What the devil is there on that ship that you've got to go back for?'

'Nothing. Nothing.' His voice quivered in tune with his nerves.

'Yes there is,' I said. 'There's something drawing you back to her as though—'

'There's nothing,' he shouted at me.

'Then why not tell the authorities where she is? What is it you're afraid of?'

His fist crashed down on the table top. 'Stop it! Questions ... questions ... nothing but questions. I've had enough of it, do you hear?' He got abruptly to his feet and stood, staring down at us. He was trembling all over.

I think he was on the verge of telling us something. I think he wanted to tell us. But instead he seemed to get a grip of himself. 'Then you won't take me out there?' There was

156

a note of resignation in his voice.

'No,' I said.

He seemed to accept that and he stood there, his body slack, staring down at the table. I got him to sit down again and gave him another drink. He stayed on to supper. He was very quiet and he didn't talk much. I didn't get anything more out of him. He seemed shut away inside himself. When he left he gave me his address. He was in lodgings in London. He said he'd come down at the end of the month and see if we'd changed our minds. I saw him out across the darkened yard and then walked slowly back through the dark shapes of the slipped boats.

'Poor devil!' Mike said, as I went below again. 'Do you think Dellimare really offered him five thousand to wreck the ship?'

'God knows!' I said. I didn't know what to think. It seemed to me that perhaps Patch might be a psychological case—a man whose balance had been destroyed because of the ship he had lost before. 'I know almost nothing about the man,' I murmured. But that wasn't true. You can't live through what we'd lived through together without knowing a good deal about a man. He was tough. He had great reserves. And I admired him. I almost wished I'd agreed to take him out to the Minkies—just to discover the truth. I told Mike the whole story then, all the little details I'd left out when I rejoined *Sea Witch* in Peter Port. And after I had finished, he said, 'It's a hell of a situation for him if the cargo really has been switched.'

I knew what he meant. He was thinking of the insurance companies, and, having worked for seven years in the marine section of Lloyd's, I knew very well that once they got their teeth into a claim, they'd never let go.

I worried a lot about this during the fitting out. But a few days after Patch had visited us, I received notification of the date of the Formal Investigation and I comforted myself with the thought that it would all be resolved then.

*Sea Witch* was ready sooner than we had dared to hope. We sailed on Tuesday, April 27, motoring down to the Solent and then heading westward under full canvas with a light northerly wind. I hadn't seen Patch again, but I couldn't help thinking that the wind was fair for the Channel Islands. Twenty-four hours' sailing would have taken us to the Minkies, and the forecast couldn't have been better— continental weather with a belt of high pressure over the Azores. We had Mike's old diving friend, Ian Baird, with us again, and with three of us working we could have got into the *Mary Deare*'s holds and checked that cargo and still got back for the Investigation. And as *Sea Witch* leaned to the breeze, her new sails gleaming white in the sunlight, I felt none of the elation that I should have felt at the start of this venture that Mike and I had dreamed about for so long.

158

The devil of it was that, now I was at sea, I remembered things I had forgotten in the bustle of fitting out. Patch had saved my life and, though he hadn't referred to it that night he had come to us at Lymington, I could remember the desperation that had prompted him to remind me of it in Paimpol. I had the sense of a debt owed, but not paid.

It wasn't only that I felt I had failed in an obligation. Sitting there, with my hands on the wheel, feeling the ship lift to the swell and hearing the water creaming past, I wondered whether it wasn't fear that was directing my course west towards Worbarrow Bay, instead of south to the Minkies. I had seen the Plateau des Minquiers in bad conditions, and deep down in my heart I knew I was scared of the place.

And the irony of it was that for four days we dived in Worbarrow Bay in conditions that were as perfect as I have ever seen them in the Channel—clear blue skies and a calm sea ruffled by only the slightest of breezes. The only limiting factor was the coldness of the water which affected us after a time, even though we were using our heaviest foam rubber suits. In those four days we located and buoyed the wreck of the LCT, cut through into the engine-room and cleared the way for lifting out the main engines, work that we had feared might take anything up to a month.

In the same time, if I had had the nerve to

159

take the gamble, we could have cut our way into each of the *Mary Deare*'s holds. I thought about it sometimes as I worked down in the green depths with *Sea Witch*'s hull a dark shape in the translucent sea above me, and at night the tally of the day's work seemed a reproach and I turned into my bunk in a mood of depression.

It was almost with relief that I woke on the Sunday to a grey dawn misted with rain and a forecast that announced a deep depression over the Atlantic moving eastward. By midday the seas were beginning to break; we got the anchors up and plugged it on the engine against a strong westerly wind for the shelter of Lulworth Cove.

I left early next morning for Southampton. It was stormy, and the downland hills, that crooked chalk fingers round the natural lagoon of the cove, were a gloomy green, shrouded in curtains of driving rain. Big seas piled up in the narrow entrance, filling the cove with an ugly swell, which broke in a roar on the shingle beach. Gusts of wind funnelled into the cove from the tops of the downs, flattening the water in sudden, violent swirls. Nobody was about. The whole chalk basin—so regular in its circle that it might have been the flooded crater of an extinct volcano—was deserted. There was only *Sea Witch*, rolling heavily, and the gulls, like scraps of paper, whirled about by the wind.

'Better set an anchor watch if it gets any worse,' I told Mike as he rowed me ashore. 'It's not very good holding ground here.'

He nodded, his face unnaturally solemn under his sou'wester. 'What are you going to do if things go against him at this Enquiry?' he asked.

'Nothing,' I replied and my voice sounded peevish against the blatter of the wind. I was tired. I think we were both pretty tired. We had been diving hard for four days. 'If I'd been going to do anything,' I added, 'the time to do it was last week, when we sailed from Lymington. The worst that can happen to him is that they'll cancel his Master's Certificate again.' Mike didn't say anything. His yellow oilskins gleamed with water in the grey light as he moved rhythmically back and forth to the swing of the oars, and over his shoulders the houses of Lulworth stood silent, with a grey, shut look, on the flank of the hill.

The dinghy grounded with a sudden jar and Mike jumped out into the backwash of a wave and hauled it up so that I could step out dry-footed in my shore-going clothes. We stood there in the rain for a moment, talking about ordinary, mundane things, things that had to be done around the boat. And then, as I turned to climb the beach, he checked me. 'I just want you to know, John . . .' He hesitated, and then said, 'As far as I'm concerned you're free to make any decision you like—whatever the risk.'

'It's very decent of you, Mike,' I said. 'But I don't think—'

'It's not a question of being decent.' He was grinning. 'I just don't like working with a man who's got something on his mind.' He left me then and pushed out in the dinghy, and I climbed the steep slope of the beach to the road where the bus was waiting for me.

## CHAPTER TWO

It was almost eleven when I reached the court. I was late and the corridor leading to the courtroom was almost empty. The letter requesting my attendance gave me the guidance of one of the officials and as we reached a small door leading into the court, it opened and Snetterton came out. 'Ah, Mr Sands.' He blinked at me. 'Come to see the fun, eh?'

'I'm here as a witness,' I said.

'Yes, yes, of course. Pity to drag you away from your diving. Heard you had started work on that wreck in Worbarrow Bay.' He hesitated and then said, 'You know, we seriously considered approaching you over the question of the *Mary Deare*. We were going to try an asdic search. But then some new information came up and it became unnecessary.'

'What new information?' I was wondering whether the *Mary Deare* had been found. The weather had been bad during most of April, but there was always the chance . . .

'You'll see, Mr Sands. Interesting case, most interesting . . .' And he hurried off down the corridor.

The official opened the door for me then and I went into the court. 'The seats for witnesses are on the right, sir,' he whispered. There was no need for him to have whispered. The room was full of the murmur of voices. I stood there in the doorway, a little dazed. There were many more people than I had expected. The whole court seemed crammed to overflowing; only in the public gallery was there any vacant space. The witnesses were crowded into the seats usually occupied by jurymen called but not serving and some of them had spilled over into the jury box itself. Patch I saw at once, sitting well down towards the front, his face pale and taut, but harder now, like a man who knows what is coming and has nerved himself to meet it. Behind him, and to the right, the crew were clustered in a little hard knot round Higgins's solid bulk. They looked awkward and ill-at-ease, a little exotic in their new shore-going clothes. Fraser, the captain of the Channel packet that had picked us up, was there, too, and, sitting beside him was Janet Taggart. She gave me a quick smile, tight-lipped and a little wan, and I wondered

163

why the devil they needed to drag her in as a witness.

And then somebody was signalling me from just behind her and, as he craned his neck up, I saw it was Hal. I pushed my way down the row and squeezed in beside him. 'I didn't expect to find you here,' I whispered.

'Very important witness,' he said. 'Don't forget that it was I who first reported the ship as a derelict hulk containing the person of my erstwhile and somewhat foolhardy skipper.' He smiled at me out of the corners of his eyes. 'Anyway, I wouldn't have missed it for the world. Going to be a damned interesting case if you ask me.'

At the time I had entered, men in various parts of the court, but chiefly on the side across from me, were standing up to give their names and state their business and who they represented. There were a surprising number of them, for, besides the insurance companies and the owners, the builders of the *Mary Deare* were represented, the Marine Officers' Association, the Radio Operators' Association, the various unions; there was even a solicitor appearing for the relatives of Captain Taggart deceased.

The atmosphere was very informal by comparison with a court of law—no wigs, no gowns, no police, no jury. Even the judge and his three assessors wore lounge suits. Across the court from where I sat the desks were occupied by the various counsel appearing for interested parties. They were very crowded. The witness box nearby stood empty and beyond was the Press desk with two reporters at it. On our side of the court the desks were occupied by the Treasury counsel and his junior and the Treasury solicitors and assistants.

Hal leaned towards me. 'Do you know who's representing the insurance people?' he whispered.

I shook my head. I had no information about the legal representatives. All I knew was that a Mr Bowen-Lodge Q.C. was chairman of the Enquiry.

'Sir Lionel Falcett. About the most expensive man they could have got.' His blue eyes darted me a quick glance. 'Significant, eh?'

I glanced down at Patch. And then I was remembering that I, too, might have to go into the witness box, and all the counsel had the right to cross-examine.

A hush slowly spread through the room. The Chairman, who had been engaged in earnest discussion with his assessors, had turned and faced the court. As soon as there was complete silence he began his opening address. 'Gentlemen. This Court meets here today, as you are well aware, to investigate the loss of the steamship *Mary Deare*. It will be the duty of the Court to examine, not only the

165

circumstances of the loss itself, but all the relevant factors that may possibly have contributed to that loss. The scope of this investigation, therefore, covers the state of the ship at the time she started on her ill-fated voyage from Yokohama, her sea-worthiness, the condition of her machinery, the nature of her cargo and the manner of its stowage, and in particular, the state of her fire-fighting equipment. It covers also the behaviour and conduct of all those concerned in the running of the vessel to the extent that they may or may not have contributed to the disaster.

'For disaster it was, gentlemen. Out of a total crew of thirty-two, no less than twelve men—over a third of the ship's complement— lost their lives. Moreover, the captain died during the voyage and a director of the company owning the vessel is reported missing. It is a sad business that we are investigating and it is possible that relatives of men who lost their lives may be present in this courtroom today. I, therefore, consider it my duty to remind you that this is a Formal Enquiry to determine the cause of this disaster and, whilst I am anxious that proper respect should be paid to the dead and that no advantage should be taken of men who, through death, are unable to testify, I would impress upon you that we are here to investigate this whole terrible business thoroughly and impartially.' Bowen-Lodge leaned a little forward. 'I will now call on Mr Holland to open proceedings on behalf of the Ministry of Transport.'

Holland might have been a banker or perhaps a stock-broker. Whereas the judge, despite his sour, dyspeptic-looking features, had comprehended the tragedy that lay behind the Enquiry and had filled the court with the drama of it, this tall, smooth-faced barrister with the sleek head of black hair had a cold-blooded urbanity of manner that suggested an interest in figures rather than the frailties of human behaviour.

'Mr Learned Chairman.' He had risen and was facing the judge and the three assessors, his hands thrust into the pockets of his jacket. 'I think I should bring to your notice at the outset that the Receiver of Wreck, in his report to the Minister, stressed that in several particulars the evidence of the survivors was conflicting. As you know, in cases of this nature, the Receiver of Wreck prepares his report on the basis of depositions in writing. These depositions are made under oath. I do not propose, therefore, to outline in detail the events leading up to the disaster or the disaster itself. I will confine myself to a brief statement of the established facts concerning the voyage and leave the details—the story as it were—to emerge from the evidence of the various witnesses.'

He paused and glanced down at his notes. Then he faced the courtroom itself and in a smooth, rather bored voice summarized the events of the voyage.

The *Mary Deare* had been purchased by the Dellimare Trading and Shipping Company in June of the previous year. She had belonged to a Burmese company and for two years had been laid-up in a creek near Yokohama. On completion of the purchase she had been towed into Yokohama for a complete overhaul. On November 18 she had been granted a seaworthy certificate to cover a single voyage to Antwerp and thence to England where she was to be broken up. On December 2 she completed coaling. On December 4 she began loading her cargo. This consisted of 148 war surplus aircraft engines of American manufacture, including 56 jet engines for a particular fighter in use with N.A.T.O. forces. In addition to this cargo, which was destined for Antwerp and was distributed fairly equally over the four holds, a large quantity of Japanese cotton and rayon goods were loaded. This part of the cargo was destined for Rangoon and was, therefore, loaded on top of the aircraft engines. The whole of the cargo, including the engines, was the property of the Hsu Trading Corporation, a very large and influential Chinese merchanting organization in Singapore.

The *Mary Deare* sailed from Yokohama on December 8. On January 6 she reached Rangoon and off-loaded her cargo of Japanese goods. A cargo of raw cotton for England, also the property of the Hsu Corporation, was not ready at the docks for loading. The ship, therefore, proceeded to bunker and then moved out into the river, where she moored to a buoy already occupied by the *Torre Annunziata*, another of the Dellimare Company ships. Four days later she moved into the docks again and loaded her cargo of cotton, the bulk of it in Numbers Two and Three holds.

She sailed from Rangoon on January 15, reaching Aden on February 4. There she landed Mr Adams, the first officer, who was sick. Mr Patch was accepted to fill this vacancy. The ship sailed on February 6. On March 2, the Master, Captain James Taggart, died, and Mr Patch assumed command of the ship. The *Mary Deare* was then in the Mediterranean, four days out from Port Said. On March 9 she passed through the Straits of Gibraltar, out into the Atlantic. Almost immediately she ran into heavy weather. She was making a certain amount of water and the pumps were kept going intermittently. On March 16 conditions worsened and it blew full gale.

'And now,' Holland said, his voice lifting slightly from the smooth monotone in which he had been addressing the Court—'Now we come to the series of incidents—mysteries you might almost call them—that are the subject of this Investigation.'

169

Briefly he enumerated them: the damage sustained by the ship in the for'ard holds, the water making headway against the pumps, the shoring of the stoke-hold bulkhead, the fire in the radio shack, the disappearance of Dellimare; and then, after rounding Ushant, the fire in Number Three hold, the abandonment of the ship by all except the captain, the discovery of the ship still afloat the following morning, her final abandonment. He punched these events home to the packed courtroom one after another in terse, hard sentences, so that the effect of them was cumulative.

'Twelve men went to their death, gentlemen,' he added, after a pause, his voice now very quiet. 'Went to their death in a mad scramble to get away from a ship that, in point of fact, was in no immediate danger of sinking. That in itself is significant.' He had turned and was facing the Chairman of the Court. 'It is not for me to attempt to influence the Court in any way, merely to present the facts. But I am entitled to draw your attention to certain points, and the points, Mr Learned Chairman, to which I wish to draw the attention of the Court are—firstly, the succession of incidents affecting the safety and sea-keeping ability of the ship, and secondly, the abandonment of a ship that was to stay afloat in gale conditions for more than 48 hours. I submit that this is one of the most extraordinary cases to come

170

before a Formal Enquiry and one that may, as a result of your decision, have far-reaching consequences for one or more of the people here in this courtroom today.'

In making that pronouncement his eyes had roved the room—to the lawyers representing the various interested parties across the floor of the court, to the public gallery, and, finally, he had turned his body round and had stared at the witnesses. His gaze was cold and hard and accusing.

Still facing the witnesses, he went on: 'I have referred to a lack of consistency in the evidence given on oath in depositions made by the various witnesses. Those same witnesses, and some others, will be giving evidence on oath before this Court. But here there is a difference; you can be cross-examined on your evidence in the witness box by myself or by any or all of the representatives of the interested parties.' He paused and then added, 'I would remind you that perjury is a serious offence.'

There was complete silence as he stared at us, and some of the *Mary Deare*'s crew shifted uneasily in their seats. Abruptly, he sat down. For perhaps thirty seconds he let the silence his speech had produced hang over the court, and then he got slowly to his feet again and called 'Gideon Patch.'

Patch was sitting quite still, his eyes fixed across the court—fixed on nothing—and he didn't move. I thought for a moment that he hadn't heard his name called. But then he turned his head and looked at Holland, and quietly, like a man who cannot believe that the moment has finally come, he got to his feet. He seemed to brace himself to meet the situation and, with a firm, decisive tread, he crossed the floor of the court and took his stand in the witness box.

The movement released the tension in the court so that there was a sudden murmur of voices and shifting of feet that continued whilst the oath was being administered and then gradually died away as Holland began his questions, Patch answering them in a voice that was barely audible.

His name was Gideon Stephen Patch. He had been educated at Pangbourne, joined the Merchant Service as a cadet in 1935, Mate's Certificate 1941, Master's Certificate 1944, first command 1945, the *Belle Isle* incident, the years on the beach; the wasted, frustrated years—Holland took him through it all, fact after fact in that same bored voice as though he were tracing the history of a parcel sent through the post. And then the technical details: Did he consider the *Mary Deare* seaworthy? Had he examined the fire-fighting equipment? Had he inspected the boats himself? Did he regard the crew as efficient? Were the officers, in his opinion, competent?

And Patch, once over the hurdle of the *Belle Isle* sinking and the suspension of his Master's

172

Certificate, began noticeably to relax and to gain confidence. It was all so impersonal. Yes, the boats were all right, he had inspected them personally. The crew were average—he had sailed with worse. The officers? He would rather not comment. Some were good, some were not.

'And the captain?' The question was put in the same flat, bored voice.

Patch hesitated, and then said, 'I imagine he was a good seaman.'

'You imagine?' Holland's dark brows lifted slightly.

'Captain Taggart was a sick man, sir.'

'Then why was he not put ashore?'

'I don't know.'

'The first officer, Adams, was put ashore because he was sick. Why wasn't Captain Taggart put ashore, if he was also sick?'

'I imagine the owners thought him fit enough to complete the voyage.'

'By the owners you mean Mr Dellimare?'

'Yes.'

'Tell me, what was the nature of Captain Taggart's illness?'

Patch had clearly been expecting that question, and, now it had come, he looked unhappy about it and for a moment his eyes glanced towards the waiting witnesses. He was looking towards Janet Taggart. And then he was facing Holland again. 'I'm sorry, sir, but I do not think I can answer that.'

173

Holland made a little impatient gesture. It was obvious that he intended to press the point, but the Chairman intervened. 'Mr Holland.' He was leaning forward. 'It seems hardly necessary for us to pursue this matter. I do not feel that the nature of Captain Taggart's illness can have any bearing on the subject of this Investigation.'

Holland had turned and was facing the judge's chair, his hands gripping the lapels of his jacket as though he were, in fact, wearing a gown. 'I submit, Mr Learned Chairman, that everything connected with the *Mary Deare* is relevant to your Investigation. I am endeavouring to present a complete picture. To do so I must give you the facts—all the facts.'

'Quite so, Mr Holland.' Bowen-Lodge's mouth was a trapshut line. 'But I see here'— and he glanced at his papers—'that Miss Taggart is amongst the witnesses in this court. I would ask you to bear that in mind, Mr Holland, and, in your references to her father, to avoid as far as possible giving her any further cause for pain.'

'Unfortunately . . .' But Holland checked himself before Bowen-Lodge's cold, official stare, and then turned to face Patch. 'I will content myself at the moment with asking you whether, in fact, you knew what was wrong with Captain Taggart?'

'Yes, I knew,' Patch answered. And then

added quickly, 'But I had no idea that it would prove fatal.'

'Quite so.' Holland turned to the cargo then. As first officer you would assume responsibility for the state of loading of the holds. Did you examine the holds yourself?'

'I satisfied myself they were properly loaded.'

'All four holds?'

'Yes.'

'You actually went into each of the holds yourself?'

'Numbers One and Four holds, yes. The other two were full of cargo, but I was able to get some idea of the stowage by looking in through the inspection hatches.'

'Before or after sailing from Aden?'

'Before.'

'Would you tell the Court exactly how these holds were loaded.'

Patch started with Number One hold and worked aft. He gave the dimensions of each— they ran the full width of the ship throughout their depth. The floor of each hold was covered by cases. He gave the approximate dimensions of the cases and the U.S.A.A.F. code numbering painted on them.

'You knew that those cases contained aero engines?' Mr Holland asked.

'Yes, I did.'

'From personal observation? By that I mean, did you at any time examine the contents of one of those cases yourself?'

'No. I had no occasion to. In any case, it would have been very difficult to get one opened—they were tightly packed and, except in Numbers One and Four holds, the cotton cargo completely covered them.'

'I see. So that when you say you knew the cases contained aero engines, you are really saying that that was how the contents were described on the manifest?' Patch nodded. 'Did Captain Taggart show you the manifest before you made your inspection of the holds?'

'I had a look at the manifest before I made my inspection.'

Holland stared at him. 'That wasn't what I asked you. Did Captain Taggart show you the manifest before you made your inspection?'

Patch hesitated and then said, 'No.'

'Had you seen Captain Taggart at that time?'

'Yes.'

'Did you ask him for the manifest?'

'No.'

'Why not? Surely if you were going to inspect the holds—'

'Captain Taggart wasn't well, sir.'

Holland hesitated. Then he half-shrugged his shoulders and turned to the ship herself. There followed nearly half an hour of technical details—her dimensions, construction, date of building, repairs, alterations, characteristics and behaviour, and her history.

She had been built on the Clyde in 1910 for the Atlantic trade. Patch had got her history from some old notebook he had found on board. He had even discovered the origin of her name; the result of some long-dead chairman's dry sense of humour, his wife being called Mary and his own second name being Deare. The ship had been torpedoed twice in the first World War, patched up and kept at sea in convoy after convoy, and then in 1922 she had hit a growler off the Gulf of St Lawrence and after that she'd been sold and for ten years had tramped the seas. The depression caught her in a Far Eastern port where she lay rotting until the shadow of another war raised shipping freights and she changed hands again and was put to work in the Indian Ocean and the China Seas. She was torpedoed again in 1941, just outside Singapore, packed with troops. She limped into Rangoon, was patched up and sailed to San Francisco. There she had the only decent overhaul in twenty years and went back to work again in the Far Eastern theatre. And then in the last days of the Japanese war, she was stranded on a coral reef under shell-fire. Half her bottom was torn out, her keel permanently kinked, part of her superstructure shot away.

'Any modern ship would have broken her back,' Patch said, and there was a sort of pride in the way he said it.

He went on to tell how she had changed hands again in 1947—a Burmese owner this time; how she had gone on struggling from port to port throughout the Far East with a twisted back and botched-up repairs until she had been discarded in Yokohama, four years later, and left there to rot until the Dellimare Company purchased her.

In telling her story, he somehow invested the *Mary Deare* with personality. If he had laid stress on the fact that she was a broken-down old hulk on her way to the scrap-heap he could have demonstrated his ability as a seaman and as a Master in bringing her up through the Bay in one of the worst sea storms of the year. Instead, he told the Court that she was a fine ship, easy to handle, and explained that it was only the repairs, carried out in poorly-equipped Far Eastern ports, that caused her to leak. His loyalty to the ship was impressive, but it lost him the sympathy he might so easily have had.

After that Holland was taking him over the details of the voyage—up through the Red Sea and the Suez Canal and into the Mediterranean; and all the time he questioned him about the crew, the officers, the relations between Dellimare and Taggart; and the picture that emerged was not a pleasant one— the crew ill-disciplined, the chief engineer incompetent, a poker addict, gambling indiscriminately with crew and officers, the captain keeping to his cabin, never on the bridge, and Dellimare roaming restlessly round the ship, feeding alone in his cabin, occasionally with Higgins, and sometimes shut up with the captain for hours on end.

The court was still as Holland reached the point at which Patch had assumed command. 'According to your entry in the ship's log, Captain Taggart died some time in the early hours of March 2nd. Is that correct?'

'Yes.'

'You had no doctor on board?'

'No.'

Janet Taggart was leaning forward, her face very pale, the knuckles of her hands white as they gripped the back of the seat in front of her.

'Did you treat Captain Taggart yourself?'

'I did what I could.'

'And what was that?'

'I got him to bed. I tried to get him to take a sedative, but he wouldn't.' Patch's voice trailed off and he glanced quickly across the court at Janet Taggart.

'Did you lock him in his cabin?'

'Yes.' His voice was scarcely above a whisper.

'Why?'

Patch did not reply.

'You state in the log that, in your opinion, Captain Taggart died of heart failure. Would you please explain to the Court what it was

179

that caused his heart—if it was his heart—to fail?'

'Mr Holland.' Bowen-Lodge's voice cut in, sharp and high. 'I must remind you of what I said before. I do not consider this relevant or necessary.'

But Holland was obstinate this time. 'With all due deference, Mr Learned Chairman, I consider it highly relevant. The witness is showing commendable restraint regarding the nature of Captain Taggart's illness. That illness, however, has a considerable bearing on the efficiency of the command he inherited and in fairness to him the Court must be informed.' And, without waiting for permission, he swung round on Patch and said, 'Now that you know the reason for the question, perhaps you will answer it. What was the basic cause of death?'

Patch stood there, obstinately silent, and Holland became suddenly impatient. 'The man died locked in his cabin. Isn't that correct?'

It was brutally put and there was a shocked look on Patch's face as he nodded dumbly.

'Why did you lock him in his cabin?' And when Patch didn't answer, Holland put a leading question. 'Is it true that you locked him in his cabin because he was raving?'

'He was delirious, yes,' Patch murmured.

'He was upsetting the crew?'

'Yes.'

'Making wild accusations?'

'Yes.'

'What accusations?'

Patch glanced unhappily round the court, and then said, 'He was accusing the officers of stealing liquor from his cabin.'

'Now will you please answer this question.' Holland was leaning forward. 'What was the basic cause, as far as you know, of Captain Taggart's death?'

Patch might have remained obstinate on this point, but Bowen-Lodge's voice cut in from high up on the judge's seat. 'Witness will kindly answer the question put to him by Counsel. I will repeat it for his benefit—what was the basic cause of death?'

Patch hesitated. 'Drink, sir,' he said reluctantly.

'Drink? Do you mean he died of drink?'

'Because of it—yes.'

The stunned silence that enveloped the court was broken by a girl's voice. It was shrill and high and quavering as she cried out, 'That's not true. How can you say a thing like that—when he's dead?'

'Please, Miss Taggart.' Holland's voice was gentle, almost fatherly. 'The witness is under oath.'

'I don't care whether he's under oath or not, he's lying,' she sobbed wildly. Patch's face had gone very white. Fraser was trying to pull her back into her seat. But she had turned towards the Chairman. 'Please stop him,' she sobbed.

And then, flinging up her head, she declared, 'My father was a fine man, a man anybody here would be proud to have known.'

'I understand, Miss Taggart.' Bowen-Lodge's voice was very quiet and soft. 'But I must remind you that this Court is investigating a disaster in which many men lost their lives. The witness is under oath. Moreover, he is not the only witness. You may rest assured that this accusation will be probed and the truth revealed. Will you please be seated now. Or if you prefer it, you may leave the court and wait outside until you are called to give evidence.'

'I'll stay,' she answered in a small, tight voice. 'I'm sorry.' She sat down slowly, her face completely white, her hands fumbling for a handkerchief.

Holland cleared his throat. 'Only one more question on this subject and then we will leave it. About how much liquor was Captain Taggart in the habit of consuming each day?'

'I cannot answer that. I don't know.' Patch's voice was scarcely audible.

'You mean you didn't actually see him consume any set quantity?'

Patch nodded.

'But you must have some idea. What was it he habitually drank—whisky?'

'Yes.'

'Anything else?'

'Sometimes a bottle of cognac. Occasionally

rum.'

'How much?'

'I don't know.'

'Had this been going on ever since the start of the voyage?'

'Yes, I think so.'

'Then, since it affected you directly as first officer, you must have made enquiries as to how much he drank. How much did you gather he consumed each day?'

Patch hesitated, and then reluctantly: 'The steward said a bottle, a bottle and a-half— sometimes two.' The court gasped.

'I see.' The sound of suppressed sobbing was distinctly audible in the stillness of the court. 'So that he was completely incapable as the Master of the ship?'

'Oh, no.' Patch shook his head. 'Towards the end of the day he would become a little fuddled. But otherwise I would say he was reasonably in command of the situation.'

'You mean to say,'—Bowen-Lodge was leaning forward—'that he was in full command of his faculties when he was steadily drinking one to two bottles a day?'

'Yes, sir. That is to say, most of the time.'

'But you admitted that he was raving and you had to lock him in his cabin. If he was raving, then surely . . .' the Chairman's brows lifted in a question.

'He wasn't raving because he was drunk,' Patch answered slowly.

'Then why was he raving?'

'He had run out of liquor.'

A shocked silence gripped the court. Janet Taggart had stopped sobbing. She was sitting quite rigid, staring at Patch with a sort of fascinated horror.

'I would like to get this point perfectly clear before we go any further,' Bowen-Lodge said in a quiet, controlled voice. 'What you're suggesting is that Captain Taggart did not die of drink, but the lack of it. Is that correct?'

'Yes, sir.'

'Do you really think absence of liquor can kill a man?'

'I don't know,' Patch answered wretchedly. 'All I know is that he lived on nothing else, and when he hadn't got it, he went raving mad and died. He never seemed to have anything in the way of food.'

Bowen-Lodge considered for a moment, his pencil tracing lines on the paper in front of him. At length he looked down at Counsel. 'I think, Mr Holland, we should call medical evidence to establish the point one way or another.'

Holland nodded. 'I have already arranged for that—it seemed necessary after reading his deposition.'

'Good. Then we can leave the matter in abeyance till then.' He sounded relieved. 'Please proceed with the examination of the witness.'

184

The next stage of the voyage was uneventful, but Patch was taken through it in detail and the picture that emerged was of a conscientious officer doing his best to pull a ship's company together with the presence of the owner a constant irritant. The incidents that came to light under Holland's steady questioning were trivial enough in themselves—the crew's mess table uncleaned between meals, cockroaches, several men lousy, the galley dirty, a lifeboat without provisions, a man injured in a fight, the engines stopped for the replacement of a bearing that had been allowed to run hot—but together they produced an impression of a ship that was badly served by the men who ran her.

Other things emerged, too. The log was improperly kept, the wells not sounded regularly, water consumption unchecked, and as often as not it was Higgins, by then acting as first officer, who was responsible. Patch showed that he was coming to depend more and more on his second officer, John Rice, and the growing sense of comradeship between the two men ran like a strong thread through the evidence.

Twice Patch referred to Dellimare. Once of his own accord, when he was dealing with the lack of supervision of the engine-room staff. 'He was encouraging Mr Burrows, my chief engineer, in his poker playing. I had to insist that he stopped entertaining Mr Burrows in his cabin. They were playing cards together till all hours of the night and it was throwing undue responsibility upon Mr Raft, the second engineer.'

'Did Mr Dellimare raise any objection?' Holland asked.

'Yes.'

'What did he say?'

'He said it was his ship and he would do what he damn' well liked and entertain any of the officers he pleased when he pleased.'

'And what did you say to that?'

'That it was endangering the safety of the ship and the morale of the engine-room and that I was the captain, not him, and the ship would be run the way I wanted it run.'

'In other words you had a row?'

'Yes.'

'And did he agree to stop playing poker with the chief engineer?'

'In the end, yes.'

'In the end? You used some persuasion?'

'Yes. I told him I had given Mr Burrows a direct order and that, if it wasn't obeyed, I should know what action to take. And I made it a direct order as far as he was concerned.'

'And he accepted that?'

'Yes.'

'Will you tell the Court what your relations with Mr Dellimare were at this stage?'

Patch hesitated. He had revealed that his relations with the owner were strained. He could in one sentence explain the reason for those strained relations and in doing so gain the sympathy of the whole court. But he let the opportunity go, merely saying, 'We did not see eye-to-eye on certain matters.' And Holland left it at that.

A further reference to Dellimare occurred almost accidentally. Patch had just assured the Court that he had personally checked all four holds as the ship ran into heavy weather off the coast of Portugal, and Holland, again being scrupulously fair to him, drew attention to the fact that he hadn't relied on his first officer's report to make sure that there could be no shifting of the cargo. 'You didn't trust him, in other words?'

'To be honest, no.'

'Did Mr Higgins, in fact, check the holds?'

'I don't know.'

'You thought so little of him that you didn't even ask whether he had checked them?'

'Yes, I suppose that is correct.'

'Did anybody, other than yourself, check the holds?'

Patch paused a moment before replying. Then he said, 'I think Mr Dellimare checked them.'

'You think he checked them?'

'Well, he was in Number One hold when I went in through the inspection hatch to check. I presumed that he was there for the same purpose as myself.'

Holland seemed to consider this for a moment. 'I see. But this was the duty of one of the ship's officers. It seems odd that the owner should find it necessary to check the cargo himself. Have you any comment to make on that?'

Patch shook his head.

'What sort of man was Mr Dellimare?' Holland asked. 'What was your impression of him?'

Now, I thought—now he'll tell them the truth about Dellimare. It was the opening he needed. But he stood there, without saying anything, his face very pale and that nerve twitching at the corner of his mouth.

'What I am trying to get at is this,' Holland went on. 'We are coming now to the night of March 16. On that night Mr Dellimare disappeared—lost overboard. Did you know that Mr Dellimare had been in the Navy during the war?'

Patch nodded and his lips framed the word 'Yes'.

'He served in corvettes and frigates, mainly in the Atlantic. He must have been through a great many storms.' There was a significant pause, and then Holland said, 'What was your impression of him, at this time, when you knew you were running into very heavy weather? Was he normal in every way?'

'Yes, I think so.' Patch's voice was very low.

'But you're not certain.'

'I didn't know him very well.'

'You had been on this ship with him for over a month. However much he kept to his cabin, you must have had some idea of his mental state. Would you say he was worried?'

'Yes, I think you could say that.'

'Business worries or private worries?'

'I don't know.'

'I'll put it quite bluntly. When you found him checking the cargo, what interpretation did you put on his action?'

'I didn't put any interpretation on it.' Patch had found his voice again and was answering factually and clearly.

'What did you say to him?'

'I told him to stay out of the holds.'

'Why?'

'He shouldn't have been there. The cargo wasn't his responsibility.'

'Quite. I'll put it to you another way. Would you say that his presence there indicated that he was getting scared, that his nerves were going to pieces? He had been torpedoed once during the war and was a long time in the water before being picked up. Would you say that his war experience was in any way affecting him?'

'No, I would . . . I don't know.'

Holland hesitated and then he gave a little shrug. He had been a man seeking after the truth, using the depositions already made as a base from which to probe. But now he changed his tactics and was content to let Patch tell the story of the night the *Mary Deare* was hove-to in the wind-spun waters of the Bay of Biscay, not questioning, not interrupting—just letting it run.

And Patch told it well, gaining from the rapt silence of the court, telling it in hard, factual sentences. And the *Mary Deare* floated into that court, rusty and battered, with the seas bursting like gunfire against the submerged reef of her bows. I watched his face as he told it straight, man-to-man—from the witness box to the Court—and I had the odd feeling that all the time he was skating round something. I looked up at the Chairman. He was sitting slightly forward with his chin cupped in his right hand, listening with a shut, tight-lipped, judicial face that told me nothing of his reactions.

The facts, as Patch presented them, were straightforward enough: the glass falling steadily, the seas rising, the wind increasing, the ship rolling, rolling steady and slow, but gradually rolling her bulwarks under as the mountains of water lifted her on to their streaming crests and tumbled her down into the valleys between. He had been on the bridge since dusk. Rice had been there, too. Just the two of them and the helmsman and a lookout. It had happened about 23.20 hours— a slight explosion, a sort of shudder. It had sounded like another wave breaking and slamming against the bows, except that there was no white water at that particular moment and the ship did not stagger. She was down in a trough and rising slowly. The break of the wave came later and, with it, the hesitation, the crash of the impact, and the sudden blur of white hiding all the fore part of the ship.

Nothing had been said for a moment, and then Rice's voice had cut through the gale's roar as he shouted, 'Did we hit something, sir?' And then he had sent Rice to sound the wells and back had come the report—making water in both the for'ard holds, particularly in Number One. He had ordered the pumps to be started in both Number One and Number Two holds, and he had stood on the bridge and watched the bows become heavy and the seas start to break green over all the for'ard part of the ship. And then Dellimare had come on to the bridge, white-faced and scared-looking. Higgins, too. They were talking about abandoning ship. They seemed to think she was going down. And Rice came back to say the crew were panicking.

He had left the bridge to Higgins and had gone out on to the upper deck with Rice. Four men in life-jackets were starting to clear Number Three boat. They were scared and he had to hit one man before they would leave the boat and go back to their duties. He had taken all the men he could find, some ten of them, and had set them to work under the bos'n and the third engineer to shore up the bulkhead between Number Two hold and the boiler-room just in case. And it was whilst he was supervising this that the helmsman had reported to the engine-room that the bridge was full of smoke.

He had taken half a dozen men and when he reached the bridge there was only the helmsman there, his eyes streaming, racked with coughing, as he clung to the wheel, nursing the ship through the crowding storm-breakers, the whole place filled with a fog of acrid smoke.

The fire had been in the radio shack, a little above and behind the bridge. No, he had no idea how it had started. The radio operator had gone below to get his life-jacket. He had stayed below to relieve himself and to have a mug of cocoa. Higgins had gone aft to inspect the steering which seemed slack. No, he didn't know where Dellimare was. He regretted that the helmsman was not among the survivors.

They had used foam extinguishers on the fire. But the heat had been so intense that they hadn't been able to get inside the room. What had finally put the fire out was the partial collapse of the roof, which had allowed the water from a breaking wave to engulf the flames.

The wind was now Force 12 in the gusts—hurricane force. He had hove-to then, putting the ship's bows into the wind with the engines at slow ahead, just holding her there, and praying to God that the seas, piling down in white cascades of water on to the bows, wouldn't smash the for'ard hatch covers. They had stayed hove-to like that, in imminent danger of their lives, for fourteen hours, the pumps just holding their own, and all the time he and Rice had kept moving constantly through the ship, to see that the bulkhead—which was leaking where the weight of water was bulging it, low down near its base—was properly shored, to keep the crew from panicking, to see that they kept to their stations and helped the ship in its struggle against the sea.

About 06.00 hours, after twenty-two hours without sleep, he had retired to his cabin. The wind was dropping by then and the glass beginning to rise. He had gone to sleep fully clothed and two hours later had been woken by Samuel King, the Jamaican steward, with the news that Mr Dellimare could not be found.

The whole ship had been searched, but without success. The man had vanished. 'I could only presume that he had been washed overboard,' Patch said, and then he stood silent, as though waiting for Holland to question him, and Holland asked him if he had held any sort of enquiry.

'Yes. I had every member of the crew make a statement before Mr Higgins, Mr Rice and myself. As far as we could determine, the last man to see Mr Dellimare alive was the steward. He had seen him leave his cabin and go out through the door on to the upper-deck leading aft. That was at about 04.30 hours.'

'And nobody saw him after that?'

Patch hesitated, and then said, 'As far as anybody could find out—no.'

'The upper-deck was the boat-deck?'

'Yes.'

'Was there any danger in going out on to that deck?'

'I don't know. I was on the bridge dealing with the fire.'

'Yes, but in your opinion—was there danger in crossing that deck?'

'No, I don't think so. It's difficult to say. Spray and some seas were sweeping right across all the decks.'

'Right aft?'

'Yes.'

'And Mr Dellimare was going aft?'

'So King said.'

Holland paused and then he asked, 'Have you any idea where Mr Dellimare was going?'

'No.'

'In view of what you have told us before, would it be reasonable to assume that he might be going aft to check that the hatches of the after-holds were still secure?'

'Possibly. But there was no need. I had checked them myself.'

'But if he had gone to check those hatches,

it would have meant going down on to the after well-deck?'

'He could have seen the state of the hatches from the after end of the upper-deck.'

'But if he had gone down, would it have been dangerous?'

'Yes. Yes, I think so. Both well-decks were being swept by the seas.'

'I see. And that was the last anyone saw of him?' The court was very still. The old ship, with her water-logged bows pointed into the gale and a man's body tossed among the spindrift out there in the raging seas; there wasn't anybody in the room who couldn't see it for himself. The puzzle of it, the mystery of it—it held them all enthralled. And behind me somebody was crying.

Then Patch's voice was going on with his story, nervous and jerky, in tune with the sense of tragedy that was seen only in the imagination and not in the cleansing, healing atmosphere of salt wind and spray.

The wind had fallen, and the sea with it, and at 12.43 hours, according to the entry in the log, he had rung for half-ahead on the engines and had resumed course. As soon as it was practicable he had ordered the hand pumps manned, and, as the bows slowly emerged from the sea, he had set a working party under Rice to repair the damage to the for'ard hatches.

He had considered putting into Brest. But, with the weather improving and the pumps holding their own, he had finally decided to hold his course, and had rounded Ushant early on the morning of the 18th. By then he had increased engine revolutions to economical speed. There was still a big swell running, but the sea was quiet, almost dead calm, with very little wind. Nevertheless, he had hugged the French coast just in case there was some sudden change in the state of the for'ard holds. Ile de Batz was abeam at 13.34, Triagoz light at 16.12, Sept Iles at 17.21. He read these times out to the Court from the log. At 19.46 the group occulting light on Les Heaux was just visible through a light mist four points on the starb'd bow. He had then altered course to North 33 East. This would take him outside the Barnouic and Roches Douvres reefs and leave Les Hanois, the light on the south-western tip of Guernsey, about four miles to starb'd. After altering course he had informed his officers that he had decided to take the ship into Southampton for inspection and repairs.

At approximately 21.20, when the steward was clearing his evening meal, which he had taken, as usual, alone in his cabin, he had heard shouts, and then Rice had rushed in to say that the after hold was on fire and that the crew were in a state of panic.

'Any particular reason for their panic?' Holland asked.

'Well, I think they thought the ship was jinxed,' Patch answered. 'In the last two days I had heard that word often.'

'And what did you think? Did you think the ship was jinxed?'

Patch faced the Chairman and the assessors. 'No,' he said. 'I thought there had been a deliberate attempt to wreck her.'

There was a stir of interest throughout the courtroom. But he didn't punch it home with any direct accusation. He just said: 'It was too coincidental—the damage to the holds and then the fire in the radio shack.'

'You were convinced that there had been some sort of explosion in Number One hold?' Holland asked.

Patch hesitated. 'Yes. Yes, I think so.'

'And the radio shack?'

'If it was an explosion, then the radio shack had to be put out of action—it was my means of communication with the rest of the world.'

'I see.' Holland paused, and then he said, 'What you are saying, in fact, is that there was somebody on board who was trying to destroy the ship.'

'Yes.'

'And when you heard that Number Three hold was on fire—did you immediately think that this was another attempt to destroy the ship?'

'Yes, I did.'

'And is that still your opinion?'

Patch nodded. 'Yes.'

'You realize that this is a very serious

197

accusation you are making?'

'Yes, I realize that.'

Holland held the court in utter silence for a moment. And then he said, 'There were thirty-one men on board the *Mary Deare*. If the fire were deliberately started, it endangered all those lives. It was tantamount to murder.'

'Yes.'

'And do you still say that the fire was started deliberately?'

'Yes, I do.'

The next question was inevitable. 'Who did you suspect of starting it?' Holland asked, and Patch hesitated. To produce the story of Dellimare's offer now was pointless. Dellimare was dead. He couldn't have started that fire, and all Patch could say was that he hadn't had much time for formulating suspicions—he had been too busy trying to save the ship.

'But you must have thought about it since?'

'Yes, I have.' Patch was facing the judge and the assessors. 'But I think that is a matter for the Court to decide.'

Bowen-Lodge nodded his agreement and Holland then got Patch back to the events following the outbreak of the fire. He and Rice had organized a fire-fighting party. No, Higgins wasn't there. It was his watch. But the second engineer was there and the radio operator and the bos'n. They ran out hoses and got them playing on to the flames through the inspection hatch whilst they cleared part of

198

the main hatch cover. They also cleared a section of Number Four hatch cover in case it was necessary to play the hoses on the bulkhead between the two holds. He had then gone down into Number Four hold through the inspection hatch.

'Why did you do that?'

'I wanted to see how hot the bulkhead plates had become. I didn't want the fire to spread aft. Also, because that hold was only partly filled with cargo, I hoped to be able to tell from the heat of the plates just how serious the fire was—what hold it had got.'

'And what did you discover?'

'It had clearly only just broken out. The bulkhead wasn't even hot. But I didn't discover that until later.'

'How do you mean?'

He explained then how he had been knocked unconscious just as he had reached the bottom of the vertical ladder. He told it in the same words that he had told it to me in his cabin on the *Mary Deare* and when he had finished Holland said, 'You're sure it wasn't an accident—that you didn't slip?'

'Quite sure,' Patch answered.

'Perhaps something fell on you—a loose piece of metal?'

But Patch pointed to his jaw where the scar still showed, maintaining that it was quite impossible for it to have happened accidentally.

'And when you came to, was there any sort of weapon near you that your assailant might have used?

'No, I don't think so. But I couldn't be certain. The place was full of smoke and I was dazed, half asphyxiated.'

'I put it to you that one of the crew—a man, say, who had a grudge against you—could have followed you down . . . hit you perhaps with his fist?'

'He would have had to be a very powerful man.' Patch was looking across at Higgins. And then he went on to describe how, when he had come to, he could still hear the men shouting as they got the boats away. He had crawled back up the vertical ladder to the inspection hatch, but the cover had been closed and clamped down. What saved him was the fact that the main hatch had been cleared at one corner and after a long time he had managed to stack enough bales of cotton up to be able to reach this opening and crawl out on to the deck. He had found Number Three boat hanging from its bow falls, the other davits empty. The engines were still running, the pumps still working and the hoses were still pouring water into Number Three hold. But not a single member of the crew remained on board.

It was an incredible, almost unbelievable story. And he went on to tell how, alone and unaided, he had put the fire out. And then in

200

the morning he had found a complete stranger wandering about the ship.

'That would be Mr Sands, from the yacht *Sea Witch*?'

'Yes.'

'Would you explain why you didn't accept his offer to take you off?'

'I saw no reason to abandon ship. She was badly down by the bows, but she wasn't in imminent danger. I thought he would notify the authorities and that it would help the salvage tug if I were on board to organize the tow.'

He told them then how he had seen me fail to regain my yacht, how he had pulled me on to the deck, and then he was telling them of our efforts to save the ship in the teeth of the rising gale, how we had got the engines going and the pumps working and kept her stern to the wind. But he made no mention of the Minkies. According to him, we had finally abandoned the ship in a rubber dinghy taken from Dellimare's cabin when she was on the verge of sinking. No, he couldn't say exactly what the position was, but it was somewhere to the east of the Roches Douvres. No, we hadn't seen her go down. The rubber dinghy? Well, yes, it did seem to indicate that Dellimare had been nervous, had not trusted the boats or the seaworthiness of the ship.

'Two final questions,' Holland said. 'And they are very important questions for you and for everybody connected with the ship.' He paused and then said, 'On reflection, are you quite convinced that it was an explosion that caused the flooding in Number One hold? I put it to you that in the conditions prevailing it was almost impossible to be certain that it wasn't some submerged object that you hit or a wave breaking against the bows.'

Patch hesitated, glancing round the court. 'It definitely wasn't a sea breaking,' he said quietly. 'It was afterwards that the next sea broke over the bows. As to whether we hit something or an explosive charge was set off, only an inspection of the actual damage could prove it one way or the other.'

'Quite. But since the ship is probably lying in at least twenty fathoms of water and we don't know quite where, inspection of the damage is out of the question. I want your opinion.'

'I don't think I can say any more than I have. I can't be certain.'

'But you think it was an explosion?' Holland waited, but getting no reply, he added. 'Having regard to the fire in the radio shack and, later, the fire in the after fold,—taking them all together, you incline to the theory that it was an explosion?'

'If you put it that way—yes.'

'Thank you.' Holland sat down and even then nobody moved. There was no whispering, no shuffling of feet. The whole court was held in the spell of the evidence.

And then Sir Lionel Falcett rose. 'Mr Learned Chairman, I would be glad if you would put one or two additional questions to the witness.' He was a small man with thinning hair and a high forehead, a very ordinary-seeming man except for his voice, which had great depth of tone and was vibrant, so that one was conscious of the power of great energy and vitality behind it. It was his voice, not the man, that instantly dominated the court. 'Witness has made it clear that he is convinced, in his own mind, that some attempt was made to wreck the *Mary Deare*. And indeed, the incidents he has related to the Court, in the absence of any natural explanation, would appear to support this conclusion. I would, however, point out to the Court, that the value of the ship herself was not such as to justify so elaborate a plot and that we must, therefore, presume that, if such a plot existed, it was directed towards fraudulently obtaining the insurance value of the cargo. I would respectfully point out to you, Mr Learned Chairman, that there would only be financial gain in such a dastardly and murderous endeavour if, in fact, the cargo had been removed prior to the loss of the ship.'

Bowen-Lodge nodded. 'I quite understand your argument, Sir Lionel.' He glanced at the clock at the far end of the court, above the gallery. 'What is your question?'

'It concerns the time the ship was moored alongside the *Torre Annunziata* in the Rangoon River,' Sir Lionel said. 'My information is that the *Mary Deare*'s crew were given shore leave, and that during that period the *Torre Annunziata* was a blaze of lights with all her winches in operation.' He looked across at Holland. 'I understand that a deposition to this effect will be introduced later and that it states that the official concerned was informed by the Master of the *Torre Annunziata* that he had been shifting cargo to make room for some steel tubing he was due to load.' He turned back to face Bowen-Lodge. 'I should like to know, Mr Learned Chairman, whether the witness heard any of his officers speak of this after he had joined the ship—whether, in fact, it had been the subject of some comment?'

The question was put and Patch answered that he had heard of it from Rice. He hadn't at the time attached any significance to it.

'But you do now?' Sir Lionel suggested.

Patch nodded. 'Yes.'

'Just one more question, Mr Learned Chairman. Can the witness tell us whether Mr Dellimare at any time made any reference to the cargo?'

The question was put and, when Patch answered, no, Sir Lionel said, 'You had no indication from anyone that the cargo might be other than that stated on the manifest?'

'No.'

'I will put it to you another way—a ship is a very tight little company of men, and in any enclosed community like that a thing popularly known as the grapevine operates. Did you hear any rumours about the cargo after you joined the ship?'

'Some men seemed to think that we had a cargo of explosives on board,' Patch answered. 'It was a rumour that persisted despite the fact that I posted a copy of the manifest on the crew's notice board.'

'You thought it dangerous that they should think they were sitting on top of a lot of explosives?'

'I did.'

'Having regard to the sort of crew you had?'

'Yes.'

'Would you say that this rumour would be sufficient in itself to cause panic amongst the crew as soon as they knew a fire had broken out?'

'Probably.'

'In point of fact Rice reported that they were panicking.' Sir Lionel leaned forward, staring at Patch. 'How did this extraordinary rumour get around the ship?'

Patch glanced involuntarily towards the waiting witnesses. 'I don't think Mr Higgins was ever convinced that we were carrying the cargo declared on the manifest.'

'He thought it was a cargo of explosives, eh? What gave him that idea?'

'I don't know.'

'Did you ask him?'

'Yes, I did.'

'When?'

'Just after we rounded Ushant.'

'And what did he say?'

'He refused to answer.'

'What were his exact words when you put the question to him?'

'His exact words?'

'Yes.'

'He said I could bloody well try and get the answer out of Taggart or Dellimare and stop bothering him. They were both dead, of course.'

'Thank you.' Sir Lionel folded himself delicately into his seat. Bowen-Lodge looked at the clock again and adjourned the court. 'Two o'clock please, gentlemen.' He rose and the court rose with him, standing whilst he left by the door at the rear of the judge's chair, followed by his three assessors.

When I turned to leave I found that Mrs Petrie had been sitting right behind me. She gave me a little brief smile of recognition. Her face was puffy and pallid under her make-up and her eyes were red. Gundersen was there, too. He had been sitting beside her, but now he had moved along the row and was talking to Higgins. She went out on her own. 'Who's that woman?' Hal asked me.

'One of the Dellimare directors,' I replied,

and I told him about my visit to the company's offices. 'I rather think she may have been living with Dellimare,' I told him.

Outside, the sun shone on rain-wet pavements, and it came as something of a shock to discover that there were people— ordinary people who knew nothing of the *Mary Deare*—hurrying about their everyday affairs. Patch was standing alone on the pavement's edge. He had been waiting for me and he came straight across. 'I'd like a word with you, Sands.' His voice was hoarse with talking and his face looked drained.

Hal said he would go on to the hotel where we had decided to lunch and Patch watched him go, fidgeting with the coins in his pocket. As soon as Hal was out of ear-shot, he said, 'You told me your boat wouldn't be ready until the end of the month.' He said it accusingly, anger and resentment in his voice.

'Yes,' I said. 'It was ready a week earlier than I expected.'

'Why didn't you let me know? I went down to the yard last Wednesday and you'd already gone. Why didn't you tell me?' And then he suddenly burst out, 'All I needed was one day. Just one day out there.' He stared at me, literally grinding his teeth. 'Don't you realize— one look at that hole in the ship's hull and I'd have known. I'd have been able to tell the truth then. As it is—' his eyes were a little wild, like something brought to bay and not knowing which way to turn. 'As it is I don't know what the hell I'm saying, what God-damn pit I'm digging for myself. One day! That was all I wanted.'

'You didn't tell me that,' I said. 'In any case, you know very well that an inspection of that sort would have to be carried out by the authorities.' But I could understand how he had wanted to be certain, to prove that his suspicions were justified. 'It'll work out,' I said, patting his arm.

'I hope you're right,' he said between his teeth. 'I hope to God you're right.' He was looking at me and his eyes were bright like coals. 'All that effort ... to put her on the Minkies ... wasted. My God! I could—' And there he stopped and his eyes, looking past me, widened, and I turned to find Janet Taggart coming straight towards us.

I once saw a painting entitled 'Vengeance'. I can't remember the artist's name and it doesn't matter now, because I know it wasn't any good. Vengeance should be painted the way Janet Taggart looked. She was pale as death, and in the pallor of her frozen face her eyes were enormous. She stopped just in front of him and struck out at him blindly.

I don't remember her words now—they came in a great overwhelming torrent of cutting, lacerating sentences. I saw Patch's eyes go dead as he flinched before the whip-lash of her tongue, and then I left them, walking quickly, wanting to get the picture of the two of them right out of my mind. I wondered if she knew what power she had to hurt the man.

We had a quick lunch and returned to the court, and on the stroke of two Bowen-Lodge took his place on the judge's seat. There were five men at the Press desk now. They were gathering like vultures at the smell of news. 'With your permission, Mr Learned Chairman,' Holland said, rising. 'I propose to proceed with the other evidence in order that the Court shall have a complete picture.'

Bowen-Lodge nodded. 'I think that a very proper course, Mr Holland. Your first witness must, however, remain in the court. Those representing the various interested parties will, I know, wish to put further questions to him.'

I had expected Higgins to be the next witness. Instead, Holland called for 'Harold Lowden' and I suddenly realized that I still hadn't made up my mind what I was going to say. Hal stood in the witness box, very erect, very much the soldier, and in short, clipped sentences told of our encounter with the *Mary Deare* and how we had found her abandoned the following morning. And when he stepped down it was my turn and I found myself automatically crossing the court and taking my stand in the witness box. I was in a cold sweat.

I repeated the oath and then Holland was facing me, smooth and urbane, asking me in that soft, bored voice of his whether I was John

Henry Sands, my business and background and why I was sailing the yacht *Sea Witch* in that area of the Channel on the night of March 18th. And as I gave the answers, I could hear the nervousness in my voice. The court was very silent. Bowen-Lodge's small gimlet eyes watched me and Holland stood there in front of me, waiting to prompt me with questions, to probe if necessary.

Across the court I saw Patch, sitting a little forward, his hands clasped, his body tense and rigid. His eyes were fixed on my face. I was telling them what the *Mary Deare* had looked like that morning when I boarded her, and suddenly my mind was made up. To tell them that the ship was stranded on the Minkies would prove him a liar. It would cut the ground from under his feet. I couldn't do it. I think I had known that all along, but the strange thing was that, once I had made the decision, all nervousness left me. I knew what I was going to say and I set out to present Patch to the Court as I had seen him through those desperate hours—a man, staggering with exhaustion, who had put out a fire single-handed and could still go on fighting to save his ship.

I told them about the bruise on his jaw, about the coal dust and the smoke-blackened haggardness of his face. I told them how we'd sweated down there in the stoke-hold to raise steam on that one boiler, how we'd got the pumps going, how we'd used the engines to keep her stern to the wind and how the seas had swept across her submerged bows in thundering cataracts of white water. And I left it at that, simply saying that we had finally abandoned her on the morning of the second day.

The questions started then. Had Patch made any comments to me about the crew having abandoned ship? Could I give the Court any idea of the *Mary Deare*'s position at the time we had taken to the dinghy? Did I think that, if there had been no gale, the ship could have safely got to some port?

Sir Lionel Falcett rose to his feet and put the same questions that Snetterton had asked me—about the cargo, the holds, Patch. 'You lived with this man through a desperate forty-eight hours. You shared his fears and his hopes. Surely he must have said something, made some comment?' And I replied that we had had little opportunity for talking. I told them again of our exhaustion, the fury of the seas, the moment-to-moment fear that the ship would go down under us.

And then suddenly it was over and I walked back across the floor of the court, feeling like a rag that has been squeezed dry. Hal gripped my arm as I sat down. 'Magnificent!' he whispered. 'You've damn' near made a hero of the man. Look at the Press desk.' And I saw that it was emptying hurriedly.

'Ian Fraser!' Holland was on his feet again and Captain Fraser was making his way across the court. It was routine evidence of how he had picked us up, and then he was released and Janet Taggart was called.

She went into the witness box pale as death, but with her head up and her face a tight little defensive mask. Holland explained that he had called her at this stage in order to release her from the painful ordeal of listening to any further statements that might be made by witnesses about her father. He then took her gently through a description of her father as she had known him—his letters, coming unfailingly from every port he visited, his presents, the money to take her on from college to university, his care of her after the death of her mother when she was seven. 'I never knew how wonderful he had been as a father until these last few years, when I was old enough to understand how he must have scraped and saved and worked to give me the education I've had.' She described him as she had last seen him, and then she read the letter he had written her from Rangoon. She read it in a small, trembling voice, and his love and concern for her were there in every line of it.

It was very painful to hear her, knowing the man was dead, and when she had finished there was a murmur of men clearing their throats and shifting uneasily in their seats.

'That will be all, Miss Taggart,' Holland said

with that gentleness that he had used with her throughout her evidence. But she didn't move from the witness box. She had taken a picture postcard from her bag and she stood with it clutched in her hand, looking across at Patch. And the look on her face sent a cold shiver through me, as she said, 'A few days ago I received a postcard from Aden. It had been delayed in the post.' She shifted her gaze to Bowen-Lodge. 'It's from my father. May I read part of it please?'

He nodded his permission and he went on: 'My father wrote: "The owner has engaged a man called Patch to be my first officer in place of poor old Adams." She wasn't reading it. She was staring straight at Bowen-Lodge, the postcard still gripped in her hand. She knew it by heart. '"I do not know what will come of this. Rumour has it that he stranded a ship once, deliberately. But whatever happens I promise you it shall not be of my doing. God go with you, Janie, and think of me. If all goes well, I shall keep my promise this time and see you again at the end of the voyage."' Her voice broke on a whisper. The court held its breath. She was like a spring coiled too tight and near to breaking.

She held the card out to Holland and he took it. 'Witness is excused,' Bowen-Lodge said. But she had turned and was facing Patch across the court. Wildly she accused him of dragging her father's name in the mud to save

213

himself. She had checked on the loss of the *Belle Isle*. She knew the truth now and she was going to see that the Court knew it. Bowen-Lodge beat on his desk with his gavel. Holland was at her side, remonstrating with her. But she ignored him, and Patch sat there, white-faced and appalled, as she blamed him for the fires, for the flooded holds, for the whole wreckage of her father's ship. 'You're a monster,' she sobbed as they dragged her from the witness box. And then she went suddenly limp and allowed herself to be hurried out of the court, her whole body convulsed with the passion of her tears.

The courtroom eased itself a little self-consciously. Nobody looked at Patch. Nobody looked anywhere until Bowen-Lodge's matter-of-fact voice lifted the tension from the room. 'Call the next witness.'

'Donald Masters!' Holland was in his place again. The court began to get back into his stride. Technical witnesses followed, giving details of the ship and its equipment, passing judgment on its age and condition, with depositions sworn by the surveyor in Yokohama and the Lloyd's official who had issued her load-line certificate. Another by the Docks Superintendent at Rangoon giving information about the *Torre Annunziata* and the adjustments to her cargo. And then Holland called 'Angela Petrie' and the court, predominantly male, stirred with interest as

Mrs Petrie went into the witness box.

She explained that the Dellimare Trading and Shipping Company had been formed as a private limited company in 1947 with Mr Dellimare, a Mr Greenly and herself as directors. It had been entirely a trading concern, specializing in the import-export business, chiefly with India and the Far East. Later Mr Greenly had ceased to be a director and Mr Gundersen, who had operated a similar type of business in Singapore, had joined the board, the capital had been increased and the business considerably expanded. She gave figures, producing them from memory with quiet efficiency.

'And the position of the Company now?' Holland asked.

'It's in process of being wound-up—a voluntary liquidation.'

'And that was arranged before Mr Dellimare's death?'

'Oh yes, it was decided some months back.'

'Any particular reason?'

She hesitated, and then said, 'There were certain tax advantages.'

A little murmur of laughter ran round the court and Holland sat down. Almost immediately Patch's lawyer was on his feet, a thin, dried-up man with a reedy voice. 'Mr Learned Chairman, I should like to ask the witness whether she is aware that Mr Dellimare was involved, just before the formation of this Company, in a case of fraudulent conversion?'

Bowen-Lodge frowned. 'I do not regard that as relevant, Mr Fenton,' he said acidly.

'I should like to answer that question.' Mrs Petrie's voice was bold and clear and vibrant. 'He was acquitted. It was a malicious accusation with no shred of evidence to support it.'

Fenton sat down a little hurriedly and Sir Lionel Falcett rose. 'Mr Learned Chairman, I should like to know from the witness whether any ships were purchased by the Company at the time of its formation?'

Bowen-Lodge put the question and Mrs Petrie answered none.

'You hadn't the capital, is that it?' Sir Lionel asked. And when she agreed, he said, 'In point of fact, it was quite a small business?'

'Yes.'

'Then why call it the Dellimare Trading and Shipping Company? Surely it was a rather unnecessarily grandiose title?'

'Oh, well, you see, Mr Dellimare was always very keen about ships, and being ex-Navy and all that, he hoped one day ... Anyway,' she added, with a flash of pride, 'we did finish up by owning ships.'

'You had the *Mary Deare* and the *Torre Annunziata*. Any others?'

She shook her head. 'No. Just those two.'

Sir Lionel glanced down at his papers. 'The

purchase of the *Mary Deare* was completed on June 18 of last year. When was the *Torre Annunziata* purchased?'

For the first time Mrs Petrie showed a slight hesitation. 'I can't remember exactly.'

'Was it in April of last year?'

'I don't remember.'

'But you are a director of the Company and this must have involved a considerable amount of finance. Do you mean to say you have no records of the transactions?' Sir Lionel's voice had sharpened slightly.

'I may have. I don't know.' And then she added quickly, 'We were expanding fast at that time and it was all fixed up at the Singapore end.'

'And you were not kept fully informed, is that it?' She nodded and he then asked, 'At what date did Mr Gundersen join the board?'

'On March 2 of last year.'

'So that these shipping transactions were a result of his joining the board?'

'Yes, I suppose so.'

Sir Lionel turned to the Chairman. 'There is just one more question I should like to put to the witness. As the Court is already aware, the *Mary Deare* was making just this one voyage and was then being sold for scrap. The *Torre Annunziata* made only two voyages and then she was sold to the Chinese. I should like to know what the margin of profit was on these transactions.'

Bowen-Lodge put the question, but she shook her head. She didn't know.

'What was the cost of acquiring these ships, then?' Sir Lionel put the question to her direct.

'No figures have yet been passed across to our office.'

'And I suppose you have no idea who put up the money?'

She shook her head. 'I'm afraid I don't know. It was all arranged at the Singapore end.'

Sir Lionel nodded and sat down. Mrs Petrie was released from the witness box and she walked back across the court. I saw that her eyes were fixed on someone just behind me, and I guessed it must be Gundersen. Her face was very white and she looked scared.

Hal leaned across to me. 'Looks as though Lionel is mounting an attack on the Company,' he whispered, and I nodded, thinking that perhaps Patch was saving his announcement of Dellimare's offer until he was questioned by Sir Lionel. It seemed reasonable. And that question by his lawyer, Fenton—it had been clumsily done, but he had made his point.

Perfume wafted over me as Mrs Petrie resumed her seat, and I heard Gundersen's voice, cold and angry, say, 'Why didn't you tell him? I gave you those figures weeks back.' And she answered him in a whisper: 'How can I think of figures now?'

And then Holland called, 'Hans

Gundersen.'

He described himself as a financier and company director and he made a strong impression on the court. He was a business man and he had all his facts and figures at his finger-tips. Without any prompting from Holland he explained to the Court exactly why he had joined the Company, why they had acquired the *Mary Deare* and the *Torre Annunziata*, how the purchases had been financed and what the expected profits were.

He explained his interest in the Dellimare Company in the cold, hard language of business. He had many interests in Singapore and other ports in the Far East. It suited his interests at that time to take a hand in the affairs of this small company. He had the chance to acquire two old ships at a very low figure. He had taken the view that freight rates were on the mend and that in a year's time it would be possible to sell the ships at a handsome profit. He had chosen the Dellimare Company as the medium through which to make the purchase because he knew Mr Dellimare and discovered that he was willing to have the Company wound up at the end of the transaction. 'In my experience,' he added, 'that is much the most remunerative way of engaging in these operations.' In the case of the *Torre Annunziata* his object had been achieved. They had sold the ship to the Chinese at a figure much higher than the purchase price. The *Mary Deare*, however, had not proved such a good proposition. Her condition had been worse than he had been led to believe. The result was that he had decided that she should make one voyage and then be sold for scrap in England. Break-up price less purchase price and overhaul would have given the Dellimare Company a small margin of profit plus the profits of the voyage. He handed Holland a slip of paper. 'Those are the figures, actual and estimated,' he said.

Holland passed them up to Bowen-Lodge and then sat down. The Chairman checked through the figures, nodded and glanced towards Sir Lionel, who rose and said, 'I should like to know from the witness who financed the acquisition of these ships and how exactly he stood to gain from the deal.'

Bowen-Lodge put the question and Gundersen replied, 'Of course. I financed the operation myself. In return I was allotted all the shares of the increased capital of the Company.'

'In other words,' Sir Lionel said, 'your motive for becoming a director of this company was profit?'

'Naturally. I am a business man, sir.'

'I appreciate that.' Sir Lionel smiled drily. 'Now, about the *Mary Deare*. You have admitted that she was not in the condition you had hoped. How was it that such a valuable cargo was entrusted to her? Did Mr Dellimare arrange that?'

'No. I arranged it through my contacts in Singapore. You must understand that I am very well known in business circles there.'

'One further question. For what reason were these two ships—the *Mary Deare* and the *Torre Annunziata*—routed in such a way that they were in the Rangoon River together from January 7th to 11th?'

'I don't understand the reason for your question, sir,' Gundersen replied. 'Mr Dellimare looked after all the details of the Company management. If a ship is sailing from England to China and another from Japan to Antwerp, then they will cross somewhere.'

Sir Lionel asked him a number of further questions, but Gundersen refused to admit any responsibility for the details of ships' schedules. 'You must understand that I have many calls on my time. This was a very small business. I do not concern myself with the day-to-day management of affairs of companies I am interested in.'

'But you flew all the way from Singapore as soon as you heard what had happened to the *Mary Deare* and have remained in this country ever since.'

'Of course. I am a director of the Company and this is a serious business. When something goes wrong, then it is necessary to be on the spot. Particularly as Mr Dellimare is dead.'

'One final question; why was it necessary for

221

Mr Dellimare to travel on the *Mary Deare* as supercargo? Surely in these days it is very unusual?'

Gundersen shrugged his shoulders. 'Mr Dellimare was in Yokohama to arrange all the details. I don't think he was a rich man, and it is cheaper to travel a long distance like that in your own ship.'

There were no further questions and Gundersen stood down. He was dressed now in a dark-grey double-breasted suit, obviously cut by a London tailor, and he looked a typical English business man—quiet, remote, competent.

More technical evidence followed, and then Bowen-Lodge adjourned the court. 'Tomorrow at ten-thirty, gentlemen.'

As I followed Hal into the corridor, a hand plucked at my sleeve. 'You're Mr Sands, aren't you?' A little, grey-haired woman was smiling up at me a little uncertainly.

'Yes,' I said. There was something about her face that I seemed to recognize.

'I thought you were, but I'm never quite certain about people—my eyes, you know. I just wanted to tell you how glad I am he has one good friend in all this terrible business. You were splendid, Mr Sands.'

I saw the likeness then. 'You're his mother, aren't you?' I was looking round for Patch, but she said, 'Please. He doesn't know I'm here. He'd be terribly angry. When he came down to

222

see me at Bridgewater, he didn't tell me anything about it. But I knew at once that he was in trouble.' She gave a little sigh. 'It was the first time I had seen him in seven years. That's a long time, Mr Sands, for an old body like me. I only had the one, you see—just Gideon. And now that his father's dead . . .' She smiled and patted my arm. 'But there, you don't want to hear about my troubles. I just wanted you to know that I'm glad he's got one good friend.' She looked up at me. 'It will be all right this time . . . you do think so, don't you, Mr Sands?'

'I'm sure it will,' I murmured. 'Sir Lionel Falcett is obviously concentrating on the cargo and the Company.'

'Yes. Yes, that's what I thought.'

I offered to see her to her hotel, but she wouldn't hear of it and left me with a brave little smile, moving along with the crowd. Hal joined me then and we went out to his car. I caught a glimpse of her standing, waiting for a bus. She was off-guard then, and she looked lonely and a little frightened.

Hal offered to put me up for the night and we collected my suitcase from the station and drove down to his house at Bosham, a small thatched place with a lawn running down to the water. I had bought an evening paper in Southampton; it was all over the front page and three columns of it inside—*Captain's Daughter Breaks Down at Enquiry; Strange Story of Loss of Mary Deare.*

It wasn't until after dinner that Hal began to ask me specific questions about Patch. At length he said, 'That day you rejoined us at Peter Port—you didn't say very much about him.' He was standing by the window, looking out across the lawn to where the water was a milky blur in the dusk. There were a couple of yachts moored out there and their masts were bobbing to the lop and the wind gusts. He turned and looked at me. 'You knew about the *Belle Isle* business then, didn't you?'

I nodded, wondering what was coming. It was very cosy in that room with its lamps and its glimmer of Eastern Brass and the big tiger skins on the floor, very remote from all that I had lived with during the past two months. Even the glass of port in my hand seemed part of the illusion of being in another world.

He came and sat down opposite me. 'Look, old chap,' he said. 'I don't want to pry into what, after all, is your concern. But just how sure are you about this fellow?'

'How do you mean?'

'Well, you've got to be damn' sure about a man ... I mean ...' He hesitated, searching for the words he wanted. 'Well, put it this way. If Patch wrecked that ship—deliberately wrecked her—then it was murder. They may only be able to pin a charge of manslaughter on him in law, but before God he'd be guilty of murder.'

224

'He didn't do it,' I said.

'Absolutely.' And having said that, I sat back, wondering why I'd said it, why I was so certain.

'I'm glad,' Hal said. 'Because, you know, all the time you were in the witness box, I was conscious that you were defending him. You were selecting your evidence, keeping things back, and at times you were a little scared. Oh, you needn't worry. I don't think anybody else noticed it. I noticed it because I know you and because at Peter Port, when you'd had less time to think it all out, you were so obviously covering up.' He paused and sipped his port. 'Go carefully, though,' he added. 'I know Lionel Falcett. Member of my club. Seen him in action, too. Don't let him get his claws into you.'

## CHAPTER THREE

It was still blowing and the streets were wet as we drove to the court the following morning. Proceedings started sharp at ten-thirty with evidence about the cargo. And then a doctor was called who showed that it was quite possible for a man who lived on nothing but liquor to die for lack of it. Through all this the courtroom was restless as though waiting for something. The public gallery was packed, the

225

Press desk crammed. And then at last Holland called 'Alfred Higgins' and, as Higgins thrust his huge bulk into the witness box, there was a sudden, expectant hush, so that the sound of a clock striking eleven was quite audible through the taking of the oath.

He was forty-three years old, Higgins told the Treasury Counsel, and, when asked for his qualifications, he explained that he'd started life on his father's barge, sailing the East Coast ports until he was fifteen; then he'd got mixed up in some smuggling racket and had stowed away on a banana boat. He'd stayed at sea after that, moving from ship to ship across the traffic lanes of the world—square-riggers, tramps and liners, tugs and coasters; he rolled the names of them out of his great barrel of a body like pages picked at random from Lloyd's Register.

He began his story back where the *Mary Deare* steamed out of Yokohama. According to him, the ship was a floating death-trap of rattling rivets and clanging plates, a piece of leaking ironmongery taken off the junk-heap of the China Seas. Of the captain, he simply said, 'The 'ole ship knew 'e was drinking 'isself ter death.' The first mate was sickening for jaundice and the third officer, Rice, was only a kid of twenty-four on his second voyage with a watch-keeper's certificate. The implication was that he, Higgins, was the only reliable deck officer on board, and though he looked like a

226

bull about to charge, there was something impressive about him as he stood there and gave his evidence in a throaty rumble.

Singapore, Rangoon, Aden—and then he was covering the same ground that Patch had covered, but from a different angle. He thought the crew 'not bad considerin' the moth-eaten sort o' tub she was.' Patch he regarded as 'a bit pernickity-like' and added, 'But that's ter be expected when a man wiv 'is record gets command again.'

And then up through the Bay of Biscay the Court got little glimpses of Patch, nervous, over-bearing, at odds with the owner, with his officers—'All 'cept Rice. 'E was the white-headed boy, as the sayin' is.' And when it came to the gale itself and the ship down by the bows and the radio shack gutted by fire, Higgins didn't give it graphically as Patch had done, but baldly, factually. He had been asleep in his bunk when the hold had started to flood. He had taken over the bridge and had remained on watch until 10.00 hours the following morning—eleven solid hours. He had then organized a more thorough search for Dellimare. No, Mr Patch hadn't ordered him to. He'd done it on his own initiative, having been relieved. He couldn't believe that Dellimare 'who was Navy an' a good bloke on a ship' could have gone overboard. Altogether he had been forty-two hours without sleep.

'You liked Mr Dellimare?' Holland asked

227

him.

'I didn't like or dislike 'im. I jus' said 'e was a good bloke, an' so 'e was.'

'Did you advise Mr Patch at one stage to abandon ship?'

'Well, yes, in a manner o' speakin'. We considered it, Mr Dellimare an' me.'

'Why?'

''Cos we knew the sort o' ship she was. We'd bin through two gales already comin' across from Singapore. Patch 'adn't. An' the one in the Bay was a lot worse than wot we'd gone through before.'

'And you thought an explosion had occurred in the for'ard hold?'

'I didn't think nothin' of the kind. I knew she was rotten an' we were takin' a helluva pounding. We didn't think she'd stand much more.' And then he said, 'If you're suggesting we were scared, just remember what it was like out there. Ten to one the boats wouldn't 've got launched in that sea, let alone stayed afloat. It took guts to even think 'o takin' ter the boats, pertikly fer Mr Dellimare who'd had a basinful o' that sort o' thing during the war. Later, when we 'ove-to, things was easier an' I thought maybe we had a chance.'

And then he was dealing with the night the fire had broken out in the after hold and they had abandoned ship. Yes, it had been about 21.20 hours. It was a stoker who had discovered it, a man called West. He'd come out of the after deckhouse and had seen smoke coming from the hatch of Number Three hold. He'd reported at once to the bridge by phone. Rice had been there at the time and Higgins had sent him to check the report and notify Mr Patch. Not once in his evidence did he refer to Patch as the captain.

'And what happened then?' Holland asked him.

'I didn't hear nothin' further for about quarter of an hour. But I knew it was fire orl right 'cos the after derrick lights was switched on an' there was a lot of activity with men running about the deck. Then Mr Patch comes up to the bridge lookin' very wild and all covered in smoke grime an' says he's ordered the boats swung out just in case. I asked him whether he'd like me ter take charge of the fire-fighting party and he said No, Mr Rice was in charge. He stood aba't fer a bit after that as though he couldn't make up his mind aba't somethin'. An' after a bit Rice comes runnin' up to the bridge in a bit of a panic an' says the fire's getting worse. And at that Patch orders him to pass the word to stand by to abandon ship. 'You notify the engine-room, Mr Higgins,' he says. 'Then take charge of the fire-fighting party. Mr Rice, you'll have charge of the upper deck. See there's no panic when I give the word.' An' that's the last I saw of him,' Higgins added.

The rest was a pattern of disaster that comes

229

from absence of command. Higgins and his men had fought the fire for a further fifteen minutes or so, and all the time it seemed to be gaining on them. The men were scared. They believed the ship was jinxed, that the cargo was explosives. Higgins sent Rice to tell Patch he couldn't hold the men much longer and Rice came back to say he couldn't find Patch anywhere. 'By then the men were near ter panic. Some were already on the upper deck, piling into Number Three boat. There weren't nothing I could do 'cept give the order to abandon ship.'

The order had resulted in a stampede for the boats. When he reached the upper deck, Higgins saw Number Three boat hanging by its bow falls with one man clinging to it. Number One boat had also been cleared. She was empty and being battered to pieces against the ship's side. By using his fists he'd got some sort of order out of the chaos on deck and he and the officers had organized the men into the two remaining boats. He had put Rice in charge of Number Four boat and had waited to see him safely clear. He had then lowered and released his own boat. Owing to the speed at which the ship was travelling he had lost contact with Rice by the time his boat hit the water and he never regained it.

'Do you mean to say,' Holland asked, 'that you took to the boats with the ship still steaming?'

230

'Yes. Acting on Mr Patch's instructions I had ordered the engine-room staff to stand by to take to the boats. When I gave the order to abandon, they didn't 'ave no instructions about stopping the engines an' afterwards none o' 'em would go below to do it.'

'But surely if you gave the order—'

'What the hell use were orders?' Higgins growled. 'Patch'd gone—vanished. One boat was already hanging in her davits, the men in her all tipped into the sea; another was bein' smashed up alongside. The men were panicking. Anybody who went below stood a good chance of coming up and finding the last two boats gone. It was as much as Rice an' I could do ter get those boats away orderly-like.'

'But good heavens!' Holland exclaimed. 'Surely, as an experienced officer, you had some control over your—'

But Higgins interrupted him again. 'Ain't you got no imagination?' he burst out. 'Can't you see what it was like—Patch gone and the crew in a panic and a fire raging on top of a cargo of explosives.'

'But it wasn't explosives.'

'Ow were we ter know?'

'You've heard the evidence proving that the cases loaded at Yokohama contained aero engines. There was no justification for believing—'

'We know now they was full of aero engines,' Higgins said quickly. 'But I'm telling you wot we thought at the time. We thought they was full of explosives.'

'But you'd seen the manifest,' Holland reminded him. 'Mr Patch even posted a copy of it on the crew's notice board.'

'What difference does that make?' Higgins demanded angrily. 'A crew don't 'ave ter believe everything that's posted on their notice board. An' let me tell you, mister, men that sail in ships like the *Mary Deare* don't go much by the manifest, pertickly in the China Seas. We may be uneddicated, but we ain't stupid. A manifest is just a piece of paper somebody's written what he wants believed on. Least, that's the way I look at it—an' I've me reasons for doin' so.'

There was no answer to that. The outburst called for a rebuke from the Chairman, but it was given mildly. Higgins was accepted for what he was, a piece of human flotsam speaking with the voice of experience. In a sense he was magnificent. He dominated that drab court. But not by the power of his personality, which was crude. He dominated it because he was different, because he was the obverse of the coin of human nature, a colourful, lawless buccaneer who didn't give a damn for authority.

'In other words,' Holland said, 'you've known a lot of strange things happen aboard ships around the world. Now, have you ever known a stranger set of circumstances than those that happened aboard the *Mary Deare*?'

Higgins pursed his lips, then shook his head. 'No, I can't say I 'ave.'

'Take the flooding of the for'ard holds. You say you didn't think it was an explosion of some sort.'

'I didn't say nuthing of the kind. I said I didn't think about it, not at the time. There was a lot of other things ter think aba't. Anyway, I wasn't on the bridge.'

'And what's your opinion now?'

Higgins shook his head. 'I don't know wot ter think.'

'And what about the fires? Were they natural outbreaks?'

'Ah, the fires—that's different.' His cunning little eyes darted a glance to where Patch sat, watching him with a tense face.

'You think they were started deliberately?'

'Yes, I reckon so.'

'You suspect somebody then?'

'I don't know about that. But,' he added, 'I knew we was in fer trouble as soon as 'e come aboard.' And he nodded his hard bollard of head towards Patch. 'Stands ter reason, a man wiv 'is record don't get the job fer nuthing—and then the skipper dying so convenient-like.'

'Are you blaming somebody for Captain Taggart's death?' There was a note of censure in Holland's voice.

'I ain't blamin' anyone. But somebody swiped the poor devil's liquor and all I say is it

233

only did one man any good.'

An excited buzz ran round the court as Holland sat down. Fenton was immediately on his feet. It was a disgraceful allegation, made without a shred of evidence to support it. And the Chairman agreed, leaning forward and asking Higgins whether it wasn't true that Taggart had accused several of the officers. And when Higgins admitted that it was, he said, 'Yourself as well?'

'The poor devil was ravin',' Higgins declared angrily.

'So he's raving when he accuses you, but not when he accuses Mr Patch, is that it?' Bowen-Lodge's voice was icy.

'Well, it didn't do me no good, him dying,' Higgins muttered.

'I put it to you that Captain Taggart just ran out of liquor.'

But Higgins shook his head. 'There was a lot of stuff brought off to 'im by a ship's chandler in Aden. 'E couldn't 've drunk it all in the time. It weren't 'umingly possible.'

'What did you think about it at the time? Did you take his accusations seriously?'

'No, why should I? When a man's ravin' the way he was, you don't know wot ter believe.' Higgins had a baffled look as though he wasn't sure where the questions were leading. 'Mebbe 'e 'ad liquor, an' mebbe 'e didn't,' he muttered hoarsely. 'Mebbe somebody pinched it—I dunno. All I know is, we searched the 'ole

234

bloomin' ship for 'im, jus' ter make 'im 'appy, 'an we didn't find a single bottle wot belonged to 'im. 'Course,' he added, 'if we'd known as 'ow 'e was goin' ter die fer lack of the stuff, there's some of us, as was plannin' ter smuggle the odd bottle through the Customs, who'd've chipped in ter 'elp 'im, as the sayin' is.'

Bowen-Lodge nodded and Fenton started to question Higgins, trying to get him to admit that Patch had never given the order to stand-by to abandon ship, trying to confuse him and break him down over little details. But Higgins was a dangerous witness to cross-examine. He made it clear with every answer that he didn't trust Patch, and he didn't budge an inch from his original testimony.

But with Sir Lionel it was different. His interest was the cargo. What had led the witness to believe that the cases loaded at Yokohama contained explosives? Had he discovered something whilst he was loading the cases? But when the Chairman put the question, Higgins said he hadn't been a member of the ship's company at the time the cases were loaded.

'When did your employment as second officer commence then?' Bowen-Lodge asked.

'The day before the ship sailed,' Higgins answered. 'By then she was all loaded up, hatches battened down an' lying out in the fairway.'

'You were shown the manifest?'

235

'No. I never saw the manifest, not till later.'

'Then what gave you the idea that the cargo contained explosives?'

'There was rumours around the docks.'

'And amongst the crew?'

'Yes.'

'Have you ever known explosives packed in cases clearly marked as aero engines?'

'Not exactly. But I've heard of explosives bein' packed and marked as other things, to avoid the regulations as you might say.'

'But you had no definite indication that the cases might contain other than what was stated on the manifest?'

'No.'

'And you did your utmost to scotch this rumour?'

For the first time Higgins showed uncertainty. 'Well no, to be honest I can't say I did.'

'Why not?'

The muscles along Higgins's neck thickened. 'Well, if it comes ter that, why should I? Wasn't none of my business.'

Bowen-Lodge glanced across at Sir Lionel with one eye-brow raised. The next question concerned the four days the ship was moored in the Rangoon River. Yes, Higgins admitted, he had gone ashore with the rest. Well, why not? It wasn't every day the owners gave a ship's company forty-eight hours ashore, expenses paid. The reason? Mr Dellimare was

236

a good bloke, that's why—knew how to treat a crew, believed in a happy ship.

'When you got back to the ship—' Sir Lionel was now putting his questions direct to the witness again—'did you talk to any of the officers or men of the *Torre Annunziata*?'

'Yes. The first officer, a bloke called Slade, came aboard for a drink wiv me and the Chief.'

'Did you ask them why they had been shifting cargo around?'

'No. But Slade tol' me they'd 'ad ter do it because of some clerical mess-up over the destination of the steel tubes they were due to load.'

'Did you talk to Adams about it?'

'No.'

'But you saw him when you got back on board?'

'Yes.'

'Did he suggest that the crew of the *Torre Annunziata* had been tampering with the *Mary Deare*'s cargo?'

'No.' And then he added quickly, 'An' if they 'ad, 'e'd've known about it 'cos when I saw 'im, 'e was up an' about an' feelin' better fer 'is two days in bed.'

'Adams being sick, I take it you were in charge of the loading of the cotton cargo?' Higgins nodded and Sir Lionel then asked him, 'Did you notice any change in the disposition of the cargo?'

'No, can't say I did.'

237

'You're quite certain?'

''Course I'm certain.'

Sir Lionel's small head shot forward and his voice was suddenly crisp and hard as he said, 'How could you be? You said you joined the ship after she was loaded?'

But Higgins wasn't easily put out. His tongue passed over the dry line of his lips. But that was the only sign of uneasiness he gave. 'I may not've bin there when she was loaded. But I was when we discharged our top cargo of Japanese cotton an' rayon goods. I took special note of 'ow the cases was stowed 'cos I guessed I'd 'ave to load the bales of raw cotton when they was ready.'

Sir Lionel nodded. 'Just one more question. You say you didn't go aboard the *Mary Deare* until the day before she sailed. How was that?'

'Well, I wasn't took on till then.'

'Who engaged you—Captain Taggart?'

'No, Mr Dellimare. Oh, Captain Taggart signed the papers. But it was Dellimare wot engaged me.'

'Why?'

Higgins frowned. ''Ow d'you mean?'

'I asked you why he engaged you. Were you the only man who applied for the vacancy?'

'Well, not exactly. I mean...' Higgins glanced round the court and again his tongue passed along his lips. 'It didn't 'appen like that.'

'You mean the job wasn't offered in the

usual way? You were engaged by Mr Dellimare privately?'

'I suppose so.' Higgins sounded reluctant.

'Perhaps you would be good enough to explain to the Court how it happened.'

Higgins hesitated. 'Well, we 'appened ter meet, as you might say, an' 'e was short of a second officer an' I wanted a berth, an' that's all there was to it.'

'Where did you meet?'

'Some bar da'n by the waterfront. Don't remember the name of it.'

'By arrangement?'

Higgins's face was reddening, the muscles on his neck swelling. 'Yes, by arrangement.' He said it angrily as though challenging Sir Lionel to make something of it.

But Sir Lionel only said, 'Thank you. That was what I wanted to know.' And sat down. He had established two things: that if the Dellimare Company were planning to wreck the *Mary Deare*, the vital shift of cargo was a possibility, and that Higgins could have been the instrument of their choice. But he had nothing definite against Higgins and that, he admitted to Hal long afterwards, was the real trouble. To justify his clients in witholding payment of the insurance claim he had to have something more positive.

It was the evidence of the other survivors that finally decided him, and the most damaging evidence was that of the helmsman,

239

Yules, who had been on the bridge with Higgins when the fire broke out. He was timid and he gave his evidence with a slight stutter. He wasn't a very strong witness, but he clung to his statement that Patch had given the order to stand by to abandon ship with unshakeable obstinacy. He even had the words off pat, and though Patch's counsel rose to the occasion and had him so terrified that he kept on looking to Higgins for support, he never budged.

He was the last witness before lunch and I didn't need Hal to tell me that Patch would have a bad time of it when he took the stand for examination by the various counsel. The Court hadn't begun to get at the truth yet. But what was the truth? Hal asked me that over lunch and all I could say was, 'God knows'.

'Dellimare couldn't have started that fire in the hold,' he said, and I agreed. Dellimare was dead by then. It had to be Higgins. Evidently Bowen-Lodge had also considered this possibility over his lunch, for, when the Court reassembled, he had Yules recalled and questioned him closely about the movements of the officer of the watch. And Yules swore that Higgins had been on the bridge from 20.00 hours and hadn't once left it. Later, Burrows, the chief engineer officer, testified that Higgins had been playing poker with him and two members of the crew who had been drowned, from 17.00 hours to 20.00 hours with

240

only a brief break for food.

One after the other the survivors went into the witness box, each from his different angle corroborating what had gone before—the certainty that the ship was jinxed, that she carried explosives and that she was destined to go to the bottom. It was the story of men carrying within themselves the seeds of inevitable tragedy.

And then at last Holland called 'Gideon Patch' and he was standing there in the witness box again, slightly stooped, his hands gripping the rail, knuckles as white as the pallor of his face. He looked worried sick and the twitch was there at the corner of his mouth.

Bowen-Lodge questioned him first—questioned him in minute detail about the orders he had given after the fire broke out. He had him go through the whole thing again from the moment Rice had rushed into his cabin to report the outbreak. Then, when Patch had told it exactly as he'd told it before, Bowen-Lodge gave a little shrug and Holland took up the questioning again. And all the time it was obvious that something was being kept back. You could sense it in the way the man stood there with that hunted look on his face and his body all tense and trembling. And the questions went back and forth with nobody making any sense out of it and Patch sticking to his statement that he had been knocked out and that the fire had been started deliberately.

'Yes, but by whom?' Bowen-Lodge demanded.

And Patch had answered in a flat, colourless voice, 'That is for the Court to decide.'

After that the ball had been tossed to the counsel representing the interested parties and they hounded him with questions about Taggart and Dellimare, about his handling of the crew, about the seaworthiness of the ship, and then finally the counsel for the Marine Officers' Association was on his feet, going back once again over the orders he'd given the night the ship was abandoned, and Bowen-Lodge was beginning to glance at the clock.

At last Sir Lionel rose, and his questions were all about the cargo. If Patch could have said that those cases were empty or contained something other than aero-engines, that would have been that and Sir Lionel would have been satisfied. But he couldn't say it and the questions went on and on until Sir Lionel had exhausted all the possibilities. He paused then and seemed on the point of sitting down. He was bending forward, peering at some notes and he looked up over his reading glasses and said, 'Perhaps, Mr Learned Chairman, you would ask the witness to tell me how he came to be on the *Mary Deare*.'

The question was put and Patch answered, quite unsuspecting, that he thought he had already explained that he had replaced Mr Adams who had been taken to hospital suffering from jaundice.

'Yes, yes, quite,' Sir Lionel said impatiently. 'What I meant was, who signed you on—Captain Taggart or Mr Dellimare?'

'Captain Taggart.'

'He came ashore and made the choice himself?'

'No.'

'Who did come ashore then and make the choice?' Sir Lionel's voice still sounded bored. He gave the impression that he was dealing with a small routine point.

'Mr Dellimare.'

'Mr Dellimare?' Sir Lionel's face was suddenly expressive of surprise. 'I see. And was it done privately, a meeting in some bar—by arrangement?' His tone carried the bite of sarcasm in it.

'No. We met at the agents'.'

'At the agents'? Then there were probably other unemployed officers there?'

'Yes. Two.'

'Why didn't Mr Dellimare choose one of them? Why did he choose you?'

'The others withdrew when they heard that the vacancy was for the *Mary Deare*.'

'But you did not withdraw. Why?' And when Patch didn't answer, Sir Lionel said, 'I want to know why?'

'Because I needed the berth.'

'How long had you been without a ship?'

'Eleven months.'

'And before that you hadn't been able to get anything better than the job of second mate on a miserable little Italian steamer called the *Apollo* working the coastal ports of East Africa. Didn't you think it strange that a man with your record should suddenly find himself first officer of a 6,000 ton ocean-going ship?' And when Patch didn't say anything, Sir Lionel repeated, 'Didn't you think it strange?'

And all Patch could say, with the eyes of the whole court on him, was, 'I never considered it.'

'You—never—considered it!' Sir Lionel stared at him—the tone of his voice, the carriage of his head all indicating that he thought him a liar. And then he turned to Bowen-Lodge. 'Perhaps Mr Learned Chairman, you would ask the witness to give a brief résumé of the events that occurred on the night of 3rd/4th February nine years ago in the region of Singapore?'

Patch's grip on the rail in front of him tightened. His face looked ghastly—trapped. The courtroom stirred as though the first breath of storm had rustled through it. Bowen-Lodge looked down at the questioner. 'The *Belle Isle*?' he enquired. And then, still in the same whisper of an aside, 'Do you consider that necessary, Sir Lionel?'

'Absolutely,' was the firm and categorical reply.

Bowen-Lodge glanced up at the clock again

and then he put the question to Patch. And Patch, rigid, and tight-lipped, said, 'There was a report issued at the time, sir.'

Bowen-Lodge looked across at Sir Lionel, a mute question to discover whether he wished to pursue the matter. It was obvious that he did. You could see it in the stillness with which he watched the man in the witness box, his small head thrust forward as though about to strike. 'I am well aware that there is a report available,' he said in a cold, icy voice. 'Nevertheless, I think it right that the Court should hear the story from your own lips.'

'It's not for me to give my views on it when a Court has already pronounced judgment,' Patch said in a tight, restrained voice.

'I was not asking for your views. I was asking for a résumé of the facts.'

Patch's hand hit the rail involuntarily. 'I cannot see that it has any bearing on the loss of the *Mary Deare*.' His voice was louder, harsher.

'That is not for you to say,' Sir Lionel snapped. And then—needling him—'There are certain similarities.'

'Similarities!' Patch stared at him. And then, beating with hand on the rail, he burst out: 'By God, there are.' He turned to face the Chairman—still angry, goaded beyond the limits of what a man will stand. 'You want the sordid details. Very well. I was drunk. Dead drunk. That's what Craven said in evidence, anyway. It was hot like the inside of an oven

245

that day in Singapore.' He was still staring at the Chairman, but not seeing him any more, seeing only Singapore on the day he'd smashed up his career. 'Damp, sweaty, torrid heat,' he murmured. 'I remember that and I remember taking the *Belle Isle* out. And after that I don't remember a thing.'

'And you were drunk?' Bowen-Lodge asked. His voice was modulated, almost gentle.

'Yes, I suppose so ... in a sense. I'd had a few drinks. But not enough,' Patch added violently. 'Not enough to put me out like a light.' And then, after a pause, he added, 'They ran her aground on the Anambas Islands at 02.23 hours in the morning with a thundering surf running and she broke her back.'

'You are aware,' Sir Lionel said quietly, 'that there has been a lot of talk since ... suggesting that you did it for the insurance.'

Patch rounded on him. 'I could hardly be unaware of it,' he said with wild sarcasm, 'seeing that all these years I've barely been able to scratch a living in my own chosen profession.' He turned back to the Chairman, gripping hold of the rail. 'They said I ordered the course and they had the log to prove it. It was there in my own handwriting. Craven—he was the second officer—swore that he'd been down to my cabin to query it and that I'd bawled him out. Later he took a fix and then came down to my cabin to warn me again, but I was in a drunken stupor—those were his

246

words—and when he couldn't wake me, he went back to the bridge and altered course on his own responsibility. By then, of course, it was too late. That was his story, and he stuck to it so well that everybody believed him, even my own counsel.' He turned his head and was looking across the courtroom at Higgins. 'By God,' he repeated, 'there are similarities.'

'What similarities?' Sir Lionel asked in a light tone of disbelief.

Patch turned to face him. It was pitiful to see how easily he was goaded. 'Just this,' he almost shouted. 'Craven was a liar. The log entry was forged. The *Belle Isle* was owned by a bunch of Greek crooks in Glasgow. They were on the verge of bankruptcy. The insurance money just about saved them. It was all in the papers six months later. That was when the rumours started.'

'And you had nothing to do with it, I suppose?' Sir Lionel asked.

'No.'

'And this man Craven had slipped a micky into your drink. Is that what you're suggesting?'

It took away from him and destroyed his defence. His muttered 'Yes' was painful anti-climax. Bowen-Lodge intervened then. 'Are you suggesting a similarity between this Greek company and the Dellimare Trading and Shipping Company?' he asked.

And Patch, fighting back, cried, 'Yes. Yes,

that's exactly what I am suggesting.'

It brought the Dellimare Company's counsel on to his feet, protesting that it was a monstrous allegation, an unwarranted aspersion on a man who was dead at the time the fire broke out in the hold. And Bowen-Lodge nodded and said, 'Quite, Mr Smiles—unless there is some justification.' He turned to Patch then and said, 'Have you any reason for making such an allegation?'

Now, I thought—now he must tell them about Dellimare's offer. Whether he had evidence to support it, or not, it was the only thing for him to do. But, instead, he drove home his accusation on the basis of motive and opportunity; the Company in liquidation and the only people who would benefit by the loss of the ship. 'Why else should the owner have been on board?' he demanded. A voyage of almost five months! It was a ridiculous waste of a director's time, unless there was a reason for his being on the ship. 'And I say there was,' he declared.

Smiles jumped to his feet again, but Bowen-Lodge forestalled him. 'You seem to be forgetting the cause of the ship being abandoned and finally lost. Are you accusing Mr Dellimare of causing the fire in that after hold?'

It brought Patch up with a jolt. 'No,' he said.

'He was dead by then?'

'Yes.' Patch's voice had dropped to a

248

whisper.

And then Smiles, still on his feet, asked what possible motive the Company could have in destroying the ship. 'She was bound for the scrap yards and in the figures Mr Gundersen has given you, Mr Learned Chairman, you will find that the scrap value was fixed at a little over £15,000. She was insured for £30,000. Is the witness suggesting that a mere £15,000 was sufficient motive to induce a company to endanger the lives of a whole ship's crew?'

'The question of motive,' Bowen-Lodge said, 'does not come within the scope of this Investigation. We are concerned solely with the facts.' He glanced towards Sir Lionel as though expecting something further from him.

'I think at this stage, Mr Learned Chairman,' Sir Lionel said, 'I should ask you to put this very serious question to the witness— Did he, or did he not, on the night of March 18, set fire to Number Three hold of the *Mary Deare*, or cause it to be set on fire?' A sort of gasp like an eager shudder ran through the courtroom.

The eyes of the two men, Counsel and Chairman, remained fixed on each other for a moment, and then Bowen-Lodge nodded slowly and turned to face the witness. Looking down on him and speaking quietly, but with great distinctness, he said, 'I think it my duty to tell you that in my opinion this whole matter of the loss of the *Mary Deare* will be the subject of

249

a case in another Court and to advise you that you need not answer this very direct question if you do not wish to. Having so advised you, I will now put the question.' And he repeated it.

'No, I did not.' Patch declared, and his voice was clear and firm. And then he added, turning to face Sir Lionel Falcett, 'If I'd set fire to the ship, why should I go to the trouble of putting it out?'

It was a good point, but Sir Lionel only shrugged. 'We have to consider that she might have gone aground on the nearby reefs, perhaps the coast of France, only partially burned out. The evidence would be better sunk in twenty fathoms of water. There was a gale coming up and then you had Mr Sands's arrival to consider—'

Bowen-Lodge gave a discreet little warning cough and Sir Lionel murmured his apologies. The Chairman looked up at the clock again and then leaned over and conferred with his assessors. Finally he adjourned the Court. 'Until ten-thirty tomorrow, gentlemen.'

Nobody moved for a moment, and even when they did, I sat there, stunned and angry at the injustice of it. To take a man's record and fling it in his face like that, to damn him without a shred of evidence . . . and there was Patch still standing stiff and rigid in the witness box—and Sir Lionel, picking up his papers and smiling at some little joke made by one of the other lawyers.

Patch was moving now, crossing the floor of the court. Without thinking I started forward to meet him, but Hal put his hand on my arm. 'Better leave him now,' he said. 'He needs to think it out, poor devil.'

'Think what out?' I asked angrily. I was still wrought up by the injustice of it.

'What he's going to say tomorrow,' Hal answered. And then he added, 'He hasn't told the whole story yet and Lionel Falcett knows it. He can tell it tomorrow, or he can tell it in the criminal courts! But he's got to tell it some time.'

The criminal courts. 'Yes, I suppose it will come to that,' I murmured. But before that, the truth had to be uncovered. And the truth, whatever it was, lay out on the Minkies. 'I must have a word with him,' I said. I had suddenly made up my mind and was forcing my way through the crowd towards Patch.

He didn't hear me when I called to him. He seemed oblivious to everything but the need to get out of the place. I caught hold of him, and he turned abruptly with a nervous start. 'Oh, it's you.' He was trembling. 'Well, what is it?'

I stared at him, horrified by the haggard, hunted look in his face. There were beads of sweat still on his forehead. 'Why in God's name didn't you tell them?' I said.

'Tell them what?' His eyes had suddenly gone blank of all expression.

'About Dellimare,' I said. 'Why didn't you

251

tell them?'

His eyes flickered and slid away from me. 'How could I?' he breathed. And then, as I started to tell him that the Court had a right to the truth, he said, 'Leave it at that, can't you? Just leave it at that.' And he turned on his heel and walked quickly away towards the exit.

I went after him then. I couldn't leave it like that. I had to give him the chance he'd asked for. I pushed through a little knot of the *Mary Deare*'s crew and caught him up in the corridor outside. 'Listen,' I said. 'I'll take you out there—as soon as the Enquiry is over.'

He shook his head, still walking towards the freedom of the main doors. 'It's too late now,' he said.

His attitude exasperated me and I caught hold of his arm, checking him. 'Don't you understand? I'm offering you my boat,' I said. '*Sea Witch* is lying in Lulworth Cove. We could be over there in twenty-four hours.'

He rounded on me then. 'I tell you it's too late.' He almost snarled the words at me. And then his eyes slid past me, narrowing suddenly and blazing with anger. I felt his muscles tense, and then he had freed himself from me and was walking away. I turned to find Higgins standing there. He had Yules with him and they were both staring after Patch walking down the corridor, fascinated by the thought that he might be guilty of sending a lot of men to their death.

I turned to look for Hal, but Higgins caught hold of my arm, so that I was instantly conscious of the colossal brute strength of the man. 'I 'eard wot you said just then.' His throaty voice was full of the smell of stale beer as he thrust his head close to mine. 'If you think you're goin' ter take 'im a't there . . .' He checked himself quickly, his small, blood-veined eyes narrowed, and he let go of my arm. 'Wot I mean is . . . well, you steer clear of 'im,' he rasped. ''E's a wrong 'un—yer can take my word for it. You'll only get yerself inter trouble.' And he turned quickly and went ploughing off down the corridor, little Yules hurrying after him.

A moment later Hal joined me. His face was serious. 'I've been talking to Lionel Falcett,' he said, as we moved off towards the entrance. 'It's as I thought. They think he's hiding something.'

'Who—Patch?' I was still shaken by what Higgins had said, wondering if he'd guessed that I'd been referring to the *Mary Deare*.

'Yes. It's only an impression, mind you. Lionel didn't say anything, but . . .' He hesitated. 'Do you know where Patch is staying?' And when I nodded, he said, 'Well, if you're absolutely certain of the chap, I'd get hold of him and tell him what the form is. It's the truth and the whole truth now, if he wants to keep clear of trouble. That's my advice, anyway. Get hold of him tonight.'

253

We went into the pub across the road and had a drink. I phoned Patch from there. It was a lodging house down by the docks and the landlady told me that he'd come in, got his coat and gone out again. I phoned him later when we arrived at Bosham and once after dinner, but he still hadn't returned. It worried me and, going to bed early, I found it difficult to sleep. Rain was lashing at the window and in the twilight of half-consciousness Patch and Higgins wandered through my mind. I pictured Patch walking the streets of Southampton, walking endlessly to a decision that would justify his cry that my offer was too late and leave him just something to be identified in a mortuary.

In the morning, of course, it all seemed different. The sun was shining and there was a blackbird singing, and as we drove into Southampton, the world was going about its prosaic, everyday life—delivery vans and postmen on bicycles and kids going to school. It was ten-fifteen when we reached the court. We had arrived early so that I could have a word with Patch before the Investigation was resumed. But he hadn't arrived yet. Only a few of the witnesses were there, Higgins among them, his big body slewed round in his seat, watching the entrance.

Across the court several of the lawyers had come in and were standing together in a little knot, talking in low voices. The Press desk was filling up; the public gallery, too. Hal left me and went to his seat, and I moved out into the corridor and stood there, watching, watching the people filing slowly in, searching for Patch amongst the faces that thronged the narrow passage-way.

'Mr Sands.' A hand touched my arm, and I turned to find Janet Taggart standing beside me, her eyes unnaturally large in the pallor of her face. 'Where is he? I can't find him.'

'Who?'

'Mr Patch. He's not in the courtroom. Do you know where he is, please?'

'No.'

She hesitated, unsure of herself. 'I'm terribly worried,' she murmured.

I stared at her, wondering how it was she had come to share my own fears. 'You should have thought of that before,' I said brutally and watched the muscles of her face contract so that the features looked small and pinched. She was different now from the sunny-smiling kid of the photograph, and the light wasn't shining on her hair any more. She looked grown up, a woman. 'He'll be here in a moment,' I said more gently, trying to calm her fears, and my own.

'Yes,' she said. 'Yes, of course.' She stood there, hesitating, her face taut. 'I went to see him last night. I didn't understand—not until I read the evidence of Higgins and the others.' She stared at me, her eyes big and scared-looking. 'He told me everything then. He was so—' She stopped there with a little shrug, uncertain of herself and what she was saying. 'You do think he's all right, don't you?' And then, because I didn't answer, she said, 'Oh God! I could kill myself for the things I said.' But she wasn't speaking to me. She was speaking to herself.

I heard the court rise. The corridor was empty. There was still no sign of Patch. 'We'd better go in,' I said gently.

She nodded, not saying anything more, and we went into the courtroom together and took our seats. Holland was on his feet. He had a piece of paper in his hand and he turned to face Bowen-Lodge as silence descended on the room. 'Mr Learned Chairman. I have just received information from the Receiver of Wreck to the effect that the *Mary Deare* is not sunk. The Harbour Master at St Helier, Jersey Island, has reported that the vessel lies stranded on the Plateau des Minquiers and that a French salvage company is endeavouring to refloat her.'

The gasp of surprise that greeted this news swept through the courtroom, gathering force as people gave voice to their astonishment. Men in the Press desk were on their feet. I caught sight of Higgins, sitting with a dazed look on his face. There was still no sign of Patch.

Bowen-Lodge leaned forward over his desk.

256

'This alters the situation entirely, Mr Holland. I take it that it means that the Receiver of Wreck will be able to make a full examination of the wreck?' And when Holland nodded, he added, 'I presume you have discussed it with him. How long before he can report to the Court?'

'He's not sure about that,' Holland answered. 'He doesn't yet know the exact position of the *Mary Deare* on the reefs nor has he any information as to the identity of the salvage company. He is making enquiries. But he informs me that the legal position may be complicated—the Minkies being part of the Channel Islands and the company concerned being French. It is a question of the Crown's rights and the rights of the salvage company. He also stated that the tides in this area, which rise and fall by over thirty feet, made the reefs particulary dangerous and, as far as the cargo was concerned, any examination might have to wait on the successful refloating of the vessel.'

'I see. Thank you, Mr Holland.' Bowen-Lodge nodded and turned to his assessors. He conferred with them, heads close together, whilst the sound of people talking broke like a wave again over the court. The Press desk was empty now. 'Well, that's that,' Hal whispered to me. 'He'll adjourn the Court now.' And then he said, 'Did you know she wasn't sunk?' And when I nodded, he said, 'Good God man! You must be daft.'

Bowen-Lodge had separated from his assessors now and he tapped with his gavel to silence the court. 'There are one or two questions, Mr Holland, arising out of the discovery that the ship is not sunk. Please recall your last witness.'

Holland nodded and called, 'Gideon Patch'.

The court was still, nobody moved.

'Gideon Patch!' And when he still didn't appear, Holland turned to the usher on the door and said, 'Call Gideon Patch.' The name was repeated, echoing in the emptiness of the corridors outside. But still nothing happened. Necks craned in the public gallery; the buzz of conversation rose again.

They waited several minutes for him, and the silence in the court was so absolute that you could almost hear the ticking of the clock. And then, after a brief discussion with the assessors, Bowen-Lodge adjourned the court for one hour. 'At twelve o'clock please, gentlemen.' The court stood and then everybody was talking at once, and down by the jury box Higgins, Yules and Burrows stood in a little bunch with their heads close together. And then Higgins broke away from them suddenly and came lumbering towards the door. His eyes met mine for a second, and they had the dead, flat look of a man who is scared.

The wait seemed a long one. There was no news. All we could learn was that enquiries

258

were being made at Patch's lodgings. 'A fat lot of good that will do,' was Hal's comment.

'A warrant and the police is the only thing now.' We had nothing to say to each other as we waited. He had accepted Patch's guilt as proved. Others took the same view. Scraps of comment came to me from the waiting crowd. 'Wot I say is, he's no better than a murderer . . . You can always tell, old boy. It's the eyes that give them away every time . . . And what about Dellimare and that poor Captain Taggart? . . . 'Course 'e did. Wouldn't you do a bunk if you'd killed 'alf the crew . . .' And all the time I was trying to reconcile the sort of man they thought he was with the man I had known on the *Mary Deare*.

At length the crowd began to drift back into the courtroom. As they did so a rumour rang from mouth to mouth—Patch hadn't been seen since the previous evening. Bowen-Lodge and the assessors entered and there was silence as Holland rose to say that he regretted he was not able to produce his chief witness.

'Have the police been requested to take action?' Bowen-Lodge asked.

'Yes. A search has been instituted.' There was a moment's silence as Bowen-Lodge fiddled with the papers on his desk.

'Would you care to re-examine any of the witnesses?' Holland asked.

Bowen-Lodge hesitated. He was looking over the available witnesses and for a moment

I thought his cold, searching gaze was fixed on me. Finally he leaned over in conference with his assessors. I felt the shirt sticking to my body. What the hell was I going to say if he recalled me? How was I going to explain my failure to tell them the ship was on the Minkies?

The minute I was kept in suspense seemed a long time. And then Bowen-Lodge said, 'I don't think there is any point in recalling any of the witnesses now, Mr Holland.' He looked up at the court. 'In view of the fact that the *Mary Deare* has been located, the assessors and I are agreed that no further purpose can be served by continuing this Investigation, particularly as the chief witness is no longer available. I am, therefore, adjourning the Court indefinitely pending examination of the wreck. All witnesses are released. You will be notified in due course should further evidence be required of you. Thank you, gentlemen, for your attendance.'

It was over, the Chairman and assessors gone, the courtroom emptying. As I made my way towards the door, Higgins stepped forward, blocking my path. 'Where is 'e?' he demanded. 'Where's 'e gone?'

I stared at him, wondering why he should be so worked up over Patch's disappearance. He ought to have been pleased. 'What's it got to do with you?' I asked him.

Beady eyes searched my face, peering at me

over sagging pouches. 'So you do know, eh? I said you would.'

'As it happens,' I said, 'I don't know. I wish I did.'

'To hell with that!' The violence inside him bubbled to the surface. 'You think I don't know what yer up to—you with your boat lyin' in Lulworth, waitin' for 'im. Well, I tell yer, if that's yer game, wotch a't, that's all.' He stared at me, his small eyes narrowed, and then he turned abruptly and left us.

As we walked down the corridor, Hal said, 'You're not going to be a fool and try and slip him out of the country, are you?' He was looking at me, his face serious, a little worried.

'No,' I said. 'I don't think it ever occurred to him that that was a way out.'

He nodded, but I don't think he was convinced. He would have pressed the point further, but as we went out into the sunshine, he was greeted by a man in a reefer with a little pointed beard and greying hair. He had a high, rather strident voice, and, as I waited, I heard him say to Hal, 'Oh, not your type, Colonel—definitely not.' There was something about a motor boat, and then: '. . . rang up about an hour and a half ago. They had her on charter a month back . . . Yes, old *Griselda*. You remember. Dry rot in the keel and rolls like a bastard.' He went off with a high-pitched laugh and Hal rejoined me. Apparently the man was a yacht broker down at Bosham. 'Odd place, this, for him to do business,' Hal said. And then he added, 'I wonder if it's the Dellimare Company, chartering a boat to go out and see what the French salvage people are up to. I wouldn't be surprised.'

We started to walk to the car and he went on talking, giving me some advice about not leaving it too late. But I was thinking of Higgins. Why had Patch's disappearance scared him?

'John. You're not listening.'

'No. I'm sorry.'

'Well, that's not surprising. Nobody listens to advice.' We had reached the car. 'But if it comes to a criminal case, see that you give them the full story, just as it happened. Don't leave it to be dragged out of you in cross-examination. They'll play hell with you and you may find yourself in real trouble.'

'All right,' I said.

We drove down to the police station then to see if there was any news of Patch. But all the sergeant at the desk could tell us was that he had been seen in a number of pubs in the dock area and had spent part of the night at an all-night café out on the Portsmouth road. He had got a lift about four in the morning in a truck headed back towards Southampton. They were now trying to trace the truck driver.

We hung around for a little, but there was no further news. 'And it's my opinion,' the sergeant added darkly, 'that there won't be any—'cept for the finding of the body as you might say. The people at the café described him as desperate—looked like death, the report says.'

Hal drove me to the railway station then, and when he had gone I bought an evening paper. Without thinking I found myself looking at the forecast. Winds moderate, north-westerly. As I stood waiting for my train I was thinking of Higgins and the Dellimare Company and the fact that the Minkies were only a day's sail from Lulworth.

# Part Three

# THE MINKIES

'*Sea Witch*! Ahoy! Ahoy, *Sea Witch*!'

Gulls wheeled, screaming, and my voice came back to me, a lonely shout in the drizzling rain. The yacht lay motionless in the crater of the cove, the reflection of her black topsides shattered every now and then as cat's-paws of wind riffled the mirror-surface of the water. The waves of a swell broke in the entrance and, all round, the hills loomed ghostly and grey in the mist, all colour lost, their grass slopes dropping to the dirty white of the chalk cliffs. There wasn't a soul about.

'Ahoy! *Sea Witch*!' A figure moved on the deck, a splash of yellow oilskins; the clatter of oars and then the dinghy was coming to meet me. It grounded with a crunch on the wet shingle and I climbed in and Mike rowed me out. I was relieved to find that I didn't have to tell him about the Enquiry; he had followed it all in the newspapers. But once we were on board with the dinghy made fast and my gear stowed, he began to ask questions—what had happened to Patch, why hadn't he turned up at the Court this morning? 'You know they've issued a warrant for his arrest?'

'A warrant? How do you know?' I asked. I don't know why, but it shocked me. It seemed so pointless.

'It was on the six o'clock news.'

'Did it say what the charge was?'

267

'No. But they've got police checks on all the roads leading out of Southampton and they're keeping watch on the ports.'

We discussed it during the meal. There were only the two of us. Ian had gone home to visit his people. Mike was to phone him as soon as we were ready to start operations again, but he hadn't done so yet because the latest forecast was wind moderate north-westerly, backing westerly later and becoming fresh, with the outlook unsettled. The thing that puzzled Mike most about the whole business was why Patch hadn't told the Court about Dellimare's offer. Not having been present at the Enquiry, but only reading the reports, it was natural, I suppose, that he should still retain a vivid impression of Patch's visit, and over coffee he suddenly reminded me of the package I had been given at Paimpol. 'I suppose it couldn't contain some vital piece of evidence?' he said.

Until that moment I had forgotten all about it. 'If it had,' I said, 'he would have asked me to produce it.'

'Have you still got it?'

I nodded and got up and went into the after cabin. It was still there in my brief-case and I took it through into the saloon. Mike had cleared a space on the table and I reached for a knife and cut the string, feeling as I had done during the war on the occasions when I had had to deal with the effects of some poor devil who'd been killed.

268

'Looks like a book of some sort,' Mike said. 'It couldn't be the log, could it?'

'No,' I answered. 'The log was in Court.'

Inside the brown paper wrapping was an envelope. The name *J. C. B. Dellimare* was typed on it and below, in blue pencil, was scrawled the one word *Collect*. The envelope had been ripped open, the tear crossing the stamped impress of a City bank. I had a vague hope then that perhaps Mike was right—that it was some sort of an account book belonging to Dellimare or the Company, something that would reveal a financial motive. And then I slid the contents on to the table and stared incredulously.

Lying amongst the supper things was a thick wad of five pound notes.

Mike was gazing at the pile, open-mouthed with astonishment. He'd never seen so much cash in his life; neither of us had. I split it between us. 'Count it!' I said.

For several seconds there wasn't a sound in the saloon except the crackle of those Bank of England notes. And when we had totalled it all up, it came to exactly £5,000, and Mike looked up at me. 'No wonder he didn't want to bring it out through the Customs himself,' he said. And then, after a pause, he added, 'Do you think he accepted Dellimare's offer after all?'

But I shook my head. 'If he'd accepted, why put out the fire, why beach her on the Minkies?' I was remembering the state of that cabin when I'd gone in to help him get out the rubber dinghy. 'No, he must have taken it afterwards—after the man was dead.'

'But why?'

'God knows!' I shrugged my shoulders. There were so many things I didn't understand. I gathered the notes together and put them back in the envelope. 'If this were his payment for wrecking the ship,' I said, 'he'd have been down here to collect it the instant he landed in England.'

'Yes, that's true.' Mike took the envelope from me, frowning and turning it over in his hand. 'Odd that he should have failed to collect it. It's almost as though he'd forgotten all about it.'

I nodded slowly. And then I went up on deck and lit the riding light. It wasn't really necessary; we were the only boat in the anchorage, and nobody was likely to come in on such a reeking night. But it gave me something to do. I lit a cigarette. It was quite dark now and we lay in a little pool of light, hemmed in by the iridescent curtain of the drizzle. The wind seemed to have died away. The water was very black and still. No ripples slapped against the topsides. The only sound was the faint murmur of wavelets on the beach. I stood there, smoking in the feeble glow of the riding light and wondering what the hell I was going to do with all that money. If I took it to the authorities, I should have to account for

270

my possession of it. Or should I send it anonymously to form the basis of a fund for the dependents of those who had lost their lives? I certainly couldn't send it to his mother, and I was damned if I was going to return it to the Dellimare Company.

I stayed there, thinking about it, until my cigarette was a sodden butt. I threw it in the water then and went below. Mike was checking over one of the aqualungs. 'Care for a drink?' I asked him.

He nodded. 'Good idea.'

I got out the bottle and the glasses.

I didn't say anything. I didn't want to talk about it. I just sat there with my drink and a cigarette, going over the whole thing in my mind. We sat for a long time in silence.

I don't know who heard it first, but we were suddenly staring at each other, listening. It came from the bows, a sort of splashing sound. 'What is it?' Mike had got to his feet. The splashing ceased and then footsteps sounded on the deck above our heads. They came slowly aft, whilst we stood waiting, frozen into immobility. They reached the hatch. The cover was slid quietly back and bare feet appeared, followed by dripping trouser legs and then the body of a man all sodden with water; he was standing suddenly at the foot of the ladder, blinking in the light, his face pale as death, his black hair plastered to his skull and water streaming from his clothes on to the grating.

271

'Good God!' I breathed. I was too astonished to say anything else. He was shivering a bit and his teeth were chattering, and I stood there, staring at him as though he were a ghost. 'If somebody would lend me a towel . . .' Patch began to strip off his wet clothes.

'So Higgins was right,' I said.

'Higgins?'

'He said you'd make for *Sea Witch.*' And then I added, 'What have you come here for? I thought you were dead.' God! I almost wished he were as I realized the impossible position he'd put me in. 'What the devil made you come here?'

He ignored my outburst. It was as though he hadn't heard or had shut his mind to it. Mike had found him a towel and he began to dry himself, standing naked, his hard, sinewy body still brown with the heat of Aden. He was shivering and he asked for a cigarette. I gave him one and he lit it and started to dry his hair. 'If you think we're going to slip you over to France, you're wrong,' I said. 'I won't do it.'

He looked at me then, frowning a little. 'France?' The muscles of his jaw tightened. 'It's the Minkies I want to get to,' he said. 'You promised to take me there. You offered me your boat.' A sudden urgency was in his voice.

I stared at him. Surely to God he didn't still want to go out to the Minkies? 'That was last night,' I said.

272

'Last night—tonight ... what difference does it make?' The pitch of his voice had risen. He had stopped towelling himself and suddenly there was doubt in his face. It was as though he had come here in the certainty that when he had arrived everything would be all right, and suddenly he knew it wasn't.

'You probably don't know it,' I said, trying to soften the blow, 'but there's a warrant out for your arrest.'

He showed no surprise. It was as though he had expected it. 'I was walking for a long time last night,' he said, 'trying to make up my mind. In the end I knew I'd never reach the *Mary Deare* if I went into that Court this morning. So I came here. I walked from Swanage and I've been up on the hills half the day, waiting for it to get dark.'

'Have you seen a paper?' I asked him.

'No. Why?'

'The *Mary Deare* has been located and a French salvage company is endeavouring to refloat her. A full examination is to be made of the wreck, and if you think there's any point—'

'A full examination.' He seemed shocked. 'When?' And then he added, 'It was announced in Court, was it?'

'Yes.'

'Who told them where the ship was. Did Gundersen?'

'Gundersen? No. It was the Harbour Master at St Helier reporting to the Receiver of

273

Wrecks. I imagine a Jersey Island fisherman sighted the wreck. He must have seen the salvage people working on her.'

'That's all right.' He seemed relieved. 'But we'll have to hurry.' He picked up the towel. 'Have you got a drink?'

I reached into the locker and got him the rum bottle and a glass. His hands shook as he poured it out. 'I'll need some clothes, too.' He knocked the drink back at one gulp and stood gasping for breath. 'Now that they know there's going to be an official examination of the boat, we'll have to move fast.'

Mike had produced some clothes out of a locker. He put them on the table and Patch picked up a vest. 'How soon can you leave?' he asked.

I stared at him. 'Don't you understand?' I said. 'There's a warrant out for your arrest. I can't possibly take you.'

He was halfway into the vest and he stopped, his eyes fixed on me. For the first time, I think, he realized that we weren't going to take him. 'But I was relying on you.' His tone was suddenly desperate. And then he added angrily, 'It was only yesterday you offered to take me. It was the one chance and—'

'But you didn't accept it,' I said. 'You told me it was too late.'

'So it was.'

'If it was too late then,' I said, 'it's certainly

274

too late now.'

'How could I accept your offer? They were going to arrest me. I was quite certain of that, and if I'd gone back into that Court this morning—'

'But you didn't.'

'No.'

'Why not? Can't you see you've put yourself in an impossible situation?' I leaned forward, determined to get at the truth. 'You've got the police hunting for you now—everybody against you. What in God's name made you decide to run for it?'

He pulled the vest down over his head and came to the edge of the table, leaning down over it. 'Something I learned last night— something that made me realize I had to get out to the *Mary Deare* as soon as possible.' There was silence for a moment, whilst we looked at him, waiting. And then he said, 'That salvage company—it's under contract to the Dellimare Company.'

'How do you know?' It seemed the wildest piece of guesswork. 'How can you possibly know when it's only just been announced that a salvage company is working on the wreck?'

'I'll tell you.' He began to get into the rest of Mike's clothes. 'Last night, when I got back to my rooms—I went up and got my coat. I was going for a walk—to think things over. And outside—I found Janet—Miss Taggart— waiting for me there in the street. She'd come. . .'

He gave a quick shrug. 'Well, it doesn't matter, but it made a difference. I knew she believed in me then, and after that I searched the pubs all through the dock area. I was certain I'd find Burrows in one of them. He couldn't keep away from the booze so long as he had money. And he had money all right. I found him down in the old part of the town, and he told me the whole thing—drunk and truculent and full of confidence. He hated my guts. That's why he told me about the salvage company. He was gloating, knowing I'd never prove anything after they'd sunk her. And all because I'd told him he was incompetent and that I'd see to it he never had charge of an engine-room again.'

He paused and took a quick drink. The wind was rising, and in the silence the sound of it whining through the rigging was suddenly loud. Then he pulled on Mike's sweater and came and sat down opposite me. He was still shivering. 'Higgins must have worked out the course of our drift for Gundersen. Anyway, they were convinced she was on the Minkies and they chartered a boat and went over there. And when they'd found her, Gundersen signed up this French outfit to salvage her.'

'But what difference does that make to you?' Mike asked. 'It's perfectly natural for the Dellimare Company to want to salvage her.'

Patch turned on him, his lips drawn back in a smile. 'They're not going to salvage her,' he said. 'They're going to have the French pull her off and then they're going to sink her in deep water.'

I saw Mike looking at him as though he were crazy and I said, 'Do you seriously imagine they could get away with that?'

'Why not?' he demanded.

'But no salvage company—'

'It's nothing to do with the salvage company. But the contract is for refloating and towing the hulk to Southampton, and Higgins and Burrows will be on board the tow. Gundersen will insist on that. And with those two on board, it's simple. Burrows has only got to open the sea cocks and the *Mary Deare* will quietly founder at the end of her tow line. They'll wait till they're past the Casquets, I imagine, and sink her in the Hurd Deep. She'll go down in sixty fathoms or more, and everybody will think it a stroke of bad luck and put it down to the state of the hull after being pounded for a couple of months on the Minkies.' He turned and stared at me. 'Now perhaps you understand. I've got to get out to her, Sands. It's my only hope. I must have proof.'

'Of what?' Mike demanded.

He looked from one to the other of us, a quick, uncertain movement of the eyes. 'I must know for certain that there was an explosion in those for'ard holds.'

'I should have thought that was a matter for

the authorities,' Mike said.

'The authorities? No. No, I must be certain.'

'But surely,' I said, 'if you went to the authorities and told them the truth ... if you told them about Dellimare's offer—'

'I can't do that.' He was staring at me and all the vitality in his eyes seemed to have burned itself out.

'Why not?' I asked.

'Why not?' His eyes dropped and he fiddled with his glass. 'You were with me on that ship,' he whispered. 'Surely to God you must have guessed by now.' And then he added quickly. 'Don't ask me any more questions. Just take me out there. Afterwards ...' He hesitated. 'When I know for certain—' He didn't finish, but looked directly at me and said, 'Well? Will you take me?'

'I'm sorry,' I said. 'But you must realize it's impossible now.'

'But—' He reached out his hand and gripped hold of my arm. 'For Christ's sake! Don't you understand? They'll refloat her and then they'll sink her out in deep water. And after that I'll never know ...' He had a beaten look and I was sorry for him. And then a spark of anger showed in his eyes. 'I thought you'd more guts, Sands,' he said, and his voice quivered. 'I thought you'd take a chance—you and Duncan. God damn it! You said you'd take me.' He was coming up again, the muscles of his arm tightening, his body no longer sagging

278

. . . unbelievably there was strength in his voice again as he said, 'You're not scared, are you, just because there's a warrant out for my arrest?'

'No,' I said. 'It isn't only that.'

'What is it then?'

I reached across the table for the envelope. 'This for one thing,' I said and I threw it down on the table in front of him so that the fivers spilled out of it and lay there, white and crisp, black-inked like funeral cards. 'You let me bring that back for you, not knowing what it was. I watched him staring down at them uncomfortably and I went on, 'Now suppose you tell us the truth—why you took that money, why you didn't tell the Court about Dellimare's offer.' I hesitated, still staring at him, but he wouldn't meet my gaze. 'You took that money from his cabin after he was dead, didn't you?'

'Yes.' His voice sounded weary, exhausted.

'Why?'

'Why?' He lifted his eyes then, staring straight at me, and they were suddenly the eyes of the man I had first met on the *Mary Deare*. 'Because it was there, I suppose. I didn't reckon it belonged to him any more . . . Oh, I don't know.' He was frowning, as though trying to concentrate on something that didn't interest him. He seemed to be lost in some private hell of his own creation. 'I suppose I was a fool to take it. It was dangerous. I realized that afterwards. But at the time . . . well, I was broke, and when you know you've got to fight a company to prove you did your best to bring a ship home that they didn't want brought home . . .' He let it go at that, his mind still on something else.

'Is that why you didn't tell the Court about Dellimare's offer?' I asked.

'No.' He got suddenly to his feet. 'No, it wasn't that.' He stood for a moment looking out through the open hatch and then he came back to the table. 'Don't you understand yet?' His eyes were fixed on my face. 'I killed him.'

'Dellimare?' I stared at him in shocked silence.

'He didn't go overboard,' he said. And then, after a pause, he added, 'His body is still there on the *Mary Deare*.'

I was so staggered I could think of nothing to say. And then suddenly he began to pour out the whole story.

It had happened on the night of the gale, just after the fire in the radio shack had been reported to him. He had gone out on to the wing of the bridge, to see whether the fire could be tackled from there, and he'd seen Dellimare making his way aft along the upper deck. 'I'd warned him I'd kill him if I found him trying to monkey with the ship. There was no reason for him to be going aft.' He had rushed down from the bridge then and had reached the after end of the deck just in time

280

to see Dellimare disappearing through the inspection hatch of Number Four hold. 'I should have slammed the lid shut on him and left it at that.' But instead he'd followed Dellimare down into the hold and had found him crouched by the for'ard bulkhead, his arm thrust down into the gap between the top case of the cargo and the hull plates. 'I can remember his face,' he breathed. 'Startled and white as hell in the light of my torch. I believe he knew I was going to kill him.'

Patch's voice trembled now as he relived the scene that had been pent-up inside him too long. Dellimare had straightened himself with a cry, holding some sort of cylinder in his hand, and Patch had moved in with a cold dynamic fury and had smashed his fist into the man's face, driving his head back on to the steel of the hull, crashing it against an angle iron. 'I wanted to crush him, smash him, obliterate him. I wanted to kill him.' He was breathing heavily, standing at the end of the table, staring at us with the light shining down on his head deepening the shadows of his face. 'There were things happening to the ship that night—the for'ard holds flooding, the fire in the radio shack, and then that little rat going down into the hold . . . and all the time a gale blowing hurricane force. My God! What would you have done? I was the Captain. The ship was in hellish danger. And he wanted her wrecked. I'd warned him . . .' He stopped

281

abruptly and wiped his forehead.

Then he went on, more quietly, describing what had happened after Dellimare had crumped up, lying in a heap on one of the aero engine cases with blood glistening red in his pale thin hair. He hadn't realized he'd killed him—not then. But the anger had drained out of him and somehow he had managed to get him up the vertical ladder to the deck. He had nearly been knocked down by a sea that had come surging in-board, but he had made the ladder to the upper-deck. That way he wouldn't meet any of the crew. But when he had almost reached the bridge housing the lights shining out of the after portholes showed him Dellimare's head and he knew then that the man was dead. 'His neck was broken.' He said it flatly, without emotion.

'But surely you could have said he'd had an accident—fallen down the hold or something?' I suggested. I was remembering the coal dust and the sound of shifting coal in the bunker, knowing what was coming.

He reached for the packet and lit a cigarette. Then he sat down opposite me again. 'I panicked, I suppose,' he said. 'Poor devil, he wasn't a pretty sight—all the back of his head smashed in.' He was seeing the blood and the lolling head again, and the sweat glistened on his forehead. 'I decided to dump him over the side.'

But he had set the body down to examine it

and when he bent to pick it up, he'd seen Higgins coming out through the starboard doorway from the bridge-housing. He hadn't dared carry the body to the rail then. But just beside him the hatch of the port bunkering chute stood open for some strange reason and, without thinking, he pitched the body down the chute and slammed the lid on it. 'It wasn't until hours later than I realized what I'd done.' He took a pull at his cigarette, dragging at it, his hands trembling. 'Instead of getting shot of the man, I'd hung his body round my neck like a millstone.' His voice had fallen to a whisper and for a moment he sat in silence. Then he added, 'When you came on board, I'd slung a rope ladder down into that bunker and was in there, trying to get at the body. But by then the rolling of the ship had buried him under tons of coal.'

There was a long silence after that and I could hear the wind in the rigging, a high, singing note. The anchor chain was grating on the shingle as the boat yawed. And then, speaking to himself, his head lowered: 'I killed him, and I thought it was justice. I thought he deserved to die. I was convinced I was saving the lives of thirty odd men, my own included.'

And then he looked at me suddenly. 'Well, I've told you the truth now.'

I nodded. I knew this was the truth. I knew now why he had to get back there, why he couldn't reveal Dellimare's offer to the Court.

'You should have gone to the police,' I said, 'as soon as you reached England.'

'The police?' He was staring at me, white-faced. 'How could I?'

'But if you'd told them about the offer Dellimare made you . . .'

'Do you think they'd have believed me? It was only my word. I'd no proof. How could I possibly justify . . .' His gaze switched to the envelope lying on the table. 'You see this money?' He reached out and grabbed up a handful of the fivers. 'He offered it to me, the whole lot. He had it there in his cabin and he spilled the whole five thousand out in front of me—out of that envelope that's lying there; and I picked it up and threw it in his face and told him I'd see him in hell before I did his dirty work for him. That's when I warned him that I'd kill him if he tried to lose me the ship.' He paused, breathing heavily. 'And then that gale and the for'ard holds suddenly making water and the fire in the radio shack . . . when I found him down in that hold—' He was still staring at me and his features were haggard and drawn, the way I'd first seen them. 'I was so sure I was justified—at the time,' he whispered.

'But it was an accident,' Mike said. 'Damn it, you didn't mean to kill him.'

He shook his head slowly, pushing his hand up through his hair. 'No, that's not true,' he said. 'I did mean to kill him. I was mad at the thought of what he'd tried to make me do—what he was doing to the ship. The first command I'd had in ten years...' He was looking down at his glass again. 'I thought when I put her on the Minkies, that I could get back to her, get rid of his body and prove that he was trying to sink her—' He was staring at me again. 'Can't you understand, Sands ... I had to know I was justified.'

'But it was still an accident,' I said gently. 'You could have gone to the authorities...' I hesitated, and then added, 'There was a time when you were prepared to—when you altered course for Southampton after rounding Ushant.'

'I still had the ship then,' he muttered, and I realized then what his ship meant to a man like Patch. So long as he'd had the *Mary Deare*'s deck under his feet and he was in command he'd still had confidence in himself, in the rightness of his actions.

He reached out his hand for the bottle. 'Mind if I have another drink?' His tone was resigned.

I watched him pour it, understanding now how desperate was his need to justify himself. I remembered how he'd reacted to the sight of the crew huddled like sheep around Higgins in the office at Paimpol. His first command in ten years and the whole thing repeating itself. It was an appalling twist of fate. 'When did you feed last?' I asked him.

'I don't know. It doesn't matter.' He swallowed some of the drink, his hand still trembling, his body slack.

'I'll get you some food.' I got up and went through into the galley. The stew was still hot in the pressure-cooker and I put some on a plate and set it in front of him. And then I asked Mike to come up on deck. The freshening wind had thinned the mist, so that the hills were dim, humped-up shapes, their shadows thrown round the cove and falling away to the narrow gap of the entrance. I stood there for a moment, wondering how I was going to persuade him. But Mike had guessed what was in my mind. 'You want *Sea Witch*, is that it, John?'

I nodded. 'For four days,' I said. 'Five at the most. That's all.'

He was looking at me, his face pale in the faint glow of the riding light. 'Surely it would be better to put the whole thing in the hands of the authorities?' I didn't say anything. I didn't know how to make him understand the way I felt. And after a while, he said, 'You believe him then—about the Dellimare Company planning to sink the ship in deep water?'

'I don't know,' I murmured. I wasn't sure. 'But if you accept that the cargo had been switched, that the whole thing was planned . . .' I hesitated, remembering how scared Higgins had been. If Higgins had started that fire and knocked Patch out and panicked the crew . . .

286

'Yes,' I said. 'I think I do believe him.'

Mike was silent for some time then. He had turned away from me and was staring out towards the entrance. At length he said, 'You're sure about this, John? It's a hell of a risk you're taking for the fellow.'

'I'm quite sure,' I said.

He nodded. 'Okay. Then the sooner we get under way the better.'

'You don't have to come,' I said.

He looked at me with that slow, rather serious smile of his. '*Sea Witch* and I go together,' he said. 'You don't get the one without the other.' He glanced up at the masthead. The burgee hadn't been taken down and it showed the wind westerly. 'We'll be able to sail it.' He was thinking we'd make better time under sail, for our engine was geared for power, not speed.

Down below I found Patch leaning back, the glass in his hand, smoking a cigarette. He hadn't touched the food. His eyes were half closed and his head lolled. He didn't look up as we entered.

'We're getting under way,' I told him.

He didn't move.

'Leave him,' Mike said. 'We can manage. I'll go and start the engine.' He was already pulling on a sweater.

But Patch had heard. His head came slowly round. 'Where are you making for— Southampton?' His voice had no life in it.

'No,' I said. 'We're taking you out to the Minkies.'

He stared at me. 'The Minkies.' He repeated it slowly, his fuddled mind not taking it in. 'You're going out to the *Mary Deare*?' And then he was on his feet, the glass crashing to the floor, his body jarring the table. 'You mean it?' He lurched across to me, catching hold of me with both his hands. 'You're not saying that just to keep me quiet. You mean it, don't you?'

'Yes,' I said. 'I mean it.' It was like trying to convince a child.

'My God!' he said. 'My God, I thought I was finished.' He was suddenly laughing, shaking me, gripping Mike's hand. 'I think I'd have gone mad,' he said. 'The uncertainty. Ten years and you get a ship and you're in command again, and then . . . You don't know what it's like when you suddenly lose confidence in yourself.' He pushed his hands up through his hair, his eyes alight and eager. I'd never seen him like that before. He turned and scrabbled up a whole pile of fivers that were lying on the table. 'Here. You take them.' He thrust them into my hand. 'I don't want them. They're yours now.' He wasn't drunk, just a little crazed—the reaction of nerves strung too taut.

I pushed the notes away. 'We'll talk about that later,' I said. 'Can you navigate into the Minkies without a chart?'

His mind seemed to snap suddenly into place. He hesitated—a seaman considering a nautical problem. 'You mean from Les Sauvages to the *Mary Deare*?'

'Yes.'

He nodded slowly. He was frowning, his mind groping for the bearings. 'Yes. Yes, I'm sure I can remember. It's only a question of the tide. You've got a nautical almanac?'

I nodded and it was settled. I had charts for the Channel. All I lacked was the large-scale chart of the Minkies. 'We'll hoist sail in here, before we get the hook up,' I said. I reached for my monkey jacket and slipped it on, and then we went up on deck and got the covers off the main and mizzen. I sent Mike to get the engine going whilst Patch and I put the battens in and hoisted the mainsail, tacking it down so that the luff was set up taut. The starter whined and the engine caught, throbbing at the deck under my feet. *Sea Witch* was suddenly alive. We hoisted the dinghy on board then and the ship bustled with activity as we got her ready for sea.

It was whilst I was up for'ard, hanking the big yankee jib on to the forestay, that I heard it—the beat of an engine coming in from the sea. I stood there for a moment, listening, and then I extinguished the riding light and ran aft, shouting to Mike to get the hook up. It might be just another yacht coming in, but it wasn't the night for yachtsmen to be risking their boats, feeling their way into a place like Lulworth, and I had no desire to be caught in here with Patch on board. We were outside the law and I wanted to get clear of the cove without being seen. I switched off the lights below and sent Patch for'ard to help Mike, and then I was at the wheel and the chain was coming in with a run as I manoeuvred *Sea Witch* up to her anchor on the engine.

The sound of the boat coming in was quite clear now, the beat of its engines throbbing back from the cliffs. The white of her masthead light appeared in the gap, bobbing to the swell. The green eye of a starboard light showed, and then the red as she turned in.

'Up and down,' Mike called.

'Leave it there,' I called to him. 'Hoist the yankee.'

The big jib floated up, a blur of white in the darkness. I hauled in the sheet and *Sea Witch* began to glide through the water as I swung her bows towards the gap. The in-coming boat was right in the entrance now. 'What do you think it is—the police?' Mike asked as he came back aft to help trim the sheets.

'I don't know,' I said. 'Get the mizzen hoisted.' For an instant I saw Patch's face, a white glimmer in the darkness as he stared seaward, and then he went aft to help Mike. I was keeping the engine throttled right back so that they wouldn't hear it above the noise of their own engine, hoping I could slip out without their seeing us in the darkness.

There wasn't a great deal of wind in the cove, but we were moving, steadily gathering way. The other boat came in slowly. She had a spotlight and she flashed it on the rocks by the entrance, holding a middle course between them. And then she was inside and we were bearing straight down on her. Under sail I had no chance of giving her a wide berth. I just had to hold my course and hope that she'd turn away.

But she held straight on and we passed her so close that I could see the whole shape of her, a big sea-going motor boat with flared bow and a long sloping deckhouse. I even caught a glimpse of the man in the wheelhouse, a dim figure peering at us out of the night.

And then their spotlight stabbed the darkness, momentarily blinding me, picking out the triangle of our mainsail in glaring white, and a voice hailed us. I think he was asking the name of our ship, but the words were lost in the roar of the engine as I opened the throttle wide, and we went steaming out through the gap. The sails flapped wildly as we came under the lee of the cliffs and the boat heaved to the swell. Then we were through and the sails filled. *Sea Witch* heeled, the water creaming back from her bows and sliding white past the cockpit as she surged forward under the thrust of power and sail.

'She's turning,' Mike shouted down to me.

I glanced over my shoulder. The motor boat's masthead steaming light and the red and green of her navigation lights were showing in the black outline of the land behind us. She was coming out through the gap.

Mike tumbled into the cockpit, hardening in the main sheet for me as I headed south on a broad reach. With the ship blacked-out—not even a binnacle light—I sailed by the wind, my head turned every now and then over my shoulder to watch the motor boat. Her masthead light began to dance as she met the swell in the entrance, and then it was swinging steadily, rhythmically as she pitched to the sea, and the red and green of her navigation lights remained fixed on us like two eyes. Her spotlight stabbed the darkness, showing glimpses of black, lumpy water as it probed the night.

'If we'd got away half an hour earlier . . .' Patch was staring aft.

'And if we'd been five minutes later,' Mike snapped, 'you'd be under arrest.' His voice sounded on edge and I knew he didn't like it any more than I did. 'I'll go and get the anchor on board.' He disappeared for'ard and I sent Patch to help him.

It was cold in the cockpit now that we were under way. But I don't think I noticed it. I was wondering about the boat behind us. It had gained on us slightly and the spotlight,

292

reaching out to us across the tumbled waters, lit our sails with a ghostly radiance. It didn't probe any longer, but was held on us, so that I knew they'd picked us out. The drizzle had slackened again and our white sails made us conspicuous.

Up for'ard Mike was coiling down the halyards, whilst Patch lashed the anchor. They came aft together. 'John. Hadn't we better heave-to?'

'They haven't ordered you to.' Patch's voice was hard and urgent. 'You don't have to do anything till they signal instructions.' He was back at sea again and a man doesn't easily give up in his own element. He came down into the cockpit. His face had tightened so that there was strength in it again. 'Well, are you going on or not?' It wasn't exactly a challenge, certainly not a threat, and yet the way he said it made me wonder what he'd do if I refused.

Mike jerked round, his body bunched, his quick temper flaring. 'If we want to heave-to, we will.'

The spotlight was switched off. Sudden blackness descended on us. 'I was asking Sands.' Patch's voice trembled out of the darkness.

'John and I own this boat jointly,' Mike flung out. 'We've worked and planned and slaved our guts out to have our own outfit, and we're not going to risk it all to get you out of the mess you're in.' He stepped down into the

293

cockpit, balancing himself to the pitch of the boat. 'You've got to heave-to,' he said to me. 'That boat is gradually coming up on us and when the police find we've got Patch on board, it's going to be damned hard to prove that we weren't slipping him out of the country, especially with all that cash sculling around below.' He leaned forward, gripping hold of my shoulder. 'Do you hear me, John?' He was shouting at me above the noise of the engine. 'You've got to heave-to before that police boat comes up on us.'

'It may not be the police,' I said. I had been thinking about it all the time they'd been up for'ard. 'The police would have sent a patrol car. They wouldn't have come by boat.'

'If it's not the police, then who the hell is it?'

I glanced over my shoulder, wondering whether perhaps imagination hadn't got the better of reason. But there was the boat, still following us. The white steaming light was swaying wildly, showing the slender stick of her mast and the outline of the deckhouse. 'She certainly rolls,' I murmured.

'What's that?'

I turned to him then. 'Did you get a good look at her, Mike, as we came out?'

'Yes. Why?'

'What sort of boat was she—could you see?'

'An old Parkhurst, I should say.' Mike's training as a marine engineer had given him a quite remarkable knowledge of power craft.

'You're certain of that?'

'I think so. Yes, I'm sure she was.'

I asked him to go down below then and look up *Griselda* in Lloyd's Register. 'And if she's in the book and her description fits, then I'd like an estimate of her speed.'

He hesitated, glancing quickly from me to Patch, and then he disappeared for'ard towards the main hatch. 'And if it is *Griselda*?' Patch asked.

'Then she was chartered this morning,' I said. 'By somebody who was in that Court.'

The spotlight was on us again and he was staring at me. 'Are you sure?'

I nodded and I could see him working it out for himself. *Sea Witch* heeled to a gust of wind and I felt the drag of the prop. Spray splashed my face. And then Mike was back. 'How did you know it was *Griselda*?' he asked me.

'I was right, was I?'

'Yes—it's either *Griselda* or a sister ship. Fifty-foot over all. Built by Parkhurst in 1931.'

'And her top speed?'

'Hard to say. She's got two six-cylinder Parkhurst engines. But they're the original engines and it depends how they've been maintained. Flat out, I'd say she might do a little over eight knots.'

*Sea Witch* was heeling farther now and the wave-tops were lopping over on to the foredeck. 'In calm water.'

'Yes, in calm water.'

The wind was rising and already the seas were beginning to break. I was thinking that in a little over two hours the tide would turn. It would be west-going then and the freshening wind would kick up a short, steep sea. It would reduce *Griselda*'s speed by at least a knot. 'I'm standing on,' I told Mike. 'We'll try and shake them off during the night.' And then I explained about the yacht broker I had met with Hal and how Higgins had warned me. 'Higgins even guessed you'd come down to Lulworth,' I said to Patch.

'Higgins!' He turned and stared aft. The spotlight was on his face and there was something in the way his eyes shone—it might have been anger or fear or exultation; I couldn't tell. And then the spotlight was switched off and he was just a black shape standing there beside me.

'Well, if it's only the Dellimare Company—' Mike's voice sounded relieved. 'They can't do anything, can they?'

Patch swung round on him. 'You don't seem to realize . . .' His voice came hard and abrupt out of the darkness, the sentence bitten off short. But I had caught his mood and I looked back over my shoulder. Was it my imagination or was the motor boat nearer now? I found myself looking all round, searching for the lights of another ship. But there was nothing— only the blackness of the night and the white of the breaking wave-tops rushing at us out of the

296

darkness. 'Well, we go on. Is that right?' I wasn't sure what I ought to do.

'You've no alternative,' Patch said.

'Haven't we?' Mike stepped down into the cockpit. 'We could run for Poole. That boat's following us and ... Well, I think we should turn the whole thing over to the authorities.' His voice sounded nervous.

A wave broke against the weather bow, showering spray aft, and we heeled to a gust so that our lee decks were awash. The sea was shallower here. There were overfalls and *Sea Witch* pitched violently with a short, uncomfortable motion, the screw juddering under the stern and the bows slamming into the waves so that water was sluicing across the foredeck. 'For God's sake cut that engine!' Patch shouted at me. 'Can't you feel the drag of the prop?'

Mike swung round on him. 'You don't run this boat.'

'It's stopping our speed,' Patch said.

He was right. I had been conscious of it for some time. 'Switch it off, will you, Mike?' I asked.

He hesitated and then dived into the charthouse. The noise of the engine died, leaving a stillness in which the sound of the sea seemed unnaturally loud. Under sail alone, the boat merged with the elements for which she had been designed, fitting herself to the pattern of wind and wave. The movement was easier. Waves ceased to break over the foredeck.

But though Patch had been right, Mike came back out of the charthouse in a mood of blazing anger. 'You seem bloody certain we're going to try and race that boat for you,' he said. And then, turning to me, he added, 'Take my advice, John. Turn down-wind and head for Poole.'

'Down-wind,' Patch said, 'the motor boat will be faster than you.'

'Well, head up-wind then and make for Weymouth.'

'It's a dead beat,' I said.

And Patch added, 'Either way she'll overhaul you.'

'What's the matter?' Mike demanded. 'They can't do anything. They've got the law on their side. That's all. They can't do anything.'

'God Almighty!' Patch said. 'Don't you understand yet?' He leaned forward, his face thrust close to mine. 'You tell him, Sands. You've met Gundersen. You know the set-up now.' He stared at me, and then he swung round to face Mike again. 'Listen!' he said. 'Here was a plan to clean up over a quarter of a million pounds. The cargo was switched and sold to the Chinks. That part of it went all right. But all the rest went wrong. The captain refused to play his part. They tried to sink her in a gale and they failed. Higgins was left to do the job on his own and he botched it.' His voice was pitched high in the urgency of his effort to communicate what he believed. 'Can't you see it from their point of view ... twelve men drowned, an old man dead, possibly murdered, and the ship herself lying out there on the Minkies. They daren't let me reach the *Mary Deare*. And they daren't let you reach her either. They daren't even let you get into port now—not until they've disposed of the *Mary Deare*.'

Mike stared at him. 'But that's fantastic,' he breathed.

'Why fantastic? They must know I'm on board. And you wouldn't have sailed if you hadn't believed my story. Imagine what they face if the truth comes out.'

Mike turned to me. 'Do you believe this, John?' His face was very pale. He sounded bewildered.

'I think we'd better try and shake them off,' I said. Patch had his own reasons for driving us on. But I knew I didn't want that boat to catch up with us in the dark.

'But good God! This is the English Channel. They can't do anything to us here.' He stared at Patch and myself, waiting for us to answer him. 'Well, what the hell can they do?' And then he looked out at the blackness that surrounded us, realizing gradually that it made no difference that we were in the Channel. There were just the three of us alone in a black waste of tumbled water that spilled to white on

299

the crests, and without another word he got the log line out of the locker and went aft to stream it astern.

'We go on then,' Patch said. The sudden relief from tension made his voice sound tired. It reminded me that he had had no sleep the night before and no food, that for days he'd been under a great strain.

Mike came back into the cockpit. 'I think we're holding them now,' he said. I glanced back at *Griselda*. Her navigation lights were masked every now and then by the marching wave-tops. 'When the tide turns,' I said, 'we'll beat up to windward and see if that will shake them off.' I got up stiffly from behind the wheel. 'Will you take the first watch, Mike?' It would have to be two hours on and four off, with one man alone at the wheel and the other two on call. We were desperately shorthanded for a hard sail like this. I gave him the wheel and went through into the charthouse to enter up the log.

Patch followed me in. 'Have you thought about who will be on board that motor boat?' he asked me. I shook my head, wondering what was coming, and he added, 'It won't be Gundersen, you know.'

'Who will it be then?'

'Higgins.'

'What's it matter which of them it is?' I asked. 'What are you trying to tell me?'

'Just this,' he said earnestly. 'Gundersen is a

man who would only take calculated risks. But
if Higgins is in control of that boat...' He
stared at me, watching to see whether I had
understood his point.

'You mean he's desperate?'

'Yes.' Patch looked at me for a moment.
'There's no need to tell young Duncan. If
Higgins doesn't stop us before we get to that
salvage tug, he's done for. When he's arrested,
the others will panic. Burrows, for one, will
turn Queen's evidence. You understand?' He
turned away then. 'I'll go and get some food
inside me.' But in the doorway he hesitated.
'I'm sorry,' he said. 'I didn't mean to land you
in a thing like this.'

I finished entering up the log and turned in,
fully-clothed, on the charthouse bunk. But I
didn't sleep much. The movement was
uncomfortable, and every time I looked out
through the open doorway I could see
*Griselda*'s lights bobbing in the darkness astern
of us, and then I would listen to the sound of
the wind in the rigging, alert for the slightest
indication that it was slackening. Twice Mike
had to call me out to help him winch in the
sheets, and at two o'clock I took over the helm.

The tide had turned and the seas were steep
and breaking. We altered course to south-west,
sheeting in the sails till they were almost flat as
we came on to the wind. It was cold then with
the wind on our faces and the spray slatting
against our oilskins as *Sea Witch* beat to

windward, bucking the seas and busting the wave-tops open, water cascading from her bows.

Behind us, *Griselda*'s navigation lights followed our change of course and the white of her masthead light danced crazily in the night as she wallowed and pitched and rolled in our wake. But a power boat doesn't fit herself to the pattern of the water the way a boat under sail does and gradually the red and green lights dipped more frequently below the level of the waves, until at last all we could see was her steaming light dancing like a will-o'-the-wisp on the wave-tops.

Mike's voice reached out to me through the noise of wind and sea: 'We've got them now.' He was excited. 'If we go about . . .' The rest of it was lost on me, whipped away by the wind, drowned in the crash of a wave bursting against the bows. But I knew what was in his mind. If we went on to the other tack, sailing north-west, instead of south-west, there was a good chance that they wouldn't notice our change of course, even though the night had become brilliant with stars. And once clear of them we could turn downwind, get to the east of them and make for the Alderney Race.

There is no doubt in my mind now that Mike was right and, had I done as he suggested, the disaster for which we were headed might have been avoided. But the changed motion induced by our heading into the wind had brought Patch on deck. I could see him sitting on the main hatch, staring aft for glimpses of *Griselda*, and I wondered what his reaction would be if we went over on to the port tack, heading back towards the English coast. Also, we were over-canvassed, and when you go about there are backstays to set up as well as the sheets to handle; one slip and we could lose out mast!

'I don't like it,' I told Mike. We were short-handed and it was night. Also, of course, in those conditions, when you are tired and cold and wet, there is a great temptation to sit tight and do nothing. I thought we were drawing ahead of them.

Apparently Mike had the same thought, for, instead of pressing his point, he shrugged his shoulders and went into the charthouse to turn in. It seems extraordinary to me now that I didn't appreciate the significance of the fact that *Griselda*'s light was no longer showing astern of us, but way out on the port quarter. Had I done so, I should have known that we were not gaining on her, merely diverging from her. She was steering a more southerly course, maintaining her speed by avoiding the head-on battering of the seas. And I for my part—as so often happens at night—thought our own speed was greater than it was.

By the end of my watch it was clouding over and the wind was slackening. I called Patch and when he came up, we eased the sheets and altered course to sou'-sou'-west. We were no longer butting into the seas then, but following the lines of the waves with a wild, swooping movement. The wind was free and *Sea Witch* was going like a train.

I heated some soup then and we drank it in the cockpit, watching the dawn break. It came with a cold, bleak light and Patch stood, staring aft. But there was nothing to be seen but a waste of grey, tumbled water. 'It's all right,' I said. 'We've left them way behind.'

He nodded, not saying anything. His face looked grey. 'At this rate we'll raise the Casquets inside of two hours,' I said, and I left him then and went below to get some sleep.

An hour later Mike woke me, shouting to me to come up on deck, his voice urgent. 'Look over there, John,' he said as I emerged from the hatch. He was pointing away to port and, at first, I could see nothing. My sleep-dimmed eyes absorbed the cold daylight and the drabness of sea and sky, and then on the lift of a wave I thought I saw something, a stick maybe or a spar-buoy raised aloft out there where the march of the waves met the horizon. I screwed up my eyes, focusing them, and the next time I balanced to the upward swoop of the deck, I saw it clearly—the mast of a small ship. It lifted itself up out of the waves and behind it came the hull of the boat itself, drab white in the morning light.

'*Griselda?*' I said.

Mike nodded and passed me the glasses. She was certainly rolling. I could see the water streaming off her and every now and then a wave burst against her bows, throwing up a cloud of spray. 'If we'd gone about last night . . .'

'Well, we didn't,' I said. I glanced aft to where Patch sat hunched over the wheel in borrowed oilskins. 'Does he know?' I asked.

'Yes. He saw her first.'

'What did he say?'

'Nothing. He didn't seem surprised.'

I stared at the boat through the glasses again, trying to estimate her speed. 'What are we doing?' I asked. 'Did you get a log reading at six?'

'Yes. We did eight in the last hour.'

Eight knots! I glanced up at the sails. They were wind-bellied out, tight and hard, solid tons of weight pulling at the mast, hauling the boat through the water. My God! it was hard that we hadn't shaken them off after a whole night of sailing.

'I've been thinking,' Mike said. 'If they come up with us . . .'

'Well?'

'There's not much they can do really, is there? I mean . . .' He hesitated, glancing at me uncertainly.

'I hope you're right,' I said and went into the charthouse. I was tired and I didn't want to think about it. I worked out our dead-

305

reckoning, based on miles logged, courses sailed and tides, and found we were ten miles north-north-west of the Casquets. In two hours' time the tide would be east-going, setting us in towards Alderney and the Cherbourg Peninsula. But that damned boat lay between us and the coast, and there was no getting away from her, not in daylight.

I stayed on in the charthouse and got the forecast: wind moderating later, some fog patches locally. A depression centred over the Atlantic was moving slowly east.

Shortly after breakfast we raised the Casquets—the north-western bastion of the Channel Islands. The tide turned and began to run against us and we had the Casquets with us for a long time, a grey, spiked helmet of a rock against which the seas broke. We thrashed our way through the steamer lane that runs up-Channel from Ushant, seeing only two ships, and those hull-down on the horizon. And then we raised Guernsey Island and the traffic in the steamer lane was just smudges of smoke where sky and sea met.

All morning Patch remained on deck, taking his trick at the helm, dozing in the cockpit or sitting staring at the grey acres that separated us from *Griselda*. Sometimes he would dive into the charthouse and work frenziedly with parallel rule and dividers, checking our course and our E.T.A. at the Minkies. Once I suggested that he went below and got some sleep, but all he said was 'Sleep? I can't sleep till I see the *Mary Deare.*' And he stayed there, grey and exhausted, existing on his nerves, as he had done all through the Enquiry.

I think he was afraid to go below—afraid that when he couldn't see her *Griselda* would somehow creep up on us. He was frighteningly tired. He kept on asking me about the tides. We had no tidal chart and it worried him. Even when the tide turned around midday, pushing us westward again, he kept on checking our bearing on the jagged outline of Guernsey Island.

I should perhaps explain that the tidal surge of six hours flood and six hours ebb that shifts the whole body of water of the English Channel builds up to an extraordinary peak in the great bight of the French coast that contains the Channel Islands. At 'springs', when the tides are greatest, it sluices in and out of the narrow gap between Alderney and the mainland at a rate of up to 7 knots. Its direction in the main body of the Channel Islands rotates throughout the twelve hours. Moreover, the rise and fall of tide is as much as from 30 to 40 feet.

I mention this to explain our preoccupation with the tide and because it has a bearing on what followed. Moreover, the whole area being strewn with submerged reefs, rock outcrops and islands, there is always a sense of tension when navigating in this section of the Channel.

Holding to our course, we were headed direct for the central mass of Guernsey. I was relying on the westward thrust of the tide to push us clear, and as we closed with the broken water that marked the submerged rocks known as Les Frettes, we were all of us watching to see what *Griselda* would do. In fact, she had no alternative, and when the rock cliffs of the island were close to port she altered course to come in astern of us.

The westernmost tip of Guernsey is marked by Les Hanois, a lighthouse set seaward on a group of rocks. We passed so close that we could see every detail of it—the cormorants standing like vultures on the rocks and the swell breaking white all along the edge; and dead astern of us *Griselda* followed in our wake, pitching and rolling with the spray flying from her bow wave. She was less than a quarter of a mile away and Patch stood with his body braced against the charthouse, staring at her through the glasses.

'Well,' I said, 'is it Higgins?' I could see a figure moving on the deck.

'Yes,' he said. 'Yes, it's Higgins all right. And Yules, too. There's another of them in the wheelhouse, but I can't see who it is.'

He handed me the glasses. I could recognize Higgins all right. He was standing by the rail, staring at us, his big body balanced to the movement of the boat. Higgins and Yule and Patch—three of the men who had sailed the

308

*Mary Deare*! And here we were, within forty miles of where the ship was stranded.

Mike was at the wheel and he suddenly called on me. 'If we turn now, we could make Peter Port ahead of them.'

It was a straight run before the wind along the southern coast of the island. We could make St Martin's Point without their gaining on us and then a few miles under engine and we should be in Peter Port. I glanced at Patch. He had stepped down into the cockpit. 'I'll relieve you,' he said. It wasn't a suggestion. It was an order.

'No,' Mike was staring at him, anger flaring up into his eyes.

'I said I'll relieve you.' Patch reached for the wheel.

'I heard what you said.' Mike swung the wheel over, shouting to me to ease the sheets. But Patch had his hands on the wheel, too. Standing, he had more purchase and he slowly got it back, holding it there whilst Mike shouted obscenities at him. Their two faces were within a foot of each other—Patch's hard and tense, Mike's livid with rage. They were like that for a long two minutes, held immobile by the counteracting force of their muscles like two statues.

And then the moment when we had any choice of action was past. *Griselda*, clear of Les Hanois rocks, was altering course to get between us and Peter Port. Patch had seen it and he said, 'You've no choice now.' He hadn't relaxed his grip of the wheel, but the tension was out of his voice. Mike stopped cursing at him. He seemed to understand, for he turned his head and stared at the motor boat. Then he let go of the wheel and stood up. 'Since you appear to be skippering this boat, you'd better bloody well steer her. But by Christ!' he added, 'if anything happens to her . . .' He stared coldly at me, still trembling with anger, and went below.

'I'm sorry,' Patch said. He had seated himself at the wheel and his voice was weary.

'This isn't your boat,' I reminded him.

He shrugged his shoulders, looking round at *Griselda*. 'What else did you expect me to do?'

There was no point in discussing it. We were committed now to go on until we reached the *Mary Deare*. But if the wind dropped . . . 'Suppose Higgins catches up with us?' I said.

He looked at me quickly. 'He mustn't. And then he added, 'We've got to get there first.'

'Yes, but suppose he does?' I was thinking that after all Higgins had got to keep within the law. 'He can't do very much.'

'No?' He laughed a little wildly. 'How do you know what Higgins can do? He's frightened.' He looked at me, sideways out of the corners of his eyes. 'Wouldn't you be frightened if you were Higgins?' And then he glanced up at the sails and his voice was quiet and practical again as he asked me to ease the sheets and he altered course for the north-west Minkies buoy.

After that we didn't talk any more and gradually I became conscious of the sound of the motor boat's engine. It was very faint at first, a gentle undertone to the swish of the sea going past, but it warned me that the wind was easing. The overcast had thinned and a humid glare hung over the water so that the outline of Jersey Island away to port was barely visible. I started the engine and from that moment I knew *Griselda* would overtake us.

The forecast announced that the depression over the Atlantic was deepening, moving eastwards faster. But it wouldn't help us. All the time the wind was dropping now and *Griselda* was coming up abeam of us, keeping between us and Jersey Island. The glare faded, leaving sea and sky a chill, luminous grey. There was no horizon any more. Patch went below to get some more clothes. It had suddenly become much colder and the wind was fluky, blowing in sudden puffs.

I sat at the wheel and watched *Griselda* draw steadily ahead of the beam, wallowing in the swell. I wondered what Higgins would do, what I would do in his place. I tried to think it out rationally. But it's difficult to think rationally when you're cold and tired and sitting alone, almost at water level, isolated in an opaque void. That sense of isolation! I had felt it at sea before, but never so strongly. And now it chilled me with a feeling of foreboding. The sea had an oily look as the big swells lumbered up from the west and rolled beneath us.

I didn't notice the fog at first. I was thinking of Higgins—and then suddenly a grey-white plasma was creeping towards us across the sea, shrouding and enveloping the water in its folds. Mike came up from below and I gave him the wheel, shouting for Patch to come on deck. *Griselda* had seen the fog, too, and she had turned in towards us. I watched her coming, waiting for the fog to close round us and hide us from her. 'We'll go about as soon as we lose sight of her,' I said as Patch came up through the hatch.

She wasn't more than two cables away when her outline blurred and then she vanished, swallowed abruptly. 'Lee-ho!' Mike called and spun the wheel. *Sea Witch* turned into the wind and through it, the big yankee flapping as I let go the jib sheet. And then the main boom was across and Patch and I were winching in the starboard jib sheet as we gathered way on the port tack.

We were doubling back on our tracks through a cold, dead, clammy world and I straightened up, listening to the beat of the motor boat's engines, trying to estimate her position, wondering whether the fog was thick enough for us to lose her.

But Higgins must have guessed what we'd do, or else we had lost too much time in going about, for the sound of *Griselda*'s engines was abeam of us, and, just as I realized this, the shape of her reappeared. Her bows seemed to rip the curtain of fog apart and suddenly the whole of her was visible, coming straight for us.

She was coming in at right-angles, her engines running flat-out and her sharp bows cutting into the swell, spray flying up past her wheelhouse. I shouted to Mike to go about again. We were heeled over, going fast and I knew that if both boats held their course we must hit. And when he didn't do anything, my throat was suddenly dry. 'Put her about!' I yelled at him. And at the same moment Patch shouted, 'Turn man! For God's sake turn!'

But Mike stood there, his body braced against the wheel, staring at the on-coming boat with a set expression on his face. 'Let him turn,' he said through his clenched teeth. 'I'm holding on.'

Patch jumped down into the cockpit. 'He's going to ram you.'

'He wouldn't dare.' And Mike held obstinately to his course, watching *Griselda* through narrowed eyes, his face suddenly white. Out of the corner of my eye I saw Higgins lean out of his wheelhouse. He was shouting and his powerful voice reached across to us through the roar of engines—'Stand by! I'm coming alongside.' And then *Griselda* was turning, swinging to come in on our bows and crowd us up into the wind.

Everything happened very fast then. Mike shouted at us to ease the sheets. 'I'm going to cut under her stern.' He turned the wheel and *Sea Witch* began to swing her bows in towards the motor boat. *Griselda* was halfway through her turn. There was just room for us to pass astern of her if we turned quickly.

But things went wrong. I eased out on the jib sheet, but Patch, unaccustomed to sail, failed to ease out on the main. And at the same moment we heeled to a puff of wind. It was that unlucky puff of wind that did it. With the full weight of it on the mainsail, *Sea Witch* failed to come round fast enough. And Higgins had throttled down to bring his boat alongside us. We drove straight into *Griselda*'s counter, drove straight into it with all the force of our powerful engine and tons of wind-driven canvas. We caught her on the port side just a few feet from her stern as it was swinging in towards us on the turn. There was a rending, splintering crash; our bows reared up as though to climb over her and then we stopped with a horrible, jarring shudder. I caught a glimpse of Yules, staring open-mouthed, and then I was flung forward against the charthouse. The boom jerked free of the mast and swung in towards me. I threw up my arm and it caught my shoulder a shattering blow, wrenching it from its socket and flinging me against the guardrails.

I remember clutching at the guardrails,

blinded with pain, and then I was lying on the deck, my face pressed close against a metal jib sheet lead and the noise of rending wood was still there and somebody was screaming. I shifted myself and pain stabbed through me. I was looking down into the water and a man's body drifted past. It was Yules and he was thrashing wildly at the water, his face white and scared, with a lock of hair washed over his eyes.

The deck vibrated under me. It was as though compressed-air drills had been put to work on the hull. I could feel the juddering all through my body. 'You all right?' Mike reached a hand down and dragged me to my feet. My teeth clenched on my lip.

'The bastard!' He was staring for'ard, his face paper-white, all the freckles showing a dull orange against his pasty skin, and his hair flaming red. 'I'll kill him.' He was shaking with anger.

I turned to see Higgins erupt from *Griselda*'s wheelhouse. He was shouting something, his great bellowing voice audible above the noise of the engines and the continuing, rending sound of wood. The two boats were locked together and he caught hold of our bowsprit, his teeth bared like an animal, his head sunk into his bull neck and his shoulder muscles bunched as he tried to tear the boats apart with his bare hands.

Mike moved then. He had the grim,

315

avenging look of a man who has seen something he loves and has worked for wantonly smashed-up. I called to him, for the fool was running for'ard up the sloped deck, yelling at Higgins, cursing him; and he flung himself from the bowsprit, straight at the man, hitting out at him in a blind fury of rage.

The boats separated then with a tearing of wood and bubbling of water and I didn't see any more. Patch had put our engine into reverse and I staggered into the cockpit, shouting at him to stop. 'Mike is still there. You can't leave him.'

'Do you want the belly torn out of your boat?' he demanded, turning the wheel as *Sea Witch* began to go astern. 'Those props were drilling the guts out of her.' Dimly I realized that he meant *Grizelda*'s props and understood what had caused the deck planks to vibrate under my body.

I turned and watched as the gap between us and the motor boat widened. *Grizelda* was down by the stern with a hole torn out of her port quarter as though a battering ram had hit her. Higgins was going back into the wheelhouse. There was nobody else on her deck. I suddenly felt sick and tired. 'What happened to him?' I asked. The sickly-sweet taste of blood was in my mouth where I'd bitten through my lip. My arm and all that side of my body was heavy and numb with pain. 'Did you see what happened?'

'He's all right,' Patch said. 'Just knocked cold.' He started to ask me about my shoulder, but I was telling him to get into forward gear and start sailing again. 'Don't lose her!' Already *Griselda*'s outlines were fading and a moment later she disappeared. Patch had put the gear lever into neutral and we could hear her engines then, racing with an ugly, grinding noise. There was a sharp report and, a little later, another. After that we couldn't hear her any more.

'Prop shafts by the sound of it,' Patch said.

Sails and mast and boat began to spin before my eyes and I sat down. Patch seemed immensely tall, standing at the wheel, and his head swung dizzily over me. I steadied myself and the roll of a swell lapped into the cockpit. I stared at it stupidly, watching the water roll back down the forward-sloping deck. And then the engine spluttered and gave out.

I shook my head, bracing myself against the dizziness that threatened to overwhelm me. There was nobody at the helm. I called to Patch and struggled to my feet. He came up out of the main hatch, his trousers dripping. 'It's up to the galley already.' And then my eyes took in the tilt of the deck, following it down to where the bowsprit was buried in the back of a wave. All the foredeck was awash. I stared at it, taking it in slowly, whilst he pushed past me into the charthouse. He came out with a jack-knife in his hand. 'She's going down,' I said. My voice sounded dead and hopeless in my ears.

'Yes,' he said. 'Not much time.' And he began slashing at the dinghy tie-ers. I watched him hoist the pram over so that she fell with her keel on the guardrails and he was able to slide her into the water.

We were still sailing, moving sluggishly through the water, and over Patch's back, as he bent to secure the dinghy painter, I caught a glimpse of the *Griselda* again, a vague shape rolling sluggishly on the edge of visibility.

'Is there any food up here?' Patch was gathering up things from the charthouse and tossing them into the dinghy—blankets, duffle coats, torches, flares, even the hand-bearing compass.

'Some chocolate.' I got it from the drawer of the chart table—three small slabs and some sweets. I got life-jackets, too, from the locker aft. But my movements were slow and clumsy and by the time I had dropped them in the dinghy the whole length of the deck was awash, the mast tilted forward and the foot of the yankee below the water.

'Quick!' Patch said. 'In you get.' He was already untying the painter. I clambered in. It wasn't difficult. The dinghy rode level with the deck. He followed me and pushed off.

I never saw her go down. As we rowed away from her, she slowly disappeared into the fog, her stern a little cocked-up, the big jib and the mizzen still set, and nothing but sea for'ard of the charthouse. She looked a strange sight—like the ghost of a ship doomed everlastingly to sail herself under. I could have wept as she faded and was suddenly gone.

I turned then to look at *Griselda*. She was lying like a log, badly down by the stern and rolling slowly to the long swell—as useless as only a motor boat can be when her engines are out of action. 'Pull on your right,' I told Patch.

He stared at me, not saying anything, his body moving rhythmically to the swing of the oars. 'For God's sake pull on your right,' I said. 'You're still not headed for *Griselda*.'

'We're not going to *Griselda*.'

I didn't understand for a moment. 'But where else . . .' My voice broke off abruptly and I felt suddenly deadly scared. He had the box of the hand-bearing compass set up at his feet, the lid open. His eyes were watching it as he rowed. He was steering a compass course. 'My God!' I cried. 'You're not going to try and make it in the dinghy?'

'Why not?'

'But what about Mike?' I was suddenly desperate. I could see Higgins struggling to get his dinghy into the water. 'You can't do it.' I seized hold of his hand as he leaned forward, gripping hold of one of the oars, pain bursting like an explosive charge in my body. 'You can't do it, I tell you.'

He stared at me, his face only a foot or two

from mine. 'No?' His voice grated in the stillness, and faint across the water came a cry for help—a desperate, long drawn-out cry. He wrenched the oar free of me and began to row again. 'If you don't like it, you can get out and swim for it like that poor bastard.' He nodded across his left shoulder and at the same moment the cry came again. This time I was able to pick him out on the lift of a swell, a black head and two dripping arms thrashing their way towards us. 'H-e-l-p!'

Patch rowed on, ignoring the cry. 'Are you going to leave him to drown?' I said, leaning forward, trying with my voice to touch some spark of humanity in him.

'It's Yules,' he answered. 'Let Higgins pick him up.'

'And Mike?' I said. 'What about Mike?'

'He'll be all right. That boat isn't going to sink.'

The oars dipped and rose, dipped and rose, his body swinging back and forth. And I sat there and watched him row away from the man. What else could I do? My shoulder had been driven out of its socket; he had only to touch it to send pain searing through me, and he knew it. I thought maybe he was right about the boat. It was only the stern that was damaged. All the fore part would be water-tight. And Higgins would pick Yules up. He had his dinghy launched now and was pulling away from *Griselda*. In the weird, fog-belt light

320

he looked like a giant specimen of those insects that are called water-boatmen. Yules had seen him coming and had ceased to thrash about in the water. He was directly between us and Higgins and he lay still in the water, not crying out any more, just waiting to be picked up.

I don't know why I should have stayed, twisted round like that, in a position that gave me a lot of pain. But I felt I had to see him picked up. I had to know that there was no justification for the feeling of horror that had suddenly gripped me.

Higgins was rowing fast, a long, sweeping stroke that was full of power, and at each pull a little froth of white water showed at the dinghy's blunt bows. Every now and then he turned and looked over his shoulder, and I knew that it was at us he was looking and not at the man in the water.

We were pulling away from Yules all the time and I couldn't be sure how near Higgins was to him. But I heard Yules call out. 'Alf!' And he raised one hand. 'I'm here.' The words were distinct and very clear in the stillness of the fog. And then suddenly he was shouting and swimming with frantic desperation, his arms flailing the water, his feet kicking at the surface.

But Higgins never checked, never spoke a word to him. He left him to drown and the oars dipped and rose with terrible regularity, the water streaming from them at every stroke as he came after us.

There was one last despairing cry, and then silence. Sickened, I turned to look at Patch. 'It's a bigger dinghy than ours,' he said. He meant it as an explanation. He meant that Higgins couldn't afford to stop—not if he was to catch up with us. His face was white. He was rowing harder now, the sweat glistening on his forehead. His words sent a cold shiver through me, and I sat there, rigid, all pain momentarily forgotten.

After that I was conscious all the time of the dinghy behind us. I can see it still, like a deadly water-beetle crawling after us across the sea, everlastingly following us through an unreal miasma of fog; and I can hear the creak of the rowlocks, the dip and splash of the oars. And I can see Patch, too, his set face leaning towards me and then pulling back, endlessly moving back and forth as he tugged at the oars, tugged till his teeth were clenched with the pain of his blistered hands, until the blisters broke and the blood dripped on the oars—hour after wretched hour.

At one time Higgins was less than fifty yards behind us and I could see every detail of his boat. It was a gay blue metal dinghy, a little battered, with the paint flaking and dulled with age, and round the gunn'ls was a heavy canvas fend-off. The thing was meant to hold five or six people and it had bluff bows so that every time he pulled it smiled an ugly, puffy smile as the thrust piled the water up in front of it.

But he had used his brute strength recklessly and he didn't gain on us any more.

The fog thinned out as night fell until it was no more than a tattered veil through which we caught glimpses of the stars. The young moon gave it a queer luminosity so that we could still see Higgins following us, little drops of phosphorescence marking the oar blades as they lifted clear of the water.

We stopped once and Patch managed to jerk my shoulder back into its socket, and a little later I moved over to the centre thwart and took the left oar, rowing one-handed. Though I was in considerable pain, we were fairly well balanced, for by then he was very tired.

We continued like that all night, holding our course by the hand-bearing compass that stood at our feet, its card glowing faintly. The moon set and the luminosity faded. We lost sight of Higgins. A wind sprang up and waves broke on the swell, slopping water over the gunn'ls. But it died away again about four and at last the stars paled in the first glimmer of returning daylight. It was one of those cold, cloud-streaked dawns that come reluctantly. It showed a lumpy sea, full of tidal swirls, and a blanket of fog lay ahead of us, clamped down between us and the coast of France.

We breakfasted on three squares of chocolate. It was half of all we had left. The woodwork of the dinghy was beaded with dew, our clothes sodden with it. Water slopped about over the floorboards as we pitched in the sea, and in our exhaustion it was becoming more and more difficult to row a course. 'How much farther?' I gasped.

Patch looked at me, his face grey, the eyes deep-sunk. 'I don't know,' he breathed. His lips were all cracked and rimed with salt. He frowned, trying to concentrate his mind. 'Tide's west-going. Be with us in two hours.' He dipped his hand in the sea and wiped salt water over his face. 'Shouldn't be long.'

Not long! I gritted my teeth. The salt was behind my eyeballs, in my mouth; it pricked my skin. The dawn's chill gripped me. I wished to God I'd never met this gaunt stranger who rowed like death at my shoulder. My mind blurred to a vision of Mike and our plans. And now the future was dead, *Sea Witch* gone and nothing in the world to think about but the Minkies, with each stroke an agony.

The sea at dawn had been empty. I could have sworn it had been empty. I had searched it carefully—every trough, every swirl, every sudden humped-up heap of water. There had been nothing—absolutely nothing. And now, suddenly, I was looking at a speck away over Patch's shoulder. The sun was coming up in a great ball of fire and the clouds that streaked the east were glowing orange and blazing to red at their edges—and all this vivid surge of colour, imprinted in the sea, seemed designed solely to show me that speck etched black in silhouette. It was a boat with two oars and a man rowing.

Ten minutes later the fog folded its clammy blanket round us again. The speck blurred and vanished. And at that moment I thought I heard a bell, very faint to the east of us. But when we stopped rowing it was gone. There wasn't a sound, except the sea. It was all round us in our grey, boxed-in world—the wet slop of water. But a little later there was a murmuring and a sucking in the veil through which our eyes couldn't see, and almost immediately the fog darkened, became black, and a shape slid past us like the towering superstructure of a battleship. It was there for an instant, blurred and indistinct, a great mass of black rock with the swell frothing gently at its base, and then it was gone as the tide hurried us on. 'My God! We're there,' I gasped.

We had stopped rowing and all around us was the murmur of the sea. Another rock appeared out of the grey curtain of the fog, a sinister pillar of rock like a crooked finger that slid stealthily by with a froth of white water at its foot as though it were sailing past us. For a moment that damnable fog almost convinced me that I was in a geological nightmare in which the rocks steamed through the water under their own power. And then a swell came up, grew big and broke suddenly. Water surged over the gunn'l and we were thrown backwards as the dinghy hit a submerged rock. The tide swung us round and dragged us clear before the next swell broke. We were soaked, the dinghy half full of water. It was hopeless to go on with the tide swirling us through a maze of dangerous rocks. We had reached the Minkies, but in an area of reefs almost twenty miles by ten we had no hope of getting our bearings. 'We'll have to wait till the fog clears,' Patch said. 'It's too dangerous—almost dead low water.'

In the lee of an ugly island of rock we found a little inlet where the water was still, like glass, tied the dinghy to an upended slab and clambered stiffly out. We stamped and moved about, but the sweat still clung to us in an icy film and we shivered under our sodden duffle coats. We ate the last of our chocolate and talked a little, grateful for the sound of our voices in that cold, dismal place.

I suppose it was inevitable that Patch should have talked about the *Mary Deare*. We were so close to her, frustrated by the fog. He talked about Rice for a bit and then he was telling me about Taggart's death. He seemed to want to talk about it. 'Poor devil!' he whispered. 'For the sake of that girl of his he'd sold his soul in every port in the Far East. He'd ruined his health and drunk himself stupid, engaging in every shady deal that would pay him more than a captain's wage. That's why they got him up

326

from Singapore.'

'Did Gundersen engage him then?' I said.

'Probably. I don't know.' He shrugged his shoulders. 'Whoever it was, they picked the wrong moment. The old vulture was going back home to his daughter, and he wasn't going to sink a ship on his last voyage.'

'And so Dellimare got rid of him—is that what you're suggesting?' I asked.

He shook his head. 'No, I don't think he intended to kill him. I think he just got hold of his liquor and was waiting until the old man was sufficiently softened up to do what he wanted. He couldn't have known he'd die that night.' He smiled at me out of the corner of his mouth. 'But it amounts to the same thing, doesn't it?' He had sat with Taggart for several hours that night, listening to a life story told in scraps of delirium—the risks and the crookery and the shady deals . . . and then two men had been drowned. That was what had started Taggart drinking. 'Like most of us, he just wanted to forget.' And he went on, conjuring up the ghost of that dreadful old man, completely absorbed in the tragedy of it, standing there on that rock like a Trappist monk, his body shivering under the limp brown folds of his duffle coat.

He switched suddenly to the daughter . . . that photograph, what it had meant to him. Her image had been his confidant, his inspiration, a symbol of all his desperate hopes. And then the meeting in St Malo—the shock of realizing that there were things he couldn't tell her, that she knew he was hiding something from her.

'You're in love with her, aren't you?' I said. We were strangely close, alone together in the eerie stillness of the fog with the sea all round us.

'Yes.' His voice had a sudden lift to it, as though even here the thought of her could raise his spirits.

'Despite what she did to you in Court?'

'Oh, that!' He dismissed it. That last night in Southampton—she had come to apologize. And after that he had told her everything—all the things he had confided to her picture. 'I had to tell somebody,' he murmured.

He lifted his head suddenly and sniffed at a breath of wind that came to us out of the dripping void. 'Still westerly,' he said, and we talked about how soon the fog would clear. He hadn't liked the look of the dawn. 'That depression,' he muttered. 'We've got to reach the salvage ship before it starts to blow up dirty.' The words were ominous.

And shortly after that we had to go back to the dinghy. The tide had risen, covering the rocks of our inlet, and it kept us constantly on the move then. We were in a strange submarine world where everything dripped water and the floor of the sea rose steadily until the towering bastion of rock had dwindled to a miserable little island barely two feet above the level of the sea. It was two o'clock then and the swell had increased and was showering us with spray as we sat huddled together in the dinghy.

I was barely conscious of time. The fog hung round us, very thick, so that it seemed as though nothing could exist in the whole world except that miserable strip of rock and the ugly, surging water.

We didn't talk much. We were too desperately cold. We took it in turns to sit and drift into a sort of coma. The tide went down again and the rock re-emerged like some monster lifting its dripping body out of the sea.

It was just after five that the fog began to clear. A wind sprang up and gradually the greyness lightened until it was an iridescent dazzle that hurt the eyes. Shapes began to emerge, forming themselves into rocks, and the sea stretched farther and farther away from us. Above our heads a patch of sky appeared, startlingly blue, and suddenly the fog was gone and the sun shone. We were in a sparkling world of blue-green water littered with rock outcrops.

We made the dinghy fast and scrambled up the barnacle-covered, weed-grown fortress of the rock. It was suddenly very warm, and from the top, which only a few hours before had been a bare, wave-worn little island, a fantastic sight met our eyes. All round us the sea was islanded with rock—mile upon mile of sinister reefs and outcrops—the Minkies at one hour before low water. Beyond the rock islands, we had glimpses of open sea—except to the south-west; to the south-west the islands became so numerous that they merged to form a solid barrier.

The beacon on Maîtresse Ile, which stands 31 feet at high water, was easily identified, and from it Patch was able to get our bearings. The rock on which we stood was on the northern side of the Minkies, about a mile inside the outer bastion of the Pipette Rocks, and he reckoned that the *Mary Deare* must lie almost due south of us. I have checked since with the large-scale chart and find that he was just about right. But the three miles that separated us from our objective constituted the main body of the reefs. We didn't appreciate this at the time, nor did we fully understand the extraordinary change in configuration of the above-water reefs that could occur in the last stages of the falling tide.

The wind was blowing quite fresh and an ugly little chop was forming on the long swell that marched steadily eastward through the reefs. Already there was a good deal of white water about, particularly in the vicinity of submerged rocks, and I think we should have been more cautious if we hadn't suddenly caught sight of Higgins. He was standing on a big rock mass not half a mile to the east of us.

It was probably the Grand Vascelin, for there was a black and white beacon on it, and even as Patch pointed him out to me, I saw Higgins move and begin to scramble down to his dinghy, which we could see bobbing about at the base of the rock, its blue paint looking bright and cheerful in the sunshine.

We moved fast then, slithering and tumbling down to our own dinghy, scrambling into it and pushing off with no time to plan our route across the reefs, knowing only that the tide, which was west-going at that time, favoured Higgins and that we had to cover those three miles and reach the safety of the salvage company's vessel before he caught up with us.

Of course we should never have shown ourselves against the skyline at the top of that rock. If we had thought about it at all, we must have known that, the instant the fog cleared, he would be standing on some vantage point watching for us. It wasn't that we had forgotten about him. You can't forget a man when he has followed you all night through a treacherous, abandoned stretch of sea with murder in his heart. But I think the fog had so isolated us mentally that the moment it cleared we rushed to the highest point to get a sight of the world that had been hidden from us for so long. It was an instinctive reaction, and in any case we were dull-witted with cold and exhaustion.

The one sensible thing we did was to put on our life-jackets and then we pushed off from the rock that had been our perch for almost twelve hours and Patch began to row, heading south-west across the tide. Away from the lee of the rock we were conscious immediately of the weight of the wind and the way the sea was kicking up; it was a west wind, blowing over the tide, and already the waves were beginning to break. It crossed my mind that this might be the beginning of the depression. The sunshine had a brittle quality and long tongues of pale cloud, wind-blown like mares'-tails, were licking out across the sky.

The tide wasn't strong, but it carried us inexorably towards the greatest mass of the dried-out reefs. The mass is actually split by two channels, but we couldn't see that and for a time Patch attempted to make up against the tide to pass to the east of it, where we could see there was open water. But then, suddenly, he altered course. I was baling at the time, using a sou'wester, and I looked up inquiringly. I thought perhaps the tide had become too strong or that he felt we were shipping too much water.

But he nodded across the stern. 'Higgins,' he said, and I turned to see the big blue dinghy emerging from behind a jagged huddle of rocks. It wasn't more than two cables behind us.

We were in open water then, in the broad channel that separates the outer wall of reefs from the main fortress mass. There were no rocks to shelter us and the breaking wave-tops constantly slopped over the gunn'ls so that, though I never stopped baling, the water in the bottom of the dinghy steadily increased. I could hear Patch's breath ecaping between his teeth and every time I glanced aft, it seemed that Higgins was nearer, the big metal dinghy riding higher and easier than ours. He was keeping a little to the east of us, heading us off from the open water, and all the time the outer rocks of the main reef were slowly closing in on us, the swell breaking all along their edge, the white water piling in over the black teeth of the outer fringe.

'You'll have to turn into the wind,' I shouted.

Patch glanced over his shoulder, still rowing steadily, and then nodded. The twenty-foot wall of rocks was very close now. But each time he turned, the starboard bow of the dinghy caught the full force of the breaking waves and water poured in, threatening to sink us. There was nothing for it but to hold our course, head for the rocks and hope for the best.

The tide helped us here, sliding us westward, along the face of the rampart, into a bay where the swell built up to 4 or 5 feet and broke on outlying ledges in a cataract of foam. Every stroke of the oars carried us deeper into the bay, making escape from it more impossible. 'We'll never get out of this,' I shouted to Patch.

He said nothing. He had no breath left to talk. I glanced over the stern and saw that Higgins had closed the distance to less than two hundred yards. Patch had to go on rowing. And then, over his shoulder, I saw the rocks at the inner end of the bay draw apart and, unbelievably, there was open water between them. 'Look!' I pointed.

Patch glanced quickly over his right shoulder, saw the gap and turned the dinghy towards it. We were in the first of the two channels with the wind behind us. The dinghy rose and fell to the steep swell. We shipped hardly any water now and I was able to bale her right out so that we rode light and easy. 'We'll make it now!' Patch's voice came to me through the wind and the noise of the sea breaking along both sides of the channel and it was full of confidence. He was grinning through his bared teeth, recklessly squandering his energy as he rowed with quick, straining tugs at the oars.

As soon as I had finished baling I took my place on the thwart beside him and we rowed in unison, not saying anything, just pulling and watching Higgins as he fell into the troughs of the endless waves and was borne aloft again on the next crest. The world smiled with the brittle glitter of white water. Only the rocks were ugly and their menace was oddly enhanced because the sun shone.

We reached the narrowest point of the

channel, guarded by a single rock outcrop, and then it suddenly opened into a broad area of water with a reef mass ahead, but plenty of water round it. It was protected somewhat from the wind so that, though the swells still surged across it, there were few whitecaps— just patches of broken water here and there.

But as we moved out into that broad patch of open water, a strange and terrifying change began to come over it. The first indication of something wrong was a swell that suddenly reared up behind the dinghy's stern and broke, slewing us broadside in the surf and very nearly turning us over. Patch shouted to me that we were on a reef and we pulled the dinghy clear of the danger spot. The swell was building up and breaking continuously at that point. And now, looking round, I noticed it was breaking at many other points—places where it hadn't been breaking only a few minutes before.

'The tide!' Patch yelled in my ear. 'Pull, man! Pull! It's the tide!'

I needed no urging. I would have pulled both arms out of their sockets to get out of that fearful place. All round us now were patches of white water, patches that joined up with other patches till there were irregular lines of surf breaking. What had been, only a few minutes ago, open water, was now, suddenly, transformed into a seething, roaring cauldron of broken water as the tide dropped like a lift to expose the rocks and gravel of the sea bed

335

contained within the ramparts of the central reef mass.

I had only just grasped what was happening when a sudden wave lifted us up and crashed us down on to a rock. The jolt of it ran right up my spine like a blow to the base of the head. Water boiled all round us, white in the sunshine, glittering like soapsuds; rocks and boulders showed for an instant and then vanished as another wave of green water swept in, lifted us up and crashed us down again. And in the instant of being uplifted I have a sort of panoramic recollection of the scene: black reefs piled round that arena and the water all brittle white and boiling mad and little sections of sea bed showing—all passing before my eyes as the dinghy was swung violently round and then finally smashed down upon a little exposed hillock of grey gravel. It was a tiny oasis in the middle of that chaos that came and went as the surf rolled across it.

We stumbled out, knee-deep in the spill of a wave, and, as it receded, we tipped the dinghy up, emptying it of water. But one glance told us that it was damaged beyond any repair we could effect on the spot—two planks were stove in for practically the whole length of the boat. 'Doesn't matter,' Patch shouted. 'We'd have to abandon it, anyway. Come on!' He bent down and removed the hand-bearing compass from its case. It was all he took. 'Come on!' he repeated. 'We walk and swim

336

the rest.'

I stood and stared at him. I thought for a moment that he'd gone mad and imagined he was Christ, capable of walking the surface of that surging carpet of broken water. But he wasn't mad. He was a seaman and his mind worked quicker than mine. Already a change had come over the scene—there was less white water, and rocks and boulders and patches of gravel were appearing as the tide receded. And two hundred yards away Higgins was ploughing through water up to his knees, dragging his dinghy after him.

I bent to pick up the painter of our own dinghy and then realized it was useless. 'Come on!' Patch said again. 'We've got to be out of here before the tide comes back.' He had started to walk south and I followed him, stumbling over hidden boulders, floundering into pot-holes, wet and dazed and exhausted.

The noise of the surf rolled back till it dwindled to a distant murmur, and in a moment, it seemed, all those acres that had been a roaring holocaust of tumbled water were suddenly still and quiet. No waves broke. Little raised beaches of boulder-strewn gravel shone wet in the sun and about them lay pools of water ruffled by the wind, and all round were the black rocks of the reef.

The sense of isolation, of loneliness and remoteness, was appalling. And it was enhanced by something that Higgins did, following on behind us. He came to our dinghy and, glancing back, I saw him pick it up in his two hands and smash it down against an outcrop of rock. The splintering crash of the wood breaking up was a sharp, savage sound. All the bows were stove in and my last contact with *Sea Witch* was wantonly destroyed.

And then Higgins started after us again, still dragging his dinghy. The tinny sound of it striking against the boulders was with us for a long time as we stumbled across stretches of exposed beach or waded through water that was sometimes so deep we had to swim. And at the back of my mind was the thought that we were twenty miles from the French coast, in an area that only a few of the local fishermen ever dared to visit. And in six short hours all this area of rock-strewn debris would be thirty feet below the sea, compressed, imprisoned, flattened by countless million tons of water. The only thing that kept me going was the thought of that salvage ship, so close now. It couldn't be more than two miles away, three at the most . . . and there'd be a bunk and dry clothes and hot soup.

I saw Patch stumble and fall. He got up and staggered on. We were halfway to the black southern bastion of the reefs, floundering over a stretch of jagged, up-ended rocks. He fell several times after that. We both did. There was no strength left in us and when a foot slipped, the muscles gave. Our sodden clothing weighed us down, tripped us up.

The sun gradually died amongst the mares' tails. Thicker clouds came up. I didn't see them come. The sweat was in my eyes. I saw nothing but what was immediately at my feet. But rock and gravel became drab and sombre. And later, much later, there was a light drizzle on my face. The sound of the sea began to come back, but by then we were crawling amongst the great up-ended slabs of rock that lay strewn about the main outcrop.

I hadn't looked back for a long time then. I didn't know where Higgins was. I couldn't hear the sound of his dinghy any more. It was lost in the noise of the sea and the drumming of the blood in my ears. And then we were clawing our way up the final slope of weed-grown rock. I paused to see Patch up at the top, leaning against a shoulder of rock and staring southwards. 'Can you see her?' I gasped.

'No.' He shook his head.

I came out on to the top beside him and stared south. It was still the Minkies. But different. More sea. There were still rock outcrops. But they were fewer, more isolated. All ahead of us was open water, dimmed and blurred by the drizzle of rain. 'I don't see her,' I gasped.

'She's there somewhere.' His voice was flat and weary. His black hair hung wet over his eyes and his hands and face were streaked with blood where he had fallen—blood and dirt and

339

sodden, shapeless clothing. He took my arm.
'You all right?' he asked.

'Yes,' I said. 'Yes, I'm all right.'

He stared at me and for the first time I saw
an expression of concern in his eyes. He
opened his mouth to say something and then
thought better of it and turned his head away.
'I'm sorry,' he said, and that was all.

'How much farther do you reckon?' I asked.

'About a mile.'

A mile to swim. I wondered whether we
should ever make it.

He took my arm again and pointed across
the litter of out-crops to a compact mass that
stood higher than any of the others. 'I think
that's Grune à Croc.' It stood on the edge of
visibility, half hidden by the drizzle, and at the
mention of its name it abruptly vanished as the
rain thickened and drove across it. Somewhere
beyond that rock lay the *Mary Deare*.

Behind us, the tide came licking hungrily
back across the beaches, coming in from the
north-west, driven by the wind and the south-
going set of the stream. But Higgins was clear
of it by then, rowing slowly, easily, to a nearby
rock, where he moored his dinghy and sat
watching us like an animal that has treed its
quarry. He could afford to wait, for with each
foot the tide rose the size of our rock perch
was halved.

We found an over-hanging slab of rock that
gave us some shelter from the wind and the

rain and still enabled us to watch him, and there we crouched, huddled close together for warmth, whilst the tide rose and night closed in. If only the visibility had been better; if we could have seen the *Mary Deare*, perhaps attracted the attention of the salvage people. But we could see nothing; we couldn't even hear them. All we could hear was the waves pounding on the other side of the reef mass and I wondered what it would be like at the top of the tide. Would the waves break right over these rocks? But by then we should be gone. Our plan was to slip into the water an hour before high tide and make for Grune à Croc. We were relying on a southward thrust from the tide coming through the main reef body to spill us out towards the rock, and though Patch had lost the hand-bearing compass, we thought the rock would be reasonably conspicuous, since it was the only one in the whole area to the south of us that would be exposed at high water.

Once we had decided what to do, we had nothing to occupy our minds. It was then that I became conscious of hunger pains for the first time. It wasn't only the pains that worried me, but the feeling that I had no warmth left in me, as though the rain and the bitter cold had reached the central fires on which my body depended and put them out. I fell into a sort of coma of misery and through bleared eyes I watched the rock to which Higgins had moored

341

slowly submerge. And then he was rowing again, and gradually the tide beat him. Oddly enough it gave me no sense of pleasure. I was too tired. As the tide ran faster so he had to row harder to keep abreast of our position. And then gradually his strokes became weaker until he was forced to steer to another rock and cling to it. But the tide rose and covered that, too, and, though he started to row again, the tide carried him slowly farther and farther from us. Night was closing in by then and I lost him in the gathering darkness.

It meant, of course, that we shouldn't have to worry about where Higgins was when we abandoned our rock and took to the water, but when you are faced with a long swim and are afraid you may be too weak to do it, then the question of whether there may or may not be a dinghy in the way doesn't seem very important. In any case, I was slipping into unconsciousness. I was so cold, so utterly drained of warmth—I had no sense of feeling left.

It was the water that woke me. It was warmer than I was and it lapped round my legs like a tepid bath. And then it slopped into my face. That was when consciousness returned and I felt Patch stir. 'Good God!' he murmured. 'It must be just about high water.'

We stood up, stiff to the joints, forcing our bodies to unbend. Was it high water? Had the tide turned already? My numbed brain groped

342

for the answer, knowing it was important, but not knowing why. The rain had stopped. There were stars and low-scudding clouds. A glimmer of moonlight made pale reflections on the ink-black water. 'Well, do we go? What's the time?' Patch's voice was no more than a croak. 'What's the time, for God's sake? My watch has stopped.'

Mine had stopped, too. There was no means of knowing the time, no means of knowing which way the tide was flowing. Jolted by sudden fear, the sleep cleared from my brain and I saw clearly that we had no alternative. If we stayed on that rock we should die of exposure—tomorrow perhaps or the next day, but we should die. After tonight we should never have the strength to swim that mile. And the water was warm—warmer than the sodden, icy clothes draped round our bodies, warmer than the wind and the ice-cold driving rain that would come again. Besides, we had life-jackets and, if the tide was wrong, there were other rocks to cling to and die on. 'Ready?' I said.

Patch hesitated and I suddenly realized that he wasn't sure of himself any more. He was a seaman. He was used to boats, not to the sea itself as an element in which to exist, body buoyed up by water. 'Come on,' I said. 'We're going now. Keep close to me and don't talk.'

We inflated our life-jackets fully and then together we stepped off the ledge of rock on which we had huddled. When we had first

343

come to that ledge it had been a thirty-foot drop to the rocks below. Now we stepped off into water, warm, buoyant water, and, lying on our backs, swam slowly south, our feet to the Pole Star, glimpsed every now and then through rents in the tattered cloudbase.

We kept abreast of each other, just two arms' lengths away, moving steadily and unhurriedly. Soon we were clear of the rocks, rising and falling gently to a big swell that was rolling in across the reefs. We could hear it pounding against distant rocks—the rocks to the west of us that got the full brunt of it. 'Storm coming up,' Patch whispered.

The wind had dropped. The swell was big, but gentle-sloped with no broken water. The sea slept, heaving as it slumbered. Yet I was sure Patch was right. Though the wind was light, the clouds were hurried and torn to shreds and the pounding of that surf was ominous, like gunfire to the west. A wave suddenly reared up out of nowhere and broke, pouring surf over us, spilling us away from it. My feet touched rock for an instant. And then everything was quiet as before and we rose and fell, rose and fell to the swell. We had crossed one of those sentinel-like pillars of rock that we had seen at low water.

The rock on which we had spent half the night was disappearing now—disappearing astern of us so that I knew we were all right. We hadn't missed the tide. Patch stopped swimming, treading water. 'I can't see Grune à Croc,' he said, and his teeth chattered. 'I think we should strike more to the west.'

So we swam on with the Pole Star and the Plough to our left and I wondered how long we could last. My teeth were chattering, too, and the sea, which had felt so warm at first, was now a cold compress chilling all my stomach. We had no food inside us to generate warmth. Soon one of us would get cramp, and that would be the end.

Our sodden clothing weighed us down. The inflated life-jackets made us clumsy. Each stroke had to be powerful to drive our bodies through the water; and power meant energy—our vital, last reserves of energy. God knows how long we swam that night. We seemed to go on and on for ever. And each stroke was imperceptibly weaker than the last. And all the time I was thinking if only I were wearing a foam rubber suit or at least had my fins on my feet. It was years since I had swum in this clumsy fashion. My mind sank into a coma, a slough of pain and deep exhaustion, in which I saw myself again ploughing down to the old tanker through clear bright Mediterranean waters that glimmered with colour—the white of the sand and the silver gleam of fish; and myself, buoyant and carefree, exactly balanced, warm and breathing comfortably through my mouthpiece.

'John! John!' I opened my eyes. Black night

surrounded me. I thought for an instant I was deep down, on the verge of going into a rapture of the depths. And then I saw a star and heard the surge of a wave breaking. 'John!' The voice called again out of the darkness.

'Yes. What is it?'

'There's a rock. I can just see it.' It was Patch's voice. Funny, I thought. He'd never called me John before. And then he said, 'You gave me a scare just now. I couldn't make you hear. I thought I'd lost you.'

The concern in his voice filled me with a sudden warmth for the man. 'Sorry,' I said. 'Just dreaming. That's all. Where's this rock of yours?' I turned, treading water, and there, not more than a hundred yards to my right, the dark shape of a rock stood out for an instant against the white gleam of a breaking wave. I searched the blackness beyond it. More waves were breaking out there and I thought I saw the solid mass of something.

And then it came to me that there would be lights on the *Mary Deare*. With a salvage company working on her there would have to be lights. I searched the blackness all round, each time I was lifted to the top of a swell, but there was nothing, not the faintest flicker of a light. Perhaps they were being so secret about their salvage operation that they didn't show lights. And then the thought came to me that perhaps they had lifted her already and towed her away. The cold came back into my body,

346

more intense now, more destructive, and I felt the muscles of my left leg begin to screw themselves together in a knot.

'There's something beyond this rock,' Patch croaked. 'Shall we make for that?'

'All right,' I said. It didn't seem to matter. To die in the water was better than to die of exposure on one of those Godforsaken rocks. I lay back, kicking out feebly with my legs, thrusting at water that was no longer warm, but icy cold, swimming automatically whilst my mind tangled itself up with the matter of those lights. There should have been lights. Unless we'd been swept back into the central mass of the reefs we should have seen lights right from the start. 'There should be lights,' I mumbled.

'Lights. That's it. There should be lights.' His voice sounded weak, a little scared. And then, after a bit—'Tell them to put the lights on.' He was back on a ship, his mind wandering. 'Put those lights on, do you hear?' And then he suddenly called 'John!' His voice was very faint.

'Yes?'

'I'm sorry I landed you into this.' He muttered something about my boat. And then I heard him say, 'I should have slit my useless throat.' Silence for a moment and then: 'They booed me, that first time. Outside the Court.' Broken water slapped my face and the next thing I heard was—'. . . kick against the pricks. I should have chucked it then.' A wave broke

347

and silenced him. He didn't speak again after that. His arms didn't move. I could just see the outline of his head, motionless.

'Are you all right?' I called out.

He didn't answer and I swam over to him. 'Are you all right?' I shouted at him. 'We're going to swim to that rock—do you hear?'

He caught hold of my arm with the iron grip of a drowning man and, as I wrenched myself free of him, he screamed at me. 'Look, man. Look at it, damn you! Tell me I'm not dreaming!'

He had raised his arm and was pointing. I turned my head and there, against the stars, I saw the tall finger of a mast and, below it, all the black bulk of her superstructure caught for an instant in the white phosphorescent glitter of a breaking wave.

We swam then, cold and exhaustion forgotten, tugging our weary, unwieldy bodies through the water. We were coming up on her bows and they were like a reef awash: the waves rolled over them, but in the troughs their shape emerged as the sea cascaded from them. And then, beyond the bows, beyond the tall finger of the mast, the bridge deck emerged and the funnel and all the line of the decks sloping upwards to her cocked-up stern.

In the trough of a wave a hard line sprang suddenly taut, catching at my left arm so that I screamed with pain, gulping in salt water; and then it flipped me over and the top of a wave engulfed me. I swam clear of the bows then, moving painfully down the ship, just clear of the streaming bulwarks, and then swam in on her where the fo'c'stle dropped to the well-deck and Number One hatch. I came in on the top of a wave that broke as it surged over the bulwarks and then I was flung down on to the hatch coaming with a force that jarred all the torn muscles of my side and my feet scrabbled on weed-grown, slippery plating whilst the wave receded in a swirl of white water.

I fetched up in the scuppers with my hand gripped round the capping of the bulwarks, and as the next wave piled in, I fought my way aft until I was clear of the water and could reach the mast, and there I clung, shouting for Patch in a high, cracked voice, for I was scared I'd lost him. That moment of panic seemed endless. I was the better swimmer. I was trained to the sea. I should have stayed with him, seen him safe on board, and I knew I hadn't the guts to go back and search for him in the darkness; I was tired, desperately tired, with all the muscles of my body curling up with the threat of cramp. And, even more, I didn't want to be alone on that ship. It was a dead ship—dead as the rocks of the Minkies. I knew it, instinctively. I could sense that it was dead through all my body and I needed him desperately. And so I clung to the mast and screamed his name and the seas came thundering in across the bows with wicked gleams of white as the water surged and swirled and poured off them in the troughs.

I didn't see him come aboard. I was still screaming his name and he was suddenly there beside me, staggering drunkenly, an ungainly, top-heavy shape in his life-jacket caught in silhouette against the break of a wave. 'It's all right,' He gasped. 'I'm here.' He reached out and caught hold of my hand, and we clung there, gasping for breath, grateful for the sudden comfort of that touch. 'There should be lights,' he said at length. There was a sort of childish disappointment in his voice, as though the salvage company had robbed him of a pleasure to which he had been looking forward.

'They've probably closed down for the night,' I said, but without conviction. I knew the ship was dead.

'But there should be lights,' he said again. And then we staggered aft, past Number Two hatch, up the ladder to the upper deck. The door to the deckhouse stood drunkenly open, crumpled and torn from its hinges. We felt our way along the alley, past his old cabin and Dellimare's and out through the empty gap of the door beyond, out on to the upper deck, where the twisted shapes of the empty davits stood like crooked fingers against starlit patches of the sky, and on, past the dim-seen hape of the funnel, crumpled and lying away from us at a precarious angle.

Squelching soggily on the steel of the deck, our bodies thin as paper in the cold night air, we traipsed the length of the *Mary Deare*, aft to the little deckhouse on the poop and back again up the starboard side, and every now and then we shouted—'Ahoy! Anybody there? Ahoy!' Not even an echo came back to us. The frail sound of our voices was lost in the cold, black night, buried in the noise of the waves surging over the bows.

No salvage boat lay alongside. No light suddenly flickered to guide us to the warmth of a cabin. We called and called, but nobody answered. The ship was dead, devoid of life—as dead as she had been the day we'd left her there.

'My God!' Patch breathed. 'We're the first. Nobody has been here.' There was a note of relief, almost exultation in his voice, and I knew he was thinking of the thing that lay buried amidst the coal of the port bunker. But all I cared about at that moment was that I was cold and wet and hurt and that, instead of the bunk and dry clothes, the warmth of food and drink and the companionship of human beings I had expected, there was nothing—nothing but the slime-covered, barnacle-encrusted shell of a wreck that had been battered by the seas for six long weeks.

'We'll get some dry clothes and have a sleep,' he said. 'We'll feel better then.' He had sensed my mood. But when we had staggered

351

back to the bridge housing and felt our way down the black iron tunnel of the alley-way to what had been his cabin, we found that the sea had been there. The door grated on sand as we forced it open and a freezing wind drove at us through portholes that stared like two luminous eyes, empty of glass. The desk had been ripped from its fastenings and lay on its side in a corner, the drawers of the bunk that contained his and Taggart's clothes were full of water and the big wall cupboard contained nothing but a sodden, gritty heap of blankets, coats and old papers.

We tried the main deck then, where the saloon and the galley were. But that was worse. The sea had swept the whole length of the alley-ways, into the officers' cabins and right aft to the crew's quarters. Everything we touched in the pitch-black darkness was sodden, filmed with slime; there wasn't a place the sea hadn't reached.

'Maybe the poop is still dry.' Patch said it wearily, without hope, and we began to move back down the port alley-way, feeling our way, bodies dead and numbed with cold, shivering uncontrollably. God, let the poop be dry! And then I staggered and hit my shoulder against the wet steel plate of the wall, thrown there by a sudden movement of the ship. I felt it through my whole body, a quiver like the first faint tremor of an earthquake. And then the ship moved again. 'Listen!' Patch's voice was urgent in the darkness. But I could hear nothing except the noise of the sea lapping at the hull. 'She's afloat,' he whispered. 'Just afloat on top of the tide.'

'How can she be?' I said.

'I don't know, but she is. Feel her!'

I felt her quiver and lift, and then she thudded back into her gravel bed. But she still went on quivering and from deep down in the bowels of her came a slow grating sound; and all the time she was trembling as though she were stirring in her sleep, struggling to free herself from the deadly reef bed on which she lay. 'It's not possible,' I murmured. The ship couldn't be afloat when her bows were submerged like a reef and the waves were rolling over them. This must be a dream. And I thought then that perhaps we had drowned out there. Did drowned men go back to their ships and dream that they shook off the reef shackles and voyaged like ghosts through dark, unnatural seas? My mind was beyond coherent thought. The ship was dead. That I knew, and beyond that, all I wanted was to lose consciousness of cold and pain, to lie down and sleep.

A hand reached out and gripped me, holding me up, and my feet trod the iron of the passage-way and climbed, without volition, up into the cold of the night air, to glimpses of stars and a drunken funnel and the unending noise of the sea. Down aft we stumbled over a

353

steel hawser laid taut across the well-deck. It thrummed and sang to the sea's roll, and the ship moved like a drunkard, tottering its masts against the sky, as we climbed the ladder to the poop's platform and vanished into the black abyss of the little deckhouse. There was clothing there in the bos'un's cabin. As I remember, it was neither wet nor dry, but it had more warmth than my own sodden clothes, and there was a dank bunk, with blankets smelling of wet like a dog's fur, and sleep—the utter oblivion of sleep, more perfect than any heaven ever dreamed of by a well-fed man seated by his own fireside.

A long time after, it seemed—many years, perhaps—the tread of a man's feet entered into that heavenly oblivion. I can't say that it woke me or even that I struggled back to consciousness. Not immediately. It was just that the tread of his feet was there; a solid, metallic sound—the ring of boots on steel plates. It was a penetrating, insistent sound. It was above my head, beside my bed, first one side, then the other, and then farther away—a slow, unhurried, purposeful tread ... the march of a dead man across the sleep of oblivion. And when it was no longer there I woke.

Daylight stabbed at my bleared eyes and a huddle of sodden blankets in the corner of the dank steel prison in which I lay, stirred and rose. It was Patch, his face ashen with fatigue.

354

'I thought I heard footsteps,' he said. His eyes looked wild, black marbles sunk deep in ivory sockets. 'I swear I heard somebody.'

I crawled out of the bunk, sweaty with the salt-heat of a soggy mass of blankets, but cold and stiff with a gnawing pain in my belly and my shoulder aching like hell. It all came back to me then, hitting me like a physical blow, and I stumbled to the door and looked out. It was true then—not a dream. I was back on the *Mary Deare*, and . . . God, she was a wreck! She was a rust-red nightmare of a ship, smeared with a film of green slime, with a stubble-growth of grey that was the barnacles. Her funnel lay over at a crazy angle and all the bridge deck was twisted and gnarled and battered. The tide was low and, beyond the wreck of her, the Minkies gnashed their black teeth, foam-flecked where the stumps of rock stuck up out of the sea. No salvage ship lay anchored off, no tug, not even a fishing boat. There was nothing—just the ugly, familiar shape of Grune à Croc and the mass of reefs beyond . . . not a single sign of life, and the sky savagely grey, with an ugly pallor that made the cloud shapes black and cold-looking.

'My God!' I croaked. Instinctively, perhaps, I knew what we had to face—what the pallor of the dawn meant and the savage grey of the sky.

And Patch, sniffing the air over my shoulder, muttered, 'There's a heap of dirt coming up.'

The sky to the west of us was sombre, a black wedge of cloud that left the horizon sharp as a line ruled between air and sea. There wasn't much wind, but the thunder of the waves on the exposed reefs had an ominous sound, and, even here, in the shelter of the rocks, the swell that slopped against the *Mary Deare*'s side was big and solid.

'Those footsteps,' I said. 'What were they?'

He shook his head, not answering, and his eyes avoided mine. God knows what he was thinking, but a shudder ran through him, and it crossed my mind that a lot of men had died because of this ship. And then a strange thing happened: a little cloud of rust rose like red steam from the well-deck bulwark as a steel hawser ran out over the side. The bight appeared, checked on the rail, and then fell over into the sea with a faint splash. When it was gone, the ship was still again—no movement anywhere, and I was conscious that Patch was gripping my arm. 'Queer,' he said, and his voice had a hollow sound.

We stood rooted to the spot for a long time, staring along the length of the ship. But everything was still and motionless—nothing moved except the sea.

'There's somebody on board,' he said. His tone was uneasy and his face was as drawn and haggard as it had been on the day I had first met him. 'Listen!' But I could hear nothing—only the slap of the waves against the ship's side and the pounding of the swell on the reefs. The wreck was as still and as quiet as the grave. A lone sea-bird drifted by, soundless on the wind and white like a piece of paper against the clouds.

Patch descended then to the well-deck and stopped to gaze at the cover of Number Four hatch. And when I joined him I saw that it wasn't the usual tarpaulin cover fixed with wooden wedges, but steel plates fresh-welded to the coaming. He had a look at the derrick winches and then we went past Number Three hatch, which was also plated over, and up the ladder to the boat deck. Here all the ventilators had been removed and lay about the deck like truncated limbs, the ventilation holes covered by rusty plating. The funnel had been cut through at the base by a blow torch, shifted to one side and the vent plated over. The engine-room skylight was screwed down tight and the water-tight doors to the port and starboard main deck alley-ways had been removed and the holes plated over.

There was no doubt whatever that the report of the St Helier fisherman had been correct. A salvage company had been working on the wreck. They had sealed off the whole hull of the *Mary Deare* and probably they had also repaired the leak in the for'ard holds. It explained the way she had lifted at the top of the tide and the rake of the decks to the cocked-up stern. The ship was watertight,

357

almost ready to float off. I found Patch standing by the port bunkering chute, his eyes riveted on the hatch cover, which had been torn from its hinges and lay abandoned on the deck. In its place a steel plate had been welded over the chute, effectively sealing the bunker off. It meant that Dellimare's body would remain there in its steel coffin until the hulk was towed into port and officials came on board with equipment to open up the ship. It meant days, possibly weeks of suspense for him, and there was despair in his face as he said, 'Well, that's that.' And he turned away, to stare aft along the length of the ship. 'They should have had a stern line out,' he said.

I wasn't following his trend of thought. I was thinking that there was all this work completed and no salvage ship. 'Why do you think they left?' I asked him.

He glanced at the sky, sniffing the breeze from the west, which was coming now in irregular puffs. 'The forecast was probably bad,' he said. 'Maybe they had a gale warning.'

I stared at the jagged reefs, remembering what it had been like before. Surely to God . . .

'What's that?' His voice came sharp and clear, and through it, beyond the barrier of the bridge-deck, the cough of a diesel engine settled to a steady roar. I could feel the deck vibrating under my feet, and for a moment we stood, quite still, listening to the music of it. Then we were running for the bridge-deck

358

alley-way. We came out at the head of the ladder that led down to the for'ard well-deck and there, just aft of Number Two hatch, stood a big suction pump, lashed to the deck. The engine was going full bat and the thick suction pipe was pulsating with the flow of water where it disappeared through a hole cut in an inspection hatch. Water was sluicing out of the far side of the pump, flooding across the deck and disappearing through the scuppers. And yet there was nobody there. The well-deck was empty and in all the fore part of the ship there wasn't a living soul.

It was uncanny.

'Try the bridge,' Patch said. 'Somebody started that pump.'

We dived back into the alley-way and up the ladder to the bridge. It was all so familiar, but horribly changed. The glass was gone, the doors smashed and the wind was whistling through it, pushing little rivulets of water across the sand-smeared platform. There was nobody there—nobody in the chartroom. And then, out on the bridge again, Patch gripped my arm and pointed. Beyond the bows a pillar-like rock stood like a bollard with the bight of a thick steel hawser round it. The hawser ran taut from rock to ship, an anchor against the pull of the tides. It was the hawser that had fouled me during the night as I swam in over the bows.

But Patch was pointing to something else—a

359

small blue dinghy pulling out from under the *Mary Deare*'s bows. It was Higgins, and he was rowing out to the rock. The peaked cap on the bull head, the massive shoulders and the blue seaman's jersey—it was all so clear in the cold grey light. It was clear, too, what he intended to do. I shouted to him, but he couldn't hear me from the bridge. I dived back down the ladder, down to the well-deck and up on to the fo'c'stle. 'Higgins!' I screamed at him. 'Higgins!'

But it was blowing quite strong in the gusts now and Higgins didn't hear me. He had reached the rock and was tying the dinghy to a snag, and then he began to climb. He reached the bight of the hawser and, with an iron bar he had brought with him for the purpose, began to lever it up the rock, whilst I shouted to him, standing up in the wind, balanced right on the slippery point of the *Mary Deare*'s bows.

He had his back to me all the time and when he'd freed the loop, he pushed it up over the jagged point of the rock and the whole line of the wire that anchored the ship right from where it ran out through the hawse-hole, went slack as it fell with a splash into the sea. Then he clambered back down the rock and got into his dinghy.

He saw me just as he'd unhitched the painter and he sat looking at me for a moment. His face was without expression and his big shoulders sagged with the effort he had made.

360

And all the time I was shouting to him, telling him to fix the hawser back on to the rock. 'There's a gale coming,' I shouted. 'A gale!' I kept on repeating that one word, trying to din it into his thick head.

Maybe I succeeded, for Higgins suddenly let go of the rock, pivoted the dinghy on one oar and began to row back towards the *Mary Deare*. Whether he panicked and was making a desperate attempt to get back on board, or whether he was moved to unexpected pity by the desolate character of the place and was trying to take us off, I shall never know, for the tide was north-going, about three knots, and though he worked like a man possessed to drag that heavy dinghy through the water faster than the tide ran, he made not more than twenty yards headway. He tired quickly and, after the first burst of energy, he made no further progress; and then, gradually, the tide took control and he drifted farther and farther away from the ship, still desperately rowing.

In the end he gave it up and steered the dinghy across the tide into the lee of Grune à Croc, and there he sat, clutching the rock, staring at the ship, his head bowed to his knees, his whole body slack with exhaustion.

The noise of the suction pump died and ceased abruptly so that I was suddenly conscious of the wind whining through the broken superstructure. Patch had switched the engine off and as I climbed down off the fore-

361

peak he came to meet me. 'We've got to flood the ship,' he called out, his voice loud and clear. 'It's our only hope.'

But there was no way of flooding her now. Every vent and hole was sealed off and we couldn't get at the sea cocks. Even the doors of the engine-room had been welded to keep the water out. The salvage company had sealed that hull up as tight as a submarine. 'We'll just have to hope for the best,' I said.

Patch laughed. The sound had a hollow ring down there in the steel vault of the alley-way. 'A westerly gale will bring a big tide. She'll float off at high water. Bound to, with nothing to hold her. She's pumped dry, all but the two for'ard holds.' His voice sounded hoarse and cracked. 'I wouldn't mind for myself.' He was staring at me. 'But it's tough on you.' And then he shrugged his shoulders and added, 'Better see if we can find some food.'

I was appalled by his acceptance of it, and as I followed him back down the alley-way to the galley, I was thinking that if only I had woken in time. The French salvage men had had her securely moored with hawsers fore and aft, and Higgins had let them go. I couldn't hate the man. I hadn't the strength to hate. But if only I'd got up the instant I heard those footsteps . . . And as though he knew what was in my mind, Patch said, 'One thing—Higgins is going to have a bad time of it out there in that dinghy.'

The galley was dark and it stank. The sea

had been there before us, and so had the French. There wasn't a tin of any sort in the place. There was a cupboard full of bread that was a pulped, mildewed mass and there was meat that heaved with maggots and butter thick with slime and sand. All we found was some cheese that was good in the centre, a jar of half dried mustard, some pickles and a broken pot of marmalade. We broke our fast on that, wolfing it down, and then we searched the saloon and all through the officers' cabins and the crew's quarters. We found a sticky mass of boiled sweets and a jar of ginger and, best of all, some stoker had gone to earth with two tins of bully beef. We took our miserable haul back to the little deckhouse on the poop and ate it, sitting there, shivering and listening to the rising note of the wind.

The gale came up fast with the turn of the tide and soon the waves, breaking against the side of the wreck, were reaching up to the bridge-deck and we could feel the stern beginning to move under us. Once, when I went to look out of the door, I saw the blue dinghy still bobbing in the lee of Grune à Croc.

By midday it was blowing full gale. All the forepart of the *Mary Deare* was being pounded and battered by huge seas, her bridge-deck hidden every now and then in sheets of white water, the whole hull quivering to the onslaught. Water swirled across the well-deck below us and the boom of the waves striking against the plates of her side was so shattering that I found myself holding my breath, waiting for them, as though the blows were being struck against my own body. The noise went on and on. It filled my head and left no room for any thought beyond the terrible, everlasting consciousness of the sea. And out beyond the sea-swept wreck of the *Mary Deare*, the stumps of the reefs dwindled as the Minkies gradually vanished in a welter of foaming surf.

I saw Higgins once more. It was about two hours before high water. The *Mary Deare* was beginning to lift and shift her bottom on the gravel bed and Grune à Croc was a grey molar stuck up out of a sea of foam with water streaming white from its sides and spray sweeping across in a low-flung cloud, driven by the wind. Higgins was moving on the back of the rock, climbing down towards the dinghy. I saw him get into it and pick up the oars. And then a squall came blurring the shape of the rock, and I suddenly lost sight of him in a curtain of rain.

That was the last I saw of Higgins. It was the last anybody saw of him. I suppose he was trying to reach the *Mary Deare*. Or perhaps he thought he could reach the mainland in the dinghy. He had no choice, anyway; Grune à Croc would have been untenable at high water.

I stood in the doorway of our deckhouse for a long time, my eyes slitted against the rain and the driving spray, watching for a glimpse

364

of him through the squall. In the end the seas drove me in and when I told Patch how Higgins had gone, he shrugged his shoulders and said, 'Lucky bastard! He's probably dead by now.' There was no anger in his voice, only weariness.

The cabin in that deckhouse was about ten feet by six, steel-walled, with a bunk, some broken furniture, a window that had no glass in it and sand on the floor. It was damp and cold, the air smoking with wind-driven spray, and it resounded like a tin box to every sound throughout the ship. We had chosen it for our refuge because it was perched high up on the stern, and it was the stern part of the ship that was afloat.

For a long time we had been conscious of movement, a rising and falling of the steel walls that coincided with the gunfire bursts of the waves crashing against the hull below us. But now there was a shifting and a grating of the keel. It was a sound felt rather than heard, for nothing was really audible except the incredible, overwhelming noise of the sea. And then gradually it lessened. Spray ceased to come in through the window. The door blew open with a crash. The *Mary Deare* had struggled free of the sea bed and was turning head to wind.

I looked out and saw that Grune à Croc was no longer on the port bow, but away to starboard. The *Mary Deare* was afloat. The movement was easier now, the noise of the sea less terrifying. The high stern was acting as a steadying sail and she was bows-on to the breaking waves. I could hear them thundering against the bridge deck, see them burst in a great cloud of spray, forcing water through every opening of the bridge housing as the broken tops swept by on either side. And all the time Grune à Croc was fading away.

I shouted to Patch that we were clear and he came out from the cabin and stood looking at the incredible sight—a wreck floating with her decks streaming rivers of water and sloped down so that all the fore part of her was below the waves. 'We're clear,' I cried. 'If we clear Les Sauvages we're all right.'

He looked at me. I think he was considering leaving me in ignorance. But then he said, 'It must be very near high water.'

I nodded. 'Just about,' I said. And then it came to me: for six solid hours after high water the tide would be north and west-going—driving us back on to the Minkies, at low water with all the reefs exposed. 'God Almighty!' I breathed, and I went back into the cabin and lay down on the bunk.

The hell of it was, there was nothing we could do—not a single damn' thing we could do to help ourselves.

We struck towards dusk in a maelstrom of white water where there wasn't a single rock showing. I don't know whether I was asleep or merely lying there on the bunk in a sort of daze, but the shock of our hitting threw me to the floor. It came like the blow of a mailed fist, a fearful crash up for'ard and then a slow crunching as the plates gave and the rocks disembowelled her; and the thunder of the seas became suddenly louder, more overwhelming.

I lay quite still where I had fallen, feeling the probing teeth of the rocks through my whole body, expecting every moment that the waves would engulf us as she slid under. But nothing happened, except that a thin mist of spray touched my face as it drifted over the ship and the grinding, gut-tearing sound went on so continuously that it became a part of the general uproar of the sea.

The cabin floor was canted over and, as I got to my feet, a sudden shifting of the ship flung me through the door and I fetched up against the bulkhead, with a sickening thud that wrenched at my arm and drove the breath out of my body. I saw the ship then, and the pain didn't seem to matter any more. She was lying heeled over, all the length of her clear against a boiling background of surf. Her bridge-deck was a twisted, broken mass of wreckage, the funnel gone, the fore-mast snapped off halfway up and hanging loose in a tangle of derrick wires. And over all the for'ard half of her the seas broke and rolled and tumbled incessantly.

367

Patch was lying, half-reclined against the steel plates of the deck-house entrance and I shouted to him: 'How long . . .' The words seemed to get caught up in my throat.

'Before she goes?'

'Yes. How long?'

'God knows.'

We didn't talk after that, but stayed there, too cold and tired and fascinated to move, watching as the first jagged points of the reef showed through the foam. The weary half light faded very slowly into darkness. We heard the bows break off; a protracted agony of tortured metal, tearing and rending up there beyond the wreck of the bridge-deck. And then the remainder of the ship lifted slightly as it was freed of their weight, shifting across the saw-edged rocks with a terrible trembling and groaning. We could see the bows then, a black wedge out in the break of the waves to port, with cargo spilling out of a cavern of a hole where the plates had been torn open. Bales of cotton bobbed about in the white water and the waves played with the great square cases that were supposed to contain aero engines, smashing them to matchwood on the reef.

Patch gripped my arm. 'Look!' he shouted. A case had been flung towards us and it was splitting open. The contents cascaded into the sea. God knows what it was. The light by then was very dim. But it certainly wasn't the solid lump of an aero engine.

'Did you see?' He had hold of my arm and was pointing. And then the sudden excitement left him as the wreck on which we stood split across at the after end of the upper deck. A great crack was opening up across the whole width of the ship. It tore the port ladder leading down to the well-deck from its fastenings, twisting it slowly as though an invisible hand were squeezing it. Rivet fastenings were torn out in machine-gun bursts and steel plates were ripped like calico. The gap widened—a yard, two yards; and then it was dark and night clamped down on the *Mary Deare*. By then the falling tide had exposed the reef, the seas had receded and the wreck was still.

We went back into the cabin and lay down under our sodden blankets. We didn't talk. Maybe we slept. I don't remember. I have no recollection of that night. It is like a blank in my mind. The sea's incessant roar, the wind piping a weird note through twisted metal and the sporadic clanging of a loose plate—that is all my recollection. I didn't feel any sense of fear. I don't think I even felt cold any more. I had reached that stage of physical and mental exhaustion that is beyond feeling.

But I remember the dawn. It filtered into the dim recesses of my mind with the sense of something strange. I was conscious of movement—a long, precipitous roll, first one way, then the other. I could hear the sea, but

369

there was no weight in the sound. The crash and roar of mountains of water smashing down on to rocks was gone, and someone was calling me. Bright sunlight stabbed my eyeballs and a face bent over me—a face that was sweaty and flushed under the greying stubble of a beard with eyes sunk deep in hollow sockets and skin stretched taut across forehead and cheekbone. 'We're afloat!' Patch said. His cracked lips were drawn back from his teeth in a sort of grin. 'Come and look.'

I staggered weakly to the entrance and looked out on a strange scene. The reefs had disappeared. The sun shone on a heaving sea, but there wasn't a sign of a rock anywhere. And all the *Mary Deare* for'ard of the well-deck had gone, vanished. The well-deck was under water, but it was as Patch had said—we were afloat; just the stern section and nothing else. And the sun was shining and the gale was diminishing. I could feel Patch trembling where he stood against me. I thought it was excitement. But it wasn't. It was fever.

By midday he was too weak to move, his eyes staring, his face flushed with unnatural colour and the sweat pouring out of him. He had been too long in the East to stand up to nights of exposure in sodden clothing without food. Towards nightfall he became delirious. Much of his raving was unintelligible, but now and then the words came clear and I realized he was back on that voyage up through the

370

Bay, giving orders, talking to Rice ... disjointed scraps that were an appalling revelation of the strain to which he had been subjected.

Towards evening a small aircraft flew over. I watched it circling low down to the north-west, its wings glinting in the setting sun. They were searching for us on the Minkies. And then night closed in and we still floated, very low in the water. There was a young moon hanging in a clear sky full of stars and the wind had gone so that the moon carved a small silver path across a placid, kindly sea that still heaved gently like a giant resting.

That night I was almost too weak to move and Patch lay like a corpse, shivering occasionally, his face still hot and his eyes wide in the faint moon-glow. Once he started up and seized my hand, trembling all over, words tumbling from his lips, words that had no meaning. But this sudden outburst—this raving—lasted only a short while. He hadn't the strength to keep it up and he suddenly fell back exhausted. I lay close against him all the rest of the night, but I had no warmth to give and in the morning he looked like a ghost, small under the stinking blankets.

I saw the Minkies again just after the sun had risen. They were on the horizon, small, jagged points of black etched sharp against the western sky. And then, much later, I heard the sound of an aircraft's engines. I had dragged

Patch out on deck to get the warmth of the sun, but he was unconscious then. The aircraft went past us. I saw the shadow of it cross the water and I pulled myself up, searching the sky for it through bleared and gritty eyes. Then I saw it turning, banking out of the sun and coming back, very low over the water. I clutched the rail for support and waved a blanket at it as it zoomed over just above my head with its engines snarling. It flew off towards the Minkies and a long time afterwards, as I lay on the warmth of the deck in a semi-coma, I heard the putter of an engine and the sound of voices.

It was the Peter Port lifeboat. They came alongside and life stirred again at the sound of friendly voices ... strong hands helping me over the rail, a lit cigarette thrust into my mouth. They stripped us of our salt-stiff, sodden clothing, wrapped us in blankets, and then sleep came to me, the wonderful relaxed warmth of sleep. But I remember, just before I lost consciousness, a voice saying. 'Want to take a last look at your ship?' And a hand lifted me up. I shall always remember that last glimpse of what was left of her. She was stern-on to us, very low in the water so that the deckhouse, in which we had lived for two nights, looked like a chicken coop floating on the surface of the water. And then, in the trough of a swell, I saw the rust-streaked lettering of her stern—*MARY DEARE*—

*Southampton.*

\*　　\*　　\*

As far as I was concerned the story of the wreck of the *Mary Deare* ended there on the edge of the Minkies. But for Patch it was different. He was more directly involved and I was reminded of this as soon as I woke in the hospital at Peter Port. I didn't know it at the time, but I had slept for more than twenty hours. I was immensely hungry, but all the nurse brought me was a small plate of steamed fish, and she told me there was somebody urgently waiting to see me. I thought perhaps it was Mike, but when the door opened it was a girl standing there.

'Who is it?' I asked. The blinds were drawn and the room all darkened.

'It's Janet Taggart.' She came to the side of my bed and I recognized her then, though she looked very tired and there were dark hollows under her eyes. 'I had to see you—as soon as you woke.'

I asked her how she had got here and she said, 'It was in the papers. I came at once.' And then she leaned down over me. 'Listen, Mr Sands. Please listen to me. I'm only allowed to stay a moment.' Her voice trembled with urgency. 'I had to see you before you talked to anybody.'

She hesitated then, and I said, 'Well, what is it?' I found it difficult to concentrate. There were so many things I wanted to know and my mind was still blurred.

'The police will be coming to take a statement from you soon.' She paused again. She seemed to have difficulty in putting whatever it was she wanted to say into words. 'Didn't Gideon once save your life?'

'Gideon?' She meant Patch, of course. 'Yes,' I said. 'Yes, I suppose he did.' And then I asked her how he was. 'Didn't somebody tell me he had pneumonia?' I had a vague memory of the doctor telling me that when he was examining my shoulder.

'Yes,' she said. 'He's very ill. But he passed the crisis last night. He'll be all right now, I hope.'

'Have you been with him all the time?'

'Yes, I insisted. I had to—in case he talked.' And then she went on quickly: 'Mr Sands— that man Dellimare ... You know what happened, don't you?'

I nodded. So he'd told her that, too. 'Nobody need ever know now,' I murmured. I felt tired and very weak. 'All the for'ard part of the ship broke up on that reef.'

'Yes, I know. That's why I had to see you before you made any statement. Don't tell anybody about it, will you. Please. He's suffered enough.'

I nodded. 'No. I won't tell anybody,' I said.

And then I added, 'But there's Mike. He knows.'

'Mike Duncan? I've seen him. He hasn't said anything yet—either to the Press or to the police. He said he'd do nothing about it until he'd seen you. He'll do whatever you do.'

'You've seen Mike?' I pulled myself up in the bed. 'How is he? Is he all right?'

'Yes, he's here in Peter Port.' She was leaning down over me again. 'Can I tell him you're going to forget what Gideon told you? Can I tell him you want him to keep quiet about it, too?'

'Yes,' I said. 'Yes, of course—there's no point in saying anything about it now. It's over—finished.' And then I asked her how Mike had been picked up.

'It was a fisherman from St Helier. He found the motor boat just before the storm broke. There was a man called Burrows on board, too. He was badly injured, but he made a statement to the police—about Higgins.' And then she said, 'I must leave you now. I want to see Mr Duncan and then I must be with Gideon when he wakes—to see that he doesn't talk. It's the sort of silly thing he might do.' She smiled wanly. 'I'm so grateful to you.'

'Tell Mike to come and see me,' I said. And as she reached the door, I added, 'And tell—Gideon—when he wakes that he's nothing to worry about any more . . . nothing at all.'

She smiled then—a sudden warmth that lit

her whole face up; for an instant she was the girl in the photograph again. And then the door closed and I lay back and went to sleep. When I woke again it was morning and the curtains were drawn back so that the sun streamed in. The police were there and I made a statement. Once of them was a plain clothes man from Southampton, but he was uncommunicative. All he would say about Patch was that he'd no instuctions at the moment to make any arrest. After that there were reporters, and then Mike arrived. The police had refused to let him see me until I had made my statement.

He was full of news. The stern section of the *Mary Deare* had gone ashore on Chausey Island. He showed me a newspaper picture of it lying on its side in a litter of rocks at low water. And yesterday Snetterton had been through Peter Port. He'd had a salvage team with him and they had left for Chausey Island in a local fishing boat. 'And I've been on to our insurance people,' he said. 'They're meeting our claim in full. We'll have enough to build to our own design, if we want to.'

'That means losing a whole season,' I said.

He nodded, grinning. 'As it happens there's a boat for sale right here in Peter Port would suit us nicely. I had a look at her last night. Not as pretty as *Sea Witch*, of course . . .' He was full of plans—one of those irrepressible people who bounce back up as soon as they're knocked down. He was as good a tonic as I could have wished and, though he still had a piece of adhesive tape stuck across the side of his jaw where the skin was split, he seemed none the worse for his thirty hours on the water-logged wreck of that motor boat.

I was discharged from hospital next day and when Mike came up to collect me, he brought a whole pile of London papers with him. 'Altogether you've had a pretty good Press,' he said, dumping them on my bed. 'And there's a newspaper fellow flew in this morning offering you a tidy little sum for a first-hand account of what happened. He's down at the hotel now.'

Later we went and looked at the boat Mike had discovered. She was cheap and sound and we bought her on the spot. And that night Snetterton turned up at our hotel, still neat, still dapper in his pin-stripe suit, though he'd spent two days on Chausey Island. They had cut into Number Four hold at low water and opened up three of the aero engine cases. The contents consisted of concrete blocks. 'A satisfactory result, Mr Sands. Most satisfactory. I have sent a full report to Scotland Yard.'

'But your San Francisco people will still have to pay the insurance, won't they?' I asked him.

'Oh, yes. Yes, of course. But we shall recover it from the Dellimare Company. Very fortunately they have a big sum standing to their credit in a Singapore bank—the proceeds of the sale of the *Torre Annunziata* and her cargo. We were able to get it frozen pending investigation. I think,' he added thoughtfully, 'that Mr Gundersen would have been better advised to have organized the re-sale of the aero engines through another company. But there—the best laid schemes . . .' He smiled as he sipped his sherry. 'It was a clever idea, though. Very clever indeed. That it failed is due entirely to Mr Patch—and to you, sir,' he added, looking at me over his glass. 'I have requested the H.B. & K.M. . . . well, we shall see.'

I wasn't able to see Patch before I left Peter Port. But I saw him three weeks later when we gave evidence before the resumed Court of Enquiry. He was still very weak. The charges against him had already been dropped; Gundersen had slipped out of the country and Burrows and other members of the crew were only too willing to tell the truth now, pleading that they had supported Higgins's story because they were frightened of him. The Court found the loss of the *Mary Deare* was due to conspiracy to defraud on the part of the owners, Patch was absolved from all blame and the whole matter was referred to the police for action.

A good deal of publicity was given to the affair at the time and, as a result of it, Patch was given command of the *Wacomo*, a 10,000-

ton freighter. He and Janet were married by then, but our diving programme had prevented us from attending the wedding and I didn't see him again until September of the following year. Mike and I were in Avonmouth then, getting ready to dive for a wreck in the Bristol Channel, and the *Wacomo* came in from Singapore and moored across the dock from us. That night we dined on board with Patch.

I barely recognized him. The lines were gone from his face and, though the stoop was still there and his hair was greying at the temples, he looked young and full of confidence in his uniform with the gold stripes. On his desk stood the same photograph in its silver frame, but across the bottom Janet had written: *For my husband now—bons voyages.* And framed on the wall was a letter from the H.B. & K.M. Corporation of San Francisco.

That letter had been handed to Janet by Snetterton at their wedding reception, and with it a cheque for £5,000 for her husband's part in exposing the fraud—a strangely apt figure! At the time Mike and I had been working on a wreck off the Hook of Holland and when we got back I found a similar letter waiting for me, together with a cheque for £2,500—*as some compensation for the loss of your vessel.*

The body of Alfred Higgins was never recovered, but in August of that year a metal dinghy, with patches of blue paint still

379

adhering to it, was found wedged in a crevice of the rocks on the south side of Alderney. It had been battered almost flat by the seas.

One final thing—an entry in the log of *Sea Witch II* made on September 8, just after we had located and buoyed the wreck in the Bristol Channel. It reads: *11.48—Freighter WACOMO passed us outward-bound for Singapore and Hong Kong. Signalled us: 'Captain Patch's compliments and he is not, repeat not, trying to run you down this time! Good wrecking!' She then gave us three blasts on her siren, to which we responded on the fog-horn.* A month later, with *Sea Witch II* laid up for the winter, I began this account of the loss of the *Mary Deare*.